Dying to Live

To Fiona,
Hope you enjoy this wild journey!
Best Wishes,

Library and Archives Canada Cataloguing in Publication

Dionne, L. J., author
Dying to Live / written by L.J. Dionne.

Issued in print and electronic formats.
ISBN 978-1-77141-131-8 (paperback).--ISBN 978-1-77141-132-5 (pdf)

I. Title.

PS3604.I65D95 2015 813'.6 C2015-904244-5
C2015-904245-3

Dying to Live

History Echoes the Future

L. J. Dionne

First Published in Canada 2015 by Influence Publishing

Book Cover Design: Marla Thompson
Editor: Jennifer Kaleta
Assistant Editor: Susan Kehoe
Production Editor: Nina Shoroplova
Typeset: Greg Salisbury

Dedicated to:

Alfred F. Dionne
My indomitable father who challenged me to write in 1998 and has never faltered in his continual support. He is truly my safe place to fall.

And to:

Kimberly A. Carey
My treasured sister who ends every conversation with, "Oh, L.J., if only you could see what I see." Every writer should have such a sister.

And in memory of:

David M. Ueland
1934 to 2006
My beloved stepfather who was the epitome of love and wisdom. I only wish he were with us today to experience his influence on *Dying to Live*.

Testimonials

"Dying to Live *is a mindful journey of good versus evil and the ethical Mr. Spock dilemma, elevating the needs of the many by extinguishing the lives of the few."*

~George Baxter-Holder, Author of *Drugs, Food, Sex and God* and Actor on *Star Trek: The Next Generation*

"Dying To Live *took me by surprise in its cinematic scope of a future world – a world that really could be our own if the lessons of the past cannot be learned. L.J. Dionne's unique voice beautifully blends metaphysical concepts with the cold, hard reality of a post-nuclear world. As with all books whose characters touch my heart and become my friends, I found myself slowing down at the end so as to keep our precious little time together for as long as possible."*

~David Tillman, Screenwriter, Director, Producer, and Distinguished Psychic

Acknowledgements

First and foremost, I thank my ever-positive, insightful publisher, Julie Salisbury, for believing the rest of the world was ready for *Dying to Live*. To my editor, an author's dream, I thank Jennifer Kaleta for her mastery of the literary world and words of encouragement. As well as Julie and Jennifer, I also thank the crew at Influence Publishing for their tireless efforts in bringing this novel to life.

During *Dying to Live's* final stages, challenging times were abundant, so many thanks to my supportive friends and family. Navigating through the brambles of trying times, there are those heroes who unexpectedly emerge; special thanks to my protective, compassionate powerhouses David Tillman and Manny Witzman. You kept me safe beyond the emotional cuts and bruises. The world needs more people like you.

Globally, thanks to the Americans for their bold drive and courage while chasing one's dreams, forever influencing us to reach higher toward that better version of ourselves. Thank you to the Canadians for their many critiques regarding American politics and lifestyles, always teaching us that success can also mean a love affair with Mother Nature and quality time spent with loved ones. Finally, special thanks to the citizens of New Zealand for their inexhaustible spiritual tolerance, and showing us how to live each ordinary day with extraordinary potential.

Contents

"The concept of war is outdated."

~ Dalai Lama

Speech from His Holiness, Denver, Colorado Peace Conference, September 18, 2006

TAINTED BEGINNINGS

Evil Awakens . . .
Kaikoura, New Zealand

Dare I speak of the past; stir regretfully those sleeping hornets? Why awaken those frenzied lunatics ready at any moment to empty their bulging sacs of poison into the unsuspecting? We have endured decades of assaults from the piously driven fanatics delivering stinging blows, one after another, as they "water-board" their myopic version of Allah down the throats of the naïve. Dare I speak of those who now lie dormant? Perhaps the mere mention of that brutal, narcissistic pestilence will condemn the next generation to repeat history. Our past lies under our feet as a foundation for growing wisdom. Each subsequent decade evolves into a more fertile place to thrive and is not intended to echo earlier times. Unfortunately, we do not always follow the wisest path. If I plant that seed of suggestion, will it rise again?

My name is Cameron Thorpe and I am an old man. Aching joints have been replaced so my elderly discomfort has diminished considerably. However more bearable, life continues to elude me. I am very tired though I have only reached my eighty-eighth year in this extremely insignificant slice of eternity. Although I rapidly approach my departure from this resilient universe, I have so much to share with the newest generation, namely my cherished grandson. And so, I forego rest. For in order to save my descendants from replicating unsavoury events during their lifetimes, it is my dedicated purpose to teach. Teach the youth not to rely on propaganda or inadequate history books destined to romanticize and sugar-coat the truth.

Teach them to think freely and build upon the greatest of our present. And most importantly, teach the youth not to be redundant.

Lachlan Thorpe, my beautiful grandson, has the weight of this complicated world upon his twenty-five-year-old shoulders. Whereas he was raised with an abundance of tolerance and practised "turning the other cheek," he was also exposed to a vile entity; one we had hoped would never surface again. Lachlan, like most peaceful youths his age, is conflicted when facing violence as the only solution. But I am his nandy. This is where I intervene, teaching him how to outsmart his opponent and save as many lives as possible. Lachlan is a new member of New Zealand's Youth Council, which consists of young adults working alongside our New World Tribune elders. After World War IV, every survivor was humbled. Collectively, we knew no one person had the answer to a meaningful, cohesive future. Via Internet connectivity, our youth had been warning the world of global conflict and consequences. Unfortunately, no one was listening. The brutal aftermaths of Worldwide War III had taught us nothing. From the ashes of WWIV, bloodied and weary, civilization arose, feeling the first twinges of wisdom take root. Tribune elders from every surviving country knew it was time to include bright, altruistic minds in the global effort toward peace and coexistence. However, like most generational sparring, the newly formed YC clashed continually with the Tribune elders.

My Lachlan paced the floor with zealous energy. He has been exposed to pure evil, and the vile father who spawned this beast. Sadly, this latest information only confirms deep-seated suspicions my colleagues and I have had for a very long time. False charisma veils the true monster beneath this individual's façade, causing the wise elders to fall for a handsome face with a silvery tongue and the promise of money in their pockets. Although Lachlan knows violence begets violence, he wants this beast dead, plain and simple. When trying to convey his evidence to the elders, Lachlan only saw rigid resistance. I am trying to soften his perception and explain that he has to convince the elders he is not naïvely reacting with youthful impulsiveness, but sound reasoning. Instead of Lachlan focusing on the elders' condescending dismissals, I have diverted his attention with the promise of assistance, with the highest level of fortitude. The key being to study the significant events that led to the demise of this vile creature's father. There are answers to be gleaned from his WWWIII reign of terror. Then, I mentioned Aerin's journals . . . now I have Lachlan's full attention.

Albeit, my grandson is not pleased with my withholding of these family journals, I assured him the timing to reveal these texts were never appropriate, until now; and some family secrets were never meant for anyone's ears. When I finish, Lachlan will possess the ammunition to fight this nefarious leader and give his generation a fair go. The toughest part of my grandson's journey will be keeping an open mind, especially during those moments when he is tempted to judge.

Lachlan closed the heavy library doors and joined me on my favourite well-worn, engulfing divan. In front of us was an antique cedar chest, which served as our coffee table over the years. I opened the chest that most family members thought only contained comfy lap blankets and the like. A musty smell, not unlike that of an attic on a warm summer's day, filled the air. My grandson raised his eyebrows inquisitively. Inside were many, many books with tattered, smudged, and stained covers. Bewildered, Lachlan stared at the treasure trove of information and shook his head.

My lap was soon covered with some of the thick, weathered journals written mostly by Aerin and other family members—critical history texts, milestone newspaper articles, and a book written by my son, Lachlan's father. I held up the oldest of Aerin's notebooks and explained that each entry in these cherished journals was lived with much passion, honour, and pure intent. While discussing this very clandestine family story with Lachlan, I stressed that none of my comments should diminish his respect for our loved ones' actions and pursuits in any way. Much of my prejudicial rhetoric would be statements pulled from these journals verbatim. I want my grandson to feel their frustrations and interactions during a time brimming with racial bigotry, a time when world peace was awry . . . near extinction.

"What could possibly have happened to question my respect?" Lachlan replied.

"A secret society, the dwindling of mankind . . . and murder."

"Involving—"

"Believe me, these secrets are not always easy to accept. Your sense of justice and spirituality will be tested, maybe even altered."

"Holy crap, Nandy, murder?"

"And much more."

"Well, you've piqued my curiosity now."

"Then let us get started." I opened a twenty-second

century history book with my liver-spotted doddering fingers and began slowly flipping through the pages. "We'll start here then progress through Aerin's oldest journal." Lachlan rolled his impatient eyes and sighed deeply. "Oh, Buds, do not worry, I am not going to drag you through some frivolous history lesson or tromp down memory lane. What I am about to share with you will surely prepare you for any worldwide debilitating quandary. I will tell the story using these sources merely as a reference, recompense the historians' injustices. Where to begin . . . we shall start with Aerin as a small boy."

"Nandy?" Lachlan viewed me with knitted brow. "A—"

"Trust me, Buds, we need to go to the beginning and crawl into Aerin's world completely. It is imperative you experience Aerin's life in its entirety. We will unravel this journey together, with precision. You see, my grandson, you exist peacefully in a world Aerin and I only dreamed of as children. We were raised with my land, your land, their land . . . it is no ones. We are simply here to rent and occupy space during our stay here on Earth. Always remember that. So many asinine arguments arise out of territorial disputes from ego-driven lines drawn in the sand. What greed shall dominate your lifetime, I wonder? What great feats will all of you accomplish? Will you continue to be fair and tolerate others' perceptions and ways? Will you continue to accommodate peace and justice . . . for all of the world's children? All I can do is offer you the building blocks then step aside. I am sure your generation will construct a future that fits your needs. So without further ado, let us absorb these past injustices. Observe as the world shattered into millions of pieces of righteous, misguided opinions: each with its neighbouring shards of cutting intolerance, a very troubled time when everyone bled. And Aerin's family was just one of many unfortunate tiny clusters of innocent bystanders. Bombing in the Middle East intensified once again, and in the midst of the blazing maelstrom lived our precious, nine-year-old Aerin. What beauty he possessed, body and soul."

Little Aerin

Poverty was an understatement when scrutinizing the Qasim family. But then, most of Aerin's hometown of Iraq lived with scarcity. Conserving food and clothing was a common, accepted way of life. Within the compact Qasim shanty, Aerin had his own bedroom, actually a converted closet. His small bed covered the entire floor. Shelving above contained Aerin's collection of threadbare books and a wooden stallion carved by his paternal grandfather. Right outside Aerin's prized bedroom was a four-drawer bureau built by his father. This was where the Qasim brothers kept their clothing. Within Aerin's brothers' bedroom, three makeshift mattresses occupied most of the floor space, leaving no room for chests or closets. However, in comparison with the rest of their limited world, they seemed just fine. Scanty living conditions did not diminish the cherished happiness of the Qasims. Love was cohesive and forever infectious. Life was simply less complicated.

A light powder covered Aerin's newly polished hand-me-down loafers. Sitting in his schoolroom chair, Aerin continued to lean over his desk and stare at his dusty shoes. He clicked his feet together and watched the dust flee from the black leather surface as particles danced within several sunbeams.

"Aerin, stop daydreaming and get your letters written, now! Arabic is Allah's language, show some respect."

Aerin jolted upright. "Yes, sir."

To avoid further ridicule from the other children, Aerin covered up most of his paper and feigned writing letters. He had finished his assignment quite a while ago and, as usual, was bored as he waited for his classmates to catch up. Trying to fit in, and not draw undue attention to himself, Aerin often played down his scholastic successes and love of learning. Lessons always completed with expediency, he filled his abundant spare time with fantasy. With all his Arabic letters printed with youthful precision, Aerin let his mind slowly drift allowing his vivid imagination to infiltrate the day. He breathed in the wonderful schoolroom aroma of paper, paste, and chalk. Fully immersed in his make-believe world, Aerin witnessed the head administrator standing over the bossy schoolmaster, rapping his knuckles with a ruler then slapping him across the face. The teacher had failed to print his letters accurately or quickly enough. Eraser crumbs covered the schoolmaster's smudged paper as he desperately tried to fix his mistakes. Aerin could not help himself; accidently he released a vengeful snicker.

"Aerin, bring me your paper!" Ripped from his rebellious fantasy, Aerin jumped to his feet with paper in hand. Suddenly he had difficulty swallowing as his mouth grew dry and a large lump swelled in his throat. Destined for yet another bout of sore knuckles, Aerin breathed in deeply and prepared himself to take his punishment like a man. He remembered what his father had told him: stand up straight and look others directly in their eyes. As Aerin marched toward the schoolmaster's desk he focused on the instructor's fixed glare and readied himself for the inevitable knuckle rapping. However, without warning a man clad in al Din military fatigues burst into the schoolroom. Face and head fully covered with a dark red and black bandana, the only visible individuality was the man's fierce eyes.

He directed his machine gun at the classroom full of nine-year-olds and screamed, "To your feet!"

Aerin stopped dead in his tracks. He felt the blood draining from his face. The al Din soldier pointed his large gun at Aerin's temple. The man reeked of stale garlic and rancid sweat. Aerin dared not wince from disgust. Instead, he held his breath.

"To your seat!" The soldier screeched.

Frightened, Aerin quickly forgot his instructor's demands, dropped his paper, and raced to his desk. His young heart pounded rapidly within his slight ribcage. Standing stiff and motionless, Aerin hoped the belligerent soldier would look elsewhere. Eerily the menacing al Din gunman moved his weapon toward those boys whose eyes were not facing forward.

"I march quickly toward my death! I am a martyr for Allah!"

Aerin and his classmates chanted the proper response. "Lend your hands to justice and to Jihad! I am a martyr for Allah!"

"Allahu Akbar!" The soldier stomped his feet as he paraded about the schoolroom. Aerin could feel the floor vibrate as one by one the heavy boots landed. Suddenly, the al Din soldier stood directly in front of Aerin. The gunman's saliva sprayed across Aerin's face as he bellowed his ideology. Immersed in fear, Aerin tried not to move but cringed ever so slightly from the rotten stench.

The children continued to scream. "Allahu Akbar! Allahu Akbar! Allah is great!"

"Death to America!"

"Death to America!" the children screamed.

"Death to the Coalition!"

"Death to the Coalition!" Aerin's voice could be heard above the others.

"The most honourable death is killing for the sake of Allah! Death to Americans!"

"Death to Americans!"

"Death to the English Coalition!"

"Death to the English Coalition!"

"I am al Din!"

"I am al Din!" cried the children.

"I follow the lighted path!"

"I follow the lighted path!"

"Lend your hands to Jihad!"

"Lend your hands to Jihad!" the children shouted.

"Die as a martyr!"

"Die as a martyr!"

Perspiration covered Aerin's brow and upper lip, but he did not dare wipe away the mounting moisture. Eyes affixed to the front of the classroom, Aerin was too terrified to even glance toward the fierce, dark brown eyes of the intruder.

"Islam will destroy all other religions through the Islamic Jihad fighters. It is our holy war. The infidel White House in America will become the Muslim House and we will replace the corrupt constitution with the Quran. The English Coalition will not continue to swallow up the rest of the world—dirty kufars, dirty non-believers, throw them into the fire! Annihilate the infidels! They are our God's enemies! Death to the infidels!"

"Death to the infidels!" Aerin and his classmates shrieked.

From the corner of Aerin's eye, he saw the enormous machine gun headed toward his face. The militant soldier shoved the tip of the weapon into Aerin's cheek. Cold metal met his trembling face. The gunman's deep voice boomed. "Death to the infidels!"

"Death to the infidels!" Aerin screeched. His knees trembled. He longed for his papa.

Still louder, the al Din soldier yelled. "I am Abu Jandal! I am the killer! I am the killer of infidels! Abu Jandal!"

The children screamed the Arabic nickname for "the killer" *Abu Jandal.*

"I am Abu Jandal!"

"I am Abu Jandal!"

Suddenly a siren began to wail. Aerin remained frozen. Al Din and the militant leader's drills were quickly forgotten. Almost instantly, the al Din soldier disappeared out the classroom door with his enormous gun. Aerin could hear his teacher shouting, but the yelling seemed far away. All he could comprehend was the deafening siren. Danger was upon his country, his city, and his schoolhouse. Other small boys scrambled about, bumping into Aerin as they raced for the exit. Aerin could feel the blood pumping in his ears. In the distance, he was sure he heard someone yelling his name. However, his feet would not move . . . that is, until the first bomb hit. The ground beneath Aerin's feet shook violently. Windows shattered sending shards of glass in all directions. Aerin was forced to his knees. Breathing in dust and debris, he could taste the dirt as he crunched grit between his teeth. From the hellish chaos, Aerin's oldest brother, Tanid, suddenly appeared. He grabbed Aerin's tiny hand in his strong protective grip, pulled him to his feet, and guided him from the dishevelled room.

Another bomb whistled in the distance and soon

exploded, pummelling plaster and metal alike. The ground shook as the boys dashed for a nearby tree. Aerin heard his own panting internally as his ears continued to ring. Panicked children and determined parents ran away from the schoolyard toward the hopeful security of their homes. The bombing grew closer. Tanid tugged at Aerin's trembling arm. Ahead, hand-in-hand, ran Rami and Balic, Aerin's middle, identical twin brothers. With both hands cupped under Aerin's armpits, Tanid lifted Aerin's feet from the ground and coaxed them around his waist. As he held his tiny brother close, Tanid ran as fast as he could. Aerin's jaw rattled with every jarring footstep. Several times, he spat the muddy build-up from his mouth. It was difficult to breathe, but Aerin continued to squeeze tightly to Tanid. Soon they were alongside Rami and Balic. The frightened foursome raced for the safety of their parents.

Dodging hysterical villagers, Aerin and his brothers weaved through the dirt-encrusted streets. Smoke billowed in dark plumes from behind the buildings ahead. Fatigued and muscles burning, Tanid let Aerin drop to his feet and run for himself. His tiny legs moved as fast as they could, but amongst such confusion, Aerin stumbled, lost his big brother's grasp, and fell forward sliding on hands and knees. He began to cry. His bleeding palms and knees stung from raw, exposed flesh. A sharp pain in his mouth and the taste of warm copper oozing onto his palate told Aerin he had bitten through his tongue. He coughed up blood upon the ground. Seeing the red viscous fluid increased his fear. When Aerin dared to look up, his brothers had vanished in a sea of oncoming people. Many of the villagers were covered in blood and wailing as they ran. Several adults nearly stepped on Aerin as they scurried past him carrying frightened, injured offspring. Abandoned, Aerin screamed as loudly as he could. Dust clung to his tear-streaked cheeks. Unknowingly, his hot, red-faced protests kept him from being trampled. Someone must have heard Aerin's desperate plea, for two large hands cupped his armpits once more and lifted him high into the air. When he turned his head, Aerin's mud-streaked face met Mr. Qasim's. Fear swam in Aerin's dilated pupils. He flung small arms around his father's neck then buried his face and breathed in his papa's nervous perspiration, as he realized fear had struck all. Aerin's father tightened his grasp on his son and continued to seek asylum within their modest home.

When the third bomb hit, Aerin, his papa, and brothers flattened themselves upon their living room floor. They waited for the ground to cease its rumbling before closing the front door to their home. Then, without hesitation, all joined Aerin's mother in the kitchen area. No time was wasted on words. Everyone grabbed a swatch of tattered cloth and began filling them with canned goods from their cupboards. Fear was held temporarily at bay as the entire family kicked into survival mode. Aerin felt very far away, his ears buzzed. However, his sore, determined hands worked quickly, tossing can after can onto the last few piles. Aerin's mother had moved to the bedroom to gather blankets and pillows. Jugs of water already lined the entrance to the family's crude underground shelter. Aerin could not wait to be safely swallowed by the darkness within the notoriously eerie room below. One by one, they crawled into the small hollowed-out confine with their collected goods. Waiting his turn, Aerin ran his tiny fingers over his wooden stallion carved by his deceased, cherished grandfather. As his papa lifted him down to Tanid below, Aerin held the Persian horse close to his chest and felt a calm wash over him. In seconds, the outside world had turned on the Qasims. It contained the enemy . . . and the enemy was getting closer.

Tiny cracks in the floorboards allowed threads of angel rays to lighten the Qasims' coarse cellar. Tanid and the twins played cards in the far corner while their mother fixed a meagre lunch. Aerin sat upon his father's lap, as he often did, and picked at the crude bandages his mother had applied to his scuffed knees.

"I don't hear the bombs anymore, Papa. Can we go upstairs now?"

"Not yet, my little one."

"What if we miss school? Won't we get in trouble?"

"Aerin, it is very doubtful your school survived the blasts. There's no need to worry."

"I'm not worried, Papa. I don't really want to go back. I hate our teachers. They yell at you and then we have to yell back."

"As I told you and your brothers, this is all temporary."

"Papa, why do Iraqis hate Westerners?"

"We've discussed this, Sweetheart. Do you remember we talked about fanatics?"

"Yes, Papa. Those that think they are being real religious, but end up hurting lots of people."

"Correct. So to answer your question, *fanatical* Muslims hate Westerners for several reasons. Prior to WWIII, the West's need of oil and gluttonous lifestyles offended these Muslims."

"Gluttonous?"

"Piggish, selfish, greedy."

"Okay. Cuz it goes against Allah to be greedy? Gluttonous?"

"Exactly. So the fanatical Muslims got tired of the Westerners, especially the Americans, sticking their noses in Middle Eastern business just to get more oil. Then following WWWIII, the West needed less and less oil, so they stayed out of Middle Eastern affairs. What happened, though, was many Iraqis lost their jobs and wealth; they began to starve. The fanatics blamed the Westerners for this destruction. Does that make sense?"

"Yeah, but how can the fanatics get mad at the Americans for buying their oil, then for not buying it?"

"I think it's easy for these Muslims to blame the West and Israelis for all their failures. Fanatics get things mixed up, Sweetheart. Because, in many ways, they are jealous of the way Westerners live. If they were completely honest, these fanatics would admit they would like a better home, more food, and safety for their families. Instead, they use their religious beliefs to make non-Muslims appear evil. They continually lash out at the *infidels*. And these fanatics claim their religion is superior, the best. Yet they teach their children to love death, not life."

"Fanatics are kinda' stupid, Papa." Aerin's mother and father exchanged smiles.

"Well, instead of stupid, let's just say they don't understand others' beliefs or lifestyles."

"I say they're stupid and mean. They love their violence. That's stupid, right? Did I tell you we have to carry a gun during our Suicide Bomber Induction Ceremony this summer?"

"Guns?" Aerin's mother entered the conversation with sudden worry.

"Saroya, don't worry, Dearest. We will be long gone before then." Soothed Mr. Qasim.

"Papa, you don't want us in the ceremony?"

"No, Aerin. As I've told you and your brothers many times, your mother and I don't believe in teaching children to blow themselves up for God's sake."

"So no gun?"

"Sweetheart, this is a way of brainwashing all of you children. You wear the al Din headbands, carry guns, and recite harsh words together. You feel a part of something bigger, protecting your country. Only when you get older will you realize how horrible these practices can be on the young. It's the worst form of child abuse."

"Brainwashing?"

"Yes, telling you lies over and over until you believe them as truths."

"Like what?"

"Well, like the English Coalition wanting to take over the world. Your Uncle Isaac sends me news from New Zealand, Sweetheart, and the Western world is doing no such thing."

"Like the Jews eating cookies with Arab blood in them?"

"They told you that?"

"Yes, Papa. They also told us the Jews have to kill a Christian child for Matza."

"That's rubbish, Sweetheart. These are all really good examples of lies . . . brainwashing."

"So no guns? No Jihad?" Aerin's brow furrowed as he lifted his sore hands into the air and flexed his biceps with all his might.

"Certainly not. Aerin, Jihad means self-struggle . . . a war inside you not against another human being. It's a battle you struggle with to make yourself a better person. There is no need for guns. Do you understand the difference?"

"Sort of . . . not really." His small shoulders slumped.

"It's that battle inside your head. You see a mud puddle while wearing your newly polished shoes. You want so desperately to jump right in the middle of that gooey brown muck." Aerin giggled. "But that little voice inside your head says 'you had better not, or Mama will give you a good tongue-lashing when you get home.'" Aerin's head jerked in the direction of his mother. He could see her smile in the haze of the minimal sunlight. "So you stand there and argue with yourself . . . a self struggle."

"And then jump in and hope Mama never finds out."

Mr. Qasim chuckled. "Precisely."

Aerin's father hugged his precocious child. He found it increasingly more difficult untangling the Gordian Knot of Islamic fanaticism every day after school. How many distortions would adhere to his children permanently? Every evening, in the utmost secrecy, Aerin's father re-taught his offspring that suicide bombings were not honoured by Allah, but by man. He taught them God was a loving ruler and the Quran, Torah, and Bible were not evil texts; it was how radical men interpreted the scriptures.

"So no ceremony, no guns."

"No, Aerin, no guns." Mr. Qasim was tired. "Okay?"

Aerin grinned. "Okay." The smile faded from Aerin's face. "But Papa?"

"Yes, Sweetheart."

"I did bad yesterday."

"What horrible crime could be carried out by someone so young, so small?" He tickled a sombre Aerin.

Without the slightest merriment, Aerin grabbed his

father's large fingers. "Um, we were kicking the ball around and I didn't get a turn. It was my turn, Papa, it really was. They kept kicking the ball away from me, so I, um, so I called them all a name."

"A bad name?"

"Yes, Papa, I called them *bastards*."

Mr. Qasim tried not to smile as Aerin stared directly into his eyes, searching for a shred of redemption.

"As much as I love your fiery spirit, Little One, it's unacceptable to talk like that. Do you understand me?"

"Um, yes, sir, Papa, I do. But, ah, there's more." Aerin's father continued to cradle his tiny child in his strong, lean arms. "I spoke with a Persian tongue, not Urdu."

"Aerin, everyone knows we emigrated from Iran."

"No, Papa, I cursed at the boys in Hebrew, not Farsi."

Horrified glances from every corner of the cellar fell upon little Aerin.

Aerin's Escape

FROM ABOVE, HEAVY FOOTSTEPS LANDED upon the weathered floorboards. Dust particles danced within the tendrils of sunshine on their journey to the cellar below. The faint stench of death crept in from the decimated streets as well and floated past the flooring's infinitesimal crevices. Aerin scurried into Mr. Qasim's arms without a sound and began to gnaw nervously on his fingernails. Wide-eyed, the entire Qasim family sat motionless.

The men above argued. "This is the house?"

"Yes, search everywhere. That door, what's that?"

"Just a closet."

For quite a while they slammed doors, pounded on walls and ripped apart every room, closet, and cupboard.

"This is the Qasim house but they are not traitors."

"Empty?"

"Yes, nothing."

"Not traitors? They speak the enemy language."

"So the little Qasim boy learned a dirty word in Hebrew. What child doesn't learn dirty words in a foreign tongue?"

"Where would he learn Jewish words if not at home?"

"No one is here. They either died in the bombings and never made it back or have intentionally vanished."

"Can we drop this now? Such a small indiscretion." Mr. Qasim finally recognized his neighbour's voice as the one pleading for their mercy.

"This isn't small! The father must be punished. We must search the streets for them . . . this isn't over."

Gradually footsteps could no longer be heard. Aerin began to sniffle.

Two weeks expired before Aerin's family thought it safe to crawl from their underground shelter. While hiding in the dark dankness, everyone had become accustomed to the mixture of dust and mildew.

Aerin was not ready to ascend; he felt safe in such close proximity to his parents. Mr. Qasim made the decision to proceed up the flimsy ladder and re-enter the insanity above. Pushing open the secret hatch, Aerin's family was struck by a putrid odour. With their front door left wide-open, a sweet stench as revolting as spoiled calf's liver, wafted over them.

On the streets, partially burnt corpses had rotted for days in the intense heat. Aerin's gag reflex retched several times as he quickly ran to the kitchen area in search of a place to vomit. He nearly made it, but bile lay thick and bitter upon his tongue causing him to lose his last meal upon the floor. Aerin spat several times. His mother brushed the soft, light-brown hair from his face. A feverish wave coursed through his body, which induced sweating followed by chills.

When Aerin was able to quit shaking, he stumbled into his tiny bedroom to find something to block the lingering odour. A well-worn bar of soap was rubbed over his upper lip until it was nearly raw. Only when the putrid smell was successfully blocked did Aerin's gagging subside. That is when he noticed his eyes ached from the excessive sunlight. Fourteen days without sunshine had retarded his visibility. Aerin wished they had stayed in their makeshift cellar.

Suddenly, intermittent bullet exchanges sounded nearby putting everyone back in motion. As rehearsed, each family member packed one, and only one, satchel with clothes and a few treasured possessions. Aerin made sure his carved horse would find a place inside his wrap. He had watched his grandfather whittle the ancient, Persian stallion especially for him. Always, Aerin's horse triggered a flood of fond memories of his favourite elder. He kissed the wooden piece then packed it between a few articles of clothing.

As he stood outside his tiny bedroom, Aerin kissed the closed door. Everyone's personal items gathered, the Qasim family left their ransacked home never to return.

ACROSS THE PERSIAN GULF, THERE was so much hatred and death it was hard to decipher the meaning behind each attack. America and their allies felt so far away. So many other enemies lived much closer to Aerin's family. The most recent bombs had been launched by the nastiest of Jews. Repeatedly they had committed heinous acts, hidden behind the United States' protective apron, and then, like spoiled children, had stuck out their tongues at their Middle Eastern neighbours. Obviously poor behaviour went unpunished, because the Israelis were forever bailed-out by the Americans—all the more reason for the Qasims to have fled their Persian homeland. With Iraq as the next hotbed of destruction, the militant Jews were getting ever closer.

For most of their days in the Middle East, the Qasims had kept a low profile. They had concealed their religious and political beliefs from their violent comrades, as well as many family secrets. At a very young age, Aerin had learned the meaning of silence and familial privacy. But such a minor slip of the tongue had banished all anonymity. Now the Qasims hid outdoors under the veil of shadowed darkness. Although the sun shone brightly, the Qasims remained cloistered and hidden in a shaded, abandoned alcove. The adjacent shattered buildings were reduced to meaningless walls and rubble. So little survived the Israeli bombs. Thankfully, no one paid the Qasims any attention as they huddled together for safety and rest. Everyone grew tired.

Aerin whispered, "Why English, Papa?"

"It's necessary."

"Always keep your friends close, but the evil even closer?"

"Why do you say the Americans are evil, Aerin? Do you know what evil even means? Who taught you that word?"

"The scary soldier with the big gun. Evil means the bad guys, right?"

"Yes, but when did you talk to this scary man with the gun?"

"He comes to our classroom. You know, the ah-deen soldier."

"Al Din?"

"Yes, Papa, al Din. He tries to teach us stuff. He shouts so much it hurts my head. He gives me an ear headache."

"What else did he say?"

"That the Americans lost their way. They worship money, not God. He said they cheat and kill for massive amounts of it. Then when they make tons of money, they want more. That makes them evil."

"Do you believe the al Din soldier, Sweetheart?"

"Sometimes. I don't know." Aerin searched his father's expression in the muted sunlight. "Oh . . . more brainwashing?"

"You got it."

"How do I know when they are lying?"

"You must always keep an open mind, see both sides of an argument. Try to see why each side is upset."

"I understand, like when Tanid and I fight."

"Yes, there are always two sides that think they are right. You have to dig for the truth, and the truth isn't always clear."

"The Americans and al Din could both be evil?"

"Sure. There are good and bad everywhere in the world. Maybe you'll get to travel to the West someday soon and find out for yourself about the Americans."

"I'll bring a gun with me if I do, Papa."

"Aerin—"

"Just kidding. I don't really like guns, so don't worry . . . no guns."

"No guns."

"Papa, I'm sorry I got you into trouble."

"Don't you ever feel badly about an innocent slip-of-the-tongue. We were planning to leave anyway. So we left a little sooner than expected; things will work out. God is watching over us."

"Do we have enough money to join Uncle Isaac and Auntie Clara in New Zealand?"

"Not yet. I'm thinking maybe a trip on a ship though."

"A ship? Oh boy, Papa!"

"Sh-h-h, Sweetheart. We must speak quietly. We don't want to draw unnecessary attention in our direction."

"Sorry, Papa. Where to? Where will we go on the big ship?"

"Far, far away from here."

Aerin smiled at his father. "Where they don't brainwash children?"

He ruffled his son's hair. "Hopefully, Sweetheart. At least soldiers won't be pointing guns in your face at school; *that* I do know. Now, settle down and try and get some sleep, Little One."

"Okay, Papa. Wow, a ship . . . a big ship."

DAYS PASSED AS AERIN'S FAMILY trudged through rubble, confusion, and death. Staying out of sight during the day, the Qasims travelled only after nightfall. When sunrise approached, the Qasims huddled together in the shade of unwanted debris or abandoned shanties for much needed sleep. One morning, Aerin watched his father's eyes closely and observed several tears seep from the corners. Aerin's small hand grasped his father's as he watched his patriarch's silent pain. Excitement surrounding the big ship was suddenly dampened by sadness. Clearly, something tormented his father. With heavy eyelids, Aerin cuddled as closely as he could to his father. Exhaustion finally overtook the entire family.

Awakened after a very long, hot day, sweat trickled down every crevice on the Qasims' bodies. Dust permeated the air. From their mother's satchel, unleavened bread was pulled and each received a modest portion. Aerin and his brothers chewed slowly as their stomachs growled with a gaseous awakening and constant yearning for more. No one spoke. They had discovered through eavesdropping on passers-by that only one day remained before the mysterious ship left Umm Qasr Harbour. Quickly they finished their scarce meal, gathered their satchels, and tried to forget the pain pulsating in their blistered feet. Fatigue and the constant fear of capture had long since devoured the boys' abundant adolescent energy. Nevertheless, the Qasims had a quest to finish, so it was essential they kept trudging forward. Dusk approached. Semi-rested and standing with belongings flung over their shoulders, each Qasim readied for yet another night-time trek.

Weak from hunger and weariness, Aerin and his three older brothers struggled to keep up with their parents as they forged a path toward the harbour. Only when they caught site of the enormous ship moored against the weathered dock did the Qasim family quicken their pace, ignoring their sore feet and escalating exhaustion. The closer they got to the Canadian ship, *Eternal Hope*, Aerin's hesitance swelled. Excitement had quickly turned to apprehension.

Dawn was upon them and legions of dirty, broken people pushed their way onto *Eternal Hope*'s gangplank. And many of these desperate souls were swiftly turned away. Those motivated to escape Iraq and Iran pushed and shoved with a renewed panic. All of a sudden, Aerin noticed his father had been pulled away, creating a distance between them.

Acting strangely, Mr. Qasim would not meet Aerin's inquisitive eyes each time he looked back at his family. Aerin screamed for his father. Lovingly, Mrs. Qasim pulled her tiniest child closer. The Qasim family stayed huddled together as Mr. Qasim appeared to be pleading for something from two filthy, shady-looking scoundrels. One man shook his fist in Mr. Qasim's face. Another man pushed Aerin's father and yanked a wad of money from his white-knuckled grasp.

When Aerin looked at his mother, he noticed her anxiety had heightened. She was losing colour in her face. Aerin's heart leapt with a renewed dread, but soon Mr. Qasim was back and herding his family toward the ship. Up the rickety steps they shuffled, Aerin glued to his father's side. Other frustrated Iraqis and Iranians continued to yell and shove.

Drenched in confusion, the Qasims slowly made their way through the zigzagging line into a crude, broken-windowed building, which led to an immigration checkpoint. Large ceiling fans blew hot sea air and an overwhelming stench of sour body odour around the crowded room. People continued to push and tempers flared. What happened next would be forever etched upon Aerin's tender soul. When it was time to enter the security scan chamber, Mr. Qasim squeezed his small son's hand once, peeled his tiny fingers free, then disappeared into the crowd of hopeless people who had been turned away from the voyage. Aerin shrieked with outrage as Mrs. Qasim hustled her offspring toward the immigration officers. She did not look back . . . she could not look back. Documents approved, Tanid helped his mother shuffle an inconsolable Aerin through a lower-deck opening onto the enormous ship. In a daze, the twins trudged in the wake of their mother and brothers. Once aboard the *Eternal Hope*, Aerin's mother searched the walls frantically for directions to the family's meagre, internal cabin on the lowest level near the noisy engine room. However, Aerin had a different agenda. He broke free from his mother's grasp, spotted the stairway up ahead, and ran upward and upward until the muscles in his legs burned. Finally, he reached the top deck and raced for the railing immediately searching for his father in the raucous crowd below.

Crying, each in their own way, the Qasim family clung to one another on one of their designated bunk beds. Mama Qasim had not wanted to take any chances loitering about the ship to say any frivolous, prolonged goodbyes, but Aerin had successfully quashed that plan. Numerous wails from separated, broken family members had been heard from all directions. With saddened waves goodbye and many blown kisses to her husband, Mrs. Qasim had eventually pried her children from the top-deck railing, herded them down the many flights of stairs, then corralled them within their windowless cabin on the bottom deck. Before long, they could feel the ship lurch forward. *Eternal Hope* pulled gently from the Arabian seaport and inched toward the Indian Ocean. It was not long before the menacing, arguing crowd on the docks grew smaller and smaller. Iraq, and the Qasims beloved husband and father faded into the distance.

Aerin's Voyage

One day into their voyage a potent influenza struck down passengers and crew alike. The virus was a resilient strain, beginning with an intense burning in the chest accompanied by a very high, relentless fever. Aerin, being so small and vulnerable, did not stand a chance. Mrs. Qasim was beside herself with worry at Aerin's swollen glands and his high temperature approaching 104° Fahrenheit. Since they had an infected family member, the Qasims, like many other families, were confined to their quarters. The boys were relieved to be quarantined, because everywhere aboard the ship people sneezed, hacked, and blew their congested noses. Phlegm had savagely overtaken the ship, turning the *Eternal Hope* into a floating Petri dish. The virus drifted from breath to breath infecting virtually everyone. Cabin crew and medical staff worked exhaustively, hoping all the while for a break in the debilitating illness. It was not long before Aerin's mother had four extremely sick children all in varying stages of influenza. She kept positive in front of her babies, but inside Mrs. Qasim was weary. Daily hacking, high fevers, and diminished appetites prevailed. Finally, very early one morning, Mrs. Qasim awakened to a chipper, ravenous Aerin writing enthusiastically in a small notebook given to him by a friendly Canadian. His amber eyes were clear and his stomach growled for attention. Mrs. Qasim was elated to see that one of her offspring was on the mend.

When the sickness lifted, the Qasims were forced to face the postponed pain of their father's absence. Since Aerin's mother could not afford any influenza relapses, the children remained sequestered. It was then Mrs. Qasim pulled a note from the satchel her husband had slipped her before their separation. She read in silence, while tears streamed down her tired face. Aerin's heart broke in half; one side ached for his broken mother and the other yearned for his missing father. The Qasim children huddled around their mother. All felt hollow.

A numb boredom set in as the enormous ship diligently weaved through the Indonesian Islands into the North Pacific Ocean. Albeit the sites were breathtaking, no one felt the slightest bit passionate about sightseeing. Nevertheless, everyone seemed rested and well fed, so a mother should not feel too badly. While spirits were down, Mrs. Qasim, actually Mrs. Saroya Ermani, felt it was time to share the contents of her husband's letter with her children. Aerin was used to all the family secrets. In fact, he had grown fond of his Arab alias, Qasim. As his father, Ari Ermani, had explained though, no longer did his family have to hide their true surname of Ermani, or the fact they were Jewish. Aerin's mother further explained that in order to get safe passage for his wife and offspring, Mr. Ermani could not let out the truth about his heritage and, therefore, had to purchase the five tickets from a bunch of nefarious scalpers. Motivated to rid their country of Jews or Jewish sympathizers, the Muslim Iraqis had ensured space for the Ermani family aboard the departing ship. However, corrupt officials took the free passes given to them by the Canadians, and forced those desperate enough to pay for their escape.

Sadly, for Aerin's family there was only enough money for five tickets, not six. It seemed the Canadians were rescuing Jews from the recent, volatile outbreak of war in the Middle East. When the Ermani family would reach the port in Vancouver, British Columbia, being Jewish would be far from a curse. Unfortunately, Mr. Ermani's fate was in the hands of a few suspicious, belligerent Iraqis. It was inevitable that Ari Ermani would be condemned for his forbidden beliefs, allowing Persian ways in his home, and, therefore, supporting the Jews. He would surely be turned in and punished for his child's Hebrew indiscretion. Hopefully, eventually, he would be freed and able to earn enough money to join his loved ones out West. Of course, Aerin's mother assured her offspring their father would join them soon. Each clung to that fragment of hope, each afraid to imagine the brutal truth.

Fatherless, forced to memorize a new last name, their true name, and headed for a foreign country, Aerin and his brothers found it difficult to indulge in any potential adventures on the high seas. They ate the plentiful meals offered them by the Canadians, listened to their mother's sweet fairy tales, and wished away the long hours with excessive sleep. Mrs. Ermani was convincing in all her assurances to her children, except one. No amount of words seemed to absolve Aerin of his guilt for speaking with a Judeo-Persian tongue. What appetite he had regained after his illness soon subsided. Imagining the horrors his father would surely endure caused Aerin to withdraw. One by one, the Ermanis worked on the tiniest of their clan. Comfort from his mother helped. All assured Aerin repeatedly that, in a way, he had saved the family. If they had not left when they did, maybe they would not have escaped Iraq . . . ever. Slowly, very slowly, Aerin gained an appetite once more. Hope of his father joining the family soon allowed Aerin's remaining remnants of nine-year-old guilt to be pushed into a secluded cavern in his brain, dormant for another time. It was not long before Aerin's smile returned as well . . . along with his inexhaustible questions.

Aerin's Canada

VANCOUVER WAS NOTHING SHORT OF spectacular. Although the Ermanis' journey was soon to end, Aerin and his brothers were free to be amazed at the enormity of *Eternal Hope* and her numerous luxuries. They had explored every crevice of the ship earlier in the morning. Once land was spotted though, the Ermani boys remained riveted with the wonders of their new city. What surprised Aerin the most was the lack of bombings and gunfire, and the many, many skyscrapers. Upon the ship's top deck, a deafening calm filled the air. Closer to shore, seagulls appeared from every direction, chirping at the new arrivals and hovering above the ship at a safe distance. Never had Aerin seen such beauty. He was awestruck. A magical city intact, tall buildings instead of rubble and ruins, and a thriving metropolis all encased inside an enormous plastic bubble. Aerin had thought dome living was unreal, science fiction fodder for fairy tales. Glued to the railing, Aerin witnessed the vast *Eternal Hope* inch closer and closer to the Pan Pacific mooring area where many Canadians milled about. Excitement pounded in Aerin's chest and tingled in his fingertips and toes. His brothers had to pry him loose from the railing and drag their protesting younger sibling to the Ermani cabin below in order to gather their belongings.

During their passage, Mrs. Ermani had received counselling from the Canadians regarding available aid, possible workplaces, schooling, and housing. Once they exited the enormous ship, Aerin's mother gathered her children and guided them to the nearest bus stop.

Although the afternoon was dark and drizzly against the downtown dome's ceiling high above, Aerin thought the city had to be the most picturesque place in the world. He was instantly in love with Canada. A very large bus, hovering above the ground, wheel-less and with paintings of killer whales and men with hockey sticks on the outside, took the Ermani family to another domed suburb known as Burnaby. Aerin was mesmerized. Automobiles whizzed past the hoverbus on either side; many floated above the ground as they moved. Those vehicles that still depended upon wheels for motion seemed to be covered in a rubbery, gooey material. Aerin would later learn these "jellywheels" were antiquated hydrogen cars upgraded with hovercraft capabilities and coated with a plastic silicone coating for increased safety. Even more intriguing for Aerin were the Vancouver homes. Canadians, one and all, lived in mansions, not tiny shacks like the hovel the Ermanis had left behind. Here they would make a new home and someday live in a mansion, as well. For the Ermanis' first night in Canada, though, a luxurious youth hostel had to suffice.

It took only two days for Aerin's mother, a tremendous cook, to find work as a waitress in a Persian restaurant that often buzzed with patrons speaking Farsi, her native language. She was thrilled; everything was falling into place as planned. They moved into a large two-bedroom apartment above the strip mall, where Mrs. Ermani worked, on their third day in Canada. Aerin and his mother shared one bedroom, while Tanid, Rami, and Balic shared the other. The enormous flat, although not nearly a mansion, became what the Ermanis would call home.

Before enrolling the children in school, Mrs. Ermani gathered her offspring for another heart-to-heart. It was time to expunge yet another family secret. In Canada, Aerin's mother was assured girls and boys received equal educational opportunities. Going forward, they would never have to hide Aerin's identity again. She could finally be the precocious, petite girl with the wispy caramel hair and amber eyes. Truly, it was time to allow Aerin to be free . . . completely free. To say Aerin was elated put it mildly. Somehow, boyish hair and baggy trousers had done nothing to feed Aerin's femininity in the past. Maybe that was why, on the first day of school in Vancouver, Aerin had chosen to learn the flute. The melodic, breathy instrument somehow pulled Aerin from sadness. Each note drew her closer to her graceful, inner self. Aerin promised her teacher and mother that she would practise her flute lessons every day, without fail. Canada had become her new saviour; freedom had taken root and the truth was liberating. Within the Western world, Aerin was an adorable little Jewish girl living in a tolerant city that embraced her uniqueness and would never think of punishing her for practising an unpopular faith or possessing an inferior gender.

To further acclimatize, after their first day of school, Mrs. Ermani had taken her children to purchase supplies and appropriate clothing. They could now throw away the handouts given to them on the ship. Mrs. Ermani's children would never have to feel inferior while living in their new country. Unbeknownst to them, their father had stashed a bundle of money in the forgotten satchel passed to their mother on the ramp during the sorrowful parting. So the Ermanis shopped. Denim blue jeans, bright T-shirts, soft, thick sweaters, flowered and patterned cotton dresses with laced collars, matching skirts and blouses, stylish dress shoes, and red, orange, green and light blue high-top tennis shoes. They experienced the Western world with no store unexplored. It had been so long since Mrs. Ermani had seen her offspring laughing and excited about something. A memorable shopping spree was exactly what the Ermani children had needed, especially Aerin. Mr. Ermani had protected his daughter's equitable future by disguising her as a boy the moment they had arrived in Iraq from Iran. He was the one that coached her nightly on the ways of survival in such a chauvinistic territory. And always, he was the one that fuelled his little girl's dreams. Mr. Ermani was everything to Aerin. Exhausted from their night out, Aerin laid her amazing outfits upon the bed. The smell of new cotton clothing filled the bedroom. Aerin closed her eyes and breathed in the unfamiliar experience. So many changes in such a short period made her reality feel like a dream. Slowly opening her eyes, Aerin stared at the bright array of garments. Never had she fantasized about possessing such beautiful things . . . new things.

A lump began to form in her throat. "Papa should be here instead of these new clothes."

Saroya hugged her daughter. "He will join us soon, Sweetheart. All you are required to do is learn and be happy. That is your Papa's only wish for you kids."

Aerin held her hands to her mouth as the tears fell. Mrs. Ermani squeezed her frail, nine-year-old tighter as they viewed the colourful display. Once again, Aerin's father had provided for his family. The Ermani children would never go hungry or want for the basics. All would have generous choices, and bright futures were theirs for the taking. Aerin's heart ached. Where was her papa? Was he safe? When would he join them? Every night Mr. Ermani's children would pray for his safe arrival in Vancouver. When her papa returned, Aerin would surprise him by wearing one of her new, lovely dresses. Surely he would beam with pride.

"Before we acquire great power,
We must acquire wisdom to use it well."
~ Ralph Waldo Emerson
Essayist and Author of *Demonology (An Essay)*

PRESS THE "RED" BUTTONS

"... set fire to the rain ..."
~ Adele
Songwriter and singer of "Set Fire to the Rain"

Deek

Outside, a crowd of locals had gathered. Opinions were abundant, but no one intervened. Inside a small convenience store, a huge Black man, covered in blood, leaned over his knifed victim and was beating him senseless. *And the rest of the non-White world wondered why White people called them niggers? Precisely, violence seemed to follow coloured individuals everywhere, even in the heart of Montana.* Now the Black man ripped open the storeowner's shirt. *Why was he robbing the poor old man?* Many dialled 911 a second and third time . . . the Fallstaff police were not moving fast enough.

The crazed, dark-skinned man continued to beat the dead storeowner. Now he screeched like a banshee. *What brought this nigger criminal to their quiet town?* When the police finally arrived, the townsfolk were ordered to step back . . . way back. Guns pointed at the Black killer, the policemen slowly made their way inside the store.

He would be late to training camp. Deek Jorgensen had endured hours and hours of interrogation, but still the officials were not listening. To end the harassment, Deek had finally lawyered-up. Alone in his jail cell, Deek focused on his predicament. How was his wife, Lourdes? Where was she? Thankfully, Lourdes had hidden in their car during the entire ordeal. Until this incident, everything had been going so well, Deek's dreams unfolding with ease and bringing him into affluence. Newly married to a gorgeous young woman and fresh from a post-honeymoon week in

Whistler, Deek thought his life was clearly on track. A second year NFL running back for the Nebraska Caribou, Deek had offered Lourdes a luxurious lifestyle. If only they had made it to Omaha. Deek blamed himself. He was the one that wanted a traditional honeymoon. Deek had also been the one to suggest driving all night in a conventional jellywheel automobile. Yes, where rubber met the road and hydrogen stoked the engine, Deek had opted to drive under the romantic moonlight. And he was the one that wanted to stop at the eerily quiet Montana convenience store and grab some coffee. True, Deek wished he had chosen to fly to Omaha instead, or driven a high-speed hovercraft, but then he never imagined things would spiral so insanely out of control.

Curled up on the undersized jail cot, Deek thought about his older deceased brother, Terrance, a welcomed distraction. He had shared Deek's love of football. Every free moment they had spent tossing the pigskin around, pretending they were scoring that all-important Super Bowl touchdown. Whether it was a humid Fulton County summer or icy frigid winter, the boys played ball. When alone, each spent time throwing the football upon the roof of their home and trying to anticipate where it would roll off, then catch it. Tall for their ages, Deek and Terrance were stars in their Pee Wee Football leagues. At six years of age, Deek was faster than the ten-year-olds and could handle the ball like no other. Terrance was proud of his baby brother's feats. He was sure Deek would play in the NFL someday. Terrance also seemed to sense that he would not. He knew somehow that his time on Earth was limited and had tried to warn Deek of this. At such a young age, Deek thought his big brother was just teasing him, an older brother's torturous sense of humour. When Terrance was shot, Deek thought his world had ended. The nights that followed his brother's death, Deek remembered staring at Terrance's empty bed. Clad in hand-me-down NFL Atlanta Falcon pajamas and cradling Terrance's treasured well-worn football, something he would continue doing into his adult years, Deek cried himself to sleep every night for months. Not even the Black gang, the Predators, "the Preds" as they called themselves for short, had been able to protect Terrance, their youngest member. The Skinheads or "Skins," a neighbouring White gang, had hunted down the Preds' leader after a drive-by shooting in their adjacent territory. Sadly though, the Skins' bullet landed in ten-year-old Terrance's chest, instead.

Instantly football had become Deek's everything. And unbeknownst to Deek, with no father, no brother, and a sickly mother, rage was deeply planted in his six-year-old psyche. Remembering every detail of Terrance's murder by some cracker Skinhead, Deek's rage festered further under his current predicament. The Preds had claimed the territory where most of the Blacks lived. It made sense at the time to defend their Atlanta, Georgia neighbourhoods . . . eventually Deek's turf. Youthful idealism had dictated the Predator creed of banding together for racial equality.

Upon Terrance's death, Deek had been recruited into the Preds almost immediately. And, of course, turf battles and revenge continued into Deek's teenage years when he naturally assumed Pred leadership. There was constant brutality due to the groups' disagreements over territorial boundaries—my street, your street, my park, your park, mine, yours, mine, yours, mine.

Deek annexed another street, historically known as

a neutral zone, causing the Skins to resist and the Preds to flex. One gang killed one of the other's members and vice versa . . . vice versa . . . vice versa. What came first, the chicken or the egg; who started the turf wars? Who started the animosity was not important; each group felt righteous and would defend their position to the death.

Whose land was it? Ownership was such a hazy notion. Each gang occupied a piece of Atlanta's Southern red clay, calling it home, but it would only be a brief time before the plots of gooey mud were relinquished to a newer generation. Yet it seemed group after group would fight for what was not theirs, merely as an excuse to fight.

The one thing that was unique for Deek, though, was he had a future. Unlike the other lost souls that joined the Preds simply to belong to something, Deek had a full-ride athletic scholarship to commence at the end of his last summer in Georgia. Football guaranteed Deek would receive a free education and a chance at his ultimate dream of eventually playing in the NFL. Not surprisingly, Deek planned to take advantage of this.

With Terrance gone and his mother's health ailing, Deek knew once he left Atlanta he would never return. For months, Deek's mother had not recognized him during his visits to the state nursing facility. He dreaded those visits. From the moment he stepped inside and breathed in stale urine and sour milk, Deek counted the minutes until he felt he had spent a respectable time with his beloved matriarch. Once outside and able to breathe in fresh air, Deek would run to his car fighting back his relentless tears.

That day when Deek decided he would no longer visit his catatonic mother was tortuous, yet necessary. There were no more tears to cry. Soon his hometown would become a part of his past and nothing else. When August arrived, the University of Southern California became Deek's ticket to liberation. Thankfully, no expectations, except playing a sport he loved so much, were imposed on him. Gang life had been for survival's sake, but while at USC, Deek had finally found freedom.

Although as a Pred he had used his fearful reputation to scare and make White people uncomfortable, Deek prided himself in never actually injuring anyone. Six foot seven inches tall and still growing, Deek's size led to intimidation tactics rather than physical brutality—a small concession that eased surfacing guilt in his adult years.

Lourdes Jorgensen struggled futilely to get legal representation for her husband so late at night. Although she was a full-blooded American, Lourdes' slight Spanish accent caused every potential defence attorney to dismiss her pleas. It was easy for them to hide at the other end of a dead phone line. Montana turned its back on whomever they believed was America's less prevalent. Raised in Southern California, Lourdes had not been a minority. Latinos ruled Los Angeles. Restaurants, schools, billboards, everything honoured the Spanish-speaking citizens and non-citizens. Bilingual, Lourdes avoided those intolerant Americans who did not appreciate hearing Spanish spoken instead of English. But in LA, Lourdes felt safe even though White people still occupied the upper echelon. Her Latino heritage surrounded her with a supportive family, especially Lourdes' three overly protective older brothers. Trapped in Anglo Montana, Lourdes once again was exposed to prejudices toward her Spanish lineage. It did not seem to matter that her non-Latina half was Irish—a very White Irish. All these locals saw was her minority half. Saturated with bigotry, Montana's law enforcement and legal system were run like a version of the failed television experiment, *Kid Nation*, where an isolated group of children made adult decisions in an adult environment. The networks were smart enough not to renew this disastrous reality show. If only Montana could be cancelled. Never had Lourdes thought her beautiful golden-brown skin and slight accent would be a disadvantage. She felt helpless, unable to free the man she loved. Imprisoned because of a local man's death was incomprehensible.

Aerin

Seven years had expired since that wonderful, confusing first week in Vancouver. Since then the Ermani family had flourished. Mrs. Ermani was promoted from waitress to head cook, and the children led the packs in their respective schools. Each had part-time jobs in addition to their studies and extra-curricular activities. Tanid had grown into a handsome twenty-year-old. Being one of his university's hockey stars ensured Tanid received a lot of female attention, although he had eyes for only one blonde Canadian, Robyn Stroud. Tanid was a strong, spirited young man who had filled the gap from his father's absence as best he could over the years. Mrs. Ermani could not be prouder.

Lanky and tall, the twins were eighteen, awkwardly cute, and heavily involved in mathematics and science. Like Aerin, Balic and Rami's reading was never enough to satiate their nagging curiosities. Firmly embedded in high school, Aerin basked in her new straight-A school status. She had just turned seventeen and was anxious to attend university. And Aerin had unequivocally decided on a career in medicine. Clad in light green scrubs every day after school, she revelled in her part-time job at Burnaby General Hospital. Going on her second year of employment, Aerin's time at the hospital had become a dream come true.

When she was not studying bodily systems, Aerin spent her quiet time with her flute. Her music sang her heart's truths. Lately, however, her playing had reflected harsher, forced tones. Educational freedom stirred a whole new form of frustration in her unrestrained thoughts. While she was younger, Aerin trusted her elders, especially her father. At school in Iraq, she and her brothers learned the ways of Islam, only to return home and undertake secret teachings of Judaism. Now, in the land of tolerance, Aerin was allowed to question everything, even religion. Living in the Western world, Aerin was free to read the Bible, Quran, Torah, as well as every radical criticism presented against these scriptures. After all, man wrote these holy texts, so how accurate could they be? She examined Hinduism, Buddhism, Taoism, Confucianism, Gnostic Christianity, and quantum physics. The more Aerin dug into the core of humanity, the more she discarded her old familial beliefs and traditions. They seemed ridiculous . . . outdated. When she had resided in the Middle East, Aerin was told the Western world was evil; Jews and Americans worshipped moolah, not Allah; and Jews, women, and dogs were lesser beings than male Muslims. Of course, these beliefs seemed to come from fanatical interpretations of Islam . . . primarily the Desert Muslims. She remembered her childhood discussions with her father regarding brainwashing and Islamic brutality. Aerin had sifted through the rhetoric over time and no longer believed a word of these radicals. Besides, why would Aerin's loving God condemn women and declare that one religion was superior, while all others were racists.

None of that had made sense to her. The universe was more comprehensible since she was able to see her Middle Eastern world through Western eyes. Privately, Aerin allowed her newfound beliefs to house her soul and heart. Cutting through man's religions and edited Books, Aerin's spirituality seemed overly simplistic, void of numerous pious rules. She had not given up on people, simply on people's religions . . . save one. Gnostic Christianity, a society more than a religion, preserved Aerin's beliefs. Pure intent, following the Golden Rule, and seeking her divine "true self" deep inside were accomplished without prejudice and void of manipulations and condemnations so hopelessly embedded in modern day religions. At seventeen years of age, Aerin Ermani declared herself not a Jew, but a child of Mother and Father God and nothing more . . . or less.

Even countries' borders no longer held importance for Aerin. Through all her readings, she had discovered a much larger picture. Although she felt proud to be a part of the beautiful Canadians, in Aerin's heart, even the North American borders had melted away. Americans and other foreigners attended Aerin's high school and they were fascinating, interesting peers as well. Besides, people from far and wide were God's children and time on Earth was only temporary, so why should pride of country be so important? Why all the fighting over a hunk of dirt or lines drawn in the sand? It did not make sense for anyone to kill another because they came from a different territory or staked claim over a piece of land that could not be taken with a person when he or she passed away. Respecting her mother, Aerin shared very little of what she knew as her new truth. The rest of the Ermani family basked in Canadian pride. Citizenship granted meant perpetual freedom. This kind country had taken a chance on these Iraqi-Iranian strangers and they were not about to take that hospitality for granted. Much like an adopted, previously abused pet, the Ermanis were forever appreciative. They knew what it was like to live in fear and under smothering oppression. There was no doubt the Ermanis would make the best of their freedom and give back to Canada.

Time heals most wounds . . . prayers are heard and often answered even after requests are long forgotten. Gathered in their favourite Persian restaurant, the Ermani offspring feasted on their mother's delicious meal. Tanid, Rami, and Balic listened with amusement as Aerin re-enacted her latest hospital tale. She had assisted her favourite emergency room doctor in removing not one, but two jellybeans from a three-year-old boy's nostrils. As funny as Aerin's antics were, all laughter came to an abrupt halt when a familiar face appeared at the restaurant entrance. Through the doors entered a very frail grey-haired man. The Ermani offspring froze. Frantically, Aerin began chewing her fingernails, a habit she had not indulged in since their arrival in Vancouver. It was as if a ghost had entered the room. In utter disbelief, all they could do was gaze wide-eyed at the elderly gentleman. Before the teenagers stood their father. Without recognition, Ari Ermani stared past his children. Instead, he searched for the loving face of his wife, Saroya.

Mrs. Ermani immediately recognized her husband when she glanced up from surveying the progress of her children's dinner. There he was straight out of her dreams. Flinging the kitchen saloon doors aside, Aerin's mother ran to her precious battered man. Although he had aged prematurely, Mr. Ermani still possessed those gentle amber eyes . . . the same eyes as his daughter. Mrs. Ermani hugged her husband; neither wanted to let go.

Gradually Aerin stood, pushed her uneasiness aside,

and approached her father. Mr. Ermani locked eyes with his youngest. With rough, scarred fingers, he brushed a lock of Aerin's silky hair from her forehead. "Oh God, my little girl." Tears spilled down his hollow cheeks. "Your hair is so long, so long . . . like liquid caramel." Mrs. Ermani stepped back to let her daughter in completely.

When Aerin hugged her father, she felt his emaciated, bony frame. Never again would Aerin re-enter the flow of an ordinary day. Repressed guilt crashed into her porcelain consciousness, fracturing it into slivers of uneasiness and each one burrowed into Aerin's tender heart. Speaking Hebrew when calling her classmates "bastards" seven years ago had caused her father unimaginable torture. Finding it difficult to speak, she finally whispered, "Welcome home, Papa."

Fanatics

Through the porous Canadian border, three vans full of handicapped individuals attempted to cross into Sweet Grass, Montana from Coutts, Alberta. Similar caravans were in line at the Peace Arch crossing between Vancouver, British Columbia and Blaine, Washington, as well as the border crossing from Fort Erie, Ontario to Buffalo, New York. Claiming to be on sightseeing expeditions, these mentally challenged passengers, many possessing prosthetic limbs, were ushered through without much consideration. Excessive drooling and poor hygiene from many of these disfigured, often forgotten souls caused the Immigration Border Patrol officers to retch with disgust or squirm with uneasiness. Some of the travellers were briefly searched for planted weapons, but, for the most part, the groaning, increasingly restless sightseers were hustled back into their vans and waved on without incident.

One hundred meters into Montana an eerie chuckle rose from one of the drooling, incoherent mental patients. And the guttural laughter was infectious. In *The Usual Suspects* Keyser Soze fashion, the gimpy, slouching men sat upright and celebrated their charade with a round of "high fives." Directive One was a success. Pumped with excessive adrenaline, all the al Din amputees and converts were ready for the next stage of their mission. They would have to conserve their energy though. Except for the van headed to Seattle, most of the men had long trips ahead of them. Sadly, America had lost her way; what the founding fathers had created long ago was long forgotten. These men were determined to initiate the United States' final destruction.

Streams of al Din-filled vans had crossed the Canadian borders into the United States during the past year. Each vehicle had headed in different directions: Seattle, Boulder, Los Angeles, Kansas City, Chicago, Miami, New York, Dallas, Atlanta, Washington, DC, and elsewhere. Only when the vans reached their sleeper cell locations did the participants feel comfortable removing wigs, pale make-up, silicone facial prosthetics, and other disguises. Limb prostheses were also removed and the amputees were returned to their wheelchairs. From inside the fake arms and legs were tightly sealed metal cylinders containing highly enriched uranium, as well as documents including bomb assembly, placement, and cell deployment instructions with one specific date in bold print. It was an aggressive timeframe for some, but everyone was energized and ready to do their part for Islam and Allah. These bomb makers, al Din's Western conduit, worked with very little sleep to meet their target date. They would never stop. Tentacles of terrorism had reached out to every nook and cranny of the globe. All non-believers would soon feel their wrath, especially the historically hated Israelis and Americans.

Deek

Everything went wrong at Deek's trial. Even with revered NFL players, White players, and Deek's coach as his character witnesses, Deek was vilified. Blinded by the defendant's dark skin, the jury deliberated for only one hour. Deek's blood boiled from all those privileged, pampered, prejudiced, pricks that had judged him . . . unfairly. Poverty and minorities to these crackerjacks were far from their reach and never supposed to crawl within their white picket fences. For the Fallstaff citizens, indigence and dark skin went hand in hand. Deek had landed in a pasty-white, Anglo American homeland of Skinhead-worshipping wannabes. The White legal system had failed him.

Weeping was minimal when the verdict was read. The guilty verdict meant Lourdes would be without her new husband indefinitely. Sentenced to life in prison, Deek would be jailed temporarily in the Fallstaff jailhouse until the following morning when he would be shipped off to a federal penitentiary more appropriate for his crime. With the overflow of prisoners, the only vacancy for him was in California. Deek would join other vile murderers in Southern California's Lompoc Federal Penitentiary. Lourdes pushed forward through the courtroom for one last caress from Deek. However, a policeman on each of her arms, Lourdes was held tightly and kept from reaching her husband. She wailed. Deek flashed his wife a dimpled smile, causing Lourdes to cry harder.

When Deek was dragged from the courtroom, several

of the bolder NFL-loving policemen had the nerve to ask him for his autograph. Deek seethed. He could still hear Lourdes screaming his name.

Lourdes' shoulders slumped. They had lost everything. What kept racing through her mind was that it would be several long days before she could inform her heroic husband that she was one month pregnant.

Aerin

Later that monumental night, the Ermani clan watched as their mother trimmed their father's stark grey hair. After he had showered, his overly tanned face no longer resembled leather; softness had invaded Mr. Ermani's appearance. Viewing his handsome family, he beamed with pride. His wife and children were strong and healthy, which was everything he had dreamed of while in his Iraqi prison cell.

At the cramped dinner table, Mrs. Ermani served warm cherry pie and vanilla ice cream to her loved ones. Slowly the inquisitive teens began to rifle seven years' worth of questions at their father. No one could understand the injustice surrounding his imprisonment. Six years of being jailed because he was sympathetic toward the Jews did not make a bit of sense. However, if they had known Mr. Qasim was actually Jewish he would have been instantly shot or hanged. Abandoning the practice of circumcision decades ago, Middle Eastern Jews had evaded physical detection. Once released after serving his treason sentence, it had taken Aerin's father a year working odd jobs at the docks before he had earned enough money for passage to Vancouver. So much confusion and conflicting emotions surrounded Mr. Ermani's bittersweet reunion. For his offspring, unresolved guilt issues resurfaced and demanded resolution — such an uncomfortable position especially for his youngest teenager. Then there were his children's immediate futures to consider. School was closing in a week for the summer months and Aerin was looking forward to another summer school session while working fulltime for the hospital. Tanid had plans to work at his mother's restaurant, spend time with his girlfriend, Robyn, and join his friends swimming and boating away his leisure time. The twins were headed for an eight-week science camp in Victoria, on Vancouver Island. All buzzed with an excited energy, never once noticing the concerned looks worn by their parents. Little did the Ermani offspring know their thwarted summer plans would be the least of their worries.

Deek

Oceans away from Aerin's homeland, the Middle East's most hated foe was fighting its hardest domestic battles. Mix American minorities with a good dose of inner-city segregation from the White majority and the result is generations of poverty, which was masked as problematic integration. Peace Provinces were far, far away from these individuals. They were living the old America, where prisons quickly filled with more and more brown and black-skinned felons, even though America's makeup had shifted considerably. What used to be a predominantly White country was now owned by minorities. At the beginning of the twenty-first century, population ratios were approximately 68 percent Whites, 14 percent Hispanic, 12 percent Black, and 5 percent Asian. Now Whites were no longer America's majority at 43 percent of the total population. Minorities made up 57 percent, including 32 percent Hispanic, 15 percent Black, and 10 percent Asian. Blame toward the White man was still ever present, which exponentially increased riots and prison deaths every year. Federal penitentiaries were at the top of that volatile list. A constant fog of Ebonics and Spanish mixed with foul language hovered within the prison walls. Questions were posed as to why fifteen percent of the "dark" population was committing forty percent of the crime. Answers ranged from hatred of "Whitey" to pale supremacist police forces entrapping innocent "coloured" men.

Hot and sweaty, Deek could not believe what he was seeing from his penitentiary transport window. The new

Lompoc prison was made entirely of glass surrounded by a protective laser fence. Deek thought it resembled something out of a hellish sci-fi movie. Vaguely, he remembered news specials regarding perpetual prison riots and the failure to eliminate them. Prison reform had massively failed. Taking a hard line only exacerbated the situation. Eliminating mediavision — MV as it was called for short — weightlifting and team sports simply left more time for breeding hatred and acting on pent-up aggression. Restructuring the building had led to plentiful sunshine, nothing more. The prisoners' demeanours remained unaffected. Even unlimited access to books resolved nothing.

All over the United States prisoners revolted, especially the African Americans. Chanting Americanized African gibberish and decorating their cells with tribal snapshots and paraphernalia kept the Black cellmates focused on hope of a country they could claim as their own someday. Authentic African attire would have been worn if allowed. Hopelessly, the Black prisoners wore their orange or blue prison garb, and wandered around the prison yard aimlessly, dreaming of a land where they led the decision-making processes and owned their futures. The militant African American behaviour behind bars affected the "free-world" Blacks as well. Relatives and loved ones of these criminals criticized the United States government, military, and all other races that had lighter skin than theirs. Whites were at the top of their list of people to blame for their misfortunes. Gang wars were at an all-time high, except within the many coveted Peace Provinces across the nation.

Inside the Lompoc confines, Deek immediately felt the tension amongst the prisoners and guards. Racial slurs rolled from their tongues alike. "Nigger, spook, coon, raisin head, moon pie", and "watermelon" accompanied Deek as he carried his bedding to his cell . . . all ridiculous words that could potentially provoke a brawl and slice through a man's soul. It was time, time for a dramatic change. Throughout history, there had been wars that seemed irresolvable . . . wars that could not be won. This racial conflict was one of those endless, mindless battles. Segregation without poverty had not solved the problem completely. Whereas the Peace Provinces were effective, they had not spread widely across the nation. To Deek and other educated individuals there was no simple solution for these angry people. Sadly, America's penal system had exhausted every option.

Waiting to board her plane in Fallstaff, Lourdes had never felt so lonely. Nowhere did she see anyone darker than the colour of paste. Despite the fact her skin was much lighter than Deek's, Lourdes still suffered the many stares . . . oh, they loved to stare with those judgmental eyes. Omaha had been accepting of Deek and Lourdes because Deek was a national football celebrity. Now Lourdes questioned the Nebraskans' hospitality. Had they really wanted to be friends or were they just indulging in hero worship, chiding with racial slurs behind Deek's and her backs? Lourdes was nauseated and not from pregnancy. With Deek's conviction, how would she be received in Omaha? Would she receive more of the same? Her life was unravelling. True, her older sister, Wandra, was already on a plane and would meet Lourdes at her Nebraska home, but it would not be easy for the two women to pack up everything for Lourdes' move back to California. Even more difficult for Lourdes would be putting a "For Sale" sign in the front yard and walking away from her enormous dream home. Lourdes' world in LA would be an unfortunate familiar one and include nothing for her, except family, and Deek's appeal process.

Kozlov

Trust was never part of their relationship. Having a common hatred was what drew Russia and al Din together. Their shared belief was that America and Israel would not be missed if obliterated from the Earth. The only real question was, how? Getting in bed together had been a long time coming for al Din and Russian intelligence. Historically, the KGB, a Russian acronym for "Committee for State Security," was the umbrella organization that served as the Soviet Union's premier security agency, secret police, and intelligence. In 1995, the president of Russia, Boris Yeltsin, signed a decree to disband the KGB, which was then replaced by the FSB, domestic state security agency of the Russian Federation. However, over the years the FSB did not instil fear in foreigners as the once-dreaded KGB had. Since the new security organization did not have the menacing reputation of the old, resembling something as benign as a Parent Teacher Association, the Russian spy industry was enhanced and specialized. Hatred toward the West or not, al Din would have never partnered with the old Russian FSB. So a super agency was formed, which inherited the old KGB name and once again instilled fear and intimidation throughout the world. Times changed and Russian intelligence was at the forefront of the spy industry yet again.

Into the room marched three men dressed in desert military garb, their faces and heads covered with black ski masks. Dark brown irises with yellowed sclera glared through the cut-out holes.

One of the men spoke. "Bogdan Kozlov, my leader, has read your KGB's proposal."

With a polished accent, Kozlov spoke perfect Urdu. "I was told Qeb al-Husri would speak with me directly. How do I know you are al Din?"

"Don't insult me."

"You could easily be from the Pakistani resurgence."

"Al-Husri cannot be put in such vulnerable situations."

"Well, I will not deal with anyone except al-Husri. Good day, sir." Kozlov stood to leave.

The other two al Din soldiers pointed Russian laser guns at Kozlov. "You're not going anywhere. Al-Husri is interested, as I told you. However, he wants assurance."

"I'm sorry. I cannot take chances. I will only deal with al-Husri.

"As you wish." The camouflaged militiaman pushed his laser gun closer to Kozlov's face and signalled for the other soldiers to grab him.

"Wait! Stop! What are you doing?" Kozlov's head was quickly covered with an opaque black, cloth sack. His arms were pulled painfully behind his back and clamped together. A searing pain pierced his upper left arm as the al Din soldier plunged a needle deeply into his flesh. "What . . . I want to . . ." Kozlov felt dizzy and stumbled. As his knees began to buckle, he lost consciousness.

Once Kozlov's ankles were strapped, the three al Din brutes lifted the solid, statuesque Russian and exited the building.

SUDDENLY THE BLACK SACK WAS ripped from Kozlov's head. His eyes darted about until they landed upon a hazy figure an arm's length away. As Kozlov tried to focus, he heard the deep rumbling of an authoritative voice. The blurred shape rose. When the massive figure passed behind Kozlov, a trailing mixture of pressed linen, dust, and sour body odour wafted about. The odour made him retch. Abruptly, Kozlov lost the battle with his drug-induced nausea and vomited on the floor.

The large man chuckled. "You Russians drink your vodka like water yet have such tender stomachs." His taunting laughter filled the room.

Kozlov spit lingering bile from his mouth. He squeezed his eyes shut tightly and shook his head, trying desperately to regain clarity. Finally, when he opened his eyes, some of the haziness had lifted. Before Kozlov sat an obese man in full Arabic attire—robe and headdress. Although his clothes were impeccable, the man beneath was not.

Upon examining the Arab more closely, Kozlov noticed a thin, grey beard covered several festering patches of acne on the Arab's neck and chin. Also troubling was the bulging Syrian's laborious breathing, which caused him to perspire profusely. Sour sweat trapped beneath the many folds of this man's blubber permeated the air. It was difficult for Kozlov to breathe without evoking another wave of nausea. Nevertheless, it was he . . . Qeb al-Husri, the al Din caliph, successor to Muhammad, who had killed millions of infidels. How had this unkempt man become the feared leader of all disgruntled Muslims? Then, Kozlov locked eyes with al-Husri. The more he stared, the more Kozlov was drawn to al-Husri. Those fierce, pale green eyes, which almost fluoresced against his olive complexion, were beautiful . . . intoxicating. Kozlov could not look away.

To break the trance-like union, al-Husri shouted, "Bogdan Kozlov, welcome! I hope your trip was restful."

Again al-Husri's deep, mocking laughter rang in Kozlov's ears.

"Where—"

He raised his hand, demanding silence. "I will ask the questions." Al-Husri switched from Urdu to Russian. "Kozlov, you wanted to meet face to face. Normally, no one is allowed in our White Mountain complex."

"Christ, you brought me to Tora Bora?"

"Your Christ cannot help you here, I'm afraid. This is Muhammad's land." Al-Husri sneered.

Kozlov knew about the supposed location of al Din headquarters. The KGB had studied the Intel regarding the cave complex in Eastern Afghanistan, near the Khyber Pass. If this was true, Kozlov was powerless . . . trapped. For the first time, he felt raw fear take root.

"So, my KGB friend, what can I do for you?"

Kozlov continued staring at al-Husri in disbelief. A drug-induced fog still clouded his thoughts. He desperately wanted to answer the man, but he was left speechless.

"Kozlov, do not look away. Look at me! You demanded my presence—"

The words finally surfaced. "Yes . . . then a syringe is slammed into my arm."

"Do not interrupt me again."

Kozlov stared at al-Husri with contempt. This time, he looked past the beguiling, alluring eyes and focused on the Muslim's tired, cold expression. His temper escalated; Kozlov sat taller. Furious over the disrespect shown him by al-Husri's men, Kozlov lashed out at the sloth with vitriolic rhetoric. "Then you have me sacked like a goddamn potato. Never would KGB disrespect you or your men in such a demeaning manner!"

"Silence!" Al-Husri stared through Kozlov. With disdain, "I made an exception for you, our KGB brethren."

Two al Din soldiers stepped closer, one brandishing a massive laser gun pointed at Kozlov's head. The other held a dripping syringe. "

"You are nothing to me, Kozlov, do you understand?" Al-Husri's stare did not waiver. "There are always KGB lackeys to be found; you should know that by now. You'd be wise to choose your words very carefully."

The Syrian's deep voice reverberated within the cement walls. Why had Kozlov not insisted on backup reinforcement? Locked away in Tora Bora in an inescapable cell with Qeb al-Husri and his men, he felt completely vulnerable, reduced to a mere pawn. Fear nipped at his reasoning. Now, unequivocally, Kozlov understood how al-Husri could command the most violent rebel organization in the world. The KGB operative's palms began to sweat.

"I apologize, al-Husri, please, please continue."

"I completely understand your hatred of the United States and Israel. I have read your internal documents and proposal and no longer have questions. What I want is proof of KGB intent."

"I have photos of the delivery of warheads into Jordan, Syria, and Saudi Arabia. Strategic locations will allow for the effective demolition of Israel. That is our intent." Kozlov pulled snapshots from a hidden pocket within his pant leg.

Al-Husri seemed unimpressed. "I will need to witness these warheads firsthand, not merely rely on a handful of photographs."

"Naturally, al-Husri." Kozlov wiped his damp palms on his pants.

"After I examine these sites I will be in touch with you."

"Sir—"

"I leave tonight. There will be no delays attributed to my suspicions."

With that, al-Husri arose. The same three soldiers hustled toward Kozlov. He viewed the articles they carried with familiarity and dread. One held a massive laser gun, the others a black sack . . . and dripping syringe.

DIRECTIVE ONE OF THEIR MASTER plan had gone down without a ripple. Russian nuclear bombs were in the final, completion stages within strategic cities in America, Great Britain, and Australia. And the American agencies, the CIA, FBI, and Homeland Security had nary a clue. Neither did Britain's MI6 Secret Intelligence Service. The English Coalition was completely clueless and ready to fall.

Lourdes' Deek

Back under the Los Angeles dome, Lourdes felt like an insect sizzling under a magnifying glass. Hot, nauseated from morning sickness, and saturated with an abundance of pregnancy hormones, her emotions had spiked beyond rationality. Lourdes waited impatiently in the pretentious lobby of Deek's high-priced attorney's office. Even though Lourdes had plenty of funds to pay the silver-haired, arrogant lawyer, he still treated Lourdes as an illegal alien, "free-holie," "beaner," "taco," "wetback" . . . all names she had internalized growing up in her country. A native Californian, within a predominantly bilingual Latino city, and Lourdes was still treated like dirt on the soles of the wealthy White men's shoes. As a little girl, Lourdes had felt the hatred penetrate her eleven-year-old world when speaking Spanish with her girlfriends. It was hard for the little girls to understand. Why had White people frowned upon the beautiful Spanish vernacular as if they had been listening to a constant flow of vulgar curse words?

Lourdes fanned her warm face with a stuffy financial magazine. She could not wait for the next hour to be over. Legal jargon spoken down to her, as if she was a Mexican illegal immigrant with no understanding of the English language, was only part of her discomfort. At the end of the session, Lourdes would have to face more humiliation and pay the fat, intelligent prick for treating her like a wetback pariah. Dark-skinned clients, especially of the Latino persuasion, had to pay on the spot; they were considered high risks for bad debt. Never mind the fact that

Deek and Lourdes' current bank balance was more than this rat-bastard would make in fifteen years. Depressingly, however, Lourdes knew the appeal process, loss of future income, as well as attorney fees, would devour that capital faster than a ravenous cancer.

EACH PENITENTIARY CELL HAD STEEL sidewalls partitioning the prisoners. The ceiling, back wall, and door to the jail cells were made of an unbreakable glass. Prison guards walked above the inmates to view any illicit behaviour. Devious activities could also be observed from a computer monitoring system. With state-of-the-art ventilation, any rebellious fire-setting could be snuffed out as well as that prisoner being immediately knocked unconscious.

The real problem brewed outside the prison walls. Constant rioting by non-inmates at the penitentiaries, nationwide, was becoming cumbersome. Decidedly, African Americans ranted, sabotaged prison workers' cars, and engaged the local press to protest their victimized loved ones' incarcerations. Never mind if these imprisoned Black derelicts killed, raped, or assaulted someone, their excuse was that corrupt police departments had set up their relative or spouse and, therefore, the inmates should go free. Besides, these protestors were still livid about the old governmental regime making the decision, driven by sheer frustration, to parade prisoners like animals in a zoo. This hard line decision had backfired; humiliation for American prisoners had not reduced crime or gang violence. Leaving belligerent offenders in glass, zoo-like cages during the daytime for U.S. citizens to view had simply evoked an undeserved sympathy. Even when the caged inmates smeared excrement or pissed on the plexiglass walls, the bleeding heart liberals were not dissuaded. They thought it inhumane to display these evil criminals for the world to view and study. Curiosity drove a lot of people to the Homo-sapiens zoo. Many were fascinated by what a serial killer looked like, but in the end, the liberals won and the zoo-like cages were turned back into private prison cells. With the changing of the current government, the new president and prison authorities had come together and made the toughest decision they would ever have to make.

An above average student while attending USC, Deek spent his first week of incarceration reading every legal book he could obtain. Engrossed in past court cases like his, Deek searched for that one racial court battle that would aid in his appeal. Time ticked by slowly. He dreaded the daily exercise hour the most. Races segregated into corners of the workout yard far from the intrusive guard towers. No one took advantage of the chin-up bar or jogging track. Instead, the prisoners wasted not one minute of human contact and crammed as much racial hatred into that daily hour as possible. Going on Deek's eighth day of imprisonment, there had been nineteen deaths—six Latinos, eight Blacks, three Whites, and two Asians.

Deek

WITHOUT HESITATION, THE SIX FOOT eight inch African American lifted the shank dripping with his own blood and plunged the ragged hunk of metal into the muscular, heavily tattooed abdomen of Lompoc's most notorious Skinhead. The wail of an impaled animal escaped the White man's lips. Blood soon covered his yellowed teeth, darkening his gaping mouth. Disbelief was etched into the man's paralyzed stare. Quickly, the other prisoners scurried like cowardly rodents away from the the man crumpled upon the ground. Deek's purple-black, sweat-covered skin glistened in the sunlight. He staggered. Warm, thick crimson fluid seeped from in between his ribs. The Black prisoners cheered in a frenzied roar as several brothers helped Deek to a nearby bench to wait for medical assistance. Deek felt as though he had nothing to lose, so he had protected himself with the only thing that these prisoners knew . . . violence. After all, he was serving a life sentence for being in the wrong place at the wrong time, and not to forget, having the wrong skin colour.

Before Deek walked away from the unmoving body, he started to spit upon the pale white skin but decided otherwise. Aggressive cheers from the ignorant lemmings were already ridiculously out of control. Vacantly, the dead man's eyes stared in Deek's direction. A mere eight days incarcerated and Deek had stabbed and killed his White attacker. Appalled by his surroundings, Deek staggered toward the building. The pungent copper smell of blood still swirled about his head. Suddenly dizzy, Deek vomited.

What followed was a battle between the Black and White prisoners' recollection of the Skinhead's attack upon Deek. Both versions included distortions to cast their prisoner in a fairer light. Shivs, sharpened from plastic utensils and toothbrushes, pierced and tore flesh. Socks filled with bars of soap, circled heads, cracking against skulls. Blood regularly plastered the walls and soaked the ground. No one was ever privy to Deek's reaction to the entire ordeal. It sickened him to remember how the skinhead had gone limp in his arms when forcing the shank farther into his abdominal cavity. As much hateful rhetoric as Deek had spewed toward the Skins while growing up, it should have felt euphoric to snuff out the hater of Blacks. On the contrary, the whole experience left Deek shaken; it had not been uplifting to watch the large White man take his last breath at Deek's hands.

How had he gotten here? His dreamlike existence consisted of Lourdes, football, and their unborn child he had just recently learned of via their last phone call . . . nothing more. Deek had a family to join and support. During his time at university, Deek had learned an alternate view of life—the world through Lourdes' eyes. Killing was never a part of him, and for the reformed Deek, neither was hatred and prejudice. The appeal hearing had to be successful; being locked within a cage would only serve to rot Deek's soul. Justice simply had to prevail.

His newly administered stitches itched beneath the sterile bandage. Sleep was impossible. Deek paced in the darkness. Then, his eyes darted toward movement outside his plexiglass jail-cell door. In the moonlight, Deek spotted men dressed in teal biohazard Hazmat suits. What was happening? A loud hissing sound came from

Deek's ventilation grate. Holding his breath initially, then breathing through a balled-up blanket became futile. A foggy vapour seeped into his living quarters and invaded his lungs. At the first sign of dizziness, panic took hold. Lying on his cot, Deek strained to focus on the subdued commotion outside. Crowds of suited men had gathered at one of the prison entrances. Deek's eyesight grew hazier. One of his last thoughts before putting his head upon his pillow was of Lourdes. Deek screamed for help inside his brain, but his pleas went unheard. Soon he would learn his appeal would never be heard as well.

Encircled, the protestors, exercising their constitutional rights continued to yell profanity at the prison guards. Clever slogans had long gone by the wayside. Nothing seemed to get the prison workers' attention except cussing and insulting racial blasphemy. Once surrounded, the canisters were opened. It took a while for the protestors to spot the men dressed in blue-green spacesuits and gas masks. The moment the crowd realized what was upon them, all they could do was lie down right where they stood. One by one, the predominantly Black, belligerent "free-world" objectionists dropped to the pavement.

Across the nation, unbeknownst to the news networks, protestors and prisoners were collectively partaking in an involuntary slumber. Any journalists present were among the bodies dotting the pavement outside the federal penitentiaries. When all awoke, they would discover their lives had been forever altered.

Visiting hours had been temporarily suspended at Lompoc prison. Protestors and journalists awakened on cots within the prison confines. Juice and crackers were offered to the confused, sleepy audience. Behind a podium in the front of the room was a well-dressed congressional-looking "suit" speaking into a microphone. He and his juice-helpers each had a gasmask dangling loosely around their necks. The speaker instructed everyone to remain calm or sleep would be induced again . . . within seconds. In disbelief, the troubled crowd rubbed their eyes and looked at one another, too groggy and scared to be enraged. Suddenly, on a large MV flat-screen behind the "suit," the president of the United States appeared.

The leader of the free world droned on with politically correct rhetoric. For many, many years, minority prisoners had wreaked havoc over their inferior station in America. Even after three Black presidents held the reins of American power, the black stallion still reared with anger. No one with light skin really understood the depths of African American pain. Whites claimed the injustice between the races was securely in the past . . . it was time to let go. Could everyone just focus on being Americans and get on with life? This cavalier, calloused simplification had enraged the United African descendants further. They were doomed to be misunderstood for eternity. Not even the three African American presidents were able to bring peace within the U.S. during their terms in office. So many governmental issues went unsolved and to the African Americans this appeared to be a massive ethnic failure. Outraged by the fact these Black presidents seemed to only represent the 43 percent lighter-skinned citizens while in office, African Americans had breathed life back into the U.S. racial conflict. Many wasted hours were spent by an enlightened few trying to get one group to truly see the others' point of view. Still, the black stallions' spirit could not be broken. To say everyone felt one particular way would be sheer ignorance. There was some improvement where American pride amongst minorities grew. However, after decades, a large portion of African Americans found it easier to internalize supposed Anglos' superiority assaults and return to victim status. Hate was so easy. To steal, rape, and murder held much more excitement than being corralled behind a desk working nine to five for the White man's greed. Touchy-feely negotiations with light-skinned folks who underneath it all were really crackers wielding the whips attempting to tame the black stallion, only served to fuel racial tensions further.

Everyone focused on the president's words. Deflated by the devastation of WWWIII, the newly appointed government had agreed to a plan to return these disgruntled prisoners to their origins, per their repeated requests. No longer would the conglomerate, called government, force unsatisfied citizens to live within the United States. Tired of gang violence, especially behind bars, the prison administration and congress negotiated with United Africa, reaching an acceptable agreement. Having an abundance of vaccinations for AIDS and cancer-fighting compounds, a frustrated United States agreed to supply United Africa with as much medication as was necessary to save the United African citizens. In return, they would allow the U.S. to empty their prisons of the African Americans and return them to their supposed homeland. The price for the prisoners' return was loss of U.S. citizenship. Albeit, they would be freed in United Africa, given a clean slate for their previous crimes, but the prisoners would never again be allowed on American soil.

A hush reverberated across the room. Relatives and loved ones of the Black prisoners had won their exhaustive fight. Behind the prison doors, African Americans would no longer reside. Ex-protestors had one week to decide if they wanted to renounce their citizenships and join the ex-prisoners in their beloved Africa. They would be secretly shipped to African territory to join their rebel pioneers and never allowed to re-enter the United States again. In the newly developed American "Big Brother" database, these individuals would be expunged, wiped clean of their birthplace.

Mu'mad's Mother

From the moment his mother felt him in her womb, she knew her son was special. An extremely difficult birth did not dissuade her either. Large dark doe eyes, framed with long soft lashes, locked upon his mother's in that first instance of maternal ownership. He was the spitting image of his father. Within those first precious minutes, the love affair had begun, an eternal bond between mother and son.

Little Mu'mad, named after the great Prophet Muhammad, would be taught to accept his birthright, and this would be forever embedded in his destiny. His life would be different from others'. However privileged, Mu'mad's life would not be easy. There was much work to be done, much responsibility. With Mu'mad's miracle birth, Islam would never be the same.

In true Canadian fashion, Vancouver had welcomed Mu'mad's mother's battered Muslim family with open arms. Fresh from the sands of Syria, she and her tiny son were allowed to set veiled roots. Adopting new identities, they were able to avoid any intruding strangers. Despite the fact she spoke perfect English, if a kind Canadian got too close, Mu'mad's mother faked incomprehension. Feigning a language barrier was an effective weapon for her strategic isolation. Tolerant of every type of person imaginable, Vancouver allowed individuals to remain as anonymous or invisible as they chose. Canadians encouraged and supported the underdog and Mu'mad's mother exploited this to the fullest. Living in a small flat in New Westminster near the new university, Mu'mad and his guarded mother began to prepare for a requited future. Certain days of the week were spent speaking only English, whereas other days were devoted to French. Of course, Urdu, the language of their people, was maintained, as well as Arabic . . . a top priority really.

When her son reached three years of age, she would begin his religious lessons. Mu'mad would learn Christianity, Judaism, and naturally Islam. Then, when the timing was right little Mu'mad would learn of his great father. All of this powerful man's work would not be in vain but passed proudly to his beautiful son. Little Mu'mad would internalize the family ideals quietly until the time was right to strike down America and Israel . . . strike back vehemently against the same murdering derelicts who had destroyed Mu'mad's father.

Secretly, Mu'mad's mother observed the nonbelievers like watching filthy monkeys in a cage. Although these Westerners were her peers at eighteen years of age, life's experiences had aged her. These dirty young adults wallowed in immaturity as they groped one another with unrestrained urgency. Female students paraded more skin than that on their pasty-white limbs. Flat, bare stomachs were a slap in the face to Mu'mad's mother . . . whores, the entire lot, all whores. She was beyond revulsion. Did these young university students not realize their sins? Their exposed bodies did nothing but provoke primal male urges. And it was their responsibility to cover up . . . calm that inevitable male arousal. Mu'mad's mother could not believe what she saw, these Western women were actually asking for rape. If a Muslim girl's virginity was despoiled, she not only obliterated her honour, but she damaged the honour of her father and all the other males in her family. There was nothing worse than to be the cause of such a familial catastrophe. Women were such easy prey in the Muslim world, so why did these infidels tempt a fate worse than death? Was it because of a few frivolous feelings of freedom or selfish expression? Mu'mad's mother had felt love before. She recognized the rumbling of an untethered heart and fire in her loins. But those foolish, self-indulgent feelings were never supposed to be acted upon. These non-believers of Islam were pathetic animals.

Mu'mad's mother sat on the college steps, her limbs and head fully covered by her burka and hijab. A group of male students climbed the steps Mu'mad's mother sat upon. Quickly she made sure her hands were covered and cowered at the sight of them. Mu'mad's mother had successfully vanished under her black veil. When the young men passed by and entered the university building, Mu'mad's mother breathed a sigh of relief. She watched Mu'mad through her sheer shield as he took his awkward steps about the expansive lawn and tossed his purple ball into the air. This was difficult, having licentious, perverted, filthy soulless Westerners so near her pure little boy.

The infidels' presence made Mu'mad's mother's skin crawl. The West boasted of love and freedom, yet their decadence only proved they were the most corrupt, money-grubbing idolatrous miscreants. That is, besides the Israelis. Had they never studied the fall of the Roman Empire? Mu'mad's mother had. In fact, she had studied a lot about the ways of other cultures. She knew who was at the root of this blasphemy and corruption. Whereas the idiotic Christian Crusaders followed along blindly, it was really the Jews who controlled the world. She understood all of that. Peace would come to the Muslims only when all Jews were eliminated.

Wallowing in a bout of heightened disgust, Mu'mad's mother had lost track of her precious boy, though mere seconds had passed. What she saw next horrified her. A sandy-haired infidel, wearing a Star of David pendant around his neck, shared apple slices with the toddler. Swiftly she was upon her son, slapping the unclean food from her child's tiny determined hand. Although Mu'mad screamed, equally from fright and anger, he had completed his first lesson in not accepting food from the light-skinned, dirty Canadians. Only later would he learn why.

Mu'mad's mother's heart raced. Everyone had stopped in his or her tracks. Eyes were focused upon the hysterical Middle Eastern woman. What had she done? Overreacting would not get Mu'mad what he needed. Besides, her overly infidel-saturated panic had done nothing for her son except to upset and confuse him, as well as draw attention to their glaring differences . . . Islamism. Mu'mad's mother held her sobbing child close to her bosom and raced from the bustling university, finding refuge in their comfortable flat. Tomorrow, in true Islamic fashion, she would work on her self-restraint. She had to be smarter than this. Just how much damage she had caused herself and her son would only play out in the days that followed.

Deek

Night descended across America. Large SST stealth fighter jets silently pierced the darkened skies, their cargo spaces filled with unconscious African American prisoners. Duct tape covered their mouths, and secured blindfolds blocked their vision. Handcuffs pinned their arms securely behind their backs. Hours and hours passed before the prisoners awakened. In the darkness, the confused mob had no idea where they were. The restraints caused many to flail about. Pain shot through their wrists as metal cut into flesh. Relieved to be alive, Deek kicked into survival mode and rubbed his face against the rumbling floor until he was free of the duct tape that covered his mouth. Quietly he spoke to the others, sharing what he had seen the night before. Falsely, he assured them everything was fine; surely, they were being transported to a new prison facility. The panicked groaning eventually ceased as resignation rippled through the crowd . . . for the time being.

Later, as the heavy cargo doors slowly opened, light seeped into the stealth transport compartments. Hundreds of thousands of blinded Black prisoners were forced to exit the stealth jets. Deek and a few others had loosened their blindfolds and only remnants of duct tape hung from their faces. They watched servicemen ripping the sticky tape from the others' mouths then removing their eye covers. Bright sunlight suddenly obstructed everyone's vision. Through squinted eyes, the prisoners could barely see the expansive grasslands spread out before them. Fresh air was a welcomed treat. Men in foreign military uniforms, fully armed, stood on the stealth platforms with bullhorns. A hush rippled across the astonished crowd. Then came the outlandish words; not only were they free from their past crimes, but they were being left in their beloved native land of Africa. Their dreams had been answered . . . finally; their United African brothers had fought for them. After generations of racial struggles, the African Americans' emotional extortion upon the U.S. government had given them freedom, at last. Incontrovertibly, the prisoners understood their time spent in the U.S. was over; never could they return home. Dropping the title of American, they were now proud to be United African and only United African.

The smallest, most abused Black prisoners were given the only knives and handcuff keys. Justice would be short-lived, however. Survival of the meanest would surely overpower survival of the delicate ones as soon as the uniformed officers departed. For subsistence and self-sufficiency, the prisoners were given grains, seeds, and an abundance of water. Also, there were boxes and boxes of canned goods, rice, noodles, and packaged foods. Bundles of African clothing, spears, and knives were left behind as well.

Watching the stealth bombers race for the skies, the freed prisoners were speechless for a slight moment. Shouts of elation exploded when what the servicemen had told them before leaving appeared to be true. They were free, in control of their lives again. Male and female ex-inmates were suddenly separated from their tainted pasts . . . and outdated country. Expelled, each and every one now had the wherewithal to start anew. The only problem was their new townsfolk included only ex-criminals with predominantly belligerent pasts.

Maktan

Paranoid over her previous behaviour toward the infidels, Mu'mad's mother watched for any suspicious Middle Eastern men hovering about her New West flat. If they had been notified of her whereabouts, they would be upon her without hesitation. Yes, the intimidating Muslims would come for her precious gem, Mu'mad. It had taken days before Mu'mad's mother revelled again in her anonymity. No one came for her or Mu'mad. She was free again to be repulsed by the infidels and continue to judge.

Another sunny day upon the university steps, Mu'mad's mother watched her son play as she listened to the students, every one of them so full of opinions and naïve idealisms. They surely did not realize so many of their theories could be easily disputed by the words of Islam. Internally, Mu'mad's mother rolled her eyes in disgust. How stupid were these Westerners?

Then came the first stinging comment. It came from a discussion between some Christian and Muslim students. In the past, they had argued through their religious doctrinal differences, but today their agreement hit with a penetrating clarity. These young idealists mulled over Islamic fanaticism, where abuse to women was barbaric and appalling.

Mu'mad's mother was fine with being labelled a victim. She had survived continual abuse from those men closest to her. It was part of her upbringing. From thirteen years of age, sexual assaults were commonplace. That was one of the reasons she had fallen so hard for her dead husband. He had taken her away from her incestuous environment at fifteen. And his sexual demands were easy in comparison. Perhaps she even enjoyed the attention more than she should have. Pregnant with her son at sixteen, Mu'mad's mother enjoyed her husband's kindness and protectiveness as he patiently awaited the birth of his male heir.

What Mu'mad's mother could not fathom was these college students labelling her a perpetrator. Evidently, by not breaking free of these mental chains, Muslim mothers were passing on fanatical views to their offspring, damning them into a diseased adulthood. Were they ruining their sons? Was it the women's fault for not stopping the abuse? What a harsh reality these impure infidels had painted. But what surprised her even more were the Muslim students agreed. How could they be so harsh on their own? Were they right?

She could not stop listening. Mu'mad's mother had no one to talk to and vent her rebuttals. She was alone . . . alone to face those seeds of doubt sprouting within. How could these frivolous non-believers have so easily ripped blinders from her eyes that were centuries old? Why was she becoming more at ease around the enemy lately? Were things more in focus or was she becoming corrupted, brainwashed by Western ways? So many questions arose that Mu'mad's mother found it difficult to answer.

These young adults were not haughty or unclean. In fact, they spoke of fairness and justice, all encapsulated in youthful freshness. Shiny hair, clean clothes, Mu'mad's mother found herself drawn closer to the unsoiled idealists of the West. She told herself she hated these infidels, but those were just words, words tattooed into her brain long ago. Something profound was welling up deep inside Mu'mad's mother. Not only did she question how her beliefs and behaviour would one day affect her son, but for the first time she was allowed to look at herself without Allah's supposed retribution crashing down upon her covered head.

The scent of jasmine was everywhere. Deep in thought, with eyes closed, Mu'mad's mother was startled when a pretty Muslim girl sat next to her on the steps. Although she wore blue jeans and a long-sleeved T-shirt, and her face was exposed, her head was covered with a colourful hijab.

"Hi there, how are you today?"

Mu'mad's mother was startled. "Oh, I'm fine . . . we're fine."

"Your English is very good. I've seen you here every day over the past few months. Your baby boy is precious. What's your name?"

"Ah, I'm Mu'mad's, Muhammad's mother."

"But what is your name?"

A tingling sensation coursed through her body. How she missed her mother and sisters back home. But it was more than that. She could not remember the last time someone had been interested in her enough to ask her name. Before she had time to think, she responded with complete sincerity. "My name is Maktan."

"I like that; it's a very strong name. I'm Irshad. Pleased to meet you, Maktan."

"The pleasure's all mine, Irshad, really."

"So your little man running around on the grass is Mu'mad?

"Yes."

"He's wonderful. Listen, Maktan, I know how hard it must be for you being in a strange country. My older cousin had quite a transition when, at eighteen, she came over from Afghanistan. Promised to a much older man of sixty back home, she escaped from marrying him by leaving her German university in the middle of the night. By way of Great Britain, my cousin changed her name and eventually disappeared here in Canada."

Maktan was appalled. "She disgraced her father and family?"

"Maktan, who cares if they were disgraced? Her father was ready to condemn her to a life of misery with a man more than three times her age."

"Aren't the men in her family looking for her?"

"No, she faked her death when she fled from Berlin. Some of her friends at university created a convincing death certificate and new identity documents for her."

"So you and your family, or community, in Canada didn't inform your relatives back home of her whereabouts?"

"Certainly not. You see there is a network of young Muslims here and across the globe that protect abused, disgruntled women. Our group is growing, too. Besides, my mother escaped from Afghanistan with her parents, many years ago. They too disappeared in the dark of the night and changed their names once they arrived in Vancouver. My mother's sister, my cousin's mother, was the only one that knew of our new family name and destination. That is how our cousin found us."

Taking it all in, Maktan was quiet for a moment. So many questions fought to get out. Maktan whispered, "Isn't she afraid of Allah's wrath?"

"What wrath, Maktan? Contrary to what you've been

taught, Allah loves women equally as he does men. This took my cousin a long time to accept. When she wore her first pair of blue jeans she thought Allah would strike her down, but there was no lightning bolt with her name on it. When she sipped her first beer, still no death bolt appeared. It took several years of unraveling the hardwired, traditionally warped, male-dominated Islam in her heart and mind."

"What is your cousin like today? What is her name?"

"She took a Western name, Annaleigh Rypien. She still practises Islam, but the non-fanatical version. Annaleigh is happily married with two little boys who she is raising to respect women and love Allah. Oh, and she is a successful pediatrician."

"How can there be two types of Islam, Irshad? The words in the Quran are the words of Allah."

"And those supposed words of Allah were written down by men years after the events occurred and Allah's words were spoken. You know, Maktan, many Muslims don't even speak Arabic, so they are vulnerable to misrepresentation of the true meanings of the Quran and have been for years. Corrupt leaders are eager to get their interpretations across to innocent followers."

Maktan was angry. "This is very unsettling. So much disrespect, Irshad."

"Perhaps, Maktan, but facts are facts. I wouldn't have understood all of this if I hadn't watched Annaleigh go through her transformation. She taught me a lot."

"How does she know she is right?"

"Because, with her new life, Annaleigh feels even closer to Allah than she ever has before. She truly feels loved by her maker."

A part of Maktan wanted to scream at this obvious infidel, whilst the other more deep-seated side wanted to rip her black, colourless burka from her own face and head and stomp it into the pavement. "Irshad, why do you even wear a hijab if you feel the way you do?"

"It is out of respect for Allah, symbolizing the veil between this world and our maker. I certainly don't wear it to dissuade male desires. I love Islam, Maktan, but want to see it get back to its loving roots as Allah had intended."

"I feel like slapping you, but I know you mean well." Confusion was etched into Maktan's face.

Irshad grinned past a row of slightly crooked, bright white teeth. "I understand, truly I do. Well, think about what I've said. I mean no disrespect." Maktan said nothing. "Hey, well, I need to get to class. Just so you know, Maktan, your eyes betray you . . . I see your wisdom even if you don't acknowledge it. Someday you will see I speak the truth. Someday you will let that powerful soul out of its mental prison. I wish you well. Got to go. Have a great afternoon."

With that, Irshad jumped to her feet and joined a mixture of racially diverse students passing by. She turned her head and waved a quick goodbye to a bewildered Maktan.

Deek's United Africa

In the African grasslands, mayhem brewed. No one listened; instead, everyone spewed opinions. Gradually, bitching and complaining became prevalent again. It was the Lompoc group's way of coping. They seemed to be comfortable when agitated voices surrounded them. Feeling entitled, perfectly healthy men sat in the scant shade and refused to help raise tarps for the betterment of the group. Women shook disapproving fingers at them and nagged incessantly, necks sore from "juking and jiving" their heads about with indignant righteousness. Nothing got done. Everyone missed his or her hot meals, air-conditioned cells, comfortable beds, and indoor plumbing. The heat threatened to suffocate them. And the millions of crazed flies were torturous . . . the more the perspiration, the more the flies seemed to multiply and hover about like a thick, itchy blanket. These flying maggots would easily condemn a sane man to lunacy. Hot, damp, and irritable, not one person would give an inch, so Deek decided to speak. Finally, a leader had stepped to the forefront, and the first order of business was silence. Deek stared at the selfish herd before him.

He took his time then bellowed. "Careful what you wish for you pile of ingrates!" No one knew how to respond. A group of outspoken females raised their voices with an incoherent tirade. "For God's sake, shut up!" The crowd did not know whether to be shocked or amused. "For decades and decades you've blamed 'white-bread' for all your problems. It pissed you off when people criticized you big Black 'bucks' for sitting around being porch monkeys, bullshitting about nothing; made you mad didn't it? Well, get a clue! Look around! Whitey isn't here, so what's your excuse now? We've been free for such a short time and look at you. The strongest of the bunch are sitting in the shade, while the women are in the hot sun doing all the work. We have to take care of one another. Do you get that? You've dreamed of Africa, wished for this very thing. Christ, you're still acting like a bunch of spoiled, victimized inmates!"

One of the shade-pilfering hulks stood. "And who elected yo' bossman, yo' cracka-lovin' college fuck?"

"Sly, if you don't like it feel free to get your lazy ass up here and lead!"

"Ah, fuck off! I ain't takin' orders from no pampered NFL Oreo. Hell, yo' veins pumpin' nuthin' but mayonnaise." The man took a couple of steps, yanked a sleeping bag from one of the women, a spear from a frail man, and grabbed a few supplies before storming off into the direction of the swaying, wheat-coloured grass.

Deek continued. "Anyone else care to join our angry friend?" No one moved. One by one, the rest of the men stepped from the shade and started to undo the packages containing tents and tarps. Instantly, an aggressive woman raised her overly parental voice. Deek stopped her. "And women, if us men are going to honour you with respect, be deserving of that treatment. There's not one of us that enjoys being ordered about with chronic nagging."

Deek moved about the crowd and helped erect the Lompoc clan's new living quarters. Once the men had the women in the shade, they organized the food and began cooking. Protectively, Deek positioned the rest of the tents surrounding the women. Enticing smells could conjure up hungry wildlife. Deek ran into a group of excessively tattooed, youthful men. He smacked a biscuit from the mouth of the largest sloth.

"Why aren't you helping?"

"We're savin' our energy for huntin' when the sun goes down."

"Bullshit. We're all hunting later. Pitch in now or none of you eat, your choice."

"Who made you the fuckin' bossman? Yo' ain't our peeps, Deek, so fuck off."

"Oh, ouch, is that supposed to hurt my precious feelings? I couldn't care less. No work, no eat."

From the waste-high sea of rolling grassland, chilling, consecutive roars erupted from all directions. Everyone stopped what he or she was doing. Then a frightful sound caused the hairs to rise on the inmates' arms and napes. A man's terrified scream pierced the stillness. Frozen and wide-eyed, the Lompoc tribe felt utterly vulnerable, with the onset of panic. Rustling in the tall grass became more violent as the screeching intensified. Deek ran toward the commotion. From the brush came a hulky Sly, his shredded shirt covered in blood. Underneath the slashed, soaked clothing were large gashes, bleeding profusely. Deek sprinted for his spear that was close by, and yelled for the rest of the men to grab their weapons. Then, from the swaying grass, a blond streak broke free. In the twilight hour, the enormous beast's fur glistened like gold. American street jungles carried enemies and those inmates they were familiar with; they knew what to expect from their foes. There were no monsters like this enormous cat. No one could move. Two more fully outstretched strides toward Sly and the muscular male lion tackled his prey. Sly wrapped his arms around his head. The cat sunk his teeth into Sly's upper arm and neck as Deek and the others launched their weapons. The ravenous lion ripped at the man's flesh just as several spears pierced the massive feline's ribcage. It screamed with a deep violent defiance then wilted. When Deek reached Sly, he and a tribesman flung the heavy lion carcass from its victim.

"Sly, Sly, hang in there! I've got you, I've got you." Deek pulled his shirt over his head and wrapped it around Sly's neck to stop the bleeding. While the men guarded the perimeter of their camp, a crowd of women brought first aid materials to Deek's side.

"Deek, let me see the wound. I was a nurse."

Sly's eyes were wide open. "Deek . . ."

"Don't talk, Sly, you'll be fine . . . you'll be fine. You're in good hands."

Suddenly, stark reality set in. To the inmates "Africa" had been a mere utopianism. Everything bad in their American lives had made their imagined Africa better . . . as unrealistic as it was, it had been their seed of hope.

Maktan

FEAR CLUNG TO MAKTAN AS she walked briskly to her and Mu'mad's flat. It had dawned on her that Irshad could be a spy for those searching for Maktan and her son. She had mentioned casually that she had noticed Maktan and Mu'mad there every day. Had that meant Irshad was observing her? Spying on her? Why on Earth had she given Irshad her real first name? By the time Maktan unlocked her front door, her rapid heartbeat left her out of breath and dizzy. Quickly, she dead-bolted her door and stumbled across the living room, clinging to a sleeping Mu'mad in her arms. Maktan's eighteen-year-old head spun. Groping items along the way, Maktan finally reached Mu'mad's crib where she put him down to finish his nap. Her knees gave way. Maktan slumped to the floor, trying to stop the spinning and catch her breath. All she could do was crawl into a fetal position upon the tattered carpet below as her full-blown panic attack took hold. Erratic breathing began. Soon after, the tears came and fell hard.

HOURS PASSED BEFORE MAKTAN WAS calm enough to function. Hungry, Mu'mad fussed continually until his mother brought him a bottle of warm milk. Maktan sat in her rocking chair and cradled her son while he ate. Well-educated, Maktan knew Irshad had a valid point of view. It was just going to take a laborious, torturous time to dissolve the bars of her cerebral cage. When Maktan was able to pierce those mental walls of her Islamic prison, she would be able to admit the centerpiece of the Quran was male supremacy and female misery. Women were deprived of a sex life and forced into a degrading, painful existence. Had she really loved her husband or was it the result of brainwashing and subtle manipulation to force her into submission?

Privately, Maktan screamed from within. She screamed for a lifetime of frustration and repression. All the abuse she had endured was suddenly released from her shackled memories. Such oppression had taken her rightful life away. Confusion banged about Maktan's brain and would not cease until clarity reigned.

She could hear her parents' arguments try to poison her new thoughts. Canada was an infidel country, whose way of life Muslims were supposed to oppose and reject. Why then was it so much better run, better led, and made for better lives than Maktan's homeland? Should not the places where Allah was worshipped and His laws obeyed be peaceful and wealthy, and the unbelievers' countries ignorant, poor, and war torn? She faced so many contradictions.

The harshest was the certainties that Muslims were superior to infidels, yet Maktan, and others like her, were not superior at all. Why were the battered women's shelters mostly filled with Muslims in New Westminster? She hated facing the fact that those societies, which respected women's rights and their freedom, were prosperous and supportive. Islam, at least for Maktan, was somehow losing its lustre. Why too were these passive, impure, infidel Canadians spewing such offensive rhetoric about her treasured Prophet Muhammad?

It was fact, according to many, that a fifty-four-year-old Muhammad bedded a nine-year-old girl. By Canadian standards, Muhammad was a filthy pedophile. And, when analyzing how Muhammad ruled, the university students asserted he was a lone ruler . . . true; an autocrat . . . true; that equalled tyranny. All in the name of Islam?

Maktan had stayed close to these students. Their free young minds gave her the information to feed Mu'mad when he was older. She would raise him knowing how the infidels thought. But why was there such emotion surging through her body during discussions of women's abuse? The Quran mandates these punishments against women . . . true. It legitimizes abuse, so the perpetrators feel no shame and are not hounded by their conscience or society. Yes, that was true too. Her head hurt.

Walks to the park had offered some happy times at the university. Plenty of sunshine helped her boy grow strong. Everything was for Mu'mad's thorough development. When he was old enough to attend school, he would go. Albeit home schooling would inevitably put him further ahead of all the other children, public schooling was essential. Keeping Mu'mad's enemies close was a tactic Maktan had learned from her deceased husband. She watched her son's rhythmic breathing as he slept soundly in her arms. Were these people Mu'mad's enemies? It was difficult to turn off the voice of her late husband. She still felt strongly that when her precious boy was grown and others trusted, loved, and were devoted to him, Mu'mad would restore the Muslim world. Islam was the future; Islam would prevail . . . but how?

Composed, yet motivated again by fear of discovery and capture, Maktan taped shut her final box. Being completely honest with herself, she would miss New

Westminster, its dome-less air, and the interesting infidel students. Maktan had enjoyed seeing her son so happy and healthy. It was equally satisfying to feel the surges inside as her soul fought to sprout new ideas and opinions. However much they would miss this suburb of Vancouver, it was time to move. Mu'mad and Maktan were entirely too exposed, maybe even compromised. Those oppressive men that had been close to her husband would easily discover her hideout soon enough. Yes, it was time to go, time to disappear.

Deek

The new United Africans ate their first meal together with little conversation. They had gotten their wish, with no knowledge of what they had bargained for. Never during their utopian dreaming had they included physical discomforts and man-eating predators.

Deek broke the silence. "So how many of you have African ancestors who were tribal hunters?" Very few hands were raised. A wave of discontent passed over the group. "How many thought hunting an outdated, distorted tradition?" A light laughter sounded. To the younger punks that were giving Deek a hard time before Sly's screams were heard, Deek spoke gently. "Hey, you four did a great job skinning that fat cat. Be sure and wash up. You don't want that bloody scent on your skin while sleeping."

Without a choice, they had found themselves on a date with the harsher side of Mother Nature. Deek and several others wrapped the remaining cooked lion and hoisted it up a tree quite a distance from camp. It was decided that rotated groups would stand watch over their campsite during their first night. Those that were not perched with spears and knives, overseeing the inmates' safety, initially dropped from exhaustion. The new United Africans' primordial first day in their new country had brought a sobering realization. Many longed for their air-conditioned prison cells.

No longer encased within the prison walls, the ex-prisoners should have enjoyed a full night of relaxed sleep . . . far from it. Living amongst unrestrained criminals, as well as monstrous cats with voracious appetites for human flesh, had given cause for most ex-inmates to sleep with one eye open.

Kozlov

On the edge of his bed sat a little girl with beautiful long blonde hair.

"Sasha?"

"Papa, where have you been?" She crawled toward her father and fell into his arms.

"At work, Baby." He patted her back.

"You always say that." Sasha pulled back and peered at Kozlov, running her delicate finger down the lengthy scar that lined the left side of Kozlov's square jawline. Her round blue eyes searched her father's. "Where? Why have you been gone so long? Why did you leave me with them?"

Concern crept across Kozlov's face. "Them? Sasha, where is Mama?"

"Some men in Egyptian robes took her." Tears welled in Sasha's eyes. "They slapped her, Papa. Over and over they hit her across the face." Kozlov's ten-year-old daughter buried her face and wept against his chest.

"It's okay, Baby. Papa will make it right."

Kozlov looked around realizing he was in his bedroom back home in Moscow. That bastard, al-Husri, had sent his men to Kozlov's home? They knew where he lived? Quickly, he scooped up Sasha, then leapt from his bed. There was a commotion outside.

As Kozlov carried his daughter to the window, he felt her racing heart against his. When he drew back the drapes and peered out, Kozlov's breath caught in his throat. No wonder his daughter clung to his neck. Far off in the distance, he saw a bulging mushroom cloud, pregnant with radiation and destruction. Air raid sirens sounded with an incessant high-pitched whine. Panicked, Kozlov was not sure which move to make next. All had gone terribly wrong. Flustered, he reluctantly let his daughter drop to her feet.

"Come, Sasha, we need to get to the fallout shelter."

"Papa?"

"Come!"

Her hand tightly in his, Kozlov guided his little girl down their luxurious, spiral staircase. As they hurried, Kozlov stole glances out the vaulted staircase windows. When they reached the bottom of the stairway, Sasha broke free and ran for the second story landing.

"Sasha!"

"Papa, I have to get my teddy!"

A bright flash blinded Kozlov. After a very short delay, a deafening explosion sounded. Glass pelted Kozlov's face. His little girl screamed.

"Sasha, Baby!" There was no answer. "Sasha!"

When Kozlov was able to peer from his damaged eyes, he noticed the skin was gone from his arms. He smelled of burnt flesh.

Kozlov broke free from a troubled sleep. His breath came in short gasps. Dampened sheets from troubled perspiration clung to Kozlov's skin. Quickly he examined the room and realized Sasha was not there. The wallpaper and drapes were not from his Moscow bedroom, either. Reality would slowly erase the angst of yet another vivid nightmare. But somehow this one was different, it lingered. Kozlov jumped from his bed and noticed, on a table next to the door, the clothes he wore from his meeting with al-Husri.

All were cleaned and pressed. Kozlov's EyeNet sunglasses lay next to his clothing. This holographic communication service, using optic-chip implants or external eyewear, and a keyboard cuff, had long since replaced cellular devices. Kozlov put on his sunglasses; no phone messages. He replaced the EyeNet device next to his wallet and gun. Feeling his confusion start to lift, he walked to the window then ripped the drapes back. Relief rushed in when he discovered he was back safely within his five-star Syrian hotel. Bile rushed into his throat. Kozlov raced for the bathroom, barely making it to the toilet before vomiting. He sat upon the ice-cold marbled floor and cried. Sasha's visit was just a nightmare . . . or was it? Cold sweat broke out on Kozlov's forehead. He stood, wobbling a bit, then struggled to fix a cold washcloth for his face. His hands shook. In the mirror, he examined the tennis ball-sized bruise on his upper arm where al-Husri's man had slammed in the needle. Queasy and dizzy Kozlov reached for the toilet and vomited a second time. Previous experience had taught him the al Din drugs caused an upset stomach and the jitters, but would soon pass. Food and water, lots of water, was the simple remedy.

Kozlov made his way to the hotel's compact concierge screen next to his bed and tapped the room service icon. He repositioned the soothing washcloth upon his forehead. As he sat on the edge of the bed and listened for a response, questions began to ricochet about his head. Had he failed? Was this al-Husri's way of saying "not a chance, time to go, Russian"?

Kozlov's thoughts were hazy, but his fear was palpable. He let his mind wander to those historical days preceding al Din's birth. Terrorism had really made its mark on the Western world on 9/11. Decades ago, al-Qaeda had terrorized and crippled the world after levelling the Twin Towers in New York City. However, to Kozlov, al-Qaeda was benign compared to al-Husri and al Din. At one time, aligned in the first decade of the twenty-first century, al-Qaeda and the Taliban had forged an alliance to protect Osama bin Laden, the worshipped Muslim that had temporarily brought the West to its knees. Though the two radical organizations shared common interests, they continued to struggle and battle for ultimate supremacy. As al-Qaeda continued to flex its fanatical muscle, the Taliban tired of its own inferior position. It was not long until al-Qaeda decided to cease the senseless bickering with its rebellious brethren. Following Osama bin Laden's assassination, with a stockpile of sophisticated weaponry and unlimited funds, al-Qaeda prevailed. While at Moscow State University, Kozlov had studied this chink in the terrorists' armour; every faction was autonomous, unable to unite. This was such a relief for the rest of the world.

For years, the mere mention of al-Qaeda caused peace-loving communities to shudder. However, as Kozlov had learned, these terrorists eventually lost their punch. He was not surprised when reading about a Sunni extremist group, ISIS, positioned in Northern Iraq and Syria, entering the scene. The KGB had become nervous when this new group cautiously aligned themselves with al-Qaeda. Centred under a united caliphate, both groups believed they shared the same Islamic political-religious leadership. ISIS, quite serious about their expansionist Islamic ideology, viciously executed Israelis and Shia Muslims in view of the world. As time wore on, al-Qaeda realized their caliphate vision of territorial jurisdiction under a caliph, successor to Muhammad, was vastly different. Ironically, even al-Qaeda found ISIS too brutal, so they disbanded. With ISIS as the new terrorist threat, al-Qaeda faded to an annoying cliché. Again, the KGB was relieved this potentially powerful group had fractured, unable to unify.

Although ISIS was horrific, they paled in comparison to Abbud al-Ypaaht's reign. While at university, Kozlov extensively researched this brutal era; it fascinated him. Al-Ypaaht made Hitler and the Third Reich seem like a pastry basket full of cream puffs. The embodiment of ancient evil, al-Ypaaht was the prophesied instigator of Worldwide War III, who globally united the Muslim extremists. This had been the KGB's worst nightmare, terrorist unification.

Al-Ypaaht had changed everything. His platinum-tongued treachery easily fooled the masses. True, al-Ypaaht conned many initially; their financial ruin and humiliation were the least of their worries however. Using biological warfare, al-Ypaaht's followers released a viral pestilence in London and New York City. The invisible killer resulted in a battle of epic proportions, forcing confinement for both metropolises. As the virus seeped beyond the quarantined borders, talks of the end of the world were at hand, so al-Ypaaht played upon that panic. While everyone was focused on the horrific, growing number of bloated, decaying corpses in these afflicted cities, al-Ypaaht struck again.

With his gift for manipulation, he tossed about false promises and padded many corrupt pockets as he cajoled countries into strategically releasing their weapons of mass destruction upon their enemies. When the atomic and nuclear arsenals were unleashed upon the distracted, self-serving international populace, millions perished from all races. The world was aglow. Many cities and citizens were reduced to rubble and ash. Frigid nuclear winters followed, which brought about food shortages, slow painful deaths, and eventually the emergence of gross birth defects. Sadly, at that time al-Ypaaht had everyone's attention.

Although the majority of survivors discovered they had a common enemy, and differences should have been forgotten, paranoia had a chokehold on the throats of the innocent, rendering them helpless. These pure-at-hearts fought very, very hard, but everyday existence became a painful struggle. Al-Ypaaht's mayhem reached every corner of existence. Russia, China, Italy, Greece, France, England, North Africa, and Israel suffered the bulk of his wrath. Loss of life was catastrophic, trust completely obliterated. Not until the "three brothers," Europe, North America, and Russia, joined forces did they cease al-Ypaaht's puppet-mastering destruction. Albeit al-Ypaaht's forces fought hard, their intense loyalty went unnoticed by their cowardly leader. In the darkest hours of early morning, the vile creature abandoned his followers and fled. Hiding like a craven cockroach in the shadows, no one ever found the instigator of WWWIII.

Kozlov's university research had taught him how the embittered, determined al-Ypaaht henchmen kept the united Arab plight alive. Hence, the emergence of al Din—the righteous, lighted path. As a young boy, Kozlov remembered that scary name, *al Din*. Later, his studies revealed just why this organization instilled fear in everyone. Al Din's global caliphate planned to overthrow political systems, cleanse the world of Christians and Jews, and implement a single theocratic one-world Islamic government.

Patient and disciplined, al Din worked toward the unification of all Muslims. After years of meticulous, clandestine organization, al Din made its debut. Noon Eastern Standard Time, CIA headquarters, in Langley, Virginia, received Intel regarding planned attacks at undisclosed sporting events. Operatives scrambled to identify scheduled NFL gridirons and baseball games at the university and professional levels. But hidden amongst a sea of sports enthusiasts were hundreds of al Din soldiers . . . with bombs strapped to their torsos. By 12:30 pm EST, 5:30 pm U.K. time, toxic vapour bombs detonated throughout the Manchester United's Old Trafford stadium. Victims dropped dead in their seats, some as they ran. Football fan fatalities were upwards of 17,000.

The world was in shock, mesmerized by the mayhem unfolding in England. The CIA and MI6 were frantic. After half an hour, at 1:00 pm EST, the next wave of poisonous bombs exploded in the New York Giants' MetLife stadium, killing 21,500 gridiron fans.

Ten minutes later, vapour bombs detonated in the Toronto Blue Jays' Rogers Centre stadium, where 11,000 baseball fans perished. But England, America, and Canada were not the real focus . . . a mere distraction.

With their allies buried in devastation, al Din's primary target was caught unaware. Al Din terrorist cells throughout Nazareth, comprised of 80 percent Muslim and known as "the Arab capital of Israel," coordinated air attacks on Israel's Northern Territory. Using Russian thermobaric bombs, al Din struck Tiberias first, reducing the city to ash and killing 60,000 Israelis.

However, the hardest hit was Israel's third largest city of Haifa. Rapid incineration by the thermobaric bombs caused 82,500 fatalities in a matter of minutes. The once-vibrant port city was levelled, shocked into silence.

For al Din, this mission was a success; in forty minutes, the infidel death toll had reached 192,000. Qeb al-Husri, in his younger years, orchestrated the entire operation. And he and al Din were just getting started.

For Kozlov, previous intrigue and fascination with al Din manifested into present-day terror. His thoughts returned to the possible rejection by al-Husri. His palms were damp. Room service had him on hold, leaving him alone with his torturous scenarios. Decades had passed since that first horrific assault, and al Din's brutality had only intensified over time. Suddenly, Kozlov could hear someone outside approaching his room. Skilfully, he rose from the edge of his bed, crept across the room, and grabbed his gun. Lurking in the hotel hallway, Kozlov's assailant came closer. Kozlov aimed his gun then froze. Underneath the door, his intruder shoved an envelope. Kozlov's heart pounded. Slowly he lowered his weapon and replaced it on the table. Reassured of his safety, Kozlov took slow staggering steps toward the door and retrieved the letter. Impatiently he ripped open the envelope, causing a severe paper cut. Blood oozed from his middle finger. He sucked away the viscous, salty build-up and, with his other hand, Kozlov shook open the folded paper. There were only three words upon the page. His heartbeat quickened, again. Kozlov reread the words then let the paper float to the floor.

Deek

EXTRACTION OF THE AFRICAN AMERICAN prisoners caused a tidal wave of behaviour reform across the United States. Jailed Latino prisoners became less vocal, less belligerent. Somehow they knew returning to Mexico was not the answer to their problems. All those years flying the Mexican flag and shoving it tauntingly into the faces of non-Latino Americans were over. If the U.S. government decided to ship Mexicans back to their homeland, their families would surely suffer greatly at the hands of corrupt Policia Federales and drug cartels. Outside, in the free world, gangs gradually disbanded . . . the threat of being deported made the gangland way of life less appealing. There were those extreme, small groups of African Americans who entered their names upon a list that "wanted out." They would be included in the next mass exodus of individuals packed off to Africa with neither a return ticket nor U.S. citizenship. Those people remaining behind in America suddenly realized their country was not so terrible, and more importantly, it would not tolerate a bunch of malice from its citizens, either. This change complemented the transformation occurring within America's political system.

The silent majority found their voices and swiftly became the outspoken. All races, especially the Whites, tried a little harder. Politically, a new party, symbolized by the Zebra, proceeded to clean up the dung left behind by previous Donkey and Elephant administrations. What emerged was a feisty striped horse . . . a tri-coloured, cuddly quadruped saturated with independence and intelligence, but equally forceful. The Zebra typified the unexploited, for it was the horse that could not be ridden. Over the years, America's government shifted most of its executive power to the legislative branch. Having the Zebra party eliminated stalemates between extremely liberal and conservative party disputes. With less governmental posturing to get to the head of the line, politicians spent their time performing their elected duties. Increased accountability caused parasitic politicos, practising ineffective, unscrupulous tactics, to move elsewhere. Perhaps these reforms were the answer to America's troubles. More importantly, history would not be in the throes of repetition . . . hopefully.

What cohesiveness that initially existed amongst the Lompoc tribe, became unhinged after the first week. How quickly they had forgotten Sly's travesty. Running a high fever, Sly's prognosis had been day-to-day. Whereas his chest and arm wounds were healing nicely, the gash in his neck was quite another story. Pus oozed from the crudely repaired tear in his throat tissue. The huge male lion had bitten and torn hard in those final seconds, before its life ended. Now, fighting back, Sly, covered in perspiration, rocked to and fro, determined to break the menacing fever. Easily forgotten, however, was empathy from Sly's tribesmen, which had rapidly dwindled.

While Deek was out with a few others searching for a better campsite, many of the ex-prisoners stopped working. Most thought themselves above the menial tasks. Arguments and aberrant behaviour took up most of their days. The stronger men terrorized and overpowered the weaker more vulnerable ones. Goods were stolen and women raped. By the time Deek's search party returned, it appeared to be an instant replay of violent American gang wars. Penitentiary groups had realigned and turfs designated through brutal assaults. Almost immediately, the new United Africans reverted to pack mentality, living like starving wolves. Some of the more desperate, frail ex-prisoners had abandoned the group in search of established United African villages. Little did they know, the natives would not welcome these Americans. Instead, death would come instantly without discussion. United Africans did not want diseased criminal attitudes and lack of scruples to infiltrate their communities. Fortunately, the Lompoc clan was not part of the violent offenders; they kept a low profile. However, they simply refused to work.

It had taken days for Sly to show signs of recovery. Although weak, Sly's appetite had returned and his neck wound was no longer abscessed.

"Sly, what's up brotha?"

"I'm one step closa ta Hell. What can I say?"

"Well, what can I say, you look like something the cat dragged in."

"Not funny, College Boy."

"Can I get you anything?"

"No, the sistas are treatin' me like a king."

"Well, your majesty, any suggestions for our new community? Everyone seems a little tense—something's up."

"From what da ladies been sayin', as soon as yo' left camp da fuckups decided ta revert back ta gang-landin'."

"That's what I heard, but I was hoping it wasn't true." Deek shook his head in disgust. "I need you better, Sly."

"I'z tryin', believe me."

"If we focus on the troublemakers, we'll have a shot at some peace."

"We got us a good bunch, Deek. They don't know no betta. Least they did no killin' or rapin'. They'z just lazy fuckas."

"Well, as soon as you're able, we've found a great location about a two-day walk from here. There's a small lake, more like an overgrown pond, lined with trees. It might be hard to defend at first because it is a watering hole for those damn lions. But once we build some kind of barricade around our camp, we'll just have to be careful outside our compound."

"Sounds like an easier go at huntin', too."

"Exactly, plenty of food will be close at hand, barbeque more of those damn cats. Well, get better, my man."

"Deek, I neva got ta thank—"

"No need. Us alpha males got to stick together, Sly. You know, outsmart these younger dumb-shits. I can't do this alone, holding our group together and all. Besides, they look up to you, Sly."

"Yo' got some educatin' ta do, that's all. Gunna take time."

"Indeed."

Outside Sly's tent, Deek surveyed the behaviour of the others. The women worked silently, while the men stood scowling at no one in particular. Uneasiness hung in the air like a thick fog. Aside from the assigned lion-watch group, cohesion seemed non-existent. Deek remained alert. Soon a beautiful, soft-spoken woman, Chandra, came bearing food.

She leaned into Deek and whispered. "Enjoy all but the stew. Those men directly behind me poisoned your food with their crap and some other chemicals. They don't know that I saw them."

"Thank you, Chandra."

Frustrated tears filled her eyes. "Don't let them ruin everything . . . please, Deek."

Restlessness grew amongst the scheming men. They paced.

Deek smiled in Chandra's direction. "You'd better get back to the others. Don't worry." Carefully Deek rose, plate and all, and proceeded to eat his dinner alone in his tent. Although a bit wobbly, Sly was able to join him. They took no chances. Sly's eats could be tainted as well. Plates empty and ruse in place, Deek and Sly proceeded to act as if nothing was wrong except for feeling a little under the weather. Both men retired early for the night.

It was difficult for Deek to stay awake for he was exhausted from the four-day, nonstop scouting journey. Several nods and Deek let his eyelids seal shut. His breathing was deep. In the corner of Deek's tent, a hidden Sly kept a watchful eye on his friend.

Maktan

OVERWROUGHT WITH SUSPICIONS OF EVERY passer-by on the sidewalk below, Maktan postponed leaving her apartment for days. Shades drawn, she peeked through the blinds to see if any Middle Eastern faces were seen casing her apartment building. Poor Mu'mad misunderstood his suddenly sequestered predicament. Progressively, he was becoming more and more restless and defiant. Incessant crying tore at Maktan's sanity. On her sixth day of isolation, she decided to take Mu'mad in the stroller and purchase some things for their escape. So far, no men from her homeland had been seen lurking about. This was as safe as it was going to get.

Outside, Maktan steered Mu'mad in the opposite direction of the university. There would be too many eyes upon them there. Irshad had noticed Maktan and her son and that was by no means good. Her pace quickened. In every direction, Maktan thought she saw a dark, Middle Eastern face in the shadows. Maktan's imagination fed her growing fear, which caused her to rush into the small department store at the nearest corner. Once inside Maktan began to grab the goods she needed as fast as she could. Thankfully little Mu'mad was amused with the rushing about. He squealed with delight. How Maktan loved her precious boy. Why had she not faked her and Mu'mad's death as Annaleigh had? Going forward she would have to be much more cautious. One mistake was one too many.

Little Mu'mad was fast asleep. Staring at her slumbering angel, Maktan plopped her exhausted body down upon the couch. Her past cried out for attention as she allowed suppressed memories and emotions to replay themselves.

WHILE PREGNANT WITH MU'MAD, MAKTAN had lain helpless in a Pakistani cave. Kept from her mother and sisters, Maktan remembered how frightened she had been giving birth around a bunch of bumbling, heartless men. Chills crept up her back when recalling those bleak days.

How foolish Muslim men could be when in the presence of a well-educated female. Prominent Syrian Muslims knew whose seed Maktan carried. Once Muhammad was born, they orchestrated mother and son's movement from Pakistan to Syria. What they had not planned on was Mu'mad's mother slipping away to Vancouver with her precious gem.

Maktan's husband had prepped her for the day she would have to go into hiding. With fake passports and plenty of Turkish lira stashed away, Maktan waited until the ignorant men became comfortable with her trips to the market. She had waited patiently for the perfect opportunity, and when it arose, Maktan fled with her son amongst the bustling crowds.

This was when Yonca and Zeren Killic, Turkish immigrants, were born. With new identities, mother and son planned to live in Canada, far away from their roots. Maktan's use of her deceased husband's secret bank account was infrequent for fear al Din would uncover the money trail, tracking her and her baby boy. Maktan knew the only reason the Syrians had spared her life was because she was still nursing her infant son at the time.

Without a doubt, they would have eventually weaned Muhammad off his mother's teat permanently. And, the

Syrian's plans for her consisted of only fatal consequences. Thankfully, no one had monitored Maktan that closely. The haughty Muslim yes-men believed she had little intelligence and no means of moving about. To Maktan it had been proven, arrogance was synonymous with stupidity.

Clad in blue jeans and a sweatshirt, Maktan's new disguise was complete. Irshad's cousin, Annaleigh, was right. Allah had not struck down Maktan because she wore infidel clothing. With Mu'mad tucked securely in her arms, Maktan trudged the seven blocks to the Royal Bank of Canada. Her personal banker had been chosen very carefully. From the moment she and Mu'mad had settled in New Westminster, Maktan had surveyed the banking institutions within walking distance. Maintaining anonymity was of the utmost importance. If not, word would travel rapidly within the Muslim community as to her whereabouts. Safety for Mu'mad could not be compromised. Maktan had escaped the fanatical clutches of the Islamic brutes once, but she would not survive a second meeting. If discovered, Mu'mad would fall into a pool of self-serving insanity, someday being used as the Islam pawn for these Desert Muslims. Maktan's husband had bigger plans for his son and had instructed her well.

Within the bank's confines, Maktan shifted her heavy, growing boy to her other hip while she searched for Candi, her blonde, green-eyed non-Muslim personal banker. A broad, white smile greeted Maktan from across the room. It had been two years since their escape from Syria. It was time to shift the remaining bulk of her financial wealth to the Canadian bank from her husband's hidden account in Luxembourg. Today, Maktan would make an aggressive move and gamble the unveiling of her and her son's location. For two years, no one had monitored withdrawals from the millions collecting dust in the tiny, financially wealthy country wedged in between France, Belgium, and Germany. No one had appeared in the dark of the night to steal away her most prized possession; no dark-complexioned men prowled about New Westminster in search of the infant who would save Islam. For a period of time, they had sunk temporary roots in this suburb, but it was time to relocate. Yes, today Maktan would shift her monies, then sign the documents for the purchase of a converted penthouse, in Vancouver, under the downtown dome. Residential skyscraper after skyscraper filled the rounded peninsula. It would be much easier to be anonymous in such a congested area. And her real estate purchase would be an investment for Mu'mad and give them both added security. They would move into two penthouse suites converted into one thirty-seven-hundred square-foot, four-bedroom, four-bath unit perched at the top of a fifty-story high-rise. An L-shaped rooftop deck would allow for an extensive garden for Maktan and plenty of room for little Mu'mad to play in the sunshine.

Money secured and condominium papers signed, Maktan walked two more blocks to a truck rental place. Mu'mad loved the moving van's rumbling engine. Back at their flat, Maktan packed up her meagre possessions and drove Mu'mad to their new downtown home. Maktan was thrilled once the last of their things were placed upon their marble floor. After she and Mu'mad returned the van to a downtown location, it was a brisk walk home, speaking to no one. When the front door was bolted and new security system engaged, Maktan finally relaxed. What a relief to be away from prying eyes. She pulled back the vaulted drapes from the many windows and took in the breathtaking view of the famous snow-covered twin Lion peaks, perched above the North Shore Mountains. She also saw the popular Pan Pacific Hotel awning, notable Harbour Centre needle, the many cruise and cargo ships inching about the water inlet, and frenzied lifestyle on the streets below. Maktan smiled. She had never lived amongst such epic beauty. Her husband would be so proud . . . she was so proud. Maktan had accomplished a great deal all by herself.

Mu'mad was sound asleep in his tiny, rocker crib. Maktan ripped open the first of several boxes of books. Eagerly she went about placing the leather-bound antiques she had accumulated while in New West into the many shelves of her and Mu'mad's old-fashioned upstairs library. She could not wait to share the contents with her grown son someday.

Kozlov

A far away, yet distinct voice could be heard from across the room. Kozlov hurried to the abandoned concierge panel beside his bed. He regained his composure and opted for a sizeable breakfast. When his order was placed with room service, he sat back on his bed and reread al-Husri's letter yet again. Those three words gave him a rush … "all is accepted."

Directive Two had taken a lot of work and carried a much higher risk for the Russian citizens if al Din decided to double-cross the KGB. Kozlov shared his nightmare of Sasha with no one, especially not his wife. He continued to work feverishly until all the Russian warheads, each identical to the American construct, had been secretly moved successfully into Jordan, Syria, and Saudi Arabia. Limited progress took week after agonizing week with covert movement happening. A forced patience was infuriating for the eager rebels. Their Jihad was long overdue. Many of the terrorists had already replaced the Russian insignia with the U.S. flag on each weapon, but there was still an abundance not yet converted. When all was complete, that is Americanized, extensive photographs would be taken of the setups and coupled with falsified U.S. Intel catapulting the ultimate plan into motion and readying the players for Directive Three.

Within the holy city of Jerusalem, top KGB leaders, including Kozlov, had met with high-level members of Israel intelligence, the Mossad. After an exhaustive day, Kozlov was anxious to board his flashjet and swiftly return to Moscow and his family. The men had not talked long, but then there was no need. What Directive Three consisted of was handing over pictures of U.S. nuclear warheads positioned throughout the Middle East and pointed directly at Israel. If top Israeli officials did not believe what they saw, the KGB would release the fabricated CIA and MI6 Intel claiming the English Coalition planned to attack Israel. This would plunge the dagger farther into an already fresh wound. The Intel explained that Israel's latest decision to oppose resolutions with Palestine had been too much for the American government to endure. The historical drama between these two territories, and distinctly different people, had become a tired, costly embarrassment for America. The false CIA and MI6 documents further claimed the U.S. wanted the KGB to engage al Din; that is, give them the bombs, but let al Din take the credit.

Most decidedly, Russia had rolled the dice, gambling that Israel's prime minister would believe the Mossad agents. If the Israeli PM retaliated by confronting the U.S. president, there would be at least a crack in the trust between the Americans and Israelis. KGB would then have to chip away at that trust further until the Israelis made an aggressive move toward the Americans. Directive Four would then be deployed. With documents successfully in the hands of the Israelis, all that was left for KGB and al Din to do was wait and hope. It was time for the world to show Russia proper respect. The arrogant Western giant and its allies would topple . . . for good.

Deek

In complete darkness, the prisoners' loved ones awaited the arrival of the SST stealth fighter jets. Surrounded by as much luggage as the group of minorities could handle, they readied themselves to flee a country that had historically not been kind and lacked adequate racial empathy. Mostly comprised of women, the group also included children of all ages and a smattering of the elderly. Everyone was anxious to join his or her deported loved ones. An eerie whirring sound came out of the darkness, as the stealth jets hovered above. One by one, they landed across the nation to escort more unhappy Americans to their new home of Africa. Blindfolded and gently handcuffed, the tired group was informed of the imperative secrecy of their trip. For the group's protection, no one could know of their location. Each complied, eager to get aboard and begin their journey. Awkwardly, Lourdes made her way into the bowels of the intimidating jet. Never did she doubt her decision to join her husband.

Like thieves in the night, several men entered Deek's tent. They would easily overpower their target, since the victim groaned from an obviously high fever. Quickly, the three men surrounded Deek's sleeping bag. One attacker grabbed his feet while another locked an arm around his throat. Again, Deek groaned. Before the third man could sink his raised knife into Deek's chest, a steadier Sly crashed a branch into the man's temple. The man crumpled to the ground. At that moment, Deek kicked at the attacker positioned at his feet, upper-cutting his assailant's jaw. The last attacker was wrestled to the ground with Sly's help. After minimal scuffling and punching Deek and Sly had the men's hands and feet tied. Gags were inserted into their mouths.

Locked down with plastic constraints, the attackers were positioned on the outskirts of their camp. Tied together, back-to-back, each man sat with swollen eyes and bloodied noses. Deek removed their gags. Then, upon their faces, Deek and Sly caked the shit-laced, poisoned stew. They had a survival choice, lick the death stew from their faces or let it dry and stand the chance its aroma would reach the hungered cats that roamed in the tall grass close by.

TWO LONG GRUELLING DAYS EXPIRED before the men were approached by any of the tribe members. Baked from the brutal sun, each man's lips were blistered and cracked. From excessive hunger, the poisoned stew remnants had long been ingested. A crowd formed around the feverish attackers. Deek and Sly cut the ropes that bound them together and dragged them to their feet. However, confessions regarding their foiled death attempt on Deek were required before the men's hand and feet constraints were removed. After the plot was revealed to the entire tribe, a vote to exile the three men was unanimous.

Sleeping bags and belongings attached to their backs, the three traitorous pariahs carried their fair share of food and supplies toward the dreaded grassland. Dizzy with sickness and fevers, the banished men would not last the day against the stalking lions hiding in the golden, swaying grass.

Aerin

One of the hardest things Mr. Ermani had to do was uproot his contented teenagers from their safe, beloved Vancouver home and move them to yet another foreign country. While each dreary, tedious day was the same for him in prison, his offspring had flourished. They had blossomed, evolved. Music, sports, politics, science, religion, and medicine: proudly Mr. Ermani's children had explored many nooks and crannies of their new existence. And there were so many more crevices for them to discover.

Was it the right decision ripping them from their comfortable home? Not only did Mr. Ermani have a job awaiting him in New Zealand, but also something inside urged him to make this move to such a faraway land. Surely, his children remembered the family discussions regarding their uncle's escape to Wellington many years before.

Marrying a New Zealander, Isaac Ermani and his Kiwi family had settled happily in their neutral country. Eventually owning a small business, Isaac had built a successful life in Kaikoura, N.Z.—a quaint seaside town on the South Island. The only thing missing was his family—his brother, sister-in-law and their four children, left behind in Iran, then years later, in Iraq.

It was not as if Aerin's father had not tried to get to New Zealand in earlier years. Fleeing from their violent Persian home, Ari Ermani had obtained falsified paperwork changing his family's surname to the Arabic name of Qasim. This had made their travels much easier, although problems arose when Mr. Ermani's money ran out. False identities were outrageously expensive. Ship and air travel to New Zealand was not cheap for six people either, especially aboard the new flashjets, which had cut air travel time by half.

His plan was to work for a while in Iraq until he had the money to purchase safe passage for his loved ones, and eventually join his brother's family in Kaikoura. The Iraqis had believed they were a Muslim family with, not three, but four little boys. Yes, all had run smoothly until that innocent Hebrew blunder by Ari's inventive, spirited nine-year-old. Aerin's outburst sent ripples of doubt through the suspicious Muslims.

Thankfully, the bombings had prompted Ari to seek inexpensive passage for five to Canada. Nevertheless, there had been many talks at mealtime about getting to Kiwi land. Was it not understood Canada was only temporary? Those old, tired discussions had started as much as twelve years ago when the kids were quite young. Had his children forgotten the family dream? Had this simply been a fantasy, an outdated dream that kept Ari alive in prison?

Even though Vancouver was wonderfully free and had moulded his teenagers into fine young adults, Mr. Ermani felt strongly it was time to move on. The previous night he had presented his plans to his wife. Exhausted and in desperate need of financial help, Saroya Ermani welcomed the plan with a bursting relief. She too was assured of work in Kaikoura; that is, until there was enough money for her to open her own Persian restaurant.

Mr. Ermani's talk with his wife had gone well. The real challenge would be convincing four incredulous young adults. Surely, his vibrant offspring would adapt. At breakfast, Aerin's father stood, took a deep breath, and delivered his disruptive news to the four eager faces before him. Mr. Ermani swung the sickle against his children's futures; and in a flash, their plans were sliced to shreds.

Aerin and her brothers were devastated. Only three weeks to say their goodbyes was not enough time. Out of respect for their father, and his torturous seven years without them, the Ermani siblings vented their anguish out of their parents' earshot. Slumping about a picnic table in a nearby park, they plotted and schemed. Tanid even offered to drop out of university, find a job, and work to raise the twins and Aerin in Vancouver. That way they could remain in Canada, ensuring Tanid a life with his high school sweetheart, Robyn. However, Aerin and the twins agreed this was not an acceptable solution. Tanid had a very promising life ahead that should not be wasted on supporting his brothers and sister. Every scenario ended the same . . . they needed the financial and emotional support of their parents and family. So their focus came back to the horrible few weeks to say their goodbyes. All four dejected Ermani offspring trudged home to plan their farewells and pack for a new home in New Zealand.

Deek

STEALTH BOMBERS APPEARED FROM NOWHERE. Hovering above, the first wave of SST jets searched for open ground to land. One by one, they descended. The prisoners recognized the intimidating machines as the very ones that had brought them to their hellish freedom. Without hesitation, the cargo doors opened. Jet engines purred. Staggering loved ones carrying and dragging their limited possessions exited the stealth jets, tired and disoriented. Whereas most passengers were greeted with a surprised delight, still other ex-prisoners ignored the crowd of predominantly women and children and rushed the planes trying to make their way aboard. Armed servicemen guarded the openings, preventing anyone's entrance. As soon as the last passenger exited, the fleet of SST stealth jets wasted no time ascending into the moonlit skies and disappearing almost instantly. Everyone was bewildered. Gradually, the squeals of surprise grew in frequency. Many of the new United Africans discovered their families had joined them.

PROTECTION BECAME A NEW WORRY. Suddenly the tribes had swelled with young attractive women and bright-eyed innocent children, a dream-come-true for rapists and pedophiles. And there were plenty of those offenders in the camp. It was only a matter of time before an incident occurred.

That day introduced itself with a sweltering madness. Oppressive heat brought lethargy and that was when fear turned into reality. A relaxing mother awakened from her nap to find her little four-year-old girl missing. Deek heard the mother's panicked screams. Somehow he knew what the commotion meant . . . in fact Deek had been anticipating the horrific occurrence, daily. Several fathers joined Deek and Sly as they ripped through tent after tent to find the child. Repeatedly they screamed her name, but to no avail. After a third of the camp was torn apart, the father of the little girl released a tortured shriek. Everyone froze. Deek reached the father's side and looked inside a dishevelled tent. His tiny unconscious daughter lay naked upon a sleeping bag, her mouth swollen and bloodied. Beside her was a naked, muscular, but slight man trying to hide his drooping erection. Thoughts of Deek's unborn child surfaced. How would he have felt if that was his little girl? In a split second, Deek lunged at the cowering pedophile and delivered the first blow. The father grabbed his baby girl and cradled her tightly. Fist landed upon the flesh of the man's face over and over before Sly could pull Deek off him.

Finally awake and, luckily, sexually unharmed, the kidnapped four-year-old clung to her parents. She was overcome with anxiety as Deek entered the family's tent. The fragile victim's father tried to calm his daughter as Deek asked him to join the other Lompoc members outside. Leaders from each tribe met to discuss the current dilemma. For starters, every member was required to drop their pants and prove to the others that he had not been convicted of rape or pedophilia. Part of their conviction process, these criminals had been branded for life. When incarcerated, they had been brutally castrated. American society had figured these perpetrators—mangled and humiliated—would no longer harm women or children if released back into society. Well, that was a massive failure. New synthetic, black-market drugs, smuggled in by these rapists, stimulated the male excitatory tissue. Testicles were not needed for erections. Deek and the other Lompoc tribe members could attest to what they witnessed. When the drugs ran out, the adults knew rape could still occur using other objects. These violators would never stop hurting women and children. They would never stop . . . unless the new Africans did something to prevent the crippling behaviour. Much discussion took place regarding punishment, but no one seemed to produce anything heinous enough to even the score. Banishment was an option, but they would still be out there, somewhere, threatening United Africa's innocent. Then a bold man from another tribal prison suggested what everyone else was thinking. Should these demented individuals be put to death? Deek could not get the image of the tiny, helpless girl from his mind. He stood.

"We're building a new society, people. Why have strikes against our peace with the constant threat of pilfering innocence? Rapists and pedophiles cannot be reformed . . . they will never quit. Their souls are stuck in a state of primal urges. Please, I beg of you, give me an alternative."

No one answered.

Aerin

Aerin sat gloomily on her bed, examining her hand-carved Persian stallion. The wooden piece had darkened from years of overhandling. Her beloved grandfather would surely be amused at how far his trinket had travelled. Aerin's finger ran down the flowing mane. Wise and gentle, Aerin's grandpa made painful events not seem so terrible. What would he think of the family's move to New Zealand? Somehow, Aerin was sure he would present the trip as an adventure full of exciting treasures. Aerin released a heavy sigh and had to smile.

Before she wrapped the memory in a microfibre scarf, she kissed the horse. "I miss you, Grandpa. Let's see what these Kiwis are all about, eh?"

Clothes strewn about, Aerin began haphazardly tossing items into her suitcases. Once the stallion was safely packed with Aerin's other valued belongings; nothing else mattered. Like her brothers, Aerin was less than enthusiastic about her future, yet she continued to pack. Unlike when the Ermanis' escaped from Iraq, each teenager was allowed two suitcases and a carryon instead of just a cloth satchel. Bulging already, Aerin's bags would be hard to close. Pensively she went through her trip preparation. Within the Ermani household that early morning, one could hear a pin drop. All goodbyes behind them, no one wanted to speak. They had three hours until their plane left Vancouver, connected in Los Angeles, then went on to Christchurch and, eventually, their final destination of Kaikoura, New Zealand. This was the best Mr. Ermani could do, the cheapest fares he could find. By the next day, Ari's entire family would be in New Zealand with his brother's family. Maybe his children's anger would diminish somewhat by then. In his soul, he knew this move was essential.

Inside the crowded coach of the flashjet, Aerin took her seat between Rami and Balic. Tanid was seated in the row in front of them with his parents. Still, no one said a thing. Aerin looked out the window next to Balic. With the dome ceiling opened for air travel, Aerin and her brothers witnessed an uncommon sight. Vancouver was just awakening with raindrops speckling the double-paned jet windows. It felt as though the city was crying out to Aerin, pleading for her not to leave.

She and her best friend, Brittany, had cried themselves into a tearless drought the previous night. Expensive EyeNet phone bills would surely be their future. With much sadness, Aerin and her family were headed to a biospheric prison, a fortified-glass maze only fit for rodent-style living.

For those lucky enough to survive the nuclear exchange of Worldwide War III, a bizarre shift in the weather, causing a "rain of milk" upon the Earth, was experienced. Millions of white radiation raindrops ate through metal and flesh alike. Dome living became essential to avoid the corrosive effects of the pervasive milky precipitation. With the loss of rain, as a water source, the desalination of seawater was necessary. Underground aqueducts brought the saltwater in, and after a mixture of filtration processes, moved purified water out to the biospheres.

In preservation mode since WWWIII, biospheres were not uncommon, and rapidly spread to many smaller communities. However, New Zealand had become the exception. A series of biospheric domes topped with firestone crystals for enhanced energy capabilities, tunnels that encompassed the entire southern island, and advanced progress in radiation studies made it an innovatively magical, yet freakish place.

Bowing her head, Aerin fought back frustrated tears. She loved her father so much but, at that moment, equally resented his return. Superior living conditions held little interest for the Canadian teenager. Surely, Aerin's papa could have found work in Vancouver; her mama had. As the engines purred, Aerin peered out the window again and let a few bitter tears escape. Defiantly, she let the aqueous trails mark her face without concealment, daring her father to turn around and witness his daughter's misery.

Deek

Deek and the other leaders disbanded with many a grave face. Angered mothers and fathers badgered this group until they were able to segregate their tribes and calm everyone down. Within the Lompoc clan, every man had to "drop trowel" again and show his previous criminal status. Those castrated, mangled individuals were cut on the forehead with a huge, unmistakable "X" to signify their intolerable past. The entire process was not completed until late in the night. For those who would not allow Deek and the others to brand them, the sexual deviants fled with only the clothes upon their backs into the feared grassland. If they somehow trekked successfully past the lions' reserve, they would be days away from any African village. What these crestfallen United Africans had not realized was they would join the weaker individuals that had escaped during the first week. A quick death from intolerant United African natives would be their destiny, as it had been for many ex-prisoners before them. As for the marked men that remained behind, within the prison tribes, they would gradually discover their fate. Sickness would keep them from any unmentionable deeds . . . until they eventually died from the traces of human excrement and other chemicals hidden in their nightly meals.

Narcissism unfortunately began to rear its menacing head. Mini tribes firmly established, identified by their ex-prisons such as Folsom, Walla Walla, Rikers Island, Lompoc, etc., began to crave power. Whose group, gang, tribe was the toughest? Friendships had formed while incarcerated, which bred a loyalty among these "brothers." Gang mentality was all that many of them knew, so aligning oneself with those who had his or her back when violence inevitably struck was understandable. The new United African, ex-penitentiary tribes flexed to show they were the toughest and meanest and, therefore, should lead. Prevailing over the others, the reigning group indulged in larger food portions and better accommodations. They received the best of everything. Freedom used to be the ex-prisoners' only dream, but now, as it used to be in the dank streets of poverty-stricken America, these hardened individuals sought privilege above others like themselves, even if it meant killing.

Every other day, flocks of helicopters passed overhead, yet no supplies were dropped. Instead, the whirlybirds just hovered. It was quite obvious the ex-prisoners were being monitored . . . evaluated by the government. What an embarrassment the Americans had become. To Deek and Sly, their United Africa was mimicking a perverse adult version of *Lord of the Flies*. Intelligence had decreased rapidly, or in Deek and Sly's case, stayed hidden. Every day, bruised and beaten bodies joined the many corpses already rotting in the sun. And right along with the deteriorating flesh was the Lompoc tribe's cohesiveness. Deek and Sly plotted to get their group away from the growing insanity.

Cleansed of perversion, these noteworthy Lompoc remainders packed their belongings and planned the laborious task of journeying in the direction of water. The small lake Deek had discovered a while back held much appeal. Conversation was at a minimum as the sombre crowd tried to pull away from the larger group without much commotion. Many were still upset with the "X"-ed out deaths. Everyone knew what had happened to the foul derelicts, but no one discussed the elimination of these rapists and pedophiles. Mothers and fathers were relieved their children were suddenly safer, but the manner in which those defiling criminals had been erased without a formal vote troubled them. Mixed emotions and fear perpetuated the silence. Why had they not been sent to a nice city like Cape Town or Johannesburg? Why had the United Africans not welcomed them? Dreams of their Africa were not measuring up to their expectations, not even in the slightest. Relatives of the pedophiles, the few that abandoned America and joined his or her loved one, left humiliated for a better life in an established city . . . such sad, naïve souls.

With the death toll rising daily, rotting bodies eventually outnumbered the living. Finally, some relief appeared after about a week. Deek and Sly lured a crowd of several hundred away from the madness. Relinquishing a large portion of their goods had been a small price to pay. After a two-and-a-half-day walk away from the violent tribes, the Lompoc group had dropped from heat and exhaustion beside the welcomed body of water. Not much was discussed amongst the ex-prisoners and their loved ones, and the hovering helicopters were not given the slightest notice. Survival was the focus, trying to keep defeat and depression at bay. This was a difficult task, because during the past week futures had become quite bleak . . . or so it seemed. However, no one was prepared for what came next.

In the darkness of the early morning, the SST stealth fighters returned. The only difference was the United

African flag appeared on the fuselage of these jets, instead of the American. Finally, the United African government was making direct contact. Relieved, the Lompoc clan felt a shift in their predicament until the stealth jets landed and Deek recognized the familiar gas masks upon the faces of the exiting United Africans. What followed was of no surprise as the all-too-memorable grey fog swirled about everyone's heads. Soon breathing became difficult and eyes began to burn. Holding their breath as long as they could and shielding their eyes, the panicked Lompoc tribe ran for their crude shelters. Clearly in vain, the new United Africans dropped to the ground one by one.

Maktan

HIDDEN SNUGLY WITHIN HER NEW downtown Vancouver condo, Maktan focused on her beautiful baby boy. Toys, books, anything to enhance his intelligence, and happiness were never denied little Mu'mad, or little Zeren. As Maktan was so young and worshipped her developing boy, she was clueless when it came to overindulgence. No matter what manipulative deceitful acts the small child perpetrated, Maktan was lovingly blind . . . like most mothers. He was just so cute. Not in the eyes of Zeren's playmates, though. They witnessed and experienced the injustice firsthand. When little Zeren did not get his way, he pinched, bit, scratched, whatever worked. He was sneaky about the pain he inflicted, too. If one of Zeren's playmates was bold enough to tattle, the adults just calmed the tears and wrote off the incident as children learning to share and play nicely together. Zeren's misbehaviour was always dismissed.

Maktan remained quiet a lot of the time around her Muslim acquaintances. It had become cumbersome when the other mothers constantly quizzed Maktan, or Yonca, about Turkey. Vague responses simply prompted more questions, but thankfully, Maktan had spent time in Istanbul. One by one, Yonca answered the personal, intrusive inquiries. Satisfied, the women moved onto other topics and pestered and probed other members of the group. Maktan knew interaction was critical for Mu'mad's growth, so she endured the trivial female banter, knowing it was a small price to pay. Life in Vancouver was proving to be more than bearable and Maktan felt safe from past threats and injustices. Watching Vancouver's skyline from her million-dollar view, Maktan basked in her son's wealth. Mother was swollen with maternal pride for her son who would be superior to all, someday. Spreading her arms out like an eagle ready to soar, Maktan tilted her head back and closed her eyes. For an instant, she felt invincible. That is, until the floor beneath her and little Mu'mad's feet began to rumble and their new high-rise began to sway.

Kozlov

Excitedly, Kozlov's wife and daughter loaded more clothes into their swelling suitcases. Since the spy industry was so all-consuming, vacations were quite rare and hardly ever included Kozlov. Holidays too were frowned upon and considered overly frivolous. Never was there an option for Kozlov to tell his superiors "no" when a task was assigned . . . actually, demanded. Responding in the negative to the upper echelon was tantamount to a death sentence and Kozlov knew the drill when one of KGB's own betrayed Russia. Hell, he had been the one to order the hits on past KGB traitors. Kozlov packed the last of his favourite shirts and zipped his bag shut.

Outside, he peered down at the black limousine that would take his family to the airport. In the moonlight, Kozlov could see the driver smoking a cigarette as he leaned against the front of the vehicle. He was surely KGB, a mere formality. No one had opposed Kozlov's request for some rest and relaxation after he had single-handedly brought Russia the future destruction of Israel and the United States. Not unexpectedly, though, Kozlov had been questioned extensively regarding his itinerary. Suspicion was a way of life in Russia, especially within the KGB. Perhaps it kept citizens more honest. Nevertheless, Kozlov was flooded with relief when his papers had been returned to him with his superior's seal stamped upon them. Neither Nederland nor Australia posed any threat to Russia. A few days in Amsterdam with Kozlov's in-laws would appease his wife and daughter. Besides, their long overdue visit was expected. So Nederland made sense, with Australia as an added bonus. No doubt, the entire time, Kozlov would be watched, perhaps beginning with the limo driver. Spying on one another was expected. Once in Australia, though, Kozlov would feel the freedom he longed for. He had planned carefully for a botched tour and staged car explosion, which had cost him plenty. But money was not important. After their staged deaths, Kozlov's family would be secretly whisked away to the West coast of the Australian continent. What the other KGB leaders did not know was the Kozlov family had new identity documents awaiting them there. Following an appropriate waiting period, the Kozlov's would fade into the fabric of everyday life within the Western city of Perth.

Kozlov let his bedroom drapes swish back into place. His eyes scanned the ornate room, recalling many pleasant memories shared with his wife. However, vague nostalgia did not stand a chance when up against a paralyzing reminder of reality. From the latest influx of gruesome nightmares, Kozlov had watched his daughter and wife die in this very room. Kozlov gathered the last of his things and proceeded to descend his spiral staircase one last time. He could hear his daughter peppering his wife with endless questions. It made Kozlov smile. Sasha was definitely her father's daughter, a persistent interrogator. Nothing went unexamined to the nth degree. Kozlov sighed. Gradually Sasha's questions faded into the background, as the only queries that pulsated in Kozlov's brain were, "Do my superiors suspect anything?" and "Whom will they send?"

Aerin

Upon arrival in Los Angeles and with heightened teenaged intolerance, Aerin felt tired and irritable. Trapped in a plane with so many clueless, rude people was quite overwhelming. Across the aisle was a Korean woman listening to a crash-course in English, out loud. Yet that was the least of Aerin's irritants. Although the obnoxiously repeated, "Hello, please take me to my hotel" over and over grated on Aerin's nerves, the two Mumbai dissidents sitting behind her took centre stage.

Not only did the men smack their snacks loudly, but also their lack of hygiene tainted the cabin air. Pungent, sour body odour, mixed with unrestrained flatulence, caused many sitting close by to gag and find anything to filter their breathing. The situation was so repulsive a male flight attendant had eventually intervened. He not only handed them aftershave lotion and told them to splash under their arms, but also was forced to deal with the men's gaseous assault. The flight attendant stammered a bit while informing both men they must cease the release of their windy arsenal.

Exasperated, Aerin shook her head in disgust. She could not believe grown men were being reprimanded for their lack of cleanliness. Keeping her vanilla lip balm close to her nose, Aerin rose quickly and stole a glimpse of the offensive culprits in the row behind her. Dark-skinned, with greasy thin hair, and oversized ears, the men's large brown eyes glanced at Aerin with an unfazed expression.

Quickly, she sat back down. Aerin rolled her eyes at

Tanid through the space in between the seats. Of all places in the plane, these rude men had to land behind her and her brothers. Of course, Tanid snickered—men enjoying their body odour and farts was so completely juvenile. Aerin could not wait for the plane to dock at the gate. There was nothing humorous about assaulting a woman's olfactory tissue.

Following the hordes of other passengers, exiting their plane, and entering the LAX terminal, Aerin and the twins lagged behind Tanid and their parents. Completely unmotivated, Aerin secretly wished she would not make their New Zealand connector. Maybe then, Canada Jetline would be forced to send her back to Vancouver. Shuffling along with their defensive attitude, the twins seemed to share Aerin's last desperate attempt to avoid their move.

By the time Balic, Rami, and Aerin arrived at their gate they faced an irate mother. Arms folded and cheeks flushed, Mrs. Ermani scolded her three youngest while hurrying them along. The topic of her rant was clearly about respect. Their father was stressed enough without having to deal with ill-mannered Western teenagers in triplicate.

Once aboard the flashjet the Ermanis quickly searched for their seats. The engines revved as the flight attendants secured the cabin door. Several passengers glared at the tardy teens as they passed by. When Aerin and the twins finally slumped into their seats, from behind Tanid popped Rami and Balic on the back of their heads. Both glanced toward Aerin and shrugged.

As the captain pulled the enormous flashjet from the gate, Aerin tightened her seatbelt. She was happy to have the window all to herself. Despite leaving Canada in the early morning, the congestion and tight layover at LAX had obliterated the afternoon. Aerin focused on the waving palm fronds that lined the outskirts of the terminal. She had never been to California. Used to the many evergreens in the Northwest, Aerin was mesmerized by the swaying trees.

A small tug on her seatbelt as the jet lurched backward yanked Aerin from her daydreaming. The takeoff began as uneventfully as it had in Vancouver. After exiting the dome's retractable rooftop, the plane continued to climb and began its path toward the Pacific Ocean. Raised to ten thousand feet, the engines calmed their churning and levelled off. Aerin peered out the window again and pondered the expensive homes clustered along the never-ending shoreline in the distance. Los Angeles grew ever smaller.

Aerin yawned. Then, without warning came a blinding, searing flash. Hellish orange flames rapidly reached for the skies. Rings of molten debris reverberated outward. Aerin gasped. The gigantic flashjet lurched violently forward. Disbelief swallowed Aerin. Was she really amidst such mayhem?

Rushing toward them were dark, ominous tendrils of ash and heat. As the distant grey, atomic mushroom cloud, swelled upward and outward, Los Angeles's expansive domed ceiling began to disintegrate. Helpless, Aerin was pushed back against her seat as the captain accelerated the jet's velocity. All the passengers white-knuckled their armrests; confusion flooded the fuselage. As the once-beautiful Los Angeles shoreline and palms shrunk in the distance, two more flashes exploded simultaneously, birthing the notoriously feared mushroom clouds, one after another. Aerin went numb.

"A fanatic is one who can't change his mind and won't change the subject."
~ Sir Winston Churchill
From *A Churchill Reader: The Wit and Wisdom of Sir Winston Churchill*, selected and edited by Colin R. Coote and P.D. Bunyan

DEATH BECKONS

Deek's Reaper Island

Ambushed again. Deek's suppositions had been correct, tumultuous times lay ahead. At gunpoint, the several hundred Lompoc tribe members, tied securely to one another, dragged their feet as they collectively exited the SST stealth jets. Because of their enormous stature, Deek, Sly, and a handful of other males were singled out for extra guards. In broken English, a uniformed man instructed the tethered group to remain quiet. Deek could feel the group's dejection return.

Emptied of their cargo, the gutted stealths' engines growled at the crowd discouraging them from getting too close. Everyone huddled together away from the intimidating, steel monsters. From the bowels of the lead jet stepped the obvious men of importance. Deek and the others exchanged glances. Tossed upon the gravelled seashell fragments was a battered wooden cube. Then, a very dark serviceman stepped onto the crude podium and cleared his throat. Bullhorn raised, he spoke in a South United African accent. "New United Africans, welcome to Reaper Island." The man forced a smile of fluorescent white teeth. Deek glanced at Sly. "Because of your criminal background, our government and many citizens have voted to have you removed from the African continent for a period of one year. After this probationary period has expired and you have proven your loyalty to United Africa, you will be removed from Reaper and relocated to the mainland. Each month we will drop care packages to assist in your survival." Some of the ex-prisoners started to shout. The commander raised his gun and fired a shot. Silence swept over the crowd. "My new United Africans, you must consider yourselves lucky . . . our chosen ones. We promised your President Walker we would keep you American prisoners safe unless violent behaviour was displayed. With all the fighting we have observed among the others left behind, we are sure they will kill one another, starve, or become food for our Lion Reserve. They are no longer any concern of the United African government. You have one year to prove yourselves." The commander outlined the specifics rapidly and with very little emotion. And he was not always kind in his delivery. When he finished, the commander gave a half-hearted salute and left the Lompoc tribe with, "Good luck, my new United Africans."

Without hesitation, the dark man left his perch and the other militia guards swiftly filed into the stealth jet behind their leader. The last man to leave grabbed the wooden cube and plunged a large machete into a patch of damp dirt. Deafening jet engines roared to a fevered pitch. Before any of the prisoners were able to grab the blade and cut his ropes, the SST stealths were airborne.

Once freed, Deek rubbed his reddened wrists then leaned into Sly. "Reaper Island? Looks like we found the Grim Reaper's residence . . . comforting."

Sly peered about rubbing his wrists as well. "No wonda he's such a grouchy mutha fucka."

"Did you see that shack at the edge of the cliff?"

"Yeah, I did."

"Let's head over there and see what's inside before one of these knuckleheads gets in there and destroys everything."

Deek and Sly left the jabbering group. By the time they reached the coarse shack, however, some of the younger Lompoc tribesmen had already entered and were flinging books out of the opening where a door once resided.

Deek shouted. "Goddamn it! Use your heads for once in your life!" He entered the flimsy shanty where three angry punks immediately stopped their tirade. "Did you ever think these books might tell us something about surviving this insanity?"

Sly shoved two of the youngsters out the doorway and grabbed a warped journal from the hands of the third. "Yo' heard Deek! Get da fuck outta here and pull your heads outta your asses!"

Deek brushed muck and remnants of mould from several of the books' covers. As he gathered his new reading material, he suddenly froze from alarm. Abruptly Deek stepped backward bumping into Sly.

"Deek, m'man, what's up?"

"See that dark crap over there covering the wall and floor? It's dried blood, Sly, lots of it."

"Could be animal blood. Yo' saw all those fuckin' sea lions."

"Yeah, but those bones over in the corner aren't from an animal. They're human remains." As they drew closer, the sweet, rotten stench became stronger; Deek and Sly covered their noses in disgust.

Sly saw the partial skeleton. "Christ! Where's da rest of his body?" He recoiled from the shack, as did Deek.

"Somebody died a violent death in there." Deek's eyes locked upon the many composition books scattered on the ground. "Let's hope the answer is in one of these."

STORIES OF THE PUTRID SHACK reached the other Lompoc members. For the younger generations, it became the one place on the island that was off limits. Moreover, they were sure it was haunted . . . possessed. Stories were instantly fabricated and rumoured throughout the tribe. No longer a place of exploration, Deek and Sly took their time cleaning up the dead man's remains.

"Deek, m' man, yo' wanna say a few?"

"Sly, I'm not much for sermon talk."

"Anythin' is betta than nothin'."

With a small army shovel, Deek packed down the sandy, shell-flecked dirt that now covered the broken skeleton from the blood-crusted shack. Sweat dripped off Deek's chin and down his bare chest. He wiped his face. "Herein lies the Grim Reaper. May your suffering be no more and your resting place go undisturbed."

"And yo' don't come knockin' on our doors."

"Yes, ah, please forget we all exist."

"Well said. Damn nice . . . uh, amen and shit."

"Amen." Deek smiled at Sly. Dark shadows framed the older man's tired eyes. In the short amount of time he had spent with Sly, Deek felt an unbreakable kinship. The older man's determination was the force behind Deek's undying hope for a bearable future. "What do you say we go rest our weary bones and read Grim's story?"

"Maybe yo' should read, College Boy, I'll listen." Sly flashed a gold-toothed smile at Deek. "I'z strong, but don't read so good, yo' know."

"Make me a cup of that disgusting honey tea of yours and you've got a deal."

"Oh, now yo' likin' ole Sly's famous brew?"

They began to walk toward camp. "It's growing on me

. . . very, very slowly." Deek put his meaty arm around Sly's broad shoulders.

DEEK FLIPPED THROUGH THE COMPOSITION books. Within the fourteen deteriorating journals was the tiniest writing Deek had ever seen. At times, he had to squint to see the words. Skimming the first journal, Deek waited for Sly to return. Already Deek had absorbed the dead man's farming failures. Evidently, the excessive seagull excrement caused the soil to be too acidic and there was mention of the offensive ammonia smell that permeated the island. For certain, the Lompoc tribe faced some troubling times ahead. However, Deek and Sly's tribe would be free on this island for the first year. The commander had stated more bundles of survival articles would be dropped by mid-afternoon. Regular care packages would be provided and when one year was completed and the ex-prisoners had proven their self-sufficiency, they would be set free on the mainland. Preferably, the Lompoc tribe's second encounter with the African continent would land them safely within a village with tolerant United African citizens, not hellbent on destroying the ex-American prisoners. As if the rugged island was not bad enough, the United African commander had peppered the Lompoc group with judgmental insults. Evidently, the United African people were vehemently opposed to these Western criminals infiltrating their towns and cities. They did not give a damn what lineage these violent people came from or what colour skin they possessed.

Sly handed Deek a steaming canteen cup. "Drink up, m'man."

"Thanks, Chief." Sly chuckled. "Well, for starters, our

Grim Reaper is actually Mr. Barry O'Malley. Yessir, our Reaper was actually a staunch Irishman who broke free from his restrictive, stodgy lifestyle."

"This gunna be good."

"And helpful—Barry has given us a head start in the field of farming."

"Well, dat's somethin'."

"Yeah, evidently seagull crap is not an effective fertilizer. So tomorrow we'll have to search for an area where the dirt is absent of bird droppings. Build a greenhouse lean-to perhaps."

"That's no problem. I can take care of organizin' dat in da mornin'."

Deek took a sip of his tea. "Wow, this brew of yours is really growing on me, Sly."

"Yo' sound surprised, College Boy."

"Maybe a little . . . okay, Chief, let's get started. I put these journals in chronological order. To start with, I found out why Barry chose to move here."

"That's fucked up. Who in their right mind would choose sucha hell-hole?"

"Barry caught the Mrs. in bed with another man."

"So get rid of da bitch! Why move here?"

"The bigger question is why would he move here and not tell anyone? It seems Barry moved here to help save the great white sharks from possible extinction."

"Fucka had some mental issues, I'd say."

"Indeed, but thanks to our certifiable Barry, we may have a chance in hell to survive this year on Reaper."

Sly raised his canteen cup. "To m'man Barry."

Deek returned the gesture. "To Barry." Deek adjusted the candle so he could read the small lettering more easily.

March 15th – I've just come from the bank. All the accounts are neatly emptied and closed. Let the bitch's new boyfriend enjoy supporting her high maintenance lifestyle. Christ, she was never a wife; instead, the bitch was a fulltime job. Now my paycheques will be used for something worthwhile, the diminishing great white sharks. I've loved these amazing creatures my entire life. Hell, they will be more appreciative than the princess bitch I leave behind. I feel so free. I'm finally rid of her. My thirty-five-foot dreamboat purchase was an easy decision. Some of the female sharks can be as long as twenty-five feet so it's a must that I have a larger craft to swim amongst these beauties.

Many of my supplies have already been delivered to the island during my many prior solo trips. No one knows of my plans; I want it that way. There will be plenty there to help me survive forever. I've spent the last of my money on champagne for the arrival on my new island. The only thing I regret is I'll miss the look on the soon-to-be ex-Mrs. O'Malley's face when she realizes she's penniless. My watch says 10:11 am. As I step upon my gorgeous aquatic craft, my ex- should be hearing from the bank right about now.

It's a beautiful day in Madagascar. A gusty wind, bright with sea spray, whips raucously over the stern of my craft leaving salt glitter that sparkles like diamonds in the dimmed morning light. For the first time in eons, I feel happy. I'm pulling from the harbour heading south, and I'm never coming back.

Sly released a huge yawn. Deek's throat was dry. "I think this one-man-show is tired and ready to turn in for the night."

"My eyes be heavy, College Boy."

Sly was asleep almost immediately. Deek ran his finger

pads carefully over the worn journal cover. The allure of O'Malley's story was much more than entertainment and perhaps his writings would be the key to their survival on Reaper. Maybe the sheer entertainment from this Irishman's adventures would keep them sane. Deek and Sly would definitely need and welcome any assistance both physically and emotionally. So far, exploration of the island and surrounding waters had revealed one thing. With the presence of large dorsal fins cleaving the choppy waters, the Lompoc tribe, if forgotten by the mainland United Africans, would most likely suffer a fate similar to O'Malley's and never escape this primitive rock.

Maktan

Below their feet the earth rumbled. In British Columbia, large earthquakes were rare; only minor ones surfaced several times a decade. Confused, the townsfolk searched for the cause of the unstable ground. North Vancouver and West Vancouver especially felt imminent doom when truck-sized boulders rumbled down the mountainside and crashed into their dome walls. Spider-webbed cracks splintered across the plexiglass. Everything shook and trembled as more and more rocks crashed into both cities' protective shells. Not until the many eyewitnesses spotted a distant mushroom cloud billowing far beyond Grouse Mountain above the North Vancouver and West Vancouver townships did they understand their fair cities were under attack. And, for once, the Canadians' detested southern neighbour would not be able to come to their aid. Angering the entire world for years, the Americans were busy defending their own homeland, however futilely. West Vancouver trembled with vulnerability. Mothers and fathers instinctively raced to retrieve their children from schools or nurseries. Many fled work abruptly for the safety of their homes, while still others were frozen, mesmerized, watching the commotion outside their shielded domes in disbelief. Screams and screeching tires filled the air. Splintered cracks in the West Van dome cover grew together, weakening the plexiglass. Soon their protective shield would cave in upon them.

News of the worldwide nuclear attacks travelled

rapidly. Government officials scrambled about making rash decisions. All veins of traffic leading into and out of North Van were halted. Ear-piercing sirens sounded on the Lions Gate and Ironworkers bridges. Red spiralling lights flashed along the fortified-glass tubes, signifying the closing of the steel doors at both ends of the bridges. The downtown dome was shut off from the North and West Vancouver domes. Outraged drivers were suddenly stranded above the waterways, their hovercrafts settling onto the bridges' surface. With EyeNet phones engaged, many furious commuters exited their vehicles. With hands sweeping through holographic images, the users' eyewear searched for an explanation. Frustrated, panicked looks made it apparent most EyeNet reception had ceased. Everyone stared through the glass tubing that now imprisoned drivers. Far north, a ring of orange blaze could be seen swelling at the base of the ominous mushroom. Grey clouds reached toward them, swallowing up remnants of blue sky. Fights broke out when several terrified drivers ripped EyeNet glasses off the faces of those who still had reception, while other heroic individuals fought to keep some semblance of rationality. When no one responded, after repeatedly pushing the large red panic buttons at the end of the bridges, a few motorists began ramming their crafts against the steel doors, blocking the entrances into downtown and East Vancouver. Frustrated Royal Canadian Mounted Police could hear the troubling screams, but were unsure of protocol. Monitors showed motorists, literally, clawing at the metal doors with bloodied fingers. Communication halted, the RCMP awaited direction from their superiors. Perspiration covered the RCMPs' concerned faces as angry Canadians honked and honked their horns from behind the steel barricades and pleaded for moral decency.

It did not take long before the police opened the downtown steel doors, just wide enough to allow a person to squeeze through. News rippled through the trapped drivers on the bridges. Parents grabbed their terrified children, while others assisted the elderly, as each abandoned his or her vehicle, rushing away from the North Van exit. One by one, bodies were rammed and dislodged through the limited opening. Petrified of the silent, airborne killer, the RCMP rapidly resealed the metal barricades as the last commuters embraced their freedom. Surely, the deadly radiation had not infiltrated the bridges' ventilation systems yet. The cheers of those rescued from the bridges assured the police, no matter what the health consequences, they had made the right decision.

MAKTAN WOULD SOON LEARN SHE too had made the right decision moving from New Westminster to downtown, all in the nick of time. Peering out her many penthouse windows, Maktan rocked her terrified toddler. Mu'mad somehow knew something was amiss and continued to scream. Vancouver's skyline was engulfed by a series of merging grey clouds, engorged with poison. Many police and ambulance sirens collided, making a deafening noise. Maktan was unsure of what to do. She ignored her neighbours' intrusive door knocking and stayed glued to the chaos outside. It was hard to avoid her morbid curiosity. The mayhem in the streets below was captivating, like a real-life nuclear snuff film. Could the fragmented news be correct? Had the ungrateful, repulsive Jews unleashed American nuclear warheads upon the Western world? Or was this the result of Maktan and Mu'mad's people? Could they have finally unloaded on the infidels? Maktan was conflicted, yet she should be elated. Nonetheless, whoever had released the bombs had put her precious boy in danger. Maktan could feel her Islamic pride eroding a bit more. Lately, human suffering of any kind tugged at her morality.

NIGHTFALL TAUNTED THOSE WITH HOMES near the edge of the domes. They were safely tucked away within the Vancouver, downtown, Burnaby, or North Van domes, protected from excessive radiation and panicked hoarders. Sadly, the West Van dome collapsed, killing many. For the remaining four domes, dull rapping noises echoed about the neighbourhoods lining the outside perimeters. Futile fists pounded against the domes' exteriors with desperate pleas from the dying.

Kozlov

Kozlov acted with speedy precision after several sleepless nights. Now, he rested comfortably inside the Amsterdam dome, with his wife and little Sasha. Although he successfully fled Moscow with his family in the wee hours of the morning days before Israel had agreed to retaliate against the United States, his mind would not ease. Major doubts had appeared to the hard-bitten agent in the form of his increasingly, recurring nightmares. Viewing the scorched body of his small child had etched those images into his wakened mind. In the past, Kozlov had killed many others' wives and babies, but it was different when annihilation reached into his own backyard. Although secure within Nederland's dome, Kozlov could not relax; all those deaths across the globe crawled inside his conscience.

Amsterdam's airport churned with excitement. People bustled about in search of their flashjet gates or visiting loved ones. Today's activities were no different than any other day except paranoia now pulsated in every cell of Kozlov's body. Two men stood at the street corner when the KGB operative and his family had left his in-laws' home. Excessive adrenalin surged in Kozlov's bloodstream. Once inside the taxi he had lost sight of the suspicious duo. Would they follow him further or report back to KGB headquarters that he had indeed arrived in Amsterdam and was heading to Australia sooner than planned? Along the path to the airport, a car behind them shadowed the taxicraft too closely. Was the hovercraft really tailing them, Kozlov wondered? How had the KGB found out Kozlov changed his family's flight plans to two days earlier? He had passed that duty to his father-in-law's secretary. Proper documents in hand, she was instructed to change the flight departures in person so there was no way the KGB could intercept such information. No phone service was used and everything was written down, then returned to Kozlov. How could the KGB find out so quickly?

Inside the terminal, Kozlov's heart just about stopped. While searching the departure screen above, he noticed the red flashing word repeated over and over beside every flight, including his own . . . *Cancelled . . . Cancelled . . . Cancelled.* Stranded people stood gawking at the news in disbelief. Kozlov's eyes darted from his wife's to every stranger standing close by, then back to his wife's. His large palm began to sweat while holding the hand of his dejected Sasha.

"Papa, eww, your hand is wet."

"Sorry, Baby, it's warm in here."

"Why are the flights cancelled?"

"I don't know—"

That is when he froze. From behind, a man poked something in the middle of his lower back.

"Hello, Bogdan. You and your family must come now. No fuss." Kozlov started to turn his head, but the agent shoved the metal object deeper into his flesh. "Eyes forward."

Somehow, Kozlov's wife knew not to question her husband and the towering Russian behind him. She grabbed Sasha's hand and whispered frantically in her daughter's ear.

Back within the home of Kozlov's in-laws, the five family members sat clustered together upon the divan. Two KGB suits stood before them, guns drawn. What troubled Kozlov most was how agitated they were. Speaking Russian between them, they spat insults and ciphers at one another. Finally, one of the men addressed Kozlov.

"So you are happy now?"

"Happy that our vacation plans are cancelled? Not hardly. What's this all about?"

"Don't play dumb, Bogdan; you led the expedition. Is this what you negotiated for Russia? How could you betray your country?"

Sasha began to weep. Kozlov's wife and mother-in-law huddled closer to the delicate child.

"What are you talking about? You're scaring my daughter."

"You knew about the bombs you brackish bastard. You spoke with al-Husri and al Din. You knew where the bombs would be positioned."

Kozlov's wife and father-in-law drew a collective gasp. He stared at his wife and shook his head. Both hands became wet with nervous perspiration.

"I am not your man."

"You are, Bogdan." The disconcerted KGB agent moved his laser gun closer to Kozlov's head.

"Can we talk in private? Get Yuri on the phone. He will tell you what my mission was. He can explain everything. You have it all wrong."

"Yuri cannot save you. Yuri is—"

"—dead," responded the other thug.

"How do you know that? What are you talking about?" Fears realized, Kozlov's heart raced.

"Moscow is gone. The mushroom bombs, Bogdan . . . the bombs took Moscow, Nizhny Novgorod, Novosibirsk, St. Petersburg, Yekaterinburg. All of our beautiful cities are gone. Russia was levelled. You beleaguered Russia, Bogdan. You did this . . . you killed her."

Aerin

Cries of hysteria filled the cabin. From the public address system, a shaken yet forceful captain's voice was barely heard over the passengers' clamour. Flight attendants yelled, "please be quiet," but no one listened. One male attendant had to resort to telling the New Zealand-bound passengers frankly to "shut up!" Finally, the captain's voice came through loud and clear. His only explanation was the world had entered World War IV; the much-dreaded nuclear nightmare was underway.

Aerin's angst over leaving her friends in Canada suddenly gave way to raw panic. Balic took her hand and squeezed with a nonverbal comfort. She looked backward, through a crack between the seats, at her father sitting in the middle. Mr. Ermani winked at Aerin, but she saw through such false encouragement. From the window, Aerin saw a crumbling, burning Los Angeles, shrinking farther and farther into the distance. She was never so glad to be trapped inside a tube of metal, with her family, high above a massive body of water. Then, the captain's voice came over the loud speaker again promising to keep everyone informed. Slowly, alphabetically, he began naming the cities that were in the throes of being levelled by man's aggression. Atlanta, Beijing, Beirut, Berlin . . . Kiev, Lima, London, Los Angeles, Manila, Melbourne, Montreal, Moscow, Munich, New York . . . Paris, Sao Paulo, St. Petersburg, Sydney . . . Tel Aviv, Tokyo, Toronto . . . on and on the list went. When the captain finished the "U's" Aerin held her fists tight and kept repeating to herself, "not Vancouver, not Vancouver."

Crying came from all directions. So many loved ones were surely deceased. And if the passengers' loved ones had survived the blasts, they were destined to suffer a flesh-rotting, agonizing existence from radiation exposure. Poisoned air, water, vegetation, and livestock would be their destiny. Information came to Aerin and the others in pieces. Thankfully, Vancouver had not made any of the lists announced to the passengers. Aerin breathed a little easier. After all, she had promised Brittany and her other Canadian friends that she would return home when she graduated from high school and reached her eighteenth year. Aerin dreamed of attending the University of British Columbia for her medical school pursuits.

Yanked from her panicked thoughts, Aerin heard the crackle of the PA system, yet again. She held her breath. Instead of just cities, the captain was now naming entire countries that had been devastated . . . Afghanistan, Algeria, Angola, Argentina, Austria, Burma, Chile, Columbia, Cuba, Finland, France, Ghana, Hungary, India, Indonesia, Iran, Iraq, Italy, Jordan, Kenya, Libya, Mexico, Morocco, Nicaragua, Nigeria, North Korea, Norway, Pakistan, Philippines, Poland, Saudi Arabia, South United Africa, South Korea, Spain, Sweden, Syria, Thailand, Turkey, Venezuela, and Vietnam . . . except for Toronto, still no Canada . . . still no New Zealand.

Shock had not waned for hours as the distressed passengers tried to comprehend what was happening. In minutes, the entire world had changed dramatically. Peeking out the window, while the rest of the cabin tossed and turned with fretful slumber, Aerin witnessed a new birth. An astonishing orange glow lined the horizon, her first New Zealand sunrise. Clouds hung low against the sea and occasional islets. Not of a wispy whimsical nature, these clouds resembled gigantic puffs of thick cotton ready to be plucked from the darkened, fertile soil below. Aerin had never seen such a cloud formation and this aerial cotton field went on forever. Such a sight gave Aerin the tiniest bit of peace. Maybe they were headed to some forgotten paradise, unscathed by nuclear bullying. Still Aerin clung to her festering anger. After all, she and her brothers' lives had been turned inside out, and now, with this nuclear catastrophe it would be that much longer before they would be able to return to Canada. Coming toward Aerin was a stern looking flight attendant, so she quickly pulled down the window shade to avoid any rebuke. Resting back in her seat, Aerin released a heavy sigh of annoyance. Everything, everything had changed. Whether awake or asleep, uncertainty clawed at everyone.

Deek

A FOG COVER BLANKETED REAPER Island. Minimal sunlight and moisture-rich air did not afford much exploration on the Lompoc tribe's first day. Instead, people huddled within visible reach. Heavy-hearted, Deek sat on a rock away from the others. Every morning and night, before bed, his first thought was of Lourdes. Those preoccupied moments, missing his wife, tortured Deek. If he contemplated those feelings for too long, Deek thought about reasons, reasons for Lourdes' decision not to join him in Africa. He could understand if it was because of her pregnancy, but then he would never know. And he would never be allowed on American soil again. This quiet morning, melancholy taunted Deek.

HIS THOUGHTS DRIFTED TO THEIR first week of dating. After a month of flirtation, and smiles exchanged during their Spiritual Studies class, Deek had succumbed to his feelings and asked out Lourdes. He was elated when she agreed to meet him after his Homecoming football game. However, the memory that gripped at Deek's heart the most was of their second date.

Walking along the Santa Monica pier, Deek and Lourdes basked in the Southern California sunshine. Their attraction was unmistakable; both knew this union would never be considered casual. As Deek and Lourdes breathed in the briny air, they strolled toward the beach. Deek was enchanted with this young woman. She conversed with such ease, poise. He was proud to be seen with her. At the end of the pier, before they stepped down onto the sand, Deek and Lourdes passed a young White man begging for change. His filthy hands gripped a tattered paper cup. Lourdes slowed her pace as she dug through her purse, pulling free a ten-dollar bill. Without breaking stride, Lourdes tucked the money into the man's free hand.

Out of the beggar's earshot, Deek stopped. "Why would you do that?"

Surprised by Deek's reaction, Lourdes replied. "He looks hungry."

"He looks like a drug addict."

"Deek."

"Well, as you mentioned on our first date, you work hard to put yourself through college. Just seems like a waste to give a street person your hard-earned cash only for him to shoot some crap into his veins."

"It's not our place to judge."

Although the conversation between Deek and Lourdes had quieted, eventually, they agreed to disagree and went on enjoying their date. The afternoon had sparked more infatuation for both. Later in the evening, when Deek and Lourdes headed for the USC shuttle to return to campus, Deek spotted a young couple sitting at a concrete picnic table, feeding their small son. Several bags of groceries crowded the tabletop. Upon closer examination, Deek recognized the father. Lourdes' gentle heart had been right; the beggar had been hungry. And he was providing for his family. As Deek and Lourdes passed by, the young man looked up from his meal. With a clean face and hands, his focus was on Lourdes. He smiled as if they shared a treasured secret. His focus was on Lourdes' generosity. She smiled back. Her satisfied grin then passed to Deek, as she laced her fingers in his. Deek never wanted to let go.

Irritated, Deek unlinked his fingers, wiped the mounting tears from his eyes, and stood. It was progressively becoming harder to ignore his yearning heart. Shaking the tender memory of Lourdes, Deek climbed from the rocks and focused, instead, on the tribe's survival. Shifting through the crowd, Deek searched for Sly. Lots of families still slept underneath tented blankets. Fatigue was understandable. Not only was the anaesthetic gas still working its way through everyone's bodies, but for the first time, they felt safe from tribal violence. Extreme cynicism and fanaticism had kept the prison gangs battling for ultimate control on the mainland, whereas the Lompoc tribe had worked together and formed an unlikely family. How quickly they had grown to trust one another. Now, securely isolated on their Reaper Island, many slept peacefully for the first time in weeks.

Ink to paper, Deek found Sly sketching out the necessities for the new Reaper Township.

"Deek, m'man, we needs fresh water. These mental giants left us water distillas, but no electricity."

"Probably solar-driven. We can take care of our water as soon as this fog lifts. Did you see this?" Deek handed Sly an instruction booklet. "Appears we have the wherewithal to create these bizarre, sophisticated lean-tos, and all are powered by solar energy." Sly flipped through the pages, focusing on the pictures. "Might work, if the blasted sun decides to shine upon us."

"Well, College Boy, yo' prepared ta supervise?"

"Indeed, as long as those crates they left behind have the components we need, we're golden."

"So what 'bout food?"

"Well, we know there are plenty of sea lions."

"And monsta sharks."

Night descended early upon Reaper Island. Everyone had worked hard that day with much pride. Tucked away in their reinforced tented homes, the Lompoc tribe fell silent. Unloading the crates earlier that day had taken longer than expected. It appeared they had everything they needed to get started. Keeping the group motivated was the real challenge; sometimes, mere survival was not an adequate incentive.

"Today was surprisin'. Hardened criminals workin' togetha sure warmed this ole man's cold heart."

"Cold heart? Come on, Sly, you're just a big softy deep inside."

"If yo' only knew, College Boy."

"Knew what? So you had a rough life and did what you needed to survive, big deal. I'm not a stranger to street living. In Atlanta I was a Predator, watched my older brother get gunned down when I was six. We killed, stole things, anything to get the respect we deserved and survive."

"I bet none of yo' pups killed their mama. She treated me like a mild curiosity . . . when she showed up. Most of da time I was just in da way."

"Jesus, Sly, you killed your mother? What happened?"

"She told me I was a disappointment and a piece of shit one too many times, College Boy. Her nasty, bitch mouth went on nonstop—naggin' and naggin'. Deek, I snapped." Sly's eyes welled-up. "I begged her ta stop yellin', stop hurtin' me. I did, I begged her."

"How old were you?"

"I was fourteen. I loved my mama, but I gotta say it felt good ta snap her neck. Everythin' went silent . . . peace yo' know? I stared at her frozen, shocked face. It took me awhile ta realize what I done. I grabbed my gun and my mutha's money and hit da streets. It became my only home."

"When did they catch you?"

"Not 'til I was an adult after killin' this drug boss and his prick partner. Tryin' ta cheat me, ya' know? At eighteen da fuckin' po-po's pulled me in. I never left da prison system afta that. Prison hell is all I knowed for da past twenty-two years. Yo' gotta small taste of that life, College Boy."

"Yeah, kill or be killed."

"Yo' know, Deek, today was different. First time in my life, I actually gave a damn 'bout othas. I've neva watched people carin' for othas like dat. When dem United Africans first dumped us here, I felt like we deserved ta be tossed out like da fuckin' trash. Hell, dat what we are, right? I didn't believe dem bastards would bring us supplies. When they dropped dem crates and everyone pitched in, I felt kinda all soft inside; maybe a chance ta do some good . . . yo' know, pay for my past sins . . . a fresh start."

"We're going to be fine, Sly, really."

"See, it's dat hope dat yo' keep feedin' us, Deek, dat makes us believe we can do this."

"Well, I'm not exempt from the need of redemption, Sly. I have a lot to work through."

"For killin' dat storeowner?"

"I didn't kill him, Sly, no bullshit."

Blood pooled around the unconscious storeowner. Deek pounded on the man's chest, but his unresponsive heart showed no sign of life. Mouth-to-mouth was impossible; every time Deek made a chest compression, blood oozed from the storeowner's mouth. Faces were pressed against the glass outside, watching Deek rip the man's blood-saturated shirt open to examine his wounds. There were three knife slits on the unconscious man's chest, but the blood appeared to have stopped pouring from the openings. That is when Deek decided he had to take drastic measures, since the man's circulatory system had clearly flat-lined. By then, more pale "crackers" lined the storefront glass. Their White, pampered, judgmental stares did not stop Deek's efforts. He had to restart the man's heart. Forcefully, Deek pounded on the storeowner's sternum, skilfully dodging the knife wounds. Again, he pounded . . . nothing. Quickly, Deek resumed the rhythmic pumping. His arms ached from the CPR compressions. Unfortunately, repeated thumps and thrusts upon the victim's chest had not produced the slightest pulse. Deek was entirely frustrated. Utter chaos was erupting outside and nary one of the nosey townsfolk had offered to help. Obviously, this lily-white town was not used to seeing an African American trying to save a White person's life. Deek stopped long enough to scream for help.

Not thinking at the time, and entirely necessary to perform CPR, Deek had pulled out the bloodied knife a couple of desperate, drug-crazed teenagers had inserted after their successful robbery. With no witnesses to the actual murder, except the teenagers he saw running from the crime scene covered in blood, Deek's fingerprints upon the murder weapon had sealed his fate. If only his Good Samaritan act had occurred in Atlanta, where the Black:White ratio was 65:35, Deek would have had a jury of his peers. They would have seen Deek was attempting to revive the storeowner. They would have used forensics to search for the spoiled, drug-crazed teenagers that had ended a man's life for a mere four hundred and five dollars. Despite the fact Georgia was still fighting the Civil War, like many other Southern states, Atlanta was different. By sheer reproductive dominance, African Americans had found a semblance of justice there; they owned Atlanta. Well, this was not Georgia but white-bread Montana, where a compassionate Deek was slapped with an unprecedented incarceration.

A gentle giant at heart, Deek's only culpability in gang crime stemmed from never stopping his Pred brothers from killing when he was younger. He had never outwardly disapproved, but then it was all he had known. Deek had never had a choice in his upbringing; violence was forced upon him by mere geography. When college was in his sights, Deek saw a lighted path ahead, without torture and murder; a fruitful safe environment where Deek's childhood guilt would gradually dissolve. Until that time came, Deek did what any other college-bound student athlete would do; he dreamed of fame, acceptance, and abundance. For the remaining Preds, their future was grim. Their adult lives became more of the same. Under the guise of justifiable turf battles, hatred continued to breed and revenge propagated. Not for Deek, though, he was headed for greater things. And he was one of the few that escaped . . . until now, when his past collided with his present.

"So yo' neva killed a man befo' that skinhead bastard back at Lompoc?"

"I never said that. While I ran with the Preds, I plotted and witnessed many deaths. Sly, I never said a word to stop the killing. I let others do the nasty deed, but I murdered whitey by the hands of others. I could whine about violence being forced upon me as a child, but that's a weak excuse. When I got older, I should have stopped the killing. Ahead of me was a bright future without murder . . . a life in college. It was a dream of football and escape from a life on the streets. I could have left my gang brothers with integrity and honour, but instead, I left without saying a word. I never looked back. My life had turned around—football career and a new wife, I was flying high. That's why I tried to save that storeowner's life. Finally I could do some good, absolve some guilt."

"Instead yo' got tossed."

"Yep, imprisoned for trying to save a man's life. Seems incomprehensible, but it happened. That's why I'm not as bitter as I could be. Perhaps I deserve all of this."

"Well, m'man, yo' helpin' me be betta. I thank yo' for that, College Boy."

"That means a lot, Sly. Thanks. And none of us here are a piece of trash . . . remember that."

"Like yo' always say, 'indeed.'"

Deek lit a candle on the small crate next to his rickety cot. "Shall we see how O'Malley fared once he arrived on Reaper?"

Snug and warm inside his sleeping bag, Sly yawned. "Yeah, yeah, let's hear more 'bout dat poor, stupid son-of-a-bitch."

March 22nd – My first storm came early; so, so early this morning. It was still dark outside. I awoke not knowing where I was. Wet and cold, I actually missed my miserable home. Yes, I missed the warm bed I shared with my ex- bitch. Mother Nature was clearly pissed off at my new decision. Hail covered the ground and was soon replaced by piercing, icy raindrops. The rain fell so fast and hard I thought I might drown, and I'm an excellent swimmer. Christ, I'm freezing.

Daylight was the best. Sunshine upon my damp skin felt so bearable. But my hellish day only got worse when I ventured out toward the beach. From the side of the cliff I observed the frisky sea lions. They seemed to be pleased with the storm's end as well. Then panic set in. My aquatic craft was missing. There were pieces of white fibreglass scattered upon the many, sharp rocks. That's when I realized what the destruction meant; my beautiful thirty-five-footer, or "Second Chance" *as I'd named her, wasn't missing at all. A Southeasterly storm pounded* Second Chance, *my new love, to a pile of fibrous matchsticks upon the rocks. Betrayed again by a disloyal woman. I will live the rest of my years on this desolate island. Tears did nothing but increase my pathetic situation.*

Snoring pulled Deek out of O'Malley's struggles. He had lost his audience. Deek whispered, "Good night, Chief."

Barely audible, Sly murmured a few incoherent words then dropped back into a heavy slumber.

Aerin's New Zealand

Aerin wanted off the flashjet. Her head hurt from the constant humming and she was tired of being caged within a rattling tin can. Not even the surrounding beauty could shake Aerin from her foul mood. Their descent into Christchurch presented a breathtaking scene of craggy peaks, dusted with powdered snow and lush greenery that framed the mountains' lowlands. To Aerin, it was just another place, very far away from home. She glued her head to the window to avoid further humiliation from the one flight attendant, with a heavy Kiwi accent, who thought it quite amusing that Aerin did not know what cassava, or Fiji, chips were. Even the Asians, who spoke little English, had laughed. Tanid had forced a chip into Aerin's stubborn mouth; such a fuss over what tasted like a lightweight pork rind. There was definitely no love affair brewing between Aerin and New Zealand.

They descended through the retracted dome rooftop without a hitch. Once on the Christchurch Tarmac, the JetAir New Zealand flashjet glided to a gentle stop. Everywhere Aerin looked she saw large, stranded jets. The only relief came from the knowledge that both the North and South Islands had escaped from being levelled by nuclear bombs, and hopefully, none were on the way. As they sat on the clogged runway, within the Christchurch dome, the plane's cabin became increasingly stuffy and humid. Stale air made it difficult to breathe. Tempers flared. The captain announced they had turned off the air-conditioning to conserve fuel. Frustration, hysteria, and irritability were not a good combination. After what seemed like an eternity, the engines ceased to churn. Soaked in perspiration, the passengers were instructed to gather their belongings and proceed to the nearest exits. Outside, Aerin saw uniformed men hastily approaching.

One by one, each passenger plopped onto the inflated slide connected to the fuselage's door. Aerin reached the asphalt below, hopped off the slide and waited for the rest of her family to descend. Uniformed security guards then ushered everyone away from the jet, where all passengers huddled together awaiting instructions. After the guards chatted with the pilots, the battered crowd began the uncomfortable trek to the terminal.

Tanid caught up with his sister. "You okay?"

"Well, let's see, the world is blowing up before our eyes; I've left my dearest friend, Brittany, behind in a city I refuse to believe is now rubble and ash; and I've arrived at the land of, ah, let's call it what it is, Oz. Yeah, Oz. Hell, I'm waiting for a legion of munchkins to burst from the bushes at any moment. Yes, Tanid, I gave up beautiful Vancouver to live within a spiked bubble. I'm just dandy, thanks for asking."

"Biospheric city."

"What?"

"Vancouver is under a dome, what's the big deal?"

"A dome no one even notices. It doesn't have a plethora of ridiculous spiked crystal caps jutting out of pyramidal and bubbled peaks." Aerin launched into one of her typical repartees. "It's Oz, Tanid, and I'm frickin' Dorothy. Not the Scarecrow, for I have a brain unlike you; nor the Tin Woodsman, for I have a heart, unlike you; and never the Cowardly Lion, for I have courage, damn it. Not enough courage to tell Papa 'no' when it came to turning our lives inside out agreeing to come to this godforsaken place, but courage nonetheless. Tanid, we are participating in a Wizard of Oz freak show."

"Aerin, lower your voice, jeez. It won't be that bad. You should be grateful we haven't been incinerated and you should love the fact that so many medical researchers and specialists have migrated here. It was you who preached about the wonders they've discovered in New Zealand. All that mumbo-jumbo about stem cell research and their successes in finding the cure for Parkinson's, leukemia, AIDS, cancer, and Alzheimer's, etc., etc., blah, blah, blah. Aerin, a little perspective, please; you're going to be exposed to the best of the best."

Aerin's teenaged angst would not subside. "Don't be so cavalier, dangling medical carrots in my face, Brother. I see right through your overly positive crap. I didn't get a choice in this move and neither did you. Look around, we're going to be living inside a ridiculous gerbil maze . . . bubbles and crystal cone-heads connected by tubes. We've been reduced to imprisoned rodents. We can't even go to the ocean."

"So the New Zealanders were inspired by the lost worlds of Lemuria and Atlantis. Balic and Rami are thrilled. They have been talking nonstop about the science and technology surrounding those crystal projections. I find it fascinating, too. Think about it, Aerin, crystals used for an added energy source, and light amplification. Kaikoura scientists are even working on channelling energy through firestone, a great crystal charged by the sun, moon, stars, and Earth itself. It's brilliant. You know, Aerin, not everything is about you." Tanid playfully shoved his sister. His grin was sarcastic, conspiratorial, yet filled with a boyish satisfaction.

"You're such a sci-fi geek. Atlantis? Seriously? I think not, it's a morbid fairy-tale, Tanid. Oz, and the only difference is when I click my heels together Vancouver refuses to appear. We're trapped . . . doomed."

"Domed."

"Not laughing."

Tanid took out his New Zealand guidebook. "Let me see, Miss Negative, my geek guide says we live in a magical place where the mountains meet the sea. There are no poisonous, venomous snakes, insects, or spiders here in Kiwi land. And biospheric living has reduced the pesky sandflies. Oh, here we go, listen to this; the Maori word for food is *Kai* and crayfish is *Koura*."

"Great, we've moved from Vancouver to Food-Crayfish, how delightful. If you don't put that damn book away—"

"And there's an abundance of farming and sheep; lots of sheep. That's so cool; I love wool. The Maori legend has it, the tiny Kaikoura Peninsula was the seat where the demigod Maui fished—"

"In case you're confused, Dear Brother, see this? This is me ignoring you. This is me walking away."

Tanid nudged Aerin again. "Come on, *Dorothy*, follow the yellow brick tarmac." The passengers had reached the airport terminal building.

"Oh please shut up, *Scarecrow*, please. Can't you see I want to wallow in my unhappiness? Can't you just let me be pissed off?" Again, Tanid lovingly bumped his sister. "Aren't you worried about Robyn?"

"Of course I am, Aerin. However, if I let myself get upset like you I just may go mad."

Aerin abandoned her moodiness long enough to consider her brother's suffering. She hooked her hand around Tanid's bicep and squeezed. "Well, we can't have that. Christ, you can be so annoying."

"Me, annoying?"

"What else does that ridiculous book have to say?"

Once inside a large, quarantined room attached to the air terminal, the passengers faced another marathon wait. No one's luggage appeared for a very long time. Christchurch Airport was nothing short of mayhem. New Zealanders with only carry-on bags were released to the radiation detox chambers and decontamination triage. Foreigners, puffy-eyed from lack of sleep and crying, were corralled into a roped-off area near baggage claim. Aerin and her family operated off pure adrenalin. No one had slept much during the very long flight. So not only were the Ermanis jet-lagged, but they had been awake over twenty hours due to insomnia from their departure woes. Mrs. Ermani and her children sat upon their carry-on luggage and waited while Mr. Ermani negotiated with the officials. Security officers guarded every exit with a mere handful working immigration. Outside the terminal, people pounded on the windows, angry they could not get to their loved ones and take them home. Confusion encircled the passengers.

Hours passed before New Zealand immigration was instructed on how to handle the tired visitors. Everyone's passports were confiscated and each was told they were not allowed to leave the country until further notice. Forwarding addresses were documented. For those unfortunate souls on holiday, with no specific destination, they would spend much of their time at the Christchurch terminal buried in paperwork and bureaucracy until N.Z. officials decided what to do with them. However inconvenient, the rest of the country dealt with isolation after all ports, beaches, and airports were closed. Immediately following the first wave of ill-fated bombs, New Zealanders sounded the sirens within their North and South island domes. Anyone enjoying activities in the mountains or ocean rushed to the nearest biosphere entrance before lockdown was triggered. Three hours passed before notification was released that every biospheric door was securely locked. Any remaining Kiwi citizens away from their homeland, and alive, would have to wait until after more was known, before returning home. News was sparse. Most people were numb and wishing this was all just a horrific nightmare.

After another hour in the never-before-used radiation detection chambers, the Ermanis were forced to shower and discard their travelling attire. They then proceeded to the decontamination triage tents. Each swallowed a small cup of opaque, orange solution and was then given a ten-day supply of pills. When the exhausted Ermanis exited the airport terminal, Mr. Ermani searched for his brother, Isaac. Aerin and her brothers slowly dragged the family's rollie-luggage behind them. Their tired legs hardly moved. Soon, a tall man, resembling their father hugged their mother. With a lacklustre greeting, the Ermani offspring acknowledged their uncle. Aerin's parents followed Isaac to an odd, chubby minivan with thick, pinkish belts of silicone surrounding it. Lasercrafts, or converted vehicles like the ones in Vancouver, also known as jellywheels, were required within the biosphere. Disinterested, tired teenaged boys stumbled the remaining couple of metres, climbed into the backseats of the lasercraft, and collapsed.

When Aerin reached her uncle's vehicle, she received a surprised "once over" and a comforting hug from her paternal relative. The men then loaded the luggage behind the zombie-like young adults and climbed into the spacious cab with Mrs. Ermani. Aerin snuggled in between Tanid and Rami. Frigid air within the vehicle started to warm from the labouring heater. Even though it was the end of spring when they had left Vancouver, the Ermanis were now engulfed by New Zealand's late fall, early winter. Oblivious to the elements, an already snoozing Balic was sprawled out, legs straddling his overstuffed backpack. While the adults discussed the bombings, the other three siblings joined their brother in dreamland.

Patiently, Aerin's uncle waited his turn to pull his craft onto the track within the northbound Coastal Tube that ran parallel to the historical Tranz Scenic railway. Isaac's passengers slept soundly. He was so relieved his brother and family had survived the nuclear holocaust. All he wanted was to get home to his wife and boys and be assured of everyone's safety. It took a while after Isaac pulled onto the laser track. Once Isaac's jellywheel was securely within the laser pod, hydraulics raised his four tires, the autopilot was engaged, and the laser mechanism became operational. When the light went green overhead, Isaac could feel his vehicle lurch forward as the laser pod began to move.

He released his hands from the steering wheel and shot his brother a proud glance. With a slight New Zealand accent, "Now we rest."

Ari gave a tired smile. "I'm speechless."

"Welcome home, Brother." Isaac released a stressful sigh. Soon he joined the others and opted for some much-needed sleep. Traditionally a four-hour trek, travelling the new

Coastal Tube would take less than two hours to arrive in Kaikoura.

Once the Ermanis arrived at the Kaikoura Tube Station, Uncle Isaac dropped his wheels, exited the laser track, and drove the short distance to his Kaikoura community. The Ermanis' neighbourhood, known as The Flats, was embedded at the base of the Seaward Kaikoura Mountain Range.

No one remembered passing through the gated entrance or being shuffled indoors. Of the days that followed, they would have hazy memories. All Aerin wanted was to catnap. Her uncle and new aunt and cousins were of no interest. During her waking hours, Aerin felt numb, making it easier to sleep away the sadness and fear. Her new family members were gracious enough to set up single mattresses for Aerin and her brothers upon the floor of their cousins' tiny bedroom. Immediately, Aerin had used her suitcases to partition her bed from the others. Darkness told her night time was once again upon the Ermani household.

Standing, Aerin noticed Balic was not in his bed. A monotonous hissing sound could be heard from the neighbouring, meagre living room. Aerin rubbed her tired eyes, stepped from her mattress, and tiptoed around and over her brothers and cousins. In the next room, Aerin joined Balic who pointed a remote control at the flat screen media monitor—click after click after click. Every channel showed black and white broadcast snow. In utter disbelief, Balic ran through every channel several times, but nothing was on the air. The clock showed 2:00 am. Obviously, no one else in the house was awake. Earlier in the day, the entire extended Ermani family had crowded around the small mediavision. Almost all of the cable networks were down and the local newscasts were scarce and completely unreliable. From what the Ermanis and their neighbours could surmise, it appeared the nuclear war had subsided . . . or the rest of the world was dead. Aerin met Balic's dull expression. At last, he conceded defeat and clicked off the MV. Both teenagers retreated to their sleeping quarters. Balic said nothing and closed his eyes in hopes of more sleep. Aerin rummaged through her backpack until she found her reading flashlight. Finding solace in her medical texts helped postpone the taunting heartache.

"So, Aerin my love, what do you think?"

"Well, let's see, the toilet water swirls in the opposite direction." She folded her arms across her chest.

"So, Daughter, is sarcasm one of the wonderful things the Western world has taught you?"

"No, Papa, that would be you. You raised me to think and talk like a boy. You raised me to have an opinion. What, now you're telling me that applies to everyone except you? Somehow, you're exempt? Sounds like a double standard to me."

"No, what it sounds like is an ungrateful, disrespectful child. Yes, I said 'child,' Daughter. Your immaturity is astounding." Mr. Ermani looked as though someone had slapped him across the face.

"Immaturity, Papa, that's rich. What exactly do you want from me? You want me to tell you everything is glorious? You abandoned us, Papa! I was just a little girl, your little girl. I had to grow up without you! Then you show up out of nowhere and rip us away from our home.

Our friends! No, you want me to think everything is wonderful, so as to ease your well-deserved guilty conscience!"

"Aerin! Your father—"

"No, Mama, you're just as guilty! You didn't even discuss our life choice with us. You were so strong raising us in Canada. Then Papa shows up and you follow him around like a lovesick puppy. Where did you go, Mama?" Mrs. Ermani gasped.

"Aerin, that is quite enough! In case you have forgotten, we are in the midst of a world crisis. Your friends—"

"My friends aren't dead! Don't you dare go there!" Aerin stormed from the room. Locked within the bathroom, she searched through drawers until she found a pair of scissors. She stared at her reflection in the mirror.

Tanid found his sister sobbing on the small mattress in the corner of the community bedroom. "Hey, Tiger, feel better? Wow, nice hair cut. Papa found your chopped ponytail. You crushed him, Aerin."

"Now he has his liquid caramel. The old Aerin is dead."

"Little dramatic, don't you think?"

"Tanid, I hate this place! Cassava chips, lollies, banana chips, ketchup that tastes like licorice; it's an insane asylum. You see the way they look at us; they hate foreigners."

"Aerin, you were too young to remember, but I felt that way about Canada at first. All the weird food and strange looks, I hated Vancouver."

"You never told me that."

"Listen, when I saw the look on your little face when Mama bought you your first dress, do you think I wanted to burst your bubble?"

"But I'm not a child anymore, Tanid. I need for you to

be on my side. Quit defending Papa and New Zealand."

"I am on your side. Just because I don't choose to join you in your misery-laden pity-party doesn't mean I don't feel the pain of this move."

"Shit, I know I'm being a colossal brat, but aren't you the slightest bit angry with Papa? Don't you miss Robyn?"

"I miss Robyn 24/7, Aerin. I can't express how much my heart is breaking, but what good does it do to lash out at Papa? He's always wanted the best for us. He went to prison while we were escaping Iraq. I hated everyone that day, Aerin."

"So the guilt is mine. I am truly an ungrateful big mouth."

"Just remember, my once well-intentioned little sister, if it weren't for Papa and Mama you would never have been allowed a precocious upbringing or to grow that big mouth."

There was a soft tapping at the bedroom door. Mrs. Ermani and Auntie Clara entered. Tanid squeezed Aerin's hand and removed himself from the room, closing the door behind him.

Auntie Clara, Kiwi born and raised, smiled at her niece and placed a necklace around Aerin's neck. Her accent was quite strong. "Sweetness, this is a hei-tiki. It is a Maori token made out of greenstone. Over the decades, we've grown to believe it brings the one who wears it good luck. All the young locals wear these. Someone has to give it to you, someone who cares for you very much."

Aerin stared at her beautiful aunt. It was so strange to hear everyone speak with Kiwi accents. Many of the phrases were quite British, but it was the vowel pronunciation that had evolved across the globe. She smiled at her wonderfully foreign aunt. Between her fingers, Aerin twirled the primitive hei-tiki figure. "Auntie Clara, I've been reduced to shameful pulp. I'm so sorry. Your house is lovely . . . truly." Tears broke free and ran down Aerin's cheeks.

Auntie Clara wiped her face dry, then, holding Aerin's face, kissed her forehead. "Tena koe, sweet girl . . . a warm Maori welcome to you. This is your home now my spirited one, give it time."

Beside Aerin sat Saroya. "Come here." She let her daughter bury her head against her bosom and proceeded to rock her lightly to and fro. "Honey, I want you to understand I haven't gone anywhere. I'm still that strong woman that raised you and your brothers."

Aerin raised her head and stared at her mother whom she adored. "But as soon as Papa entered the picture you lost your voice. You know how I hate submissive females."

"Oh, my sweet girl, I haven't lost my voice. Please understand the relief I felt when your father walked through the door that first night. I am so tired. For seven-and-a-half years, I had to be mother and father to all of you. Aerin, it was so nice to let someone else lead for a change. I welcomed your father's strength. At night we discussed your futures and felt they would be much fuller here."

"But you act so weak in Papa's presence. It infuriates me."

"That's the way I was raised, Aerin. It's what I'm comfortable with. Your father doesn't demand this behaviour; it's simply a part of who I am. I rather he lead."

"Yet you raised me to feel differently."

"The Western world encourages women to be strong. Why shouldn't you have all that and more?"

"I've been so cruel to Papa."

"Know this, my daughter, an enormous part of your father is extremely proud you speak your mind. He has living proof he did the right thing, raising you as a boy in your early years. Don't ever forget that."

"Looks like I owe him a big, fat, submissive, girlie apology."

"It certainly wouldn't hurt. Work with your wisdom, Love, not emotions." Aerin wiped away the remnants of tears from her face, then proceeded toward the door. Saroya stopped her. "Hey, I have to say, your spiked hair agrees with you. You're quite stunning, you know?"

"And you're quite biased . . . and a terrible liar."

Deek

By mid-afternoon the vaporous veil sluggishly lifted. Muffled sunlight strained to reach the ground. Four days into their stay on Reaper Island and Deek and Sly had identified individuals eager to be in charge of gardening, creating fresh water, hunting for food, and assembling crude food storages out of prefabricated buildings left behind by the servicemen. The mood for the time being was hopeful. Days before, choppers could be heard overhead, readying the many crates to be lowered to the ground. Deek had supervised the logging of the contents. Every necessity they needed for self-sufficiency seemed to be included. That day was filled with the sound of hammering, muffled conversations, and occasional laughter.

All was calm, until a distant scream pierced the air. True, the hunting squad had found food, but when Deek arrived with Sly at the shoreline, the food had taken chase against the hunters. Men scattered in every direction as they dodged the enraged elephant sea lions aggressively pursuing them.

Barking sea lions deafened the Lompoc group. Then Deek saw the bloodied man whose screams were drowned out by the frenzied outbursts. The hunter volunteers ran from the larger male sea lions as Deek cautiously approached the beached victim. He was minus a large chunk of meat from his right, upper leg. To keep the snapping sea lion from him, the panicked man jabbed his spear at anything that came too close. Deek signalled for the other fleeing men to stop. Back and forth, the largest bull lion rocked from fin to fin, his head raised upward. Spear readied, Deek took another step closer to the alpha sea lion. There were many scars marking his enormous body. Deek took two more steps closer, which ceased the enormous male's barking. His large, suspicious brown eyes stayed locked upon Deek.

The injured man was still in a panic. "Get me the fuck outta here!"

"Lower your voice, you fool."

"Fuck you! Get me outta here!"

Swiftly, the bull sea lion lunged to his right, grabbing the shouting victim by the throat. The bleeding man released a scream angering his attacker further. Shaking his head back and forth, the sea lion began to maul his victim's head. Neck ensanguining from a severed carotid artery, the bloodied mangled man finally ceased screaming when abruptly the bull lion's large canines snapped his lower jaw. What terrified the silenced victim more than his head injuries was his attacker dragging him toward the breaking waves. Like many of the Lompoc tribe, childhood swim lessons were non-existent and he was one of those who had never learned to swim. Trying to scream was futile. Garbled, gurgling sounds were all he was able to muster.

Deek released his spear, merely nicking the seven hundred pound animal. The bull sea lion continued to drag the bloodied man into the water. Deek ran to retrieve his spear. Angered sea lions began to bark and lunge at him, while the other Lompoc tribe members launched their spears, hitting a few seals.

By the time Deek was able to ready his arm to throw his spear again, the enormous bull lion and mutilated victim were submersed in the churning surf. Deek hesitated, his target unclear. He felt completely helpless. There were no swim lessons for him as a child, either; all Deek could do was stare at the flailing man in the white-capped water.

A larger pool of maroon fanned out into the ocean as the sea lion pulled his prey under the ravenous waves. Then, with a flicker of disbelief, an explosive whitish-grey flash rose from the water. Fins and a powerful tail whipped about. Wedged within the huge triangular teeth of the twenty-six foot great white shark was the head of Deek's decapitated tribesman, along with the top half of the severed sea lion.

In an instant, the hunter had become the hunted, yet again. Deek could not breathe. When the large body of the female shark splashed back into the ocean, a bright reddish-orange pool of blood swelled across the surface. Two huge glistening dorsal fins broke the choppy water and sliced through the battling waves. Both sharks proceeded to rip apart the now-small-in-comparison carcass of the bull sea lion.

At that moment, it all made sense; it explained why the herd of sea lions huddled desperately upon the rocky shoreline. Once inside the water they became the chosen meal for the handful of great whites that lurked along Reaper Island's waterline.

Deek knew with certainty his Lompoc tribe would never escape this place. No wonder the United Africans that left them here were so anxious to return to their mainland. The ex-prisoners were trapped, and never would they consider this unrelenting pile of rocks home.

Aerin

After much rest from her inevitable outburst and suddenly in an explorative mood, Aerin crept quietly from the house. She sat in an oversized rocking chair upon the porch and studied her relatives' surroundings. Repeatedly, she tried to reach Brittany, and others, on her EyeNet phone. Each attempt returned a dead connection. Aerin sighed as she pocketed her EyeNet glasses.

Her eyes scanned the front yards of the Ermani farm and their neighbours. Sophistication was a relative term, relative to one's environment. Too tired to get excited, Aerin sat alone, dreamlike, as she rocked. Albeit her aunt, uncle, and cousins were considered to be in a poorer state than other South Islanders, they were far from struggling. Dew completely dissipated, Aerin marvelled at the perfect lawn bordering the front of the tiny Ermani farm.

Suddenly, Aerin noticed two apparatuses come alive on opposite sides of the plush grass near the front end of the property line. A red laser beam shot across from one side to the other. Both mechanisms slowly began moving toward the porch. With the red, connected beam travelling along, all the taller blades of grass were lopped-off. When the lawn was perfectly trimmed, the laser beam shut off and the two mechanisms returned to their initial positions. From the side of the lawn farthest from their neighbours, small nozzles arose much like automatic sprinkler heads; only these little gadgets were blowers. As they blew the newly cut blades of grass toward the other side, lawn-vacs sucked the debris into a trapping gutter. Aerin would later learn these gutters sucked the piled contents into a container for composting.

A grin crawled across her stubborn expression, as she revelled in the wonderment of an ingenious environment. Originally, she had assumed New Zealand would be archaic, far behind the Canadians. After all, Vancouver was far more advanced when compared to Iraq and mirrored the fast-paced American lifestyle. How naïve Aerin had been. Home always seemed to be the best place on Earth. She shook her head in amazement. For so many years, Aerin's family had lovingly mocked the many letters sent to them by their Uncle Isaac's household. He had bragged about New Zealand's advancements, but surely, no place was as sophisticated as North America. How utterly ridiculous Aerin felt.

Fully awake and avoiding her grief, Aerin decided to venture off the porch for more Kiwi wonders. She shoved her vestigial EyeNet glasses farther into her baggy pocket and headed next-door. Their neighbours, the Whibleys, had lots of livestock—a few cows and many, many sheep that seemed fat and happy. Sheep shearing would not begin until the summer months, October through December. Inside the barn, Aerin wandered about and examined more closely the feeder stalls. Everything was mechanized, of course. Water bins were automatically filled and levels maintained. On the other side of the wall, Aerin heard voices. Balic and Rami were being shown how the feeders worked by their cousins Kendall, twenty-two, Quentin, twenty, and Evan, fifteen. Again, she swam in a sea of Kiwi accents.

"All we have to do, twice a day, is toss discarded fruit and vegetables into this vat. Completely automated, the molasses and various grains are mixed in with the produce, and the muck is distributed to the livestock feeders on the other side of the wall." Kendall had the twins' full attention. They proceeded to pepper him with numerous technical questions. Their favourite wonder was the fact these high-tech machines ran off animal waste. Balic and Rami were suddenly alive with scientific challenges.

Before Aerin, wiggling enthusiastically, were the Whibleys' two large Border collies. Aerin bent down and let them smother her with head-butts and brief kisses to the face.

A shy Harrison Whibley spoke softly with his strong accent. "Will you look at that; our two boys lose all perspective in the presence of a lady."

"They're great, Harrison. What are their names?"

"This one, with the black face, is All Blacks—named after our national rugby team. His brother, the blue merle, is named Scrum."

"You all sure love your rugby here. Back home, Tanid and the twins were obsessed with hockey."

Uncomfortable, Harrison did not know how to respond.

"What's a scrum anyway?"

Tanid appeared inside the barn. "It's like a face-off in hockey." Aerin still shook her head. "You know, when they drop the puck between two players?"

"Okay . . . sorry, Harrison, I'm not much into sports."

"It's Harry, Aerin." Tanid chided.

"Oh sorry, Harry."

"Actually, I rather like Harrison. Whatever you prefer."

"Then, Harrison, you'll have to be patient with me. All these sports references throw me a bit."

"Yeah, if these two mutts were Aerin's, Harry, she would have named them Penicillin and Stem Cell."

Harrison grinned. Aerin fluffed the fur around Scrum's beautiful dappled grey and white face and stared into his cold, powerful, powder-blue eyes. "Scrum, eh? Wow, you are a beauty, aren't ya'? Aren't ya'?" Not to be forgotten, All Blacks nudged in for some of Aerin's affection, knocking her to the seat of her pants. Harrison and Tanid had a good laugh at her expense. Aerin pretended to be angry until the two Border collies competed for her attention further, knocking her about. She could not maintain her feigned anger and soon burst into laughter, joining the guys. All Blacks won the battle and wormed his huge, shiny, black and white body into Aerin's lap. She was smothered with furry bodies and limbs. Scrum licked her face then nipped at All Blacks. Aerin hugged All Blacks' neck. When he wriggled free, Aerin grabbed his large silky, predominantly black head and finally noticed his piercing golden eyes. "Whoa, Handsome, you've got the eyes of a lion. Harrison, they really are gorgeous dogs. Their eyes are so intense."

"Yep, yep . . . now you see why the sheep don't give them any flack during mustering."

"I can see that; I bet they're fierce. Wow, they're really something."

"You're lucky, Aerin; Scrum and All Blacks don't take to everyone. In fact, they're both a couple of snobs. Just goes to show you they have good taste."

Bored out of her mind from recycling talk, Aerin walked toward the back of the house with All Blacks and Scrum in tow. Her father and Tanid stood with Uncle Isaac, examining the cushy, rubbery exterior of the family's chubby jellywheel. "We don't have accidents anymore. This silicone makes fender-bender incidents more like a spastic case of bumper cars."

Aerin's father acted much like Balic and Rami. "Talk to me about these prefab houses I see everywhere."

"Ari, you wouldn't believe it, everyone's homes are made of stone and a flame-retardant synthetic wood over reinforced steel. The roofs are made of tiles and solar panels."

"Isaac, you said you were still struggling here. You have a beautiful two-story home with an amazing farm surrounding it."

"Well, you should see the wealthy whose homes are made from the same prefab material, but are much, much larger, three and four-stories. And they have a central computer that operates the security system, as well as a bunch of other fancy features. They even have robots that perform mundane chores."

"Fascinating."

"Okay, ready, watch the roof." Isaac pressed a button on a remote control he held in his hand. Everyone looked upward. Two of the large solar panels retracted. "Come on, this is brilliant."

Still uninterested, Aerin stayed put as the men climbed an outside stairway to the rooftop. From the looks on their faces, Aerin decided against going into the house and remained focused on what was hidden in the attic area of the Ermani home. Her uncle, father, and brother disappeared into the hole in the roof. Soon, a whirring erupted from inside. Then, Aerin was astounded. Floating quietly above the house was a large magenta, silicone-coated hovercraft. Uncle Isaac brought the craft down to Aerin's level. Tanid and her father beamed with a renewed excitement. There were no tires.

Tanid yelled. "Hop in, Aerin, we're off to see the wizard!"

Aerin slid into the backseat next to Tanid. When her Uncle Isaac steered the hovercraft upward, toward the dome's ceiling, Aerin had to admit she felt a freewheeling happiness for the first time since her father had announced their move to New Zealand. Back home in Vancouver they had not known many people able to afford the expensive hovercrafts. Only the wealthy seemed to possess these vehicles and they lived in the exclusive West Van area, quite a distance from Aerin's suburb. For the Ermanis, hovercraft rides had been scarce. Now, so high in the air, it felt like an untethered rollercoaster. Below, Aerin took in the entirety of their gated, predominantly Jewish, neighbourhood. As they rose higher, she could see other gated communities. It appeared people had willingly segregated themselves into clusters. Aerin had witnessed the Western world evolve in this direction, as well. Culturally, religiously, individuals chose to live where they felt happiest and to hell with what the rest of the world thought. Ironically, minorities were being associated with poverty less and less. Tolerance of diversity was everywhere in Kaikoura. As long as foreigners tried to fit in and not disrupt the peaceful lifestyle they were welcome.

Uncle Isaac dodged an oncoming hovercraft. Everyone waved at one another and let laughter push away any nuclear dread. Yes, Aerin had to admit, they had moved to a magical place. If only she could truly appreciate New Zealand's remarkable accomplishments and cease her yearning for Vancouver.

Deek

Sea lion tasted odd. There was so much fat laced within the strands of meat that one might as well chew on a hunk of blubber. The Lompoc group overcooked the awful sea lion to eliminate as much grease as possible. Preventing the hovering birds from pilfering chunks of the roasted meat from the fire pits became a challenge. For days and days, Sly and Deek tried different ways to land some fish or one of the sharks.

Using globs of bloody sea lion as bait, Deek and a few other robust men were finally able to land one of the great whites. Stubbornly, Deek would not relinquish the cable that ripped through his hands as the shark raced toward deeper water. Once he had tightened his grasp, Deek was unexpectedly yanked into the churning surf. He gulped seawater. Panic set in when Deek realized that not only was he beneath the surface of the ocean, but the previously taut cable within his bleeding palms was loose and doubling back toward him. Deek flailed about in great white territory. He dropped the line and clawed at the powerful current. His lungs burned from lack of air. Above, he saw the swirling waves through salt-burned eyes. Frantically, Deek fought to get within the turbulence of the next breaking wave. He clawed and clawed for the surface, then something rammed into Deek's ribcage. Pain shot through his thoracic cavity, flipping him over and over, until his last somersault landed him upon the beach. Saltwater spurt from Deek's nostrils and poured from his mouth as he violently vomited.

Sly's face was pale. "Christ almighty, Deek! I'z thought yo' was shark bait. Christ, oh Christ Jesus. No mo' fishin', College Boy . . . no mo' fishin'."

Deek's chest burned. Again, he vomited then repeatedly coughed. Before he was able to talk, Deek dry-heaved several more times and finally collapsed from exhaustion. His ringing ears shut out the barking of the agitated sea lions. The smell of sea air kept him nauseated. Sly and the other defeated fishermen stayed close.

"College Boy?"

"I'm thinking sea lion meat doesn't taste so bad."

"Yeah, fuck dem big fish."

"Indeed."

Their botched attempt at catching a great white shark forced the Lompoc men to concentrate their efforts upon the frantic seals. Although a suicide mission, many seals scattered from the attacking hunters and launched themselves into the churning ocean. Dorsal fins surfaced from every direction. It was not long before a bloodbath occurred in the choppy waters. Everyone watched in horror as his or her hunting efforts ceased.

Deek looked at his mangled hands then up at Sly. "I think I'm ready to head back to camp."

"Here, let me help yo'." As Sly assisted Deek to his feet, he ordered several of the stronger more skilful men to resume the attack on a sea lion for dinner.

Before retreating from the beach, Deek sighed. "I never want to be that close to a shark ever again."

"No doubt. Neva seen a fish ram someone like dat."

"I'm just lucky its jaws weren't open." Sly did not have the heart to tell Deek that in fact the great white's mouth had been wide open, exposing row after row of enormous, triangular teeth.

Deek's mended hands throbbed beneath the bandages. His bruised ribs ached with every movement. By reading more of O'Malley's adventures to Sly, Deek was able to ignore the pain.

April 1st – Yes, I made it to April. Somehow calling me a fool on Fool's Day is redundant; my foolishness never ceases to amaze me. It has no limits. Yesterday I fancied myself Ahab, hunter of the great white whale. Pathetically, the only white prey I conquered was an injured seagull whose days were already numbered. Although my belly is full this morning, I'm paying the price. Tearing about the barnacle-covered rocks wore a hole right through my prematurely weathered boat shoes. Only when I'd been victorious with my catch did I realize shell fragments had pierced my rubber soles and proceeded to mangle the once-tough skin on the balls of my feet. It will be days before I'll be able to walk again. True the corrosive seawater conspires against everything I own, but thankfully it also assists in mending my tender, broken flesh.

You might ask, why a damn bird when there is food-a-plenty swimming about the surrounding ocean? Put simply, try and reel in a two-thousand pound fish from the sea that houses a mouthful of pearly-white razors and is covered with metal-flecked skin that serves as a grater against its pursuer's skin. I'll put up with mangled feet and meagre morsels of meat from a menacing bird over landing an enormous beast any day.

Deek yawned. He was sore and tired and wanted to sleep away the rest of his horrifying day.

Aerin

Immediately Aerin's extended family kicked into protective mode when WWIV began. The Ermani land in between their trusted neighbours, the Whibleys, contained sectioned plots for vegetables and fruit, whereas the Whibleys' spacious backyard was used for their two cows, a herd of sheep, and an expansive chicken coop. Between the two families, they had the ideal setup. The Ermanis and Whibleys decided to share everything as they always had. Both families prepared for the worst. For years, the Jewish Ermanis and Catholic Whibleys had learned to live cooperatively, next to one another. Their first year of cohabitating within the same gated community, Pete and Isaac had not fared so well. Every discussion seemed to provoke disagreement. Whether it was religion, rugby, politics, or world affairs, it did not matter; one bellowed black and the other white. After months of bickering, Victoria and Clara had had enough. Peace was declared under threat of unbearable consequences at home, absolutely no affection. As the months passed, avoidance became impossible, so Pete and Isaac learned to treat one another's opinion with a modicum of civility. Regardless of how nasty their conversing became, at the end of the day each was determined to rise above their differences and offer a handshake to the other.

While the women sat around the Ermani breakfast table, sipping tea, the men congregated in the living room talking over one another. A knock on the door ceased the kitchen chatter.

Aerin's Auntie Clara peered through the backdoor window then opened the door. "Cheers, Pete, come in, come in. The men are in the living room."

With his usual rugged swagger, beer in hand, Pete Whibley joined the others.

"So, Isaac, you think it was as simple as that?"

"Well, they've been acting like a bunch of sociopaths for years."

Pete chimed in. "Who are we discussing, mates?"

"The Americans."

"Ah, sheer lunatics, eh?"

"See Pete agrees, Ari. It's poetic payback, actually. Generations upon generations of Americans have been raised on false beliefs, claiming their country is the best, superior to all. These poor, lied-to individuals swallowed all that damaging propaganda fed to them. Hell, they believed every word. Governments, political parties, and politicians became more and more deceitful and greedy. Personal gain was at the top of their lists. What trickled down to the common citizen was a sense of entitlement and grandiose distortion of self-worth. You know, grab your slice of the capitalistic American pie, mate, at whatever the cost. And since they were such a superior nation, any failure should be blamed on others. If they could divert attention from themselves, it was a success. Sweep any indiscretions under the proverbial carpet, accept no responsibility, and show no remorse. Empathy became extinct. Sadly, gentleness was viewed as a sign of weakness, so strength was measured in how one could manipulate and charm others to get one's own way. Culturally, Americans were raised to be a bunch of sociopaths, Ari. Their role models taught them this behaviour. Maybe if the Americans had held honour with the rest of the world, as they once did years and years ago, Israel wouldn't have bombed them."

"As I said, the Americans were a bunch of lunatics."

"No they aren't, Pete." Exasperated, Aerin entered the living room from the hallway where she had overheard every prejudicial word. It had become impossible to remain quiet. "What an ignorant thing to say." She folded her arms across her chest.

"Well, look who's here, our newest little wahine."

"What did you call me?"

"Relax, Aerin, it's Maori for woman."

Pete pulled a swig from his beer, almost emptying the bottle. "Aerin, the Americans were lunatics. Look what was on the news day after day. This actor is going to rehab, this one shaved her eyebrows, and this one's sleeping with this one—"

"And you think because there were a lot of American journalists and newscasters trying to make money off pathetic moments in people's lives it gives you the right to condemn the entire nation to lunacy? American press and paparazzi hold the majority of the crazies in their realm. The way you're acting, Pete, your narrow perception is one of the reasons the United States got such a bad reputation. Americans aren't lunatics and the only thing they were once guilty of was unilateral thinking, but that wasn't their fault. Engraved into every American is the belief they are the best, the most intelligent, that's true they're taught that. So listening to your judgmental comments, Pete, you think you're superior. I guess that means you're acting American. Hello . . . pot calling the kettle black, much? Then by your definition that makes you a lunatic."

"Cheeky one, eh, Ari? Aerin, my little spitfire, America displayed their own so ridiculously—"

"Don't judge a nation by the absurd few in front of

the cameras. I went to school with Americans, Pete. They are smart, full of hope, and not afraid to chase after their dreams. That's what makes them the best a lot of the time. Here's a newsflash for you; they hate those asinine gossip channels as much as you do. And quit talking about them in the past tense. You don't know if they're all dead."

"So you agree the Americans were, are, a misguided bunch?"

"That's a vast generalization and not for me to say . . . the ones I know are good people. I will say this, if they all perished in the war, it is truly a travesty. There are many, many amazing individuals in the United States. Once their global blinders were ripped from their eyes, they were the first to recognize they were victims of political propaganda and then criticize their own country's failings. And it's not easy to lead the world in innovation. It is easy, however, to sit on the sidelines, suck down beers, and criticize. Enlightened Americans certainly did not deserve to die, if in fact they did, especially by the very country they coveted and protected for so many years."

Raised in Sydney, Australia, in his early years, Pete, a large ex-rugby player with weathered skin and dirty-blond hair, was the quintessential rugged "down-under" bloke. "No need to get your petticoat ruffled, Little Sheila. Wow, so emotional." Pete laughed.

"Petticoat? How old are you? In case you haven't noticed, I'm wearing jeans just like you, and thank God, that is where the similarities end. Wow, you're such a relic, Pete."

"Aerin, don't be so disrespectful."

"Disrespect is a two-way street, Papa."

Pete wore a satisfied grin. "Maybe you should join the

other wahines in the kitchen. Exchange some recipes, or better yet, get your Uncle Pete another beer."

"Fat chance. It's a good thing you don't have daughters, Pete. You know, you're no better than the Middle Eastern men who think that small dangling flap of skin between their legs entitles them to a life of superiority over women."

"Aerin!"

"Ari, let her talk, mate. I'm quite enjoying this. Aerin, your warped point of view is a Western myth, believing women are superior."

"It's no myth. I am superior to men like you."

Pete laughed again. "Aerin, sweet passionate Aerin, you are two sammies short of a picnic if you think Sheilas have the upper hand."

"As you Kiwis say, 'bugger off,' Pete. Women have something you 'thinker' types don't have. We have brains and feelings. You haven't a clue as to what's really important in life. Hell, you haven't a clue where to find your own heart inside your bloated chest."

"So all blokes—"

"No, men like you, not men like my father or uncle. They get what is important. Men like you who overvalue your maleness are living in the past. I'm sure you would rather I just feed you beer after beer and become a deaf-mute."

"Yeah, that'd be right. Ideal, actually." Pete looked around at the other men clearly amused. Ari and Isaac were clearly not.

"Wow, I hope you're kidding. Scary to think you might be a complete fossil, incapable of deep thought."

Pete chuckled. "I never joke about the superiority of men."

"Seriously? I thought men like you were extinct.

Honestly, Pete, I think you would drown in my stream of consciousness."

"But I'm a strong swimmer. Bring it on, Little Sheila."

"You're going to need more than a life preserver or swimmies to stay afloat. The foul, trite string of words that seeps past your lips has you dog-paddling in a puddle of naïveté."

"Crikey dick, Ari, you've raised this one with quite a mouth on her."

Aerin stood to leave. "I'm bored. Papa, I sure hope you aren't going to waste too much time splashing about in this shallow end of unintellectuality. No offense, Uncle Isaac."

"None taken, Sweetheart."

"Dear Daughter, you know me better than that."

"Do I?"

"Such a biting tongue, though."

"Oh, Ari, we're just having a bit of fun here—little generational sparring."

"I can assure you, Pete, my daughter is not being playful. Her acerbic sarcasm is meant to sting."

Aerin placed her hands on her hips and held her head high. "Thank you, Papa."

"Honey, that was not exactly a compliment."

"To me it was."

"Speak your mind, Little Sheila, Uncle Pete here can take it."

"All right then, Aerin, fill the man's ears. God help us all." Ari gave Isaac a withered glance.

Aerin sat back down on the sofa. "Enlightenment 101." Aerin rubbed her hands together. "Let's begin." Her grin quickly vanished from her face as she stared through her new nemesis. "So, Pete, do you have any idea just how hard it is to move to a foreign country? It's bad enough I had to leave my friends behind, but then I have to listen to a grown man run down good, caring people. You sit there in your laid-back easy chair, sucking down beer after beer and make bold judgmental accusations regarding the American way of life. They're hard-working people, Pete, capitalism's a tough business. Americans barely get two weeks holiday a year. If they 'fight the system' in any way, there are a hundred citizens or more waiting in line to take their jobs. That's pressure."

"So find another job."

"It's not the job; it's the way they were raised. In Western society 'sky's the limit,' so it's ingrained in Americans not to fail. They're raised with, 'Push harder, be the best.'"

"Canadians aren't like that."

"My point exactly, they were raised differently."

"Like loony-left liberals."

"That's a pejorative generality. There are a lot of liberal Canadians, but they are nowhere near the derogatory meaning attached to American politics. The handful of loony lefts in America use liberal rhetoric but do not practise what they preach, and man do they feel the need to preach. Many get on their 'green' soapboxes and bark about how to save the environment, yet they own six or seven houses that are in no way energy-efficient. They rant and rave about gun control, but think they are exempt with their gun-toting bodyguards. Liberalism in Canada is a way of life. They are taught how to live more peacefully, in harmony with Mother Nature."

"So your little American friends weren't taught how to get along with people or their environment?"

"Oh, Pete, you do try to give me a migraine. It's not

that Americans are out of touch with their environment so much as the emphasis is skewed toward reaching the pinnacle of one's dreams . . . and this push to be the best starts at a very young age. It's not forced upon American children; it's more a subtle social manipulation. As I said before, they were brought up with the attitude 'don't settle for second best.' That's a lifetime of extreme expectations. On mediavision, American children are shown what kind of lifestyle they could have if they become famous, land at the top of their game. Doesn't leave much room for failure. Ralph Waldo Emerson said, 'America is another name for opportunity.' So raised with that pressure to follow one's dreams and be successful, the Americans have succeeded as a nation and reached great heights. Ask any young person from a foreign country, hellbent on obtaining his or her dreams which country would be the best place for this to happen and most always the answer is America."

"Not anymore."

"If that is true, what a travesty . . . and have a little respect for the dead."

"Listen, Aerin, I always say if you can't stand the heat, get out. If the Americans hated the pressure they were raised under, they should have stopped trying to be a world leader. New Zealand never tried to outdo Australia. Our country relishes its unassuming tranquility. And look who survived WWIV."

"It's hard to lead, but it's even harder for Americans to avoid being the best they can be when the whole premise of the United States is to be free and enjoy success without oppression."

"True. But—"

"Then do you see how hypocritical your stance is, to sit

in that relaxing easy chair and judge those fearless enough to try to be the greatest? The high school we attended had a lot of Americans. It was embarrassing when the Canadian students were so hateful toward them. Yet they gobble up U.S. products. America and Canada are sibling countries, each with their similarities and differences. Consumer-wise, for many of the larger Canadian chain stores, they are America Lite . . . American stores with a maple leaf plastered on the logo. They reap the benefits of being America's younger sibling yet complain about the familial responsibilities that go along with that relationship."

"But you can understand that, Aerin. The Canadians were tired of going to war because of the United States sticking their noses in where they did not belong."

"I get that, Uncle Isaac. Canadians have every right to be pissed about fighting American wars, especially when they don't agree with the U.S. government's motives for engaging in battle. However, when Canada got attacked by terrorists in Toronto at the onset of WWWIII, who was the first military strength to join the Canadian troops? The Americans, without hesitation, without complaints. Those whiney Canadians conveniently forget that bit of history.

"Don't get me wrong, I'm not saying one country is better . . . each group of citizens is just raised differently. As I said, Canadians emphasize living in harmony with their environment, such efforts as serious as recycling are engrained in us. We were taught to recycle trash, clothing, and even wood for furniture and floors, and paper for kitchen countertops, if you can believe it. My Canadian friends were reared with success always being an option, but they seemed to have an easier place to fall if they never reached unrealistic pinnacles.

"They seem to live less stressful lives in general and

are kinder to the less fortunate. It's just those embittered Canucks who ruin it for everyone else by constantly bitching and complaining about the U.S. They are what the famous comedian, Stephen Colbert, used to call 'maple-suckers' and 'ice-holes.' My American friends have said many times, 'it is very difficult to be the unpopular leader, having your every move scrutinized and criticized.'

"Some of my Canadian classmates were complete ice-holes with their passive-aggressive behaviour toward competition with the U.S. They revelled in their relaxed upbringing yet whined incessantly when the Americans beat them at sports or employment opportunities. You can't have it both ways; you either work yourself to death and end up as a top contender, or you enjoy a peaceful way of life with less stress, happy with second place. As sibling countries, we should share, taking the best from each other.

"Sadly, most Americans are unaware of their bitter younger siblings' hatred toward them. And I bet most of those critical Canucks haven't even ventured past the Canadian border into the States. Instead, they rely on distorted news reports like you do, Pete. I'm sure you've never trekked outside the 'land down-under,' except maybe to play a bit of rugby."

"Who can afford to travel otherwise?"

"Yet you judge. My American friends often find success but not a lot of peace or calm. Then foreigners like you come along, watch some show on the rich and ridiculous, and think you're justified in saying Americans are lunatics."

Uncle Isaac was fully engaged. "And how were you raised, Aerin? How would you categorize your upbringing?"

"I was raised around penis-worshipping misogynists, initially; then in a Western environment, that values education. I value wisdom and freedom. Therefore, I take advantage of my opportunities."

Pete finished yet another beer. "Do you compete with the boys and try to be the best?"

"Always."

"Then you're saying you are an American lunatic."

"Nice, Pete. I am a wonderful combination of both countries. My drive to be a doctor is quite obsessive, but if I fail, I have alternatives to fall back on. I won't be left with a hollowness deep inside, feeling somehow inadequate because I did not become the Nobel Laureate in Physiology or Medicine. And how were you raised, Pete, milking cows and shovelling horse crap?"

"Pretty much."

Aerin wore a sarcastic grin. "Like you, Pete, there are those Canadians who sit back and mock the Americans while they wear their clothes, listen to their music, or watch their MV shows and feature films."

"What's the harm in disliking Americans yet consuming their products?"

"It's hypocritical, that's what. If you hate these leaders in fashion, music, and film then don't be a part of their successes. Sit in your maple-saturated or, in your case, beer-saturated world and be happy with it."

"I just don't see the big deal. The Americans are getting what they want . . . the mighty dollar."

"Because those ice-holes are being fake. And they go on and on. Bitter much? I wish they'd just stifle the bitching about their southern neighbours. However, there is hope. The wise Canadians embrace other countries' accomplishments and enjoy the fruits of their success and hard work. Instead of bloviating, Pete, you should be appreciative that Americans, and a group of gutsy Canadians, are brave enough to step up and try leading the world. And if you don't like what the leaders are doing, then step in and lead yourself, by all means. Otherwise, lock your lips shut."

"But Aerin—"

"You're not exempt from overgeneralizing either, Uncle Isaac. Sociopaths? Seriously? Have you ever met an American, Uncle?"

"No, I can't say that I have. But many of my friends have and they share the same opinion."

"Your Jewish friends?"

"Well yes, except Pete."

"And with a brief exposure to his opinions, I can safely say he doesn't count."

"Aer—"

"It's true. I'm not even going to discuss Pete's obvious disregard for women's feelings, because I'm not sure if his attitude stems from a hotbed of wilful misogyny or simply a well of stupidity. I'll just state now, I feel sorry for Victoria and thankful as hell you two don't have any daughters."

"Aerin, you can't focus on my words always. I'm eighty percent hot air and fifteen percent sarcasm."

"And I'm trying desperately to appeal to that intelligible five percent, Pete. Uncle Isaac makes a comment judging the Americans, calling them sociopaths, and you blindly nod. At least Uncle Isaac has travelled to Canada. You, I bet, have not."

"No I haven't."

"Then, instead of thoughtlessly agreeing, open your ears. Uncle Isaac, I'm just curious what your definition of sociopath is."

Isaac drew in a deep breath. He knew he was now in the

hot seat. "Well, Dear Niece, it's a person who perpetuates a sense of superiority and entitlement using any means to obtain that lifestyle. The Americans are charming, manipulative, and lie with no remorse across the globe as they stick their noses into other countries' skirmishes . . . all justified in the name of democracy. With a holier than thou mentality, Americans don't care who they hurt and will never take the blame for their behaviour."

"But Uncle, are you talking about Americans or the American government? Sounds to me like you are condemning a nation because of a group of narcissistic, corrupt politicians."

"Fair point. I am guilty of overgeneralization, but when are the American people with a conscience going to take back the reins and run the country honestly and in the spirit of what the founding fathers had intended?"

"Of course, I can't answer that. All I can say is give that powerful nation a chance. Until you walk a mile in an American's shoes, don't criticize. Here's the other problem with your strong opinion: the cold, hard truth is, by your definition, American-born Jews are especially sociopathic."

"Aerin, that's completely out of line."

"No, Uncle, it isn't. My American friends whose parents struggled in the entertainment industry said American Jews, basically, flipped the proverbial bird at its new country, many times over. Americans stuck up for the persecuted German and European Jews during and after World War II by taking them into the U.S. And how did later generations thank their country? By looking after other Jews, not other Americans.

"Making choices based on Judaism doesn't ensure the most intelligent or most talented are chosen in the work force, either. Nepotism . . . favouritism . . . sounds like discrimination to me. What we truly witnessed with this crazed nuclear WWIV was a war of entitlement. Not to be offensive, Uncle, but I truly believe one spoiled group unleashed upon another, resulting in death for many innocents.

"First, you have Jewish Americans with their subtle sense of superiority and, secondly, you have the Israeli Jews with their sense of entitlement given them as special allies of the U.S. Both groups used our Jewish ancestors' brutalized history with the Nazis as a way to extort sympathy from the rest of the world. The Holocaust was so horrific that Americans spoiled those Jews within their borders and protected the Jews living in Israel. Things went awry as passing generations failed to appreciate this special status.

"Jewish Americans, initially so appreciative of their freedom, raised their children to think they were the chosen race. They were told they were special, Uncle; that they deserved the best cuts of meat and weren't forced to eat, say, mushroom stems. What the spoiled Jewish American offspring weren't told is every religion thinks they are the chosen ones. They didn't tell the distracted youth that if they are receiving the best cuts of meats, some inferior group is receiving the scraps and that throwing away half of their mushrooms was downright wasteful. So the Jews, treasuring their beautiful children, created spoiled brats with a sense of superiority and sat in wonderment as the Jews once again became despised by many.

"In the entertainment industry, especially, these American Jews have dominated for decades and decades. Jewish offspring many, many times were given the best acting parts, even when they possessed less talent. True,

America was based on being 'the land of dreams,' but where the Jewish Americans went wrong is they didn't give back so others could fulfill their dreams, others with the most talent. They were too busy giving too much to their 'special' children. What wasn't explained to the younger Jews is, if society fails as a whole, so does the individual."

"Dearest Aerin, why so harsh toward your own? You're talking about the Hollywood crowd, Aerin, such a small group of our people."

"God, I hate it when you say *our people*, Uncle Isaac. I don't give a crap what DNA they possess. I told you, I went to school with lots of Americans and observed some Trust Fund babies from the entertainment industry. I can say with all civility that they were nauseating pukes. They didn't even take their faith seriously, Uncle. To the disappointing Trust Fund brats, Judaism was never important until there was a perk they could exploit from belonging. None of the faith-based rituals made sense until it was convenient for individual advancement. After all, they belonged to the superior Jewish clubhouse, non-Semitics not allowed. I would never claim them as *my own*, Uncle. Over the years, other Americans also grew sour toward these self-serving citizens. So many Americans worked themselves to death, taking very little holiday, with much resentment brewing inside and out. They didn't have Trust Funds."

"But those are the exceptions."

"Then let's talk about the Israeli Jews. Tenderhearted toward Israel for generations, the American government backed and protected our ancestors. This created a long list of enemies in the Middle East. For so long, Israeli Jews acted aggressively, with their distorted sense of entitlement, then hid behind Uncle Sam's coattails, tongues out, giving the raspberries to Palestine and the rest of the world. When the U.S. no longer needed Middle Eastern oil and grew tired of the constant battles in this territory, trust between the two countries began to crumble. Israel eventually threw a nuclear temper-tantrum after America said 'no' to their increasing demands. They were guilty of forgetting, as were so many non-Jews too, that neighbours must care for neighbours, communities for communities, and countries for countries. What irony that our American Jews were pummelled by their own native country."

"See, Isaac and Ari, you should convert to Catholicism. Jesus is a proper mate." There was an ignorant sincerity in Pete's steely-grey eyes.

"I suppose you think your religion superior, too? Remember, you're following a Jew, Pete. Jesus wasn't a Christian. Otherwise, he would have followed himself around. Catch the irony?"

"So I'm a lover of Jews. What can I say?"

Isaac struggled with his anger. "Aerin, how can you say such hurtful things? Have you forgotten your own Jewish heritage?"

"What's my *own*, Uncle? Born Jewish? Born Persian? Or are my *own* Canadians? New Zealanders now? Women? Spiritualists? Doctors? What's my *own*, Uncle? By which category do you wish to define me? Aren't we all God's children?"

"Ari, you've allowed your daughter to become an apostate. I can't listen to this."

"Isaac, I allowed my daughter to find her own beliefs. She has a point; we are all God's children are we not?"

"And that makes my people everyone. Uncle Isaac,

what if you awakened blind tomorrow, would you recognize your own? Would you feel their faces to see if their eyes were close together or far apart, their noses hooked or widespread? What would you search for? Would you ask for their last name? Careful, Uncle, many Jewish Americans changed their surnames. Listen, the point I'm making is the minute a group chooses to take care of their own they are being prejudicial against the rest of the world. The minute this group decides to protect for no other reason but because they have similar genealogy, they isolate and stagnate. They miss out on soul diversity. And Uncle, the very nature of choosing the *group*, your *own* as you say, you're telling the rest of the world you believe your people superior. That feels very prejudicial in my skin."

Isaac was aghast. "Aerin, the Jews have suffered horribly in the past. The Nazis—"

"Uncle Isaac, I've heard it all, believe me. This is present day."

"It's hard to hear you speak of our ancestors like that. It's extremely disrespectful."

"But it's okay for you to be disrespectful toward the Americans?" Aerin paused as she stared at her uncle, unflinchingly. "See how horrible I sounded using vast generalizations? I don't believe those harsh words I've thrown at you regarding the Jews."

"So this was all a cruel lesson?" Isaac's face was flushed.

"Bigotry is a cruel business, Uncle. I had to get your attention . . . you weren't listening. I just threw every shitty thing I've ever heard about Jewish people into my diatribe."

"Well it was hard-hitting." Isaac glanced at his brother. "And why are you smiling?"

"Can't a father be somewhat proud?"

"Not at my expense." Ari laughed.

"Sorry to shock you so, Uncle. And please know I have immense compassion and respect for our ancestors. However, I will make this broad statement, I'm not so sure our ancestors would respect their Jewish relatives of today."

"My dear niece, you have shocked and equally shamed me . . . I guess you are never too old to learn."

Pete chimed in to clear the tension. "Aerin's right, Isaac. I can tell you many stories of what rude wankers the Israeli tourists could be. The dags I dealt with mucked up their hotel rooms, lived like pigs, and expected everyone to tidy up after them. And demanding . . . whew . . . especially the Sheilas. I never wanted to punch women so much in my life, a nasty lot. But Aerin, I wasn't aware American Jews were such a pain in the arse."

"Pete, after that long-winded, mock-argument, and that is all you gleaned? Did you not hear how I was talking nonsense and forcing a point?"

"Yes, but they were valid points, eh?"

"I was massively generalizing and using the spoiled entertainment Trust Fund babies to exaggerate my argument. And Trust Fund brats come from all walks of life. Powerful words, true or false, can damage lives. There are a lot of good people in America, of all races, nationalities, and religions. No one deserved to be obliterated by WWIV. It's shallow opinions like yours, Pete, which got the world blown up." Aerin stood. "I can't believe you three are not setting a proper example for my generation. Instead of crotch grabbing and worshipping each other's maleness, a little wisdom, please? Uncle Isaac, I meant no disrespect . . . really. I just don't want you to get buried in your Jewishness or anti-Americanism." Aerin sighed. She was partially exhausted yet equally emotionally charged. Before anyone could stop her, Aerin left the living room. The emptiness from missing Vancouver still remained. Once out the front door, she again became lost in her smouldering teenage angst and began pacing the porch.

"Isaac, Ari, I'm sorry mates. I thought we were sparring, thought we were getting on. I didn't intend to upset Aerin. Just having a bit of fun. Most women ignore my big mouth. I know Victoria doesn't take me seriously most of the time."

"No need to apologize, Pete. As much as I am proud of my precious daughter's intellect, I do fear the Western world has somehow tainted her. Aerin's generation doesn't seem to be at all familiar with decorum."

"You know, Ari, it is hard to be a woman in today's society. Besides, you remember what it was like to be a teenager, so full of emotions and idealisms."

"Isaac, you're telling me that? I raised Aerin as a boy in her early years. I, of all people, know how hard it is for my intelligent daughter."

"You forget we asked for her opinion, Brother. Her words were passionate but painfully true."

"I didn't raise her to be disrespectful, though. She trapped you in a humiliating corner, Brother, without regard for your feelings. Although I was amused, I am equally troubled by her callousness."

"Ari, her intentions weren't malicious. She was simply voicing her beliefs. As hard as it was to hear, a lot of what Aerin said I respect. They're valid points."

"Even by running down her own people? You said yourself, Aerin has become an apostate."

"But at the end, she retracted what she said, only reprimanding Pete and me for bashing the Americans."

Pete felt terrible. "Listen, mates, Aerin spent time in the Western world, saw things we haven't. We can't view Aerin's behaviour as overly cheeky just because her opinions are different from ours. Ari, you've given her the freedom to fly, stay proud of that. Isaac's right, teenagers are fuelled by emotions. My son, Tucker, is a prime example. Teenagers don't have all the answers; they just passionately think they do. Aerin's actually quite refreshing. I don't have a daughter but would be proud to have one like her, mouth and all." He chuckled.

Tanid entered the room and sat on the couch to listen to the news on the mediavision. "So what's the news this hour?"

All the men were ready for a subject change. Uncle Isaac replied, "Bits and pieces, Tanid, but it seems the local broadcasters report something only to recant their statements by the next broadcast. Pete, earlier we were discussing how to further protect ourselves."

"Protect yourselves? From whom?"

Ari chimed in. "Pete, when in Iraq we experienced what can happen after a massive bombing. People get desperate and act like panicked animals."

"My brother speaks the truth. Looting and beatings can occur without much help from an overworked police force. We want to avoid any violence, if possible, eh?"

"Yep, yep. What do you have in mind?"

"Build a modernized fortress around our property. It won't take long for radiation-infected outsiders to find the vent portals, especially the one near the lookout off Scarborough above Avoca Point. That's a well-known escape route for the younger generations when seeking sunshine on the beach."

"How do you propose we wall off the property?"

"We're headed to the dump and hardware store. From what we have observed, the public is staying calm and hasn't gone insane yet."

"Would you consider a fortress or barrier that surrounds both our properties? I have barbed wire and lots of cement, mates. Besides, your produce and our livestock complement one another, if we're buggered for a time. We've discussed that. Hell, together we can be self-sufficient for months."

North Vancouver

A WEEK HAD DRAGGED BY since the nuclear devastation; still the bridges were clogged with abandoned vehicles. Passage from Vancouver to North Van was forbidden until further notification from local government. Those stranded, yearned for their homes and loved ones across the waters of Vancouver Harbour. However, they were considered fortunate. Against the outside of the domed walls, starved, diseased, desperate people pounded with bloodied fists night after night. They stood upon layers and layers of loathsome yet unnoticed decaying corpses. For the select individuals caged within the domes, it was disturbing. They were unable to give these dying souls food, water, or medicine. The RCMP had threatened Vancouver's domed citizens with banishment for opening any dome door, a sentence to a short life among the diseased. On both sides of the fortified glass, the citizens felt helpless, embroiled in such a cruel dilemma. No one inside complained, though. They were appreciative of landing within the Burnaby, Vancouver, downtown, or North Van domes, spared the fate of those poor souls outside clawing to get in. For many, the question remained, "Were the dome-dwellers free or prisoners disguised as the lucky ones?"

DUE TO OVER CROWDING AT Lions Gate Hospital's Triage Centre, a town meeting was held at Sutherland High School. The North Vancouver auditorium was packed. Frustrated, tired citizens wanted guidance, a morsel of reassurance. Commissioner Wyatt of the RCMP addressed the crowd. "Everybody, I have lots of information to convey. I need everyone's attention, please!" An irate crowd did not hold back. The noise level hovered at a painful level. "Please, please, hear me out. Then we can work with what obstacles arise. Please, sit down everyone! I'll wait!" Agitated voices quieted to a rumble. "Thank you. Okay, we are just beginning to find out what has happened globally. It seems we are victims of what the media is calling WWIV, as many of you already know. My officers are collating a list of names for those held inside the downtown, Burnaby, and Vancouver domes. This will be distributed as soon as possible. We also have scientists working to determine if it's safe to clear the bridges. As it stands, reuniting with our loved ones confined across the water will have to wait." The crowd became restless. "Okay, many of you have asked about EyeNet service; obviously this has not been restored yet. Communication analysts have met to resolve this issue."

An angry man shouted, "Is it true Mayor Lemieux abdicated? If so, who's in charge? Who's making these decisions?"

"Yeah, who's running things?" Added another citizen.

"Quiet, please! Mayor Lemieux lost his wife and four children; they were in Whistler when the bombs hit. The rumour that he renounced his mayoralty is completely false. Mayor Lemieux, despite his grief, has worked long hours alongside other officials to solve temporary housing, food rationing, water purification, and RDXM issues." Commissioner Wyatt paused. "Any other questions or can I continue?" Everyone quieted for the moment. "We will continue to house people in school auditoriums." Discussions began again. "People, this is temporary. We are looking into vacant condo units in the new Harbour View building. Very few owners have moved in. Listen, a lot of work has to be done . . . this too will be temporary, of course."

Conversations from the tired group grew louder. A weary Commissioner Wyatt waited. "Now, health issues . . . How many are showing signs of radiation poisoning? I'm talking about skin lesions, nausea, vomiting, and any bleeding from the rectum." Reluctantly, hands began inching into the air. "Don't be shy; this is about survival, people." It appeared almost everyone was part of the infected group. "The good news? Lions Gate's Triage Centre has a stockpile of radiation detoxification medication, RDXM, to combat any deteriorating affects. And efforts to accelerate the manufacturing of this drug are being addressed by Mayor Lemieux and his team. We have to hit radiation poisoning head on, though. Bad news? Those showing obvious signs must be quarantined."

Another verbal eruption burst from the crowd. "Quiet! My officers are here to escort those infected individuals to Campbell High School for comprehensive detox treatment. Listen! It's imperative you get the proper medication. Besides, the health officials know how to relieve any nausea and painful oozing from cracked skin. There is no deception in what we're telling you. People, please! If you do not receive medication, you will suffer like those poor souls we've heard about outside the domes."

No one moved. A blister-faced teenager shouted from the group. "You're just trying to get rid of us sick folk, eh? Quarantine the wretched diseased so as not to disturb you wealthy bastards."

"And you, young man, have radiation on the brain.

Wealth has nothing to do with this. Now, sit down, damn it. It's hard enough getting information and assistance to all of you. I don't need widespread panic . . . I said sit down!" Quickly, the troubled teen dropped to his seat.

"All of you are aware Britain, America, and us Canadians have been working with the scientists from New Zealand. They have always been on the cutting edge of health cures. Well, our Kiwi cousins passed their knowledge on to the English Coalition and worked with other allied countries on innovative health cures and improvements. So I'll say again, those infected who want to survive and join their loved ones eventually, please proceed into the next room. Those not showing signs of infection, please take a one-month supply of RDXM on your way out. Oh, and while saying your temporary goodbyes to your sick loved ones, avoid saliva transfers and any contact with broken lesions . . . please."

"Honey, I do love you, but the man said no kissing."

"He said no saliva swapping. I've just found you and now I can't touch you . . . love you."

The pale man, with dark red circles under his eyes, abruptly pulled affixed gauze from his throat area. Many clusters of oozing blisters now faced his beautiful wife. Horrified, she recoiled putting her shaking hand to her mouth.

"See, I'm a walking mushroom cloud. My saliva will kill you. My radiation-infected cells are just waiting to crawl inside your skin, Honey."

"Why didn't you tell me?"

"That's why I stayed hidden this past week. Believe me, you don't want this surging through your body. This crap cuts through your DNA and rewrites your genetic code, a corrupted code that becomes a recipe for cancer. It compromises your immune system where suddenly you're afraid of a stranger's whisper of a cough. I'm lucky to be alive, Honey. I've been focused on surviving. I was hoping for treatment and now it's here. Honey, I didn't need to drag you through all the gory details of my sickness."

"Oh God, does it hurt? I want so badly to hug you."

"In time, Honey, we'll hug again."

MAKTAN PEERED OUT HER LIVING room window in the direction of North Vancouver; all seemed quiet, unscathed. However, Maktan had experienced war and devastation before. She recognized this eerie silence, when primal behaviour intervened and trust was obliterated. Everyone outside her home posed a threat. Casserole dishes containing a vast variety of Indian, Chinese, and Western cuisine found their way to Maktan's doorstep. Suspicious of her neighbours' motives at first, she let much of the food pile up, only to be eventually dumped in her garburator, untouched. A week of being trapped at the penthouse level within her high-rise with nothing to feed little Mu'mad, Maktan had finally succumbed to her son's hunger. Ravenously, Mu'mad devoured a mound of warm, gooey macaroni and cheese. Maktan had to admit the buttery-cheese sauce mixed with the chewy pasta was surprisingly satisfying. Western food was not horrendous. Nervously, Maktan had allowed the first morsel of humanity into her home . . . anything for Mu'mad's survival.

Aerin

After verbally accosting Pete and insulting her father and uncle, Aerin avoided the men. However, since they were the ones making all the decisions lately, she stayed within earshot. Aerin could not believe what she had just overheard. They were considering cutting themselves off from the rest of the South Islanders? Why all the paranoia and worry regarding a lunatic fringe? Aerin rolled her eyes in disgust. Forbidden to go outside alone, a rule Aerin planned to break frequently, she sat in a chair in the living room by a window and softly played her flute. Clueless about World War IV, the birds outside happily chirped and flew about the treetops. Some tilted their heads as they listened to Aerin's sweet music. For the first time in her life, Aerin wished she had been born feathered, with wings. She would fly far away from this place. Tanid touched his sister's shoulder.

"Hey, Sis, howzit?"

Aerin put her flute down. Tanid followed his sister out the front door onto the porch. "Sick of those narrow-minded cavemen inside."

"Ah, Pete and Uncle Isaac aren't so bad."

"Pete's pure annoyance. He uses humour to try and cover up his ignorance and judgmental ways. And Papa and Uncle Isaac are so busy being Jewish; it's nauseating."

"Aren't you judging them, Aerin?"

"Absolutely, it sucks to be right. Besides, they've gone too long worshipping their own opinions. It's time someone rattled their cages."

"Perhaps, but try not to get upset while educating the old farts. You okay otherwise?"

"Numb, depressed, brain-dead would be accurate depictions; or, maybe comatose; yeah, a walking corpse . . . depressed walking corpse; or more like a disheartened hopeless bumbling cadaver; a—"

"Sorry I asked."

"Always did know how to shut you up. Hey, Tanid, on a more serious note, you think Robyn is safe in Vancouver?"

"I don't know. Stubbornly, I keep searching for EyeNet service; as if, by some miracle, I am able to make a connection."

"I'm so sorry. I miss my friends but that doesn't compare to someone you are in love with."

Ari came onto the porch from the living room. His eyes did not meet Aerin's. "Hey you two, we're hooking up the trailers and going with Mr. Whibley to the dump. Tanid, care to join the men?"

"Papa, are you excluding me because I'm a woman?"

Cautiously, Ari answered his daughter. "Well, ah, yes. I don't trust desperation; we need to get past this precipice, Aerin. Please don't turn this into a gender battle."

"Do you forget I'm a surgical genius? Anatomically I could slice circles around any attacker. Eviscerate the infidels before they know what hit them, right? Give me a surgical blade and I could non-surreptitiously pummel the angry crowd."

"Such disturbing words fly from that beautiful mouth of yours, Daughter. I never know when you are kidding."

"What can I say? I take after my father."

"Papa, you've truly created a walking headache." Tanid was relieved his father and sister were finally speaking.

"Both you men should be proud of who I am." Aerin stared through her father.

"I am proud of you . . . but you still can't go with us, Honey." Mr. Ermani put his arm around Tanid's shoulder. "Let's go, Son."

"Pete, I hope you're happy. Your chauvinism is rubbing off on my father." Aerin chided.

"Glad to be of help, Little Wahine." Pete tipped his leather brimmed hat and winked at Aerin.

Tanid peered over his shoulder. "Hey, Sis, try out the shower."

"I smell just fine, thank you."

"Just do it. After the water turns off, stand really still."

Ari dragged Tanid toward the trailer-hitched lasercraft.

"Tanid?"

"Really, you'll love it!"

As she watched Pete and the Ermani men leave, Aerin played a melancholy tune on her comforting flute. She had successfully feigned congeniality with the adult men. Inside, parts of Aerin still seethed. Only when boredom had peaked yet again did she consider Tanid's suggestion. With the men gone, the house was quieted with calm, muffled female voices.

When Aerin readied herself inside the stone-tiled, circular shower, water trickled from the spigot in front of her. Aerin felt the temperature and touched the green square labelled "approve." Suddenly multiple jets from all angles shot warm water upon Aerin. She giggled as she lathered up her hair and body from the various soap dispensers. What a surprise. This was a welcomed indulgence. After conditioner was rinsed from Aerin's hair, she touched the red "off" square . . . and waited. Thermal lights flash-dried Aerin in less than ten seconds. "Unbelievable," she said to herself. Aerin stepped from the shower, clean and dry, carrying a grin plastered across her face. Boldly, Aerin shoved her semi-damp head within a smoke-tinted fishbowl. Pressing the lever, she braced herself. Warm, soothing air blew her hair in all directions. Aerin mumbled to no one. "I wonder if there's a gadget to brush my teeth for me. Ha, squeaky-clean in fifteen minutes. Great, more time to spend utterly pissed off at the world."

Hours churned by as Aerin, her mother, Auntie Clara, and Victoria waited impatiently for the men to return.

"Have you met my sons yet, Aerin?" Victoria smiled pleasantly.

"I have chatted briefly with Harrison. Seems I've been too busy barking opinions at my family or sleeping in to meet Tucker though."

"Well, no fault in that, eh? I believe Tucker is your age, eighteen?"

"Balic and Rami are eighteen, I just turned seventeen."

"Oh, so you're in between my boys. Harrison just turned sixteen. It's nice you're all close in age."

Struggling engines and crunching gravel were heard from outside. The women jumped from their chairs and politely pushed single file through the backdoor. Four jellywheels, with attached trailers, pulled into the Ermanis' backyard. The flatbeds and trailers bulged with an assortment of metal objects for the planned stronghold. As the twins and Tanid pulled weathered sheets of aluminum from one of the trailers, Aerin spotted two large silver pods. The twins carted them off, one at a time, to the nearby vault in the Ermanis' backyard.

Saroya leaned into Aerin and whispered. "What on Earth are those?"

"They look a lot like tanning beds. Tanid, what are those for?"

"Papa's attempt at pacifying the twins' scientific curiosities. They went berserk when they spotted them at the dump."

Aerin trotted toward the vault that housed the family's unused storm cellar. She too was intrigued.

Deek

Following a few days of an exhaustive blame fest, Deek and Sly used every bit of reason to remind these new United Africans they were on trial. One year of perseverance and they could leave Nature's prison. Unfortunately, no one listened.

"For the love of God, shut up! Do you not see that your chronic complaining and shitty attitudes got you here in the first place?"

If Deek had not been so angry, there might have been protests from the crowd. Instead, silence prevailed. "You bitched about America, about the White man holding you down. You committed a crime that put you in prison. And the shittiest part of this whole ordeal is most of you perpetrated atrocities against other Black people, against your own. Yet you continue to complain and blame others. The intolerant White government grants your request to leave the United States and frees you in Africa and still you bitch. You whine for your free meals, cable MV, and temperature-controlled cells. What in the hell did you think the United Africans would do with a bunch of violent criminals? They don't trust us . . . not one of us, so get over it! Christ, what a bunch of crybabies! If freedom means we have to prove to our new government that we can create a peaceful community within a year's time on this goddamn rock, then so be it! For once in your life, grow up! And the next time you point that finger of blame at anyone, start with yourself. After all, you got yourself here. I, on the other hand, love America. I didn't ask to be shipped off to a foreign country. Do I whine or bitch and blame all of you? I'll probably never see my wife and unborn baby because of you America-bashers! So goddamn it, if I can suck it up, so can you! Just, please, shut the hell up!"

Deek stormed away from the group. He sought refuge in O'Malley's dilapidated shack. However fumigated and restored, the dwelling was still very crude. Deek did not care. All he sought was solace. As he sat on the cot, Deek held his head and rocked to and fro. Somehow, speaking the words of his lost Lourdes had evoked repressed emotions tenfold. His yearning for his wife was immense.

As Sly approached O'Malley's shanty, he heard deep sobbing. Instead of interrupting Deek's sorrow, to let him know his speech had motivated the others to pull together for the moment, he let his young friend privately mend some internal wounds.

There was a pleasant thundering in the distance. It had been three days since Deek had chastised the Lompoc tribe. He peeked between the clapboards and discovered the skies were bright and clear. There was no threat of a storm. A piccolo-type chirping joined the rhythmic pounding. With dusk's approach, Deek left O'Malley's shanty and journal, letting the native music draw him closer. The drumming grew louder, driving Deek's rejuvenated heartbeat. As the gentle giant made his way to the top of a mound of ragged rocks insulating the Lompoc Township, his breath caught in his throat. Surveying the scene below, he discovered many new prefab structures had been erected. What seized Deek's heart, though, was, in the centre of the growing Lompoc village, a ceremony that would make the United Africans' tribal ancestors proud.

Fire torches danced about as the singing blended with the amateurish music, creating primal artistry. Deek could feel his mother around him. She dearly loved thunderous African melodies. Tears ran down the ex-NFL player's cheeks. He was part of these tough, proud survivors. Never was Deek so honoured to be a Black man, with so much love and hope emanating in all directions. From the raging bonfire, Deek felt currents of warmth reach his face; he closed his eyes. For the moment, Deek let the native music fill his soul.

Aerin

For the next eight days the Whibley and Ermani men moved dirt, converted cement into blocks, erected fences, and installed barbed wire and laser deterrents to perfect their collective barrier. Many sacks of rice, oats, wheat, and flour were stockpiled in the newly weatherproofed sheds, behind both houses. Jugs of distilled water, canned goods, batteries, candles, blankets, bedding, clothing, and dried meats were stored in the vault's underground cellar, shared between the two families. The women planted an array of vegetables, pruned fruit trees, made jams, churned butter and cheese, and collected eggs. Everyone worked until they dropped at the end of each day. Sleep was always welcomed, and in short supply. Although the families were isolated, they felt safer. If greedy, crazed invaders got past the enormous blockade, they would have to contend with Scrum and All Blacks, the canine barrier the Whibleys and Ermanis seemed to share. At the very least, the Border collies would announce their approach.

On the porch, the guys spent their ninth day resting. Saroya, Clara, and Victoria finished up their last batch of canning jams and pickles.

Saroya peered out the kitchen window; a wave of despondency washed over her. "Look at Aerin in the garden. It feels as if my poor daughter is slowly rotting away. We used to chat about everything. Aerin loved to tell stories about what she witnessed at the Burnaby hospital, impossible surgeries, time spent in the ER, saving lives, spiritual absurdities, anything that was on her mind. Now I look into my sweet girl's eyes and they seem dead . . . she just refuses to talk anymore."

"Saroya, give her time."

"It doesn't help that she's the only girl among the kids. Kendall, Quentin, and Evan have Victoria's boys, Tucker and Harrison, and my sons to do things with. Aerin sadly has just us older women, not a good substitute for her friends back in Vancouver." Saroya forced a smile. "I'm going to finish up her chores for her. Maybe I'll pull out some of her favourite books; oh, how she loves to read."

Bundled in one of her thick sweaters, Aerin dug through the suitcase that was filled with nothing but her beloved books. The one her mother brought her had been perused during her flashjet trip. And Aerin did not want to be reminded of that nightmarish moment. Not surprisingly, after much rummaging, she settled on her favourite thick surgical text laying beside her mattress. In the past, Aerin had always found comfort losing herself in the voluminous physiological mysteries. Hugging the massive book against her chest, along with a well-used notebook full of her thoughts, Aerin joined the men on the porch. Of course, they were discussing battle scenarios. Pete's jovial, boisterous voice could be heard above the others. Aerin shook her head in disgust; that man was sheer annoyance. For about thirty minutes, she read and wrote. When the women called everyone in for dinner, Aerin whispered to Tanid that she would be in soon. However, food was the last thing Aerin craved. Bookless, she trudged down the driveway with journal in hand. The closer she got to the newly constructed barricade, the more she wanted her freedom. Looking back several times toward the house, Aerin waited until there was no movement at the windows. The dogs ate their dinner, seemingly disinterested in Aerin's whereabouts. Slowly, she keyed in the combination to turn off the laser barriers, undid the heavy gate, and tried to inch out of the Ermanis' yard. Movement was suddenly restricted. Aerin's clothing was snagged on something. When she looked behind her, she discovered why she could not move. Scrum had his teeth locked onto the back of her baggy sweater.

Aerin whispered gruffly. "Scrum, let go!" She popped him lightly on the head with her journal. All Blacks had manoeuvred himself in front of her, obstructing the exit. "All right, you two, back, back ... yard, yard, go!" Reluctantly, both Border collies let Aerin pass but commenced barking.

Without hesitation, Aerin walked briskly down the rest of the driveway. She was free. Far above, the crystal peaks sparkled in the winter twilight. It was difficult for Aerin to get a clear perspective of the skies. She squinted. Two seagulls flew about peering out the glass ceiling as well. Realizing she was outside the Ermani/Whibley fortress completely, a much-invigorated Aerin burst into a freedom-motivated jog. Several times, she looked back over her shoulder to ensure no one had followed. That is when she ran ... ran like she never had before. Aerin only slowed for a brief moment when passing through their community's security gate. Peering about and sure no one had seen her, Aerin started to run again. Adrenalin surged through her bloodstream. Aerin's heart raced. Now she was truly free, free to resume her race for freedom. With no planned destination, she headed in the direction of the lookout, somewhere above Avoca and Kean points. The roads and skyways seemed empty, absent of crazed looters running amok. Aerin's pace quickened. Remembering her uncle's words, she headed toward Scarborough in pursuit of the previously mentioned vent portal. Crazily, uncaringly, Aerin sprinted, kilometre after kilometre.

WINDS MOANED FIERCELY THROUGH THE ventilation ducts. Smells of the sea wafted past Aerin's face. Faster and faster she went as she weaved through the maze of tunnels to the bent portal vent. What she was running from, or to, she was not sure. Ahead was a dead end. Aerin squeezed stealthily through a tiny opening, secured a very long time ago by the local Kaikourans. Now she was truly free. Ha, Aerin thought, she had finally escaped the crystallized Land of Oz without having to click her heels three times. She breathed in the wonderful sea air. More than an hour had passed since Aerin snuck from her family prison. Darkness descended. Only the full moon illuminated Aerin's surroundings. Gusts of wind began to pound against her, Mother Nature's way of reminding Aerin of her insignificance. Below her, the sea appeared troubled; angry white-capped swells fought to reach the shoreline. Aerin found it hard to walk amidst the blustery wind, so she sat upon the first rock she reached and watched the surf's amazing battle. Aerin felt so small. Waves crashed, one after the other, against the dark, pebbled shoreline. Far off in the distance, snow-capped peaks fluoresced the Seaward Kaikoura Mountain backdrop. Manakau, haloed with a glowing cloud ring, stood proud above the other sharpened summits. The view was spectacular.

Feel something, Aerin demanded of herself. So much beauty surrounded her, yet nothing mattered. No tingling in her fingertips or upon her skin. All Aerin was able to conjure was the heavy heart of a homesick teenager. Her pen lay motionless in her hand. Aerin's journal beckoned, but she was unable to write. They had given up everything for relatives she never knew, and not one of them could soothe her restless soul. Even after two weeks in New Zealand, Aerin still missed Brittany, her friends, her school, the diner, and Burnaby General Hospital. Aerin's heart ached for Canada. With no postal service, EyeNet, mediavision, or Internet, she had not heard if her Vancouver friends were even alive. WWIV halted the world. True, they had their father back and the family was finally united, but sometimes family was not enough. Resentment over their move to New Zealand was still fresh even now, long after their trip across the Pacific Ocean. Other emotions, ranging from fear, to helplessness and anger, depressed Aerin. It had taken several years for her and her brothers to become Canadian citizens. Quickly and enthusiastically, they had absorbed the culture, the freedom. But just when the Ermani siblings were filled with Canadian pride, they were again ripped from their home. Stability was snatched from beneath their feet, leaving them with pummelled dreams and that all-too-familiar feeling of insecurity.

Thoughts ricocheted about Aerin's head. Her spirituality had certainly been challenged in this new environment. In Canada, Aerin had discarded every religious belief she had ever entertained. Freedom of education had brought new beliefs, and with that, an unspoken pressure to keep her newfound secrets. Perhaps, Aerin was not hiding her new way of life so well. Her Uncle Isaac had called her an apostate, how perceptive. Still, she would not let him know just how deep those renouncements ran. Staunch religious practices had always been shoved down her young throat. The last family confrontation, when Aerin had at last spoken from her heart, had left her uncle unnerved. Her father was clearly frustrated with her, as well. No one understood. Judaism and all its flaws choked her spiritual growth. While in Vancouver, Aerin had adopted a positive attitude toward every incident, her view of the world forever transformed. There were no coincidences in life, so why become despondent when unpopular things happened? Her readings taught her to look for the lesson in every situation or be patient until its message was clear. Always choosing the positive path, Aerin envisioned her desired outcomes, prayed for them, and meditated on how it felt to have her dreams come true. All seemed to be on track, until this . . . living in Oz, her beautiful, detested fairy-tale. The absence of friends and making every effort to remain religiously mute, catatonic, so as not to appear ungrateful, had twisted Aerin into emotional knots. As much as she tried, Aerin was not able to untangle the negativity that had prodded her to escape the biospheric prison and flee to the comfort of the Kaikoura shoreline.

Not only had her world been shredded beyond recognition, but Aerin and her siblings were also in the midst of their second consecutive winter. Seasonally, New Zealanders prepared for frigid temperatures and precipitation, not the warm winds of summer back home. Time would not be spent sleeping in or attending summer school, either. Instead, the Ermani offspring were collectively forced to work. Wherever they were needed, they filled in, reluctant or not. Many of Aerin's memories of those postwar days were a blur. Very much in survival mode, and somewhat in shock, every family member had gone through the motions of rebuilding their new township. Where was a future in all of this? Again, Aerin's thoughts replayed every negative, depressing incident she had experienced. Nothing good would emerge. She threw a pebble into the fierce waves. Numbness clung to Aerin's heart. She sat upon her rock and watched the waves rip angrily at the glistening pebbled shoreline. Still, the wind pushed and pulled as it tried to pry Aerin loose, but not even Mother Nature could get Aerin's full attention.

Deek

RAIN CEASED ALL ISLAND WORK. Spiteful winds and punishing rain made it impossible to venture outside the prefab lean-tos. Warmth was the ultimate challenge for the day. Tucked within O'Malley's shack, Deek was immersed in one of the dead man's journals.

APRIL 17TH – TENDER FEET DIDN'T do so well when matched with brine-spattered stones. My feet have not completely healed since I got here. A few unhealed cracks in my skin let the stinging salt remind me to take it easy. Duct tape, glue, and pieces of dried sea lion pelts pilfered from already dead elephant seals, I used to layer upon the souls of my tattered tennis shoes. Once they are dry, I'll torture them instead of my delicate, healing flesh. God, my sores smell horrible; they smell of infection.

The small bit of lumber I brought with me and what's left of my craft will be perfect for my new abode. It has been sunny these past few days. Sore feet or not, I must build some shelter. What's worse than weathering the storms is dealing with the abundance of bird shit. Thousands and thousands of seagulls and murres call this island home. I'm learning how to confiscate the strange-tasting eggs without receiving pecks on the head by the many nose-diving mama birds. These aviary neighbours are fascinating to watch. There is definitely a pecking order, pardon the pun! Ha! How pathetic, I'm the only one who laughs at my lame jokes these days. Skilful assassins, the gulls, pummel the murres and even kill their own with a cannibalistic fervour. That's why it's easier to hunt the seagulls for food rather than the skittish murres. I just wait until the gull starts his/her attack, then I launch my crude spear. It took me two days before I was successful. I'll get better at it. My effort was worth the trouble; bird meat tastes better than their unborn. What ridiculous sacrifices I've made for my beloved, endangered great whites lurking about the cove below. Patiently I await each lesson they have for me. There are so many secrets these sharks have held for centuries. These beasts somehow warm my heart. But I cannot research them if I perish. Tomorrow I will gather some of the seagull and murre guano and add it to the soil I've been pampering for a garden. Before, I was convinced the ammonia was toxic, but I was wrong. Massive amounts of phosphates from this bird excrement have nourished the growth of the grapes, tomatoes, potatoes, and apricots I have planted.

Aerin

What morsels of clarity Aerin gathered were quickly swept away upon the winds. Powerful gusts ripped at the Fyffe House, an old whaler's home, positioned behind Aerin. A continuous whistling sound raised goose bumps on her skin, but eeriness soon turned to irritation. With a heightened exasperation, Aerin felt dared to challenge Mother Nature further. She climbed down the hurricane seawall to the waterside.

Vancouver had implemented these steel titanium, alloy-like walls as well. Weather changes had increased hurricane and tidal wave activity prompting countries to take precautions against the churning after-effects. These seawalls had proven to bend but not break with gale-force winds, saving lives that would otherwise have been swept away by violent waters.

Aerin sat upon some damp rocks, where she fruitlessly attempted to collect remnants of her old self. It was high tide. Maudlin feelings closed around Aerin's heart, like a compressing fog, as she took inventory of her missing friends. Oh, how she missed Canada . . . her home. While in Vancouver, excursions outside dome living were a common occurrence. Aerin missed the gentle breeze and the feeling of chapped cheeks from the winter air. Now she could not even feel the frigid wind tearing at her face and clothes. All Aerin wanted to do was scream "I'm dying inside!"

Going through the motions of life, nothing held any meaning. Aerin was not present and this went way beyond sadness or grieving. Aerin had lost the most precious gift from a peaceful existence . . . hope. When her mother had asked about her wellbeing, Aerin had successfully hidden her emotions, or so she thought. Over the past weeks, hopeless, suicidal feelings were deeply buried in her subconscious, resulting in an acceptable lie. To the outside world, Aerin was fine . . . quiet, but fine.

In desperation, she rubbed her greenstone hei-tiki. How on Earth had her life become so bleak? There was no warning either. Squabbling nations were the norm. The daily news was filled with these indicators. Yet after WWWIII, no one could fathom another nuclear catastrophe. Aerin, as many others, never saw WWIV coming. But more importantly, she never noticed the moonlit shadow growing behind her.

"PAPA, SCRUM AND ALL BLACKS are going nuts! They keep pestering us guys, then taking off toward the gate. Aerin is no longer on the porch." Tanid seemed agitated.

"She's not in our bedroom either." Balic announced.

"Saroya?"

"Ari, Honey, Aerin went to read on the porch with all of you men. She wasn't interested in dinner. Why, what's wrong? Where is she?"

Mr. Ermani began to pace. "Boys, we need to search the yard."

Everyone headed for the door. Nowhere the Ermanis and Whibleys searched produced Aerin; their hunt was in vain. Scrum and All Blacks relentlessly barked their secret.

"Isaac, get the van! Look at the dogs, they're glued to the front gate!"

"Ari, you don't think Aerin ventured out of the complex, do you?"

"There's no other explanation. She knows the alarm code and we had left it unchained."

Clara and Victoria tried to console a frantic Saroya.

All the boys jumped into the back of the hovercraft, as the three men, Ari, Isaac, and Pete, crowded into the cab. Holding the massive gate open, Harrison scolded Scrum and All Blacks as they tried to escape the confines of the yard and join the search party. When the gate slammed shut, Tanid reset the alarm. He quickly joined the boys in the back of the van. Uncle Isaac hit the throttle and raced the rest of the way down the path of the gravel driveway.

"Which way, Ari?"

Tanid shouted, "Water, Uncle Isaac, head for the vent opening!" To himself he added, "Aerin loves the ocean."

"WHERE DID SHE GO? WHY did she go? Aerin usually tells me everything." Saroya sobbed the tears of a helpless mother whose infant has been ripped from her breast.

"Saroya, come now, it'll be all right. Aerin is smart and very responsible. She's not the reckless type. She won't stumble into any danger."

"But the guys said some of the townspeople were starting to loot, steal, and act aggressive. Constable Kittelty said he's had to call in backup from Nelson and Christchurch."

"Sweet Saroya, please calm down. The entire town hasn't gone mad."

"Not yet. It only takes one lunatic to start a tirade. I've lived it, Clara. I've seen how desperate people can go insane in an instant."

"Okay, not helping. Saroya, Clara's right, Aerin is resourceful. She'll be fine."

"I would love to believe you both, Victoria, but I know my Ari. When he returned from town, I saw in his eyes a familiar anxiety. The men saw something to be afraid of and they're not telling us."

The shadow reached across Aerin's lap and crept toward her feet. Cold chills crawled up her spine and her breath became shallow. Sour body odour, laced with a familiar desperation, yanked Aerin back to her days in Iraq before their escape. The stench adhered to Aerin's nostrils. Someone was behind her and getting closer. To her right, Aerin could see a large, brown foot. Speaking Urdu, a raspy whisper came from the pungent man. "Infidel, you insult Allah. You don't cover your skin."

Aerin's heart pounded like a hammer inside her chest as she tilted her head backward. "What did you—?"

He was upon her. Long fingers clamped around Aerin's throat. Harder and harder the stranger squeezed. Aerin clawed at the man's hands, then his face, groping for his eyes. The man continued to push on Aerin's windpipe. Panicked, Aerin kicked while ripping at the strangler's fingers. Sinking her nails into his flesh, Aerin drew blood but still could not breathe. She needed air. Suddenly, Aerin felt far away, somehow floating above herself. Battling for her life seemed so unimportant and the pain in her neck had vanished. Peacefully, her body went limp. Just before darkness consumed her completely, Aerin felt a release on her throat. The pain returned, but that did not matter. Starved for air, she sucked in a huge gasp, then drank in as much air as she could. Breathing was the only thing on Aerin's mind. Before she was able to focus on her attacker, a scorching pain exploded against her left temple. Darkness hit with a brutal finality.

Deek

MONTHS WENT BY AND THE promised care packages from Johannesburg ceased. To Deek it was quite clear his community was abandoned. No more grains, batteries, blankets, fresh vegetables and fruit, clothing or bottled water were replenished. However, earlier shipments had included solar kits and distilled water purification devices. Deek called a community meeting; it was way past the time to get serious. They had been double-crossed before, so the United Africans' behaviour was of no surprise. At least they had each other, good and bad. Reaper Island was their new home and there was no other alternative except to make it work. Brewing tempers provoked already fragile psyches to unravel further. Bad habits were hard to break; bitching and complaining rose to an all-time high.

Upon a rock covered in bird droppings stood Deek. Peering out at the sea of negativity before him, Deek scaled the pinnacle of his frustration, yet again. Pejorative comments against President Walker and his predominantly White administration, were jarring and unfounded. Based on historical prejudices, the Lompoc group vilified White America. President Walker must be behind this new injustice; the United Africans would never treat their ancestors poorly. A fiery ball of anger could be no longer contained as it burst past taut lips. "Seriously? You are making this a Black/White issue? Every bad thing in your life is due to whitey? Shut the fuck up! You make me embarrassed to be a Black man!"

Sly's head whipped around to see his explosive friend's

eyes closed and both ears covered. All that was heard was the chirping seagulls and waves crashing in the distance.

"Why do you always resort to negativity? God, quit your incessant whining! You just loooove to be victims!"

"Where are the supplies those mutha fuckas promised us? Every time we start ta trust, we get slapped down! That white-bread fuckin' president neva cared 'bout us brothas. He's behind this, sho-nough; and I'z fuckin' tired of it! So don't yo' stand up there and give us yur College Boy mayo bullshit!" Jeers came from all directions. The tirade against Deek went on and on.

With eyes ablaze, Deek stared down the young gang-banger leading the pack. When the rest of the group quieted, Deek let his deep voice rumble, "Boo-fucking-hoo. Poor mistreated little Black punk!" The young man's fists tightened. "What, you want a piece of me? Want to throw a punch? Solve yet another predicament with violence? Bring it on, Ghetto Boy! Come on up here and show everyone just how stupid you really are!" Deek's massive build quivered with anger. No one moved.

When he was calm enough to continue, Deek said, "So you've had it rough . . . we all have. At home, you fought the Whites; now, you blame them for the Africans' betrayal. Do you know how insane that sounds? Constantly feeling victimized clouds reality. Don't you get that? Your points of view are distorted. Do you really think having white skin guarantees an easy life? Those of you nodding your heads are even more ignorant than I thought. Have you ever, just once, let yourself crawl in whitey's shoes? I didn't think so. It's much easier to be the poor unfortunate underdog. To spend your entire life wallowing in your comfortable misery and self-pity, you avoided having to break through the fear that successful people have to overcome to get ahead in this world. I know; I've been there.

"Yeah, you evaded those pressures of others always wanting a piece of your success; the success you and only you earned. But you wouldn't know what that feels like. You're too busy hating, yet loving negativity. You'ld rather sit with your hand out and a sense of righteous entitlement to remedy history's injustices. Those very inequities you've perpetuated by accepting an inferior station have kept you from finding your true selves.

"Poor, pitiful Black you! Why don't you step into the shoes of others, lots of others, and walk for miles before you decide to spew prejudices in the direction of those gallant enough to pay the price for a better life? Christ, quit using your skin colour to make excuses. That way of thinking rots your soul. Instead, take responsibility for your whereabouts. And think, don't react; the United African government may be testing us. Think positively for a change. Otherwise, you become a colossal waste. No wonder White people, and brown for that matter, are sick of the sight of you! Hell, I can hardly stand to be around you!"

"Shut up, yo' prick bastard!"

"Yeah, fuck off, Deek! We're United Africans now!"

"Fuckin' crackers sold us to slavery! Otherwise we be home, not on this fuckin' rock!"

"Sorry to burst your self-righteous bubble, my friend, but your greedier African ancestors sold you into slavery initially. It's amazing how you love to leave that part out of your daily rant. And you committed a crime . . . that's why you're on this fucking rock!"

"Shut the fuck up, Deek! We're sick of yo'! Yo' nothin'

but an Uncle Tom! Just rememba, whitey landed your Black ass in jail!" The young gang-banger basked in his smugness.

"Oh no, whitey didn't! You did, and you and you and you! After years and years of fifteen percent of the population playing victims and bitching about how they don't have fifty percent of what America has to offer, whitey got their bellies full! You were culpable! Yes, you helped whitey hate Black people! I love America! It's fucked up people like you who have ruined my life! So you're sick of me? Then you deal with each other! You lead, tough guy, I'm out!" Deek stormed from the group a second time. Not even Sly tried to stop him.

Aerin

Towering over Mr. Ermani's little girl was a dark, thin man. In the moonlight, blood spatter shone black on the stranger's dirty shirt . . . the blood of his daughter. Aerin lay motionless upon the dampened rocks. The pages of her journal snapped and fluttered in the violent wind. What began as a night-time trek of an emotionally charged teenager had turned into the fatal chapter of her life. Before Isaac had completely stopped the hovercraft, Ari and Pete were already out of the cab and racing toward the murderer. The rest of the Ermani and Whibley men in tow, they quickly cornered the perpetrator. There was nowhere for him to run. Mr. Ermani landed the first blow to the vile man's jaw, knocking him to the ground. Weakened from his journey to Vancouver, then New Zealand, Ari drew his strength from pure adrenalin. Quickly, though, his punches became ineffective. Pete gladly took over without hesitation, his powerful fists landing successive blows to Aerin's attacker. A drooping, bloodied head told the rest of the group that Pete had conquered the Arab. Tucker, with the help of Kendall, pulled his father off the crumpled body. Ari began to kick his daughter's murderer over and over. When he began to pound on the unmoving Arab, Quentin and Evan pulled him away. Tucker, Kendall, and Isaac held a struggling, ill-tempered Pete.

While Aerin's murderer was brutalized, Tanid, the twins, and Harrison worked to resuscitate Aerin. Tanid, always the closest to her, gingerly held Aerin's bruised head as Balic performed mouth-to-mouth and Rami administered chest compressions. Harrison held Aerin's hand and when Rami tired, Harrison took over. Bitter tears streaked the boys' faces. Frantically they worked, but sadly, nothing happened. It appeared no air entered the lungs of a fragile Aerin, so Tanid tilted his sister's head farther back. He could not pry his eyes from her swollen throat, blackened by horrible handprints. Suddenly her chest rose with forced air. Harrison and the twins were astounded. They worked with a renewed vigour, hoping they had witnessed a sign of life.

North Vancouver

Deranged faces peered into the confined Vancouver, downtown, Burnaby, and North Van domes. Large oozing sores covered their skin. Pleading with those who looked their way, these desperate souls just wanted in; wanted a chance. Occasionally, a desperate, pleading smile would appear exposing bloodied gums holding loosely to darkened teeth. Contaminated air and water made it impossible to be rational. They pounded on the plexiglass barrier. Those Canadians trapped inside Vancouver's safe environments were forced to ignore the threatening crazies. Any sympathy was mistaken for encouragement, which only made things worse. Although they felt badly for the deteriorating suburban citizens, those inside the domes could not help but want to get far, far away from the domes' walls. However diminishing, aid had been given to Vancouver, including downtown, Burnaby, and North Van. The tough decision to exclude those suburbs surrounding the four domes haunted everyone. It continued to be against the law to allow radiation-infected individuals to enter the encasements. Not until six or seven months passed would the desperate tapping hush and fade to an eerie silence.

A tall handsome man stood in the doorway facing his elated wife.

"Oh, my God, look at you!" She pulled the faded Canucks hockey jersey, a token of Vancouver's forgotten sport, from his neck area exposing pink skin. "Your blisters are all healed. Oh, Sweetheart, you look fantastic."

He hugged his lovely wife like it was their first embrace. It had been such a very long time before they had been allowed to touch. Their lips met with a fumbling awkwardness, at first. Then he held his love's face and kissed her fully on the mouth. Very quickly, like starved teenagers, their bodies fell together in sync. Husband and wife relished in their long-awaited intimacy.

They lay intertwined on a makeshift bed in their converted flat. WWIV had destroyed their expensive home in Port Coquitlam. Work had brought them both across the water to North Van that awful day. Now the couple shared a high-rise with many other displaced, trapped families. It was a blessing the building had been finished shortly before the nuclear decimation. The vacant skyscraper was deemed perfect when Mayor Lemieux, and his team, searched for temporary-to-permanent relocation sites.

"Honey, this place is really nice. I'm surprised actually, we even have a view of downtown Vancouver."

"It is nice isn't it? I was so scared, though. At first, I didn't believe the RCMP when they wanted to quarantine all of you. I thought I would never see you again."

"Well, I'm here, Honey, healthy and whole. I'm no longer a walking mushroom cloud. My saliva won't cause your eyeballs to light up."

"Very funny. I'm so thankful you're here . . . and well."

The husband peered into his wife's eyes. "Oh, Christ, I hate to spoil this special occasion, but I can't hold it in any longer."

"Oh, God, it's about Brittany isn't it?"

"It is, Honey. The updated Vancouver list came out."

"Is she on it?"

"She is, but . . . but they put her up in Kitsilano near

her old Starbucks job right after the bombing."

"Where those people are dying, mysteriously, from liver disease?"

"Yes, Honey, the very place where they found a slow air leak in the Van dome a while back, and no one realized they were slowly being poisoned."

"Oh, God, is she sick? She's sick, isn't she? But she took the RDXM medicine, right? My baby is dying? Is my Brittany going to die?"

Deek

"America isn't the land of the free, Sly. It let its historical guilt from slavery ruin its balance. The bitter Blacks with their caustic demeanours, brandishing guns and weakness of spirit, have lessened any sympathy America may have had toward their plight. Normally Americans are empathetic and encouraging when people face loss and difficult life lessons with honour and class. However, not this screeching, belligerent group. Quick to blame every other race but their own, the Blacks held America hostage in the past."

"But brotha, they don't see dat. Hell, I'z havin' a hard time seein' yo' point of view. Dem folks, includin' me, only know hurt. Dat's all we knows."

"You mean that's all you focus on. When you have fifteen percent of America's population bitching and killing because they don't get handed more than their fair share of what the country has to offer, the remaining eighty-five percent of Americans roll their eyes in disgust and turn a deaf ear toward the black-skinned crybabies. Sly, my wife is half Latina, half Caucasian, and when she was younger she did runway . . . modeling, fashion shows?"

"Oh, yeah, yeah."

"She said there were three Black girls that were pissed off because the designer wanted only one Black model and the rest lighter skinned in his show. Evidently, the Blacks felt all three of them should be chosen. After all, in their opinion they were prettier than the others. Christ, Sly, these high-powered models are all gorgeous. Anyway,

Lourdes got into it with these girls. She said they were shocked when she defended the Whites, as well as the Latinas. Evidently, this designer wanted a full representation of all women, you know, to enhance his diverse line of clothing. He was looking at skin and hair colour especially. Sly, Lourdes has the most beautiful golden skin, long legs that won't quit, and the deepest navy-blue eyes; she takes my breath away." Past due tears invaded Deek's eyes. He looked away from Sly as he choked back the emotion then cleared his throat. "So this designer fella lumps two of the Black girls in with the Latinas because of their light-brown skin colour. Needless to say, they lost out to my beautiful woman. Lourdes stands five foot eleven inches with the shiniest brown hair; she's gorgeous. There's no wonder she was chosen. Anyway, the ousted Black chicks became so belligerent they had to be escorted from the premises. And Sly, Lourdes said this was a common occurrence, every time there was controversy there was one or more Black models at the core of it. You know, heads juking about, bitching about how unfair they were being treated, and no one able to get a word in."

"I'm not followin' yur point, College Boy. As a race we been taught ta fight back."

"Not fight back, just fight whenever it suits you. Ghetto temper-tantrums are more like it. Look, Sly, if the non-Blacks are eighty-five percent of the population, including Whites, Latinas, and Asians; and Blacks are fifteen percent, why out of say ten girls should three be Black? That's thirty-three percent. Yeah, that's what the nasty Black chicks were barking. As Lourdes tried to explain initially, why shouldn't there be four or five Whites, all divided up between redheads, brunettes, and blondes, three Latina, one Asian and one or two Blacks? Well, the Black chicks went ballistic. Never could they see Lourdes' explanation or understand the designer was simply trying to sell his clothing line. Oh, no, Lourdes was prejudiced, plain and simple. They weren't fighting for equality, Sly; they were fighting for three of the ten slots, if not more. Our race can be the most discriminating, prejudicial group I've ever been exposed to . . . and they can't see beyond their own self-centredness. Anger paralyzes a person, Sly. It keeps him or her stuck. So our people condemn their offspring with the same debilitating emotions. Their futures are limited to drowning in a massive pool of rage as they are condemned to repeat the lives of their narrow-minded parents."

"But dem Black women had a point. It's been decades of holdin' Blacks down dat got us in an inferior position, da mayonnaise always gettin' da best jobs. So what if they was askin' for half da positions. 'Bout time things was slanted in da other direction; da Black direction."

"So whitey should give the Blacks their way in every argument? Let them have the better jobs when not earned? That's ridiculous. Keep lying to yourself, Sly, but remember mass generalization against the Whites is as prejudicial as calling a woman a bitch or a Black a nigger. Mass generalization is mass stupidity. Whereas you are innocently choosing comradeship and identification within the Black man's fight for justice, Sly, you are, at the same time, condemning anyone with light skin. So stomp all over other Americans to make way for the poor abused Black victims?"

"It's a start."

"You really don't get it do you, Sly? Plain and simple

. . . you're prejudiced, you are a racist. You're just another Spears lover, like the rest of the Lompoc group." Deek released an exasperated sigh.

"What? Spears lover?"

"Derogatory nickname for that Black movie director, Spears somebody, from a long time ago?"

"Well, least dat Spears dude fought for his own."

"More like he used his colour to promote his movies."

"I'z proud to be a Spears lover then."

"That old time director claimed he was fighting for the brothers' rights. In reality, Sly, his ridiculous antics caused whitey to resent Blacks even more. Spears wanted representation even when not appropriate."

"Whatcha mean, College Boy? Yo' is givin' this ole man a headache. Dat Spears dude musta been a great man, he looked out for da Black brothas and sistas back then."

"When Spears wasn't orchestrating a self-serving publicity stunt, he was squawking about putting Blacks in movies even when it was an historical incident involving only Whites. That was his unwavering argument. But what it really came down to was he wanted inequality against the Whites. Just like those models Lourdes had to deal with, Spears' bullshit soon landed on deaf ears. Whitey got smart and demanded he practise what he preached. They asked for roles in his Black films, do you remember that? He had a damn fit. Not only did he become the brunt of a lot of jokes in Hollywood, in a lot of ways it ruined his career."

"I'z proud he fought for us, though."

"Even when it wasn't justified? That is as idiotic as a White actor demanding to be cast as a native tribesman in a Shaka Zulu film!"

"Ha. Good point. Truth is, I neva listened ta da mayos wheneva there was a racial matta. I always lumped those damn cracka mutha fuckas together; figured they all had betta lives than all of us. I didn't care what dem mayos had ta say."

"Our Lompoc group thinks as you do, Sly. You're all Spears lovers, with one-dimensional thinking. You operate off emotions not reason. We have to pull this Lompoc group into a three-dimensional world, Sly . . . black, white and any shade in-between."

"Then yo' need to explain it ta 'em, College Boy."

"They don't want to hear the truth. Did you know that in the American prisons we have thirty-six percent Whites, twenty-one percent Latino, three percent Asian and others, and a whopping forty percent Black? So we have fifteen percent of the population producing forty percent of the criminals!"

"Now wait a damn minute!"

"No! You say harsh things about the Whites, but you can't take it when someone dishes it back!"

"But yo' was railroaded into jail by the fuckin' mayos! Yo' don't think otha brothas got the same bad rap? It happens every day, Deek! Why ain't yo' bitta?"

"Look at the facts, Sly, all the facts. Most of the arrests come from Black-on-Black crimes. Yet you all still blame the crackers, the mayonnaise! Whitey didn't put the gun in your hands and force you to pull the trigger. I was thrown into the penal system because of ignorance and fear, most of which was created by a history of Black violence and hostile attitudes. Fear of the Black man got my dark ass thrown in jail. And who instilled that fear? I don't blame the Whites anymore, Sly. I've seen the bigger picture for most of my adult life. You tease me about college, but I witnessed a lot in that environment and learned from it. And I believe my appeal will go just fine. I know Lourdes is working on getting me out of this predicament. But while I am here, I'm not going to wallow in self-pity and play the victim. My wife and time at the university taught me just how screwed up our race is in America. Black Americans can't even stop the violence in their own neighbourhoods, yet they expect other races to come in and clean up their messes. Chronic, nasty attitudes have never fostered empathy and support, either. Why am I the only one who understands this?"

"Most of us was raised on hate."

"I wasn't. My mama wouldn't let it step an inch inside our home. And I married outside of my race, which is an even bigger eye-opener when listening to Lourdes' experiences."

"Well, yo' is one of da lucky ones then, Deek. It's really hard ta try and understand da mayos when we can find so many things ta hate 'em for."

"That hatred keeps you imprisoned in ignorance, you realize that?"

"Maybe it does, College Boy, maybe yo' right. I don't know if yo' gunna get these battered brothas ta listen."

"Then they can leave me out of the decision-making process. It's all theirs; they can lead. I'm not forcing my views down anyone's throats. I just know there's a better life out there, for all of them, and it starts with a different perspective, different attitude. Spears' plantation mentality is so, so outdated. It was outdated then and it's severely outdated now."

Days passed before Deek would even consider speaking to another soul besides Sly. Even their conversations were limited and a bit strained. Sly was not used to another Black point of view. Deek was left exhausted, isolation his only course of action. Mama Jorgensen used to tell Deek that sometimes the most powerful words were those unspoken. So he remained silent. During that tense period, several men had tried to lead the Lompoc group and just as many mutinies followed. With bruised, battered faces and egos, the fractured community scrambled up the hill, one by one, to Deek's cabin.

Sly convinced Deek to peek through a crack in his shack's wall, a small space converted into a crude window. There stood many defeated pairs of eyes. Sly too had the swollen eyes of a sleepless man. It did not take Deek long to exit his domicile.

The punk gang-banger who had challenged Deek days before stepped forward. His face was covered with scabs and bruises. "Deek, man, we need yur help."

"Yeah, Deek, I don't wanna raise these babies 'round violence."

"Who you callin' violent, bitch?"

A string of angry rebukes escalated in tone. Deek took one look around, sighed, and turned to re-enter O'Malley's shack. Gradually, the voices ceased until not a word was uttered.

One woman shouted, "We feel safe with you, Deek! You've kept us alive!"

Deek did not budge.

"Please, Deek."

He wheeled about. "Boo-fucking-hoo! Poor bunch of stupid niggers!" Deek seethed. He folded his arms and stared down those giving into uncontrollable outbursts yet again. “You’re not ready.”

Deek walked away.

“Wait!” Chandra stepped forward.

“We are ready, Deek.”

“Are you sure? I called you the worst derogatory name and you lost your heads . . . again. Those names are just words. You’re giving them too much power. I called you the horrendous ‘N word’ and you’re still here. You didn’t crumble or suddenly fall apart. I don’t see any bruises or broken bones on your bodies. Nigger, nigger, nigger . . . my Black ass didn’t fall apart, or suddenly vaporize. If I’m to go any further you all collectively need to suck it up and toughen that thin black skin of yours.”

A mass exodus of offended Lompoc inmates descended down the hill. Ashamed for her brethren, Chandra let her head droop in disgust.

Aerin

Above her body, Aerin floated. Pain ceased to exist as a pleasant wave of calmness and overwhelming peace blanketed her. Several times she attempted to tell Tanid and the twins she was fine, but they ignored her. Why were they so upset?

Tanid yelled, "Don't crush her chest, Rami!"

Desperately trying to get Tanid's attention, Aerin shouted and waved her arms frantically in his face. No one seemed to hear her. Completely frustrated, Aerin grabbed at Tanid's arm. Horrified, she watched her hand go right through her brother's limb, as if nothing was there. Aerin tried again and again to grasp Tanid, but nothing worked. She struggled to feel him but could not. Instead, her brother's arm was the consistency of gelatin with an electric current running through it. From her voracious reading, she recognized this phenomenon. Taken aback, Aerin screamed inside her head. There was no other explanation. Quite simply, Aerin was dead. Accepting the inevitable seemed to increase her sense of self-identity, for Aerin felt free all of a sudden, entirely and utterly free to be her complete self. Fear instantly faded to bliss and understanding. Then a tugging sensation pulled her toward an engulfing portal, a tunnel. With a *whoosh*, she let herself pass, spiralling, weightless, through the darkened, horizontal passageway. At the end of the tunnel was a brilliant white light that pulsated warmth, a light brighter than anything Aerin had ever experienced. Despite its intensity, the illumination did not hurt her eyes. Fascinated, Aerin refused to look away. The white light emanated peacefulness, an overpowering love, rarely felt on Earth. That is when Aerin saw the many colours spread across an indescribable vista. Before her was an amazing field of tulips, roses, and lilies in all her favourite hues. There were colours she had never seen before. Past the tapestry of flowers, an astonishing city lined the base of stately mountains. In the foreground stood three majestic Greco-Roman buildings with white marbled pillars. Expansive domes spread across the tops of the classic structures. Immediately, Aerin knew from her studies she was witnessing the Halls of Records, Wisdom and Justice. Of course, the book descriptions paled in comparison; these buildings took Aerin's breath away. Beautifully manicured gardens were everywhere. Aerin recognized the two identical Towers directly behind the Halls. Very tall, contemporary monoliths of white marble and blue glass reached for the sky. Drawing closer, Aerin saw the waterfalls whispering down the walls of these reverent structures. She sighed, for everything surrounding her exuded serenity. Aerin could happily remain amidst the surreal sights, forever. Her dream-state heightened when she noticed an elderly man approach. He was beautiful. The closer the man got Aerin's disbelief grew. Did her eyes deceive her or was this a welcomed dream? All Aerin could do was stare. There before her was her beloved grandfather . . . a happy, healthy younger version of him.

DRENCHED WITH SWEAT, AERIN'S FATHER struggled against Evan and Quentin's grasps to reach his daughter's murderer.

Isaac squeezed his brother's shoulder. "Ari, stop now, you and Pete did the job. It's not worth taking another life, mate."

Ari's inexperienced knuckles were bloodied and

bruised. Each hand had started to swell. Unable to look at the progress of his children, he instead focused on the battered young miscreant at Pete's feet. For the first time, Ari really focused on Aerin's attacker. He could not be much older than Tanid. Bending down, Isaac checked the young man's pulse. Aerin's murderer was still alive.

"So, MY LITTLE PEANUT, HOW lovely you've become." It was he! It truly was her cherished grandfather. She had not heard her childhood nickname since she was a very, very small child. Aerin stared at her favourite elder with suspicious disbelief. Why was he here? She wanted him to stay. Startled, she heard his deep, comforting voice, but noticed his lips never moved. "My little peanut, you will be all right."

"Grandpa, it's really you! You're here . . . you're really here! I still have the stallion you carved for me. Oh, I have so much to tell you. I'm going to be a doctor—"

"I know, my precious girl. I have witnessed your amazing journey. You see, I visit you frequently and am so very proud of who you've become."

"How—"

"I keep a close eye on you, Aerin, that's how."

"You visit me?"

"Frequently . . . Sweetheart, you know you need to go back."

"But—"

"Search your heart. You know you cannot stay, it isn't your time yet."

"Oh, Grandpa, how I've missed you."

"Just remember I'm always with you . . . time to go, Peanut."

"I know. I have lots of work to do . . . and my family needs me."

A beautiful blonde came forward eager to talk. Aerin was stunned. The last time she had seen this familiar face was back in Vancouver . . . she too must be dead.

Much was discussed between Aerin and her visitors. It was Aerin's grandfather who finally ended the loving exchange. "Peanut, it's time. It won't always be easy, but you are going to do great things. You have much to do. Tell the others I love them."

An overpowering, unconditional love ran through Aerin; a love she knew now would never leave her. Enlightenment was a one-way street, not to be reversed. Aerin internalized what she already half-heartedly believed, love and knowledge were all that mattered; the only "things" one could take with them to the afterlife. Undeniably, without a doubt, Aerin knew there was life after death . . . Heaven . . . Home. She had read about such things and now felt them deeply embedded in her own skin. Those enlightened, wise souls were right; what a powerful, comforting feeling it was to experience "the other side." Aerin realized that religious persons followed the teachings of the church, whereas spiritual individuals followed the guidance of his or her enlightened soul. And one's spirit guide and angelic legion was always nearby, offering assistance. Formal religions added dogma and doctrine . . . so many rules of do's and don'ts. This experience confirmed a sacred awareness, which was always latent in Aerin. She had never balked at the divine, but now she had proof. Not irrefutable evidence she could discuss with others, but an infused soulfulness that would carry her throughout life until she joined her grandfather once again. Everything was, and would be, all right.

Aerin soared, spiralled through the tunnel once again, faster and faster. With great reluctance, she felt sucked back into her battered body. Instantly, her throat and chest burned with a searing pain. It hurt to breathe. Sharp pangs struck her upper body, but somehow, Aerin knew she was safe. In her mind, she would view the world differently going forward . . . somehow life's purpose was no longer a stranger.

Then came a wonderful sound. Gasping and coughing was heard from behind Ari and Isaac. Aerin's father wheeled around to see his daughter breathing, with open eyes, searching for her loved ones.

Any shred of despair that was in Aerin was forever gone. Fear and teenaged angst had become obsolete. A renewed energy surged within her unbattered soul. Why waste time was her first thought. Life was so precious, so short. Aerin drank in these new feelings like a thirsty child. With her renewed perspective, she planned to share this fantastic knowledge with those ready to listen, pass it past parched lips and abolish pessimism, once and for all.

"Papa, listen to Uncle Isaac, it's not worth taking another life." All stared at Aerin in shock. "And Tanid, Rami wasn't crushing my chest."

Ari raced to his daughter's side. "Oh, my sweet girl. You gave us such a scare. Oh, thank you, God, thank you."

With a raspy voice, "Don't forget to thank Azna, too."

"Honey?"

"Mother God?" She searched her father's eyes. "Never mind."

"Honey, listen are you all right?"

"Papa?"

"Yes, Baby."

"I'm so, so sorry."

"Honey, save your vocal cords."

"No, I need to say this."

"Take it slowly. I'm not going anywhere." He held his daughter's hand.

"I was so mad at you, you and Uncle Isaac. I thought we were moving to New Zealand to satisfy your paranoia. Ouch, oh my neck hurts."

"Be still, Honey. Maybe your uncle and I are a bit paranoid. I'm so sorry I tore your young lives apart. I just always—"

"Papa, don't you dare apologize. Kaikoura is a great home, I see that now."

"Yes, yes it is."

"I'm so very sorry." It hurt Aerin to swallow. "I needed some space and—"

"It's okay, really; you're here and alive; that's all that matters."

"I'm so happy now, sore but happy. I have so much to tell all of you."

"Save your voice, Honey. I need to get you home to your frantic mother, if you're sure you are done spreading your wings."

"I'm done, I promise. Home sounds really good. Papa?"

"Yes, Honey."

"Sorry about cutting off my hair."

"I raised you to be a strong person, Aerin. I never dreamed how strong you might become, though. You wear your hair any way you like. The spiked look is actually growing on me."

It was time to get Aerin home. While the young men headed for Isaac's vehicle to fashion a crude bed for Aerin in the back, Harrison climbed down to the rock where

Aerin sat earlier and retrieved her blood-spattered journal.

Pete gently pushed past Ari and gingerly lifted Aerin's aching body. She winced with unimaginable pain. Almost passing out, Aerin began to fade. Pete's gruff voice rumbled in her ears. "Stay with us now, Little One."

"Pete . . . Uncle Pete . . ."

"Don't talk, Sweetheart." Aerin's body went limp.

Kozlov

Barely able to see his towering assailants past swollen black eyes, Kozlov grew tired of his own futile pleas. The blackened bruises surrounding his eye sockets, engorged with excessive blood, throbbed relentlessly. How had the bombing escalated so completely out of control? Russia was never supposed to be a target. All those millions upon millions of deaths . . . Kozlov was deeply saddened. He would never forgive himself. Now, his family was without a country. Orphaned and living in Amsterdam, they would forever be void of the Russian culture. Nothing they had known would matter to the remainder of the existing world. Kozlov felt numb from his attacking brethren's blows. Yet he welcomed the fists against his skull. Longing to abate his overwhelming guilt, Kozlov silently dared the KGB operative to end his misery.

Slumped before him, the KGB agent realized Kozlov was unconscious. He paced. Was what he said true? Had Russia simply been in the crossfire, part of China's and the U.S.'s retaliatory list if they were ever bombed? Why had the KGB not anticipated this? Still he paced. Kozlov breathed erratically. Was he dying? In a panic, the operative grabbed the battered Kozlov like a rag doll.

The agent flopped Kozlov's body on the divan across from his panicked family. Mrs. Kozlov jumped from her chair, pushed the less muscular KGB operative aside, and rushed to her husband's aid. Sasha burst into tears, again. Too frightened to move, she remained in between her protective grandparents.

Hovering in a thick fog, Kozlov was sure he heard his wife's voice in the distance. He was frustrated that he was neither able to move nor answer her. "Try, Bogdan. Answer her," he told himself. Who was crying? Was that Sasha? His loved ones' voices sounded farther and farther away. Kozlov finally surrendered and let the pain and commotion fade.

Aerin

Aerin's attacker was secured within the cellar. Chains binding his ankles and wrists were anchored to rings Balic and Rami had cemented into the floor. He would go nowhere. During the nuclear bombardment, and right before a mushroom cloud or two formed in the Australian skies, a ship full of Middle Eastern immigrants was denied port in Melbourne, then later, Auckland. For days and days, they had drifted about Eastern Australia and now roamed the southern waters of New Zealand's South Island.

The Royal N.Z. Naval Base in Christchurch spotted the ship on radar and launched a patrol boat to investigate. Having prior run-ins with Australia's Coast Guard and N.Z.'s North Island naval patrol, the Arabs knew they had little time. Frustrated, angered, and running out of supplies, the Desert Muslims searched for a bit of vacant shoreline. They were hellbent on claiming new destinations. Finally, the time came; they spotted the beach north of Kean Point. There were no docks, just a pebbled, deserted shoreline; so the Arabs helmed their ship into the surf. Out of nowhere, search lights ablaze, a patrol boat approached from behind. It was a race to the shore.

Cresting one last wave, the Arab ship surged forward and then collided with the beach. Before long, the patrol boat skidded ashore. However, before the patrol squad could exit their vessel, the Arabs, bruised and shaken, had quickly abandoned their ship and scurried for the shadows. To the Arabs, this was the perfect scenario. Guided by

Allah, of course, these "chosen ones" were on a mission to take whatever war-free-zone suited them.

Once aground, feet firmly planted upon new soil, they had scattered for the darkness to wait. Never mind the fact they were the very groups that fought violently against the Jews for centuries over land they felt was theirs; never mind the fact that New Zealanders felt the same sense of ownership about their native country; and never mind the fact these Desert Muslims planned to take land that was not theirs. Allah had somehow told them to move on . . . take what they needed. Laden with their sense of entitlement, the Desert Muslims would soon claim their property.

It took hours, but the N.Z. patrol squad apprehended most of the Desert Muslim immigrants. Fatigued, the squad wanted to believe they had captured all of the intruders. Pushing past the pounding surf, the patrol boat carried its crew and prisoners back to Christchurch.

Considered victors, Aerin's miscreant and others who evaded seizure roamed Kaikoura's shoreline in search of their spoils of WWIV. That is when he had spotted Aerin, disrespectfully flaunting her hair and limbs. It had been too much for Aerin's attacker; the English Coalition's habits would not be tolerated in his new "chosen land." Allah would be respected above all else. And this whore infidel would feel his wrath . . . all brutality in the name of Allah.

"Aerin, how did you know what I said to Rami? And you knew what Uncle Isaac said to Papa. You heard these things, but you weren't breathing, Aerin. You were, ah—"

"Dead? When I was dead?"

"Well, yes."

"Tanid, you wouldn't believe it if I told you. Life doesn't end after our Earthly bodies cease to function. And . . . I see things."

"Shut up."

"I'm serious, Brother. You have to have an open mind . . . actually, more than an open mind to accept all this."

"I do."

"No, you don't."

"I will, I promise. Keep talking."

"Tanid, are you sure you want to hear this? All of this?"

"Why wouldn't I?"

"It's not only a tough topic, especially for you, but the news isn't all good."

"Aerin, I'm a grown man—spill it."

"Well, for starters, there is an afterlife. And Heaven is our real Home, only a home that none of us remember."

"What?"

"See, you're already freaking out. Shut off that thinker-dominated side of your brain. You know I've read extensively about the *other side*. Now I can say I got to experience it firsthand."

"Well I'm not freaking out, so continue."

"Look at you; you're trying so hard not to laugh. Smugness will come back to bite you, Dear Brother."

"Okay, sorry, sorry. It just sounds so ridiculously farfetched."

"Close your mind and try to listen with your soul."

"I didn't know a soul had ears." Tanid couldn't contain his laughter any longer.

"You're an ignorant ass, so typical of you mental, non-feeling boneheads."

"I'm not ignorant. Come on, Aerin. Grow a sense of

humour. Okay, okay, go ahead, I'm listening. I've heard all this psychic crap in school, I just don't happen to believe it."

"Well, the good news is I got to see the future, Tanid. Of course a lot of it doesn't make sense, but I saw great things ahead for you and me."

"Could you be more vague?"

"Absolutely. All kidding aside, we are destined to make this world a better place."

"You're high, Little Sister."

"I do feel euphoric."

"That's not what I meant, wacko."

"And I knew you were going to say that."

"Shut up."

"And that."

"Leaving now, Crazy Girl."

"Love you, mean it."

"Okay, no bullshit, give me the specifics."

"Even if it's bad?"

"Especially if it's bad."

"Then you need to sit down, Tanid." Aerin's brother complied, sitting upon the sofa next to his sister's chair. "I spoke with Grandpa—"

"Aerin—"

"I spoke with grandpa . . . and Robyn. She's here now." Tanid went silent for a bit. There was no trace of a smile on his face.

"That's cruel, Aerin. So you had a lack of oxygen to your brain and hallucinated. Grandpa? And saying Robyn is here indicates she's dead and that is just mean-spirited."

"Robyn says she found the engagement ring you left her on her favourite lavender, satin pillow." The colour drained from Tanid's face. "Robyn was wearing your ring when the bombs struck Seattle. She was visiting her family in Kirkland when the nuclear arsenal arrived."

"How could you know that?"

"Tanid, Grandpa and Robyn are so happy and they love us all so much. Robyn loves you, that doesn't end."

"Aerin—"

"The ring was yellow gold with a teardrop diamond."

"There is no—"

"She told you the morning we left Vancouver that she wasn't pregnant."

"Aerin!"

"And you planned to earn enough money in New Zealand, buy a plane ticket, and leave all of us to return to Canada to be with her."

"Okay, okay . . . I don't get this. How could you know all those details?"

"Psychic visions are real, Tanid. I just wanted you to know what I see is real, not a dream or hallucination."

"So my Robyn is dead."

"I'm afraid so. Though she felt nothing when the bombs detonated. No one in her family felt a thing. Angels were there to take them Home." Pooled stubborn tears fell from Tanid's eyes. "They're all happy and awaiting our return. Yes, Tanid, Robyn is Home yet keeping close to you."

"She can see me?"

"Robyn's standing next to you now. Can you feel her touch your cheek?"

"My skin feels a little tingly, but I can't see her of course."

"You have smelled her perfume haven't you?"

"Yes, yes that's true. I just thought it was my overactive imagination."

"Robyn says she also comes to you in your dreams."

"I do dream about her, but that's just my mind dealing with missing her so much."

"They're vivid dreams, aren't they?"

"Very vivid . . . I do smell her, Aerin, out on the porch."

"That makes her happy when you realize her presence. Don't be afraid to tell her you love her. She hears you."

Tanid fought the menacing lump building in his throat.

"Oh, Brother, you hold so much in."

"I'm so sorry I wasn't there to protect her."

"Tanid, try to shift your way of viewing death. It's not a bad thing; dying is great. We are greeted with an overpowering love on our way Home. No pain, no sadness . . . basically, Tanid, if hell was a real place then hell is here on Earth."

Before Aerin sat her heartbroken brother, a truly hollow vessel. The vacant look upon his face and slouched shoulders was all that was left. He had been reduced to a vulnerable, motherless child. Past opinionated quips and cockiness—from the security of having someone to run to or someone to join with in criticizing the world—had vanished. Tanid's partner-in-crime had abandoned him to face human cruelty alone. And it threatened to swallow him whole. Robyn had been his everything. Looking back, he had used that security to flip-the-bird at the world. As long as he and Robyn had each other, screw everyone else. An officious attitude toward others, the couple took one another's side during any familial or political rant. Yes, everyone could go straight to hell. Now his partner was gone; Tanid was an army of one. But he still had Aerin. Forever close, however, not even his little sister could mend the lingering heartache. Life had changed in an instant and Tanid wanted to press *rewind.* He wanted more time with Robyn. Although, with deep sincerity, when Aerin told her big brother she was "here for him," the threadbare cliché seemed trite.

Tanid wiped his eyes. "Give me those books you swear by."

Aerin handed Tanid a couple of books she had been rereading since her rebirth. "Use that potentially open mind of yours, not your smug logic, and read all of these. Try to think outside your comfort zone and consume it all. When you become stubborn and incredulous, doubting what you read, smack yourself. Then, read on. When you've ingested every word, Brother, come back and we'll chat."

"Yeah, sure. Near-death experiences?"

Aerin slapped another spiritual paperback against Tanid's chest. He did not respond. "Read, Tanid, read. Apostasy can be invigorating. And if you breathe a word of this to anyone else, I'll strangle you."

"Not funny—there will be no more stranglings in this family." Tanid touched the yellow-green bruise that had pooled at the base of Aerin's neck. Without much else to discuss, Tanid collected his new reading material and left the room.

"Hurry back . . . enlightened, Big Brother." Still, Aerin was unable to make Tanid smile. It was apparent that Aerin's once-esoteric, inner knowledge was meant to become exoteric, shared with all who would listen.

"Beware of those who would rob you of your hope, for they diminish your light by planting seeds of fear within you."

~ Kyron

American channeller, speaker and author, Lee Carroll, from channelled entity "Kyron"

HOPE SWELLS

Aerin

It took two months to organize the electricity and water filtration plants. Everything had remained operational, but it was the dogged interaction of the people that had caused system failures. In a desperate pursuit of some form of leadership, several overly confident men reluctantly stepped forward . . . armed, of course. With these luxuries intact, New Zealanders felt their world returning to some sense of normalcy. Then, approaching three months of postwar holocaust, just when the islanders were functioning beautifully together, all hell broke loose. Ship upon ship of aggressive survivors hit the North and South beaches in droves. Evidently, the rest of the world was discovering those few countries that continued to flourish despite global contamination.

Secured within the Ermani/Whibley compound, the young adults pursued their interests as best they could. Whereas the twins and Tanid, with his newfound spiritual beliefs, busied themselves in the Ermani/Whibley storm cellar creating something out of the confiscated tanning beds, Aerin spent her time reading and rereading her many medical books. Humanitarianism drove Aerin after her near-death experience. Life suddenly had a purpose and a career in medicine held new meaning. Whenever nearby neighbourhood battles quieted and the injured were extricated and unable to make it to the hospital, they were brought to Aerin for treatment. Many of the local doctors refused to assist with injured refugees, which gave Aerin many patients. Appreciative of Aerin's assistance, supplies magically found their way to Aerin's father and uncle. It started with bandages and ointments, but before long, the donations grew to include all varieties of medicines, sutures, needles, IVs, and syringes. Eventually, random medical-related things such as oxygen tanks and a microscope miraculously arrived at Aerin's makeshift clinic. She was sure the local doctors sent the supplies; and they were generous. You name it and Aerin had it stocked in her newly converted vault. At first, she had been nervous removing bullets and stitching up torn blood vessels and tissue. However, with such support from her community, Aerin quickly adapted. Her patients healed beautifully, which reinforced her confidence and became the groundwork for Aerin's medical education. To the unwanted immigrants, Aerin was their vanguard medical welcoming committee. Word was on the street and spreading rapidly that Dr. Aerin, as she was affectionately known, had become the teenager saving the unwanted.

Tanid was extremely proud of his baby sister. He had read the books she fed him as instructed. As hard as it was for Tanid to understand these spiritual, ethereal concepts, it was, very slowly, accepted. How to bring these beliefs into the tangible world? Tanid schemed and brainstormed with his younger brothers as they sketched, created, and tested for hours, days, and weeks. The young Ermani men were alive with purpose. And Tanid could build anything. He was a genius at creating a machine out of spare and unrelated parts. Balic excelled at mathematics whereas Rami was the family's mechanical engineer. Together, they mixed chemicals, snipped wires, added tubing and metal plates, repaired non-functioning parts, and cohesively worked to create something astounding, something that would change the world Aerin foresaw. With her medical and spiritual input, they would have everything they needed. And across the room sat their first guinea pig, their hostile prisoner . . . the very man that had killed Aerin.

Deek

A WEEK HAD PASSED SINCE Deek attempted to jar the stubborn, stuck minds of the Lompoc tribe. The short speech he had thrown at the departing group had been harsh with brutal honesty.

"So are we going to try this again? You all look tired. First, I would like to apologize to everyone. I know my words cut deeply, and I'm certainly not perfect. The first thing I learned at university is just how much I don't know. All I was trying to do was explain that instead of feeling proud of being an American, you all gave up. You renounced America and claimed Africa, an Africa that still doesn't understand your lifestyles. When they bring us all back to the mainland, you will still be a minority. You may have similar skin colour, but your attitude is American. You were not raised in United Africa with African traditions. And your own ancestors chose to isolate you from them. Understand that these United Africans respect those Americans—white, black, and brown—who have assisted their country with aid, vaccines, and cures for crippling diseases. What do you bring to them, a rap sheet? You can't give up this go-around and resort to quick fixes like crime and violence. Impress the United Africans with your uniqueness, people. How will you add to their society?"

Defeated faces stared back at Deek. No one seemed to know what to say.

"Look, I have been extremely hard on all of you to get your attention. I know many of you have had it rough, rougher than should ever be inflicted upon another human being, but that is over. Where there is bitterness, happiness needs to breed. You've got to find a way to forgive the past and let it go. You are poisoning your future and those around you with perpetual cynicism. Keep that cycle spinning and it's only a matter of time before people act out against you making life rough once again. Seriously, you bring in what you dwell upon."

Deek looked around at the confused faces. The young gang-banger pleaded past puffy, scabbed lips. "How do yo' do that, Deek? How do yo' forget the past? It's always there."

"By staying present." Blank faces stared back at Deek, yet no one left. "How many of you are weary, tired of being angry, tired of hating? Be honest." Everyone raised a hand. Some were reduced to exhausted tears. "Okay then, bear with me, I'll explain the best I can. At the university, I majored in medicine, and of course football, but minored in Spiritual Studies. You see, I wanted to be the best doctor around when I finished . . . pure ego on my part. Plus, that was my wife's field of study, spirituality. Yes, I'm ashamed to say my enlightenment came about because of a beautiful face and the longest brown legs you could ever imagine. Of course, I told myself otherwise. I thought I could broaden my medical expertise by fusing Eastern and Western medicine; then I would be head and shoulders above the others, the 'White' others. I thought I was so clever. I was going to beat whitey at his own game. The med students thought I would slide through my courses because I was a dumb jock superstar. So secretly, I studied my ass off. I'd show those mayos who was more intelligent. Ha! The joke was on me, people. I fell in love and stumbled upon my true self in the process." Deek sat down on a huge rock behind him. His crowd grew closer and got comfortable as well.

"My spiritual studies covered the practice of getting rid of one's ego. That egoless process was like dislodging rust and calcified deposits from the prejudicial, decomposing plumbing in my brain. I discovered a new way of viewing life. It's this simple, release the ego and live in the now. Don't be judgmental, let things and others just be. When you are able to do that, you can release the past and those tiresome, ever-changing plans for the future. This will dissolve sadness, bitterness, stress, and pressure. Living in the now brings much peace. One of the masters, Eckhart Tolle, stated our human minds are predisposed for negativity. It's as if we are born with a collective mental illness, it's our inherited dysfunction. We all have it. The human mind in its normal state generates suffering, dissatisfaction, and misery. Yes, even White people, brothers and sisters. Inside, there is no colour difference." Finally, Deek saw a few smiles.

"We have to sit quietly when that whacky brain of ours starts stirring up negative scenarios. The ego must die. We purchase or steal stuff for prestige. At the end of the day, this stuff really doesn't hold any meaning. It's all connected to the ego. 'I have more shit than you, therefore I am the shit!' Really, stuff is all bullshit; we need very little to exist. Think about it, many millions of men and women perish or are maimed and disfigured so a group can gain a few miles of dirt . . . dirt they can't take with them when they die. Instead, they leave it to their offspring to fight over, keeping the cycle of violence going. What's the point? Greed, power, and war are all about ego. It's a collective insanity, which intensifies and accelerates until we almost annihilate ourselves completely. War ends up being a group of dysfunctional, unconscious minds battling with other dysfunctional, unconscious minds. Religion is another example. Each believes they are in sole possession of the truth, their truth. Again, it's all ego-driven. I'm right, so therefore I have the sacrosanct secret. However, if someone or some religion is right, all the others must be wrong. That's a ridiculous judgment. Don't cast judgment in any situation if you want to remain conscious, in the now. It's hard to do at first, but believe me, it becomes liberating. All of us need to care for one another and live in harmony. You all still with me? You look lost."

"Nah, man, we gettin' it."

"Yeah, keep going."

"Please, Deek."

"Okay, so we're all suffering from this same mental illness. Once you recognize the ego in the world and avoid it, the easier it is to remain non-reactive toward it. Don't take someone else's 'ego pain' personally. Ego implies unawareness, or unconsciousness, and the two cannot coexist in our minds. And pay close attention to this part; Black people typically suffer from even bigger 'pain-bodies' within. We have what Tolle called a collective grievance. We each have a pain-body that resides in our minds and feeds off negativity. Now we bring together a group of similar pain-bodies and that burden inside strengthens. This common thread intensifies our individual pain. We become carriers of a very, very heavy burden, or constant pain inside . . . that is, if we listen to this insane brain of ours. It's that simple.

"So you missed your opportunity to own a peaceful existence in America. You made your country the enemy. At times, you held whitey hostage because of ancestral guilt you threw his way. That was pure manipulation.

Think about it, those perpetrators of slavery are long dead. Our race assigned each one of us as a victim. This bred hatred and bitterness, which created your suppressed reality. If you only knew, for every shitty White person that has tried to hold you down there are hundreds, maybe thousands, of White folk who would love to see you succeed . . . even help you along your journey. It's all perception. Don't judge people by their governments or skin colour; don't judge the many by the few. Remember, the only evil perpetrator on this planet is human unconsciousness. Negativity is unintelligent, toxic. And most importantly, whatever you fight, you strengthen; what you resist, persists." Sly stood and clapped loudly. The rest of the crowd slowly joined in.

"So now you understand why I had such a hard time being around all of you pessimistic bastards! Also, according to Tolle, those with heavy pain-bodies usually have a better chance to awaken spiritually and find peace. Release that ego and see who surfaces. There's hope for you poor sons-of-bitches yet!" Slowly the Lompoc tribe began to celebrate their exalted hope.

"One last word, this lack of supplies by the United Africans may merely be a test, as I mentioned before. Let's accept this challenge and make the best of hard times. We know how to hunt meat and eggs, successfully. We have new growth in our green shack. It won't be long before we have plenty of fruits and vegetables. My brothers and sisters, we can do this. Rationing will be necessary since our supplies have been cut off; but bottom line, it's time to care for one another. And once again, those of you who refuse to work, you will receive an adult timeout. No work, no eat. Who's with me?"

Sly was the first to yell. "Count me in, yo' mayonnaise-loving, mutha fucka!"

"Thanks for that, Sly. By God, people, if our ancestors

can survive slavery and years of persecution, we can survive this absurd rock we're on. So, New Africans, just be."

With that, the Lompoc members began to dance about foolishly. They were eager to disregard a past filled with such a suffocating unhappiness. Everyone clapped and strutted around in unison. In calm, semi-hushed voices, the Lompoc group chanted. "Just be, just be, just be, just be . . ." Life had to be different. They were ready to experience a rebirth not as United Africans, but as their unique group of New Africans.

Aerin & Glowworm

Being psychic carried an unspoken burden. Aerin had been given a gift from God. Ever since her near-death experience, she had been able to see into a person's soul. It was as if a video played in her mind's eye; past and present events of the person in question were shown to Aerin. And there were dreams, vivid dreams. Aerin gradually learned these were actually premonitions. With the slightest touch, Aerin could immediately tell if a person was a "white," "grey," or "dark" soul. Those light-filled or "white" souls were concerned about their destinies, how they were affecting others, always wondering if they were on the right path to goodness. However, the "dark" souls viewed themselves as sheer perfection. They blamed others for their indiscretions, hurt as many "white" souls as they could, and never wasted a nanosecond worrying about their future. Then there were those wavering "grey" souls, those individuals that sat upon the fence between good and Earth-bound evil. Sadly, most of these people were enticed toward the darkness. Why not? It was easier.

That is where Aerin's gift came into play. She was on a mission to convert those grey beings into lighter entities, and her efforts appeared to be working. Their first case had been extremely stressful. Once Ari's offspring had placed Aerin's attacker into the near-death machine, constructed from the converted tanning bed, her brothers stepped back to let their sister take over. Aerin inserted an IV containing a deadly cocktail into the man's vein. His hate-filled eyes locked upon her. Impatiently, Aerin waited for their prisoner to lose consciousness. Once the Arab's eyes shut and his mouth was agape, Aerin intubated him with a breathing tube then attached it to a gadget on the inside wall of the near-death machine. After she closed the lid, everyone glanced at one another then held their breath. Their aqua-glowing machine eventually sucked the life from the prejudiced, narrow-minded Arab. After a prescribed time, the breathing mechanism was initiated inside the near-death machine. Carefully opening the lid, Aerin quickly inserted antibiotics as well as epinephrine, to stimulate the heart, into the man's IV. Then they waited . . . and waited. When the man's eyelids finally fluttered and he gasped for more air, Aerin, without hesitation extubated her patient and turned off his IV. His dark eyes darted about. The man was back . . . back to life with a new look about his face. It appeared he was viewing the world for the first time through clear eyes. The Ermani siblings were amazed.

His second breath as a new man came in a bout of coughing. Once he was calm, however, he delivered a surprisingly heartfelt apology to Aerin. She smiled, before her lay a reformed non-fanatic. Thankfully, the continuation of her Middle Eastern studies allowed her to converse with this once-repulsive young man. Never again would her attacker be obsessed with suicide bombings and the promise of seventy virgins. Those beliefs suddenly seemed ludicrous, outdated. He was once a mere pawn for Islam, but eventually he would be transformed into a master of spirituality. What he had seen and experienced had to be deciphered. All the man could tell Aerin was he somehow felt different. His fanatical Islam, like radical Christianity or Judaism, was a cold business. If he had shown the slightest weakness, he would have been struck down, excluded from the pack like a bitch dog pushing away the runt in hopes it would perish. What a loss of unique individuals, all under the guise of following proper Islam.

Aerin was fascinated with the man's instantaneous, infused wisdom. So much was discovered in such a short period. They chatted for hours, compared notes, and revelled in their new understandings. Each had specific experiences that were exhilarating to the other.

More interested in science than spirituality, Tanid, Rami and Balic were high on their machine's success. They complimented one another and discussed what they would add to improve the process. Morbidly, they could not wait for their next victim.

Tanid beamed with pride. "So what shall we call it?"

Balic rubbed his chin. "That emanating aqua glow reminds me of those creepy glow-worms Uncle Isaac showed us in the Waitomo caves on the North Island."

Exasperated with her brothers' narrow-mindedness, Aerin chimed in, "Seriously? Can we possibly focus on what miraculous event just occurred? Hello!"

Tanid grinned at the twins. "Okay, Aerin, okay, we're focused." To his brothers he whispered. "Glowworm it is." They exchanged quiet "high fives."

Several conversations began simultaneously and grew in intensity, until Aerin's mother entered their domain. In shock, she dropped the plate of food she had brought for the prisoner. "Tanid, what is he doing out of his restraints?"

"Oh, Mama, relax, there's a perfectly not-so-logical explanation."

Aerin jumped up and helped her mother to a nearby stool while the prisoner, or Ahmed as Aerin had discovered, began picking up the broken plate that had contained his lunch.

Saroya felt faint. "Aerin?"

"Mama, if we tell you what we've been up to, you have to promise not to tell Papa, or anyone else."

"Honey—"

"Promise me or I go no further."

"I have to get lunch ready for everyone. If I don't get back to the house, your father will come looking for me."

"Promise me."

"Okay, but you and your brothers have a lot of explaining to do. Tanid, you watch out for Aerin." Saroya glared at Ahmed.

"I will, Mama. If you don't mind, we'd like to eat our lunch out here . . . with Ahmed."

"Do I have a choice?"

"Not really." Tanid helped his mother to her feet and hugged her. He kissed his mother's temple. "Trust me when I say we are doing something monumentally good here. We've actually had a scientific, and spiritual, breakthrough."

"Should I be concerned?"

"No, you should be immensely proud." Mrs. Ermani could not take her eyes from her daughter's murderer as she headed for the door. "And you'll understand if we lock everyone out of the cellar for now."

"I'll knock four times when I bring you your picnic basket." She shook a fist at Ahmed and through clenched teeth spoke Urdu. "You will not touch my Aerin." Ahmed nodded. "Tanid, please be careful. Your father—"

"Mama, you promised!"

"You children are going to be the death of me."

Balic laughed. "That's okay; we'll just toss you into Glowworm and have Aerin bring you back." Saroya was not amused.

Deek

Deek's group showed signs of improvement. Together they coached one another when times seemed bleak. Refresher discussions kept everyone on track, for it was not an easy process. Focused on optimism, the Lompoc clan did not notice Deek's troubled state. He was perplexed. His tribe was progressively getting sicker and it was far worse than starving bellies.

Deek finished his exhausting day with O'Malley's journal. This poor son-of-a-bitch had it rougher than the Lompoc tribe did, by far. Deek and Sly found a perverse comfort in that.

May 9th – I've just lived through the storm of all storms. This morning I was minding my own business prior to Mother Nature's tirade. With fascination, I observed my cherished three hover patiently along the shoreline for an unsuspecting elephant seal. My great whites, Joan of Arc, free-spirited and often defying common behaviour by lurking several feet suspiciously below the ocean's surface and possessing the most haunting doll eyes; Lizzie Borden, whose dorsal fin looks as though someone has taken an axe to it; and Marie Antoinette, who appears to be seeking some kind of revenge by beheading or ripping limbs from her prey. There they swam, enormous and majestic. That's when I noticed the growing, dark grey clouds poised along the skyline like tanks readied for impending battle. A distant rumbling announced their approach. The mood of the day had done an about-face. Soon the wind began its assault upon the water, churning the sea into violent, slashing swells. The air was armed and loaded with moisture. Fog tendrils pawed at my feet, before its entire arsenal attacked my island. By the time explosive waves crashed upon the beach I'd somehow found my way to my meagre shack through the heavy murkiness. The war had begun. Thunder cracked overhead and pounding waves shook the ground. All I could do was hide and attempt to stay warm by huddling inside my sleeping bag. I envied Joan, Lizzie, and Antoinette, so safe beneath the violent surface.

For hours I held my breath each time I heard the crackling of yet another giant wave, unfolding upon the battered beach. Each swell reached for my shack with angry retribution, only to smash into millions of salty droplets, like Second Chance *had against the rocky shoreline. Serenity finally came at 2:00 am.*

Aerin

Slowly, painfully New Zealand's hellish behaviour quieted. Albeit resentment remained toward any intruding foreigners, almost everyone realized the world, as they knew it, would never return. Whether the North and South Islanders cared to admit it or not, the truth was there had been a definite brotherhood with the Canadians, Americans, Australians, and British. Music, movies, media-vision shows, and fashion had always been shared—maybe not in their entirety, each group had their unique qualities and tastes, but for the most part, there was a sharing of ideas, commodities and on a smaller scale, lifestyles. These brothers lived miles and miles apart yet were not so different; only minor variances in their interpretation of the English language left obvious distinguishing features. But differences and commonalities no longer mattered. The current inhabitants of New Zealand were quite diverse and knew they had to pull together if they were to survive. Slowly, painfully the "new" New Zealanders repaired their towns. Natural leaders stepped to the forefront. Those men and women who were most trusted organized the townships. However, the tempo of business life was a watered-down version of the past. Broadcasts had come by radio alone. Property lines were redistributed for many New Zealanders, who would never return to their native country. Like-kind races flocked, actually clung, together. Trust was slow-going and confined within small groups. Food was grown locally, dairies resurrected, and various small grocery stores were constructed. Day by day, New

Zealand redefined itself post-WWIV. Citizenship was granted to all current occupants. That is how the Ermani family instantly became a part of the Kiwis.

They had worked hard through fall, and now winter was in full swing. Gradually, the Ermanis and other township citizens pulled together to ward off arriving pirates or militant greed-mongers. Everyone had a common goal, the will to survive collectively, harmoniously. Those that were hellbent on complaining about the past were simply told to shut-up and get to work. New Zealanders kept it simple when confusion gnawed at their infrastructures. Troublemakers, especially criminals, were exiled. If these useless individuals were not able to survive in the "rough" zones outside the biospheres, they perished. Life was hard enough on the inside, let alone being ostracized to fend for oneself on the outside of dome living. Yes, the "new islanders" seemed to have evolved a bit. They learned to tolerate the intolerable, each throwing away their mental scorecards of injustice and set examples for the unenlightened.

Gradually, the word spread across the South Shore. Not only did the locals consider Aerin a promising young doctor, but she was also the talk of the town with her prisoner conversion. Never mind her alleged psychic abilities, that topic took a backseat to her healing powers. The Ermani/Whibley compound had evolved into a place of hope, changing hostile prisoners into peaceful, contributing citizens. Aerin's group moved the Glowworm machines to a more secure location deep within the cellar to a secret room dugout from the hillside. The offshoot of their cellar is where Aerin and her team could process more and more fanatics without interference. Gradually, too, Balic and Rami were contracted by Aerin to build two more transformation Glowworm cocoons.

When the Ermani children had convinced their mother they were doing great things, they began to work toward telling their father and uncle. Possessing typical male rigidity, they would be the hardest to convince. If the Ermanis could change their patriarchs' minds, they could get any of the family members to believe. Hope kept them driven.

Although transportation was safer, more convenient, and no longer poisoned the skies, another occupant dominated the air. Smog had been replaced with a silent killer. This contaminant lingered on the winds waiting like a murderer with a restrained patience . . . quiet and deadly. Unspoken fear had long taken root in everyone's mind. After the nuclear bombs had been discharged and the initial panic subsided, radiation effects were briefly mentioned. It seemed survival took precedence. But the invisible killer had started its global journey immediately. Everyone held a vague picture in his or her mind of the horrors of radiation poisoning. What had not been taught in school was acquired from news snippets, feature films, mediavision shows, and documentaries. And many had walked the literary roads of realistic fiction. Whatever the source, each individual had a mental picture of his or her nuclear doom and gloom. But not one, not one depiction got even close to describing the horror of living through the thermonuclear aftermath. And then, that day arrived. The silent killer crept along the tranquil waterfront, refusing to be ignored. Yes, upon the winds did that silent killer float, permeating every crevice of the world.

When a scarred cruise ship filled with radiation-infected

Filipinos, Koreans, and British docked at the deserted South Shore wharf, the observing New Zealanders were speechless. The vessel's captain had avoided larger ports at Wellington and Auckland, opting for Kaikoura, where his passengers had a better chance for acceptance. However intimidating they were, the naval servicemen stopped the advancement of these unfortunates onto the seldom-used dock. The guns aimed at these frail survivors were hardly necessary. It was not as though the diseased immigrants had the energy for aggression; pain held them captive. Dropping their weapons, the service men and women approached with their radiation-detection equipment. Sweating in their stuffy biohazard Hazmat suits and running their wands over the new arrivals, they weeded out the radiation-rich individuals. Those hopeless souls would be given pain medication, nothing else. Rapidly approaching death, this doomed group would be kept comfortable in their final days. However, those that had a chance of survival were given permission to plant their tender feet firmly upon New Zealand soil.

Even after four post-war months, these survivors still had not healed properly or completely. Isolated upon their ship, they had been unprepared for such catastrophic medical needs. Such a horrific sight, there stood the nuclear bomb victims hair frizzled, glued to their heads with bloated faces, dark red from excessive burns. Bloodstains covered their scorched clothing, and the worst of the horde had large pieces of skin that had healed grotesquely about their limbs. Upon closer examination by volunteer medical healers, including Dr. Aerin, the nightmare revealed far worse debilitations. Heavy, keloidal skin had surfaced next to irreparable, charred epidermis.

Many had purplish subcutaneous hemorrhaging, bleeding from the gums, hair falling out, high fevers, and atomic bomb cataracts. Stumbling, these landed immigrants had difficulty seeing past the opacity near the centre of their irises. Those grappling with recent radioactive attacks on his or her immune systems were the worst. So many oozing, pus-engorged infected wounds created a rotting flesh stench that caused nausea among the militia and medics. Gag reflexes were innocently evoked over and over. Others yanked their Hazmat hoods free and vomited. Rotting flesh, cloudy eyes, these suffering victims were nothing short of modern day zombies.

Aerin saw the entire incident as a once-in-a-lifetime opportunity to absorb these people's stories. Tales of the ominous mushroom clouds were compared to what she had witnessed when leaving Los Angeles. Ear-splitting explosions and blinding, eye-searing flashes had ended with the all-telling yellowish-orange, black mushroom clouds. Morbid curiosity had held their fearful gazes as they had watched the bomb's destruction. Unmentionable pain had followed stemming from seared corneas and scorched skin. Then came the devouring flames, levelling buildings. Smells of searing flesh, mixed with horrific screams and hysterics, filled the congested air, while survivors frantically searched for loved ones. In a matter of minutes, smoking corpses and torched cities were reduced to ash. Everyone had their version of genocide, the obliteration of their society. Aerin's psychic abilities allowed her to feel and see the suffering and sadness of her patients. Each exposure to World War IV added to the appeal of Aerin's new home in New Zealand. The Ermanis were blessed, spared the agonies of war. To say she felt gratitude was a monumental understatement.

Local scientists poured their efforts into the reversal of nuclear and atomic bomb afflictions. They worked tirelessly, knowing hell was upon the suffering. Performing their once-routine jobs with renewed energy, the scientists felt a rare appreciation; a sense of community prevailed over individuality that was once important. Life was less complicated in some respects. True, as the citizens rebuilt their homeland that invisible killer hovered about ready to infect the unsuspecting. Floating radiation dust had long since arrived on the shores of N.Z., though no one knew the full extent of its murderous effects. True, New Zealand had the magical drug RDXM, but other complications were on the rise. Yes, sadly, the silent killer was not done. More medical mysteries lay ahead.

Thankfully, the North and South Islands were not downwind of Australia's catastrophe. Strong northwesterly winds had initially spared the Kiwis from breathing in massive amounts of the invisible reaper. With the arrival of the tainted cruise ship, the scientists had their human guinea pigs. Each victim welcomed treatment, even experimental. Residual radioactivity would soon bring thyroid cancer, leukemia, cirrhosis of the liver, stomach, bladder, intestinal, and lung cancers. But then what? Medical researchers worked non-stop. They had a purpose, one that had a fatal expiration date.

Although her post-war patients intrigued Aerin, part of her exhilaration was of a scientific nature. All this changed arriving home very late one night. Her vestigial EyeNet glasses beeped with life. Hope of a message from home prodded Aerin to keep the eyewear charged. As time passed, she had forgotten about her once-relied-upon connection to her friends. But there it was, an occasional beep relaying to Aerin that she had voicemail. She rushed to receive the message. When she heard the familiar voice and saw Brittany's thin face from her holographic recording, Aerin's knees buckled beneath her. Surely her ears deceived her. Out of the blue, Aerin's best friend from Vancouver had phoned.

Hey, Aer, it's Bri. I'm hoping you still have EyeNet reception. Oh how I hope you are all right. I miss you so much. Bombs landed far north of Vancouver; Whistler was levelled. No more skiing, that's for sure. Well, I don't know how to tell you this, but I'm really sick. Yeah, that sneaky radiation somehow got inside me. It seems this hypersensitive body of mine couldn't handle the dreaded silent killer. Aer, I have advanced liver disease and no hopes of a transplant. Not enough healthy organs floating about these days. At least my parents are with me now. Sorry to share all this drama over the phone. I just needed to talk to someone . . . talk to you. Can you believe it, Aer? I'll never live to see my eighteenth birthday. Sorry to leave such dire news. You know I'm no drama queen. Never could stand the princess wannabes. I just needed my best friend. If only you were already a doctor and were here to cure me. Oh well, such is life. I love you, Aer. If by chance you get this message please, please call me. Mahalo, aloha hoaloha.

Those all-too-familiar nicknames, "Aer" and "Bri," were what Aerin and Brittany's classmates had called them. And then there was Brittany's love of Hawaii. "Aloha, hoaloha." That was how Aerin and Brittany had ended every conversation between them. Brittany dreamed of vacationing in Maui and often spoke the native language.

Aloha hoaloha, goodbye friend—Aerin wanted to cry. An ache grew ever stronger in Aerin's chest. It was hard to breathe from the growing lump in her throat. Aerin sobbed.

In Vancouver, Brittany had been her sounding board. She was unlike the other girls. Labelled a cute tomboy, Brittany shared Aerin's dislike of weak, spoiled women. The two best friends could not fathom why so many women aspired to be snotty, lazy, and worthless when God had blessed them with healthy brains and hearts. Wanting to be princesses, waited on hand and foot, these stunted, narcissistic women were stuck in a twelve-year-old's fantasy. Aerin smiled. She loved those times in high school when Brittany had verbally knocked the tiaras off the much-disliked bitchy girls, dripping with their undeserved sense of superiority. How Aerin missed her friend. They knew each other's deepest, darkest secrets, good and bad. When the war began, Aerin was sure she would never see Brittany again. Now she was back but only for such a short, pain-ridden moment. Aerin's previous fascination surrounding the horrors of radiation was suddenly trashed. Science be damned. Her best friend was dying of the very killer she now battled on the shores of New Zealand. Aerin had to beat this murderer . . . especially for Brittany. On her EyeNet cuff, she hit Brittany's speed-dial number. Sadly, Aerin's best friend would never answer her phone again.

Inferno Killer

Years ago, Whale Watch donated part of Kaikoura's South Peninsula to build a small college. Hidden on the premises was the clandestine, worldwide "Think Tank." Migration to this facility was gradual over the years. Its existence was rumoured in the foreign press, but for decades, the world's curiosity was more frivolously spent paying homage to rock stars, pro athletes, and actors. These powerful geniuses, who had congregated so far from their homelands, were used to being anonymous, invisible. In fact, they welcomed the intellectual solitude. Many of the Kaikouran locals thought the college was simply a ruse, a front for the prestigious research centre for these top scientists, environmentalists, and medical experts. This was the reason enrolment at the college dwindled as time passed. Clearly, it was much sexier for New Zealand's youth to learn abroad or attend the world's elite film and entertainment university in Wellington on the North Island.

Except for the comings and goings of the quiet, unassuming research participants, there was little activity on Kaikoura's South Peninsula. For years, the Kaikoura Police Station, part of the Tasman District, was a sole-charge-station with one policeman overseeing the entire area. In the past eight months, with the increase of prominent professionals and their critical research, the Kaikoura police force was increased to three police officers. Pre-WWIV, Kaikoura's territory had been the calm before the storm with nary a murder. Finally, the criminal cyclone had arrived. That is why Constable Kittelty was not at all shocked when a frantic 111 call came through dispatch claiming a corpse had been found.

"There's a body . . . oh, bloody hell! Not mine . . . not my . . . not a farm body . . . smells of kerosene . . . bloody hell . . . not mine!"

Constable Kittelty put down his cup of hot tea. "Dr. Zetterberg, please slow down, sir. You found a burnt body?"

"Yah, yah, please hurry! I . . . I—"

The line went dead. Constable Kittelty raced from the police station toward the South Peninsula in his shiny blue hovercraft, one of the fastest vehicles on the South Island. Seldom were his police craft's flashing lights ever engaged, but this late night his siren and blue and red twirling lights were in full force.

Lately, there had been an increase in bizarre happenings. With the increase in foreigners, there had been a correlated increase in missing persons. Additionally, Kaikourans had witnessed violent prisoners returning from their medical treatments somehow reformed, with drastically improved attitudes. Now this, a scorched corpse dumped at the body farm. Unexplainable madness on the South Island had found fertile ground.

PUNGENT WAVES OF AN ODIOUS stench attacked Constable Kittelty. The smell was so repulsive; he held his untucked shirttail to his mouth and nose. Still, the sweet, rancid burnt flesh odour, mixed with gasoline, penetrated and clung to his clothing. Several gag reflexes jumped in Kittelty's throat.

"Um . . . not one of mine . . . not my body."

Dr. Zetterberg, all of five foot three inches, stood over the blackened corpse. Visibly shaken, the pale delicate

Swedish doctor pulled at his thinning blond hair and continued to stammer.

Towering over the doctor at six foot four inches, Kittelty felt sorry for the small, shaken brainiac. Before he focused on the charred body, he scanned the entire enclosure. Kittelty's eyes widened when he realized he and Dr. Zetterberg were not alone in the otherwise sterile, temperature-controlled laboratory. Rows and rows of bodies suspended in transparent thermal suits lay before him. Their chests moved in unison as the collective respirator helped these living corpses breathe. An element of Dr. Zetterberg's research included the effect diseases, viruses, and toxins had on terminally ill patients that had donated their limited lives to research. His body farm, where he and his colleagues harvested stem cells and more, was well known and respected by the locals. Dr. Zetterberg's epic studies and cures had saved many lives.

However, most Kaikourans, including Kittelty, had never seen the suspended bodies or the complicated life support system.

"Dr. Zetterberg, how do you know the corpse is not one of your bodies?"

"My machines wouldn't do this . . . my machines keep bodies alive not maim . . . or kill them."

"Do you have records on all these, ah, people?"

"Yah, yah, and I don't have any record for this one. See, this is not my body."

"So you came into the room and saw the corpse? What time did you say?"

"I was here before dinner and everything was fine. After a few of us ate in the cafeteria, we went back to the research lab. You see, we've had a breakthrough with our revised cure for MRSA."

"MRSA?"

"Methicillin-resistant Staphylococcus aureus . . . the 'superbug' that keeps mutating . . . the flesh-eating disease?"

"Oh, yes, yes, continue, Doctor."

"So I needed more live tissue around ten forty-five, that's when I came in here, yah?"

"And you saw the corpse?"

"Nay, Constable, . . . I smelled it."

Deek

Deek and Sly stood above a slight ravine and stared at a very disturbing sight. Many piles of dead murres and seagulls lay before them.

"Damn, I wondered why there seemed to be less birds flying about."

"So these birds gettin' sick like our peeps."

"Seems so. I wish I had access to my pre-Med texts from university. Then I'd have a clue as to what is killing our women and children . . . and these birds. Sly, you'd think O'Malley would have mentioned any sickness or diseases he experienced here."

"College Boy, I ain't gotta clue. Maybe we dyin' from ammonia poisonin'. Maybe dem birds died from their own shit fumes."

Deek laughed even though worry lines were etched deeply into his face. "You know, we aren't sure what killed O'Malley. From the looks of his remains, it had to be brutal, though. It wasn't a peaceful death, that's for certain. If only we had the journal of O'Malley's final days."

"Maybe he was too sick ta write."

"Possibly. Might have been some kind of bird flu. O'Malley could have died of sickness and someone or something tore apart pieces of his corpse."

"Christ, Deek, this be pure hell. We ain't gunna last a year at this rate."

"What do you think about building a boat?"

"Are yo' nuts? This be Black folk yo' talkin' 'bout. No one's gunna volunteer for dat trip. None of these mutha fuckas can swim worth a damn, if at all."

"We don't need good swimmers. We need someone who can man a sailboat. We need outside medical help, Sly, whether it's from United Africans or whomever else we may come in contact with. There's no way around it, we have to venture off Reaper. We have to build a boat."

Aerin

MUCH LIKE THE ANIMOSITY FELT toward the great British explorer, James Cook, and his crew, the locals were not affable regarding foreigners bringing contaminants into their country. In 1770, when Cook discovered New Zealand, his sailors brought venereal diseases to the Maori natives causing many unnecessary deaths. During these modern times, the locals revisited those feelings of isolationism. Why allow more worldly contaminants to annihilate the already struggling New Zealanders? That is why Aerin tried to keep a low profile with her foreign patients that had moored their cruise ship on the Kaikoura shoreline and dragged their battered bodies ashore. Keenly aware of the prejudice toward them, and being a non-native herself, Aerin was overly secretive and protective. It had not taken long for these poor souls to worm their way into Aerin's heart.

Especially favourite was her South Korean patient, an eight-year-old boy named Ryu Byung Hyun. Everyone referred to him by his surname, Ryu, pronounced Lyu, or Lou when spoken quickly. Amongst the hospital staff he became known as Little Lou, an accepted foreigner and their ray of sunshine. This fragile child came to Dr. Aerin with terrible burns upon his back. Patches of a floral pattern from a Hawaiian aloha shirt had been burned into Lou's otherwise porcelain olive skin. Initially, Aerin had fought to keep a dehydrated Little Lou from drinking too quickly. How he had cried for more water. The poor little guy was so thirsty, but too much too fast could have killed him. That is when Aerin brought Little Lou to the hospital; she needed help.

Eventually, Little Lou's high fever and diarrhea had subsided. That was when he began eating better. Aerin was elated seeing the child smile for the first time and was assured Little Lou's pain had diminished significantly. Another indicator was one morning to Aerin's surprise, the adorable boy answered her plethora of daily questions with perfect English.

He explained an atomic bomb had unexpectedly hit the Philippines where Lou's cruise ship was docked, on the island of Cebu. Gleefully, Little Lou and his playmates had run about the streets of Cebu City, keeping a close eye on their parents but so oblivious to the rest of their surroundings . . . and the approaching bombs. At that fateful moment, Little Lou kicked the big, green ball to his cousin as an ear-splitting crack exploded and a blinding light flashed. A second later, Little Lou heard haunting screams and smelled burning skin . . . his skin.

For the days that followed, Little Lou translated stories for Dr. Aerin from some of the non-English-speaking survivors. One female victim's story especially haunted Aerin. On the way to town for some fresh fruit, this middle-aged woman had spotted a distant bright light that quickly filled the air. A red ring of fire grew upward toward an enormous mushroom cloud then turned into a pillar of fire. Deeper into the heart of the city, the woman witnessed unbelievable atrocities. People ran past her with burned and shredded skin hanging from their bodies. Others had died instantly. Lining the streets were bodies with crusted skulls, eyeballs hanging out of their heads and many burned beyond recognition. Surrounding her was a sudden sea of fire; flames had swallowed the many buildings. The river leading into town was clogged with ash and dead bodies. The odour was atrocious. Soon black rain began to fall, bringing radiation-rich residue to the ground. Hell was upon them. Completely traumatized, the woman was numb when the second bomb hit. An even brighter flash filled the air. A thunderous crack caused the woman to grip her ears as a wave of heat hit, launching her into the air. When she regained consciousness, everything was black and silent for a while. Pain seared through her limbs. Skin dangled off her burnt arms. It was hours before she was rescued. While she waited for some shred of sanity, the woman had regained her sight and witnessed many burned, swollen faces with hollow eye sockets staring back at her. Perhaps the worst image that would be forever etched into the woman's mind was a hysterical mother running frantically about with a headless infant in her arms. These shared images visited Aerin in her sleep for weeks to follow.

Dr. Aerin was elated that her Little Lou seemed to be healing so well. He was such a delightful child. With his expressive eyes and shiny pitch-black hair, always sporting a defiant tuft standing at attention at the crown of his head, Little Lou lived to make others smile. He was more than adorable. Although initially seldom seen, Little Lou's magnetic smile rendered many defenceless when it crept across his beautiful face. Little Lou had soon learned that in this strange country he possessed no enemies, only that hidden enemy that had long since ceased to lurk in the shadows.

One dark morning, Aerin entered Little Lou's hospital

room only to find an empty bed. Upon further examination, Dr. Aerin discovered a clump of his silky hair resting upon his vacant pillow. In the middle of the fitted sheet were splotches of fresh blood. The radiation poisoning had crawled deeply into Little Lou's frail body before the medical staff had been able to retard the cancerous progression. Aerin's guard dropped as she succumbed to her grief. All this time she thought her small patient was healing with a reduction in pain. Loss of hair and bleeding from his rectum indicated otherwise. Being his initial doctor, why had Aerin not seen the signs of Little Lou's suffering?

When Aerin's sadness subsided a bit, she was able to actually see Little Lou in her mind's eye. Thank God for her psychic abilities. There, standing before her was his bright smile, as he stood hand-in-hand with his deceased parents. Yes, he was happy and Aerin was so appreciative knowing Little Lou was finally free of pain.

Deek

OCTOBER 31ST – HOW ABOUT THAT, it's Halloween. I've proven great whites are not rogue, meat-eating murderers. Seven notable ones, including my favourites Antoinette, Joan, and Lizzie, have left the waters around my island only to return as a group. How misunderstood are sharks, especially great whites.

I observed another attack today by Marie Antoinette, by far the largest of the three at twenty-six-plus feet. She is gargantuan. A bold elephant seal swam underwater toward the rocks, eager to join its family. There was an eerie calm when Antoinette breached the water and locked her jaws entirely over three-quarters of the seal. Engulfed within her jaws, freshly shredded seal meat fluttered in the gushing scarlet waters as she emerged. In constant movement, when Antoinette rocketed out of the churning sea, exposed upper and lower rows of treacherous teeth shone bright against the highly oxygenated blood. The beautiful great white flapped her mighty tail about in the air then landed with an explosive crack against the bloodstained water.

Elated gulls chirped and swirled above the commotion. Soon they began to swoop in and tear flesh from the remains of the slowly submerging elephant seal's carcass. Focused upon Antoinette and her well-crafted kill, I didn't notice the small boat trying to avoid the shark's path. I couldn't move. Had someone found me? Suddenly, Joan of Arc inched closer to the surface. Her enormous body swam underneath dwarfing the vessel. The fishing boat bobbed like a cork in the shark's wake. Panicked, the boat's captain manoeuvred the bow away from the agitated great whites.

Gaining my senses, I jumped to my feet and began

frantically waving and yelling. Still the boat pulled away from me. My hands shook as I quickly unbuttoned my red flannel shirt. When I waved the garment above my head, I'm sure my breathing stopped for a moment. I gave it all I had. Standing upon that cliff, waving my shirt and yelling I experienced a fleeting flash of hope. It was apparent life around my ex-wife, ex-beast, wouldn't be so bad in comparison to my current living arrangements. Hellbent on escaping their frightening situation though, not one of the boat's occupants saw my distress signal. Or, if they had, they chose to turn a blind eye in my direction. When viewing that wonderful craft bobbing about on the vast ocean it seemed such a mere dot upon the horizon. I never felt so alone.

December 8th – I have been despondent for weeks. That's when I decided to build my own boat. If I could get past the feeding zone of the sharks, I could sail back to Madagascar. Having those people so close in proximity changed me. I need human contact, ex-beast and all . . . or die trying to get it.

An ammonia-fuelled cloud settled tent-like over the Lompoc Township. Layer upon layer of whitish-grey bird excrement covered the many cabins like icing upon gingerbread houses. Deek expelled more toxic air from his lungs. Their tribe had been so focused on killing elephant sea lions and tearing down cabins from deceased members for boat materials, they had shirked their routine roof cleaning duties. Stepping outside past his cabin door, Deek stretched his sore muscles. Building a seaworthy vessel was hard work. O'Malley's journals had given them much direction, but nothing was mentioned about the sweat and agony that was needed as a crucial component.

Everywhere Deek looked was spotted with seagulls and the amusing murres. As O'Malley had described, murres were duck-sized with tuxedo, penguin-like markings and sleek heads like a loon. They always looked as though they were dressed for a dinner party. After months on Reaper, the softball-sized murre eggs had actually become moderately tasty, although Deek preferred their meat. Each seabird death also meant just that much less bird crap to handle. Deek coughed again. There had to be in excess of ten thousand birds, even after observing the piles of dead murre and seagull carcasses a while back. They had continued to die off but recently had accelerated their reproduction with renewed vigour. Deek knew the real owner of Reaper Island; and it would only get worse. The Lompoc family, merely temporary visitors, would never be able to kill enough birds or eat enough eggs to reduce the population of their pesky, feathered neighbours significantly.

Slowly, one by one, lean-to doors began opening. It seemed Deek's coughing brought the community to life. The building of their boat had brought hope anew to these survivors. Motivation was at an all-time high.

Sly pulled a faded sweatshirt over his head. "So O'Malley thinks dem fucked up monstas swimmin''round out there actually have brains larga than a pea?"

"Seems so. Not only can they eat us whole, but they can skilfully plot our demise."

"That freak show, O'Malley, was actually in love with dem beasts even though they woulda made a meal outta him. Hell, maybe they did . . . eat a part of him. I pity da poor bastards dat end up in our boat, no matta how good we build it."

"Don't worry; I'm going to volunteer for the voyage.

I trust we'll make a sturdy-as-hell seaworthy craft. And you'll need to remain behind to watch over this crazy bunch, so don't worry about those sharks. Hey, how's that rash on your arms doing?"

"It's spread ta my legs. I did as Vera said and rubbed some of that first aid ointment on my elbow sores."

"Maybe you should take today off. The sea lion hides have been dried and treated. We're ready for O'Malley's next step, creating our massive sails."

"Fuck dat, no sissy skin rash gunna hold ole Sly down. I'm ready ta get some mo' buildin' done."

"After breakfast, how about you avoid some of the moisture on the beach and supervise bird crap clean-up?"

"The hell yo' say!"

"Seriously, Sly, I need you healthy. Those sores get infected further and high fevers will follow. Then what good are you to the townsfolk and me?"

"Listen, College Boy—"

"Sly, are you going to let a bunch of birds bury us in shit? Please, Sly, let's get your skin healed."

"Goddamn yo' iz a bossy son-of-a-bitch."

"Call me any name you like, I'm just tired of breathing ammonia-laden air."

"The rooftops will be brown by da time all of yo' return for suppa . . . bank on it."

"Thanks, Chief."

Deek went back into his cabin and searched for his first aid kit. He grabbed the tube of Polysporin® and gingerly proceeded to cover the oozing blisters on the palms of his hands. Once he had bandaged the sores, Deek pulled on his awkwardly made sea lion gloves. After releasing a pain-filled sigh, Deek left his cabin for another tough, challenging day. Once outside, the faint smell of fried eggs pushed past the odorous pungent bird excrement. Deek forgot about his aching hands as his stomach released a demanding growl.

Kozlov

Money talks the loudest and, in Kozlov's case, money shouted the loudest. In his current predicament, with Nederland still using currency for commerce, Kozlov had slowly discovered his captors' predictable moral decline. Talks of their precious Russia had eventually turned to complaints about the lack of luxuries and missed lifestyles. Weeks and weeks of brutality and isolation could not bring back an annihilated Russia, so Kozlov offered the KGB thugs five million Euros for his release. All previous offers had been snubbed. If only he had known the KGB thugs' magical price for freedom. Five million Euros and Kozlov was on his way to joining his family. It was not surprising how quickly the two thugs had forgotten their grievances and national loyalty. For foreigners trapped inside the Amsterdam dome with such wealth, this was an appealing alternative.

Kozlov left the bank relieved. The thugs had revealed all, rendering no more bargaining tools. Euros in hand, the KGB bruisers were instructed to never show their faces around his family again. If so, they would have the Dutch police on them, instantly. Or, better yet, they would never see the light of day again. Yes, Kozlov had found the men's weaknesses and exploited their greed. An heir of Old Russian money, Kozlov had grown up knowing nothing but wealth. How easily tough situations ended when payoffs were involved. Kozlov's father had taught him that at a very young age. Yes, money talked. And when one was raised on monetary security, one kept that currency close.

His nightmarish premonitions had prompted Kozlov to transfer his fortune to the Bank of Nederland days before leaving Russia. He was brilliant in protecting his family, physically and financially. However, when it came to emotional support Kozlov had failed miserably.

His summoned driver raced through the streets of Amsterdam per his instructions. Kidnapped and abused for months, Kozlov had to get to his in-laws' house and repair the damage from the menacing KGB intruders and that which he had caused from a lifelong career in the KGB. Kozlov was out of his element, but he would not cease to try to mend the broken hearts of his wife and daughter. Although they knew Kozlov was alive the entire time, his girls were never certain if he would be released. Frightened beyond anything they had ever experienced during the past months, his wife and daughter had also lost, in an instant, everyone they had left behind in Russia. And what was most terrifying to Kozlov was they believed he was the cause of WWIV. This was one situation he would not be able to buy his way out of.

Cameron

After a year of community rebuilding, Ari and Saroya had found it feasible to purchase their first plot of land and slowly build their small prefab, two-story house. It seemed overnight New Zealand had become home. Lush and providing the sense of being off the world's beaten trail, the land of the Kiwis held a comforting mystique, even for the tough Ermani offspring. Infrequently trodden paths were still the norm, unlike the rest of the world's overpopulated pre-war megalopolises. Everywhere on the South Island seemed the road less travelled. Used to a comfortable poverty, the Ermanis' first home was small but acceptable. With the success of the Ermani children's societal contributions, the family was able to pool their money together and buy the land next to Aerin's Auntie Clara and Uncle Isaac's compact farm. All worked diligently to build a quaint five-bedroom, three-bath home. The young adults had their own bedrooms. That was a first. Mrs. Ermani had a reasonable version of the kitchen of her dreams, and Mr. Ermani had a pottery hut behind the house for his artistic pursuits. It had not been a burden to anyone to put his or her passions on hold to build this new refuge. The Ermanis happily spent every spare moment constructing, hammering, sanding, tiling, and painting. Jobs were done with vitality. Thoughts of Vancouver were long faded. Time had conveniently buried the pain of the past.

While the old and newfound Kiwis adapted to their

fresh beginning, the Kaikoura Police spent many a sleepless night trying to solve the murder of the burnt corpse, which was quickly becoming a stale cold case. Even after calling in other officers and detectives, from Nelson and Blenheim within the Tasman District, and forensic experts, from the Christchurch Police Station of the Canterbury District, Constable Kittelty was no closer to solving the mystery of the charred John Doe than he had been months earlier. The only definitive conclusions were, the victim was a man, and he was not New Zealand born. For the past twenty years, as in most countries, all Kiwis were required to register DNA samples and iris scans at birth. Forensics was able to extract some viable genetic evidence from the corpse, but the results provided no matches from the N.Z. CODIS database. As no eye tissue remained, the N.Z. SCAN database was of no use either. Constable Kittelty surmised the victim was most definitely one of his foreign missing persons. He tossed the tattered John Doe file into a near-empty filing cabinet behind his desk. Life had returned to some form of normalcy. Boredom, once known as peacefulness, taunted Kittelty. He was not used to leaving any loose ends at work. Instead of sitting down for a latte bowl from the Encounter Café and a chat with the locals, the constable took his steamy daily boost to go and chose to cruise the streets of Kaikoura, especially the South Peninsula. What he searched for was not entirely clear.

To Professor Cameron Thorpe, the "think tank" property held much promise for educational purposes, not simply a notorious murder site. The once semi-popular Christian college was being converted into what Cameron hoped would be a major university someday. The six buildings could be easily transformed. However, the small library and athletic facility would take considerable work to enlarge. And if enrolment went as planned, construction of several dormitories would be required to join the two existing brick dorms. Box-shaped, with the library in the centre and the current gymnasium at the west end of the campus, Cameron sketched in three more academic buildings angled about. Two existing dormitories on opposite north-south ends of the campus would be joined by new additions, one near the enhanced athletic facility and two at the university entrance. It was an exquisite layout. Cameron's vision was aggressive but doable. He became yet another new Kiwi citizen envisioning greatness for a blossoming New Zealand. A premiere university would, without a doubt, fuel future advancements.

For Aerin, there seemed to be no time to pursue anything else, until that memorable day when she met the fresh, seasoned Australian professor and designer of the proposed new South New Zealand University (SNZU) on Kaikoura's South Peninsula. It was not his flawless tanned skin, stark blond hair or transparent, light blue eyes that made time stand still for Aerin. No, what caught her attention at the town meeting was his passion for education and the building of a prestigious university. Charisma had been instrumental in getting the township to realize SNZU had a future, with the need for mental stimulation and improvement. He pled his case with exuberance. Soon, Professor Thorpe had the support of the townsfolk, all the townsfolk. Yes, Aerin's time was about to become overcrowded with a preoccupation toward an intelligent Australian who possessed the most penetrating powder-blue eyes.

Deek

Many calloused palms and infected sores later, an odd-looking boat sat propped upon a few rounded logs, postured for its first splash into the churning surf bordering Reaper Island. Screams of elation mixed with sporadic masculine tears escaped the shipbuilders.

"Goddamn I'z prouda us!" Sly waved his covered arms above his head. The celebration grew louder. One of the few whose "island rot" skin had healed, Sly remained covered to avoid a moisture-induced relapse. Long since out of Polysporin®, almost everyone had patches of rashes and/or sores upon their limbs and neck. Once the boat was launched, everyone would retreat to his or her shanties to avoid the moisture and ward off further dermatitis. What terrified the Lompoc New Africans more than irritated skin was when the disease went inward. Vomiting, nausea, loss of hair, and bleeding from any number of orifices meant death would soon follow. Those that died were cremated and their small cabins torn apart. Wood not used for their escape boat was stored for firewood. Deceased islanders' sleeping bags had been used for the boat's life preservers, warmth, and general comfort. Nothing was wasted on Reaper Island.

After such a laborious endeavour, the crude sea craft was ready. Elation soared. No more would the Lompoc townsfolk wait for the United Africans to appear. They had taken their future into their own hands.

"Are you sure you want to do this? Weren't you the one saying you were afraid of the water?"

"Listen, College Boy, I fear nothin'. What I said was I'z a shitty swimmer. I ain't plannin' on enterin' da water, not with those mutha fuckin' sharks eyein' me fo' dinna."

"Sly—"

"Deek, yo' our leada. These good folk trust yo'. O'Malley spelled it out for us. I can handle that fuckin' boat, no problem."

"About O'Malley, Sly, there's an entry I read a while back that I have kept from you. If you're hellbent on leading this expedition then I need to read that entry to you tonight."

"I'z our captain, for sure."

"You might not be after you hear O'Malley's words."

"It's 'bout dem damn sharks ain't it?"

"Yeah, one in particular."

Everyone pushed, but the boat was much heavier than anticipated. With Sly aboard, and brimming with supplies, it seemed impossible to budge the awkward craft even an inch. Still, they struggled, both men and women. It felt as though they were pushing against a steadfast boulder. Flushed faces and clenched jaws, the Lompoc townsfolk willed the vessel to move. Hope quickly vaporized as panic swept over the group. This was their only chance for survival. But what if they were unable to move their creation? There were no other salvation options. This makeshift sea vessel was all they had. Fear crept in; soon adrenalin overpowered their bloodstreams. Perspiration poured out of determined foreheads. Deek let out the first screech of frustration . . . and the rest followed. From the boat above, Sly peered down at his friend, feeling totally helpless. He joined in with the yelling. And then, ever so slightly, there was the tiniest give in the standoff. The Lompoc tribe pushed harder and yelled louder. Upon the log rollers, the boat began to creep toward the breaking waves.

Sly screamed, "Fuck, yes! Don't stop!"

Deek repositioned his feet in the sand and continued to push. The others rapidly mimicked their leader. Everyone's muscles from back to legs burned from fatigue. As they pushed and pushed, the craft moved another foot. Three other smaller Lompoc tribesmen scrambled aboard the beached vessel. Again, Deek and the others strained with all their might. Excessive adrenalin finally launched their vessel of hope into the frightening ocean ahead.

Deek yelled. "Brace yourselves! Ready the sail then drop the rudder!" Sly and the others clung to one another near the mast as they met the first wave head on. Water crashed over the bow and exploded in all directions. Deek cupped his hands to his mouth and hollered. "God speed, Chief! God speed!"

Their blessed boat raced down the backside of the next wave, disappearing from sight. Each and every Lompoc member held his or her breath.

Aerin & Cameron

Her hand shot into the air. Despite such little time left in each day, Aerin had found several hours to volunteer for the library renovation with the intriguing SNZU professor. What with books, all kinds of books, and an attractive associate, Aerin was a euphoric wreck. Piles and piles of used books covered most of the library's tiled foyer floor. Citizens had graciously donated their personal stockpile for the students. So it went for the next month, house decorating, saving people at the hospital, converting fanatical heathens, and categorizing and labelling books for Professor Thorpe. For Aerin, an abundance of energy had surfaced past a thick fog of depressive lethargy after Little Lou's death and lack of further communication from Brittany. Mrs. Ermani had spoken to her daughter about love and its wonderment, but Aerin had dismissed the silly banter. Love was pure emotions and frivolous, something Aerin never had time for in the past. But now her body mocked her. No longer in control, Aerin's pulse quickened, hands moistened with sweat, and she suddenly became exceedingly clumsy when around the tall Aussie. Thankfully, Cameron had been oblivious to Aerin's bodily changes. Actually, the stalwart professor had not noticed much of anything except the birthing of his educational institution. However, this did not discourage Aerin. She was too energized to realize she was flying solo in the jet stream of affection. No matter, this male-female thing was quite entertaining and limitless. If Professor Thorpe had asked Aerin to recreate the Dewey Decimal system from scratch, she would have attempted it without even flinching at the absurdity of it all.

Saroya enjoyed the renewed closeness with Aerin. Auntie Clara and Victoria, neither having been blessed with daughters, treasured being involved in Aerin's love turmoil, as well. Amorous feelings were so foreign to an eighteen soon-to-be nineteen-year-old Aerin. She had bypassed the high school sweetheart phase, always claiming there was never enough time to waste upon the opposite sex. Sharing her daily pursuits with her mother, Auntie Clara, and Victoria, Aerin found she appreciated having an unspoken membership to their mysterious women's club. Before, being female had felt like a curse. While growing up in the Middle East she had been reminded constantly of her inferior gender. During her Iraqi upbringing, Aerin had avoided belonging to that pool of second-class citizens thanks to her father's charade. Vancouver had certainly been accepting of women, but still there was an underlying tension with some of the chauvinistic men in the hospital's upper management. Detest for the weaker sex was just subtler in the West than it was in the Middle East. Besides, Aerin had been more interested in her intellectual freedom than flirting with a bunch of pimple-faced high school boys. Now, though, her heart betrayed her. Aerin had discovered the male gender on a different level. As foreign as the feelings were, she relished every unpredictable, exciting aspect of them.

Sly

O'Malley's last words reverberated inside Sly's head. It was not Deek's intention to scare him and his three-man crew, rather to prepare them. The first calm afternoon became the worst day of their journey. Repeatedly, the giant dorsal fins sliced through the glassy, rolling waves. Nausea overtook two of Sly's crew. Even past the men's dark skin, one could see the darker circles under their troubled eyes. To keep the nauseated men distracted, Sly introduced his crew to Lizzie Borden, Joan of Arc, and especially Marie Antoinette. They studied each great white's quirky behaviour. Lizzie, the scariest in appearance seemed to be the least threatening. She liked to swim alongside the boat and roll her eyes about studying the shipmates. Fortunately, Lizzie never made aggressive movements toward the vessel. However, Joan of Arc was not so accommodating. She lurked beneath the vessel much of the time, only to surface and aggressively bump the crude craft on several occasions. Her furtive behaviour kept everyone on edge, never knowing when she would spring from the dark depths of the ocean. Although frightfully scary, Joan was not the great white to fear the most. Marie Antoinette was the cantankerous one. How the men's eyes had widened with astonishment when Sly retold O'Malley's tale. For days, no one ventured toward the sides of the boat. But how easily one forgot when the urge to vomit arose. Before Sly could stop his seasick mate from spewing bile over the side, Antoinette had already started her vertical ascent from deep in the sea. Powerful muscles drove the gigantic shark upward as she remained locked and focused on her target. When she burst free of the ocean, jaws wide open, it took only a split-second to decapitate the vomiting crewman. Blood spurted from the gaping neck, spewing viscous, magenta fluid about the crude vessel until the slumping body realized the battle for life was over. Horrified, Sly and the others sank deeper into the bottom of their craft. Frozen with disbelief, no one spoke for quite a while.

Anger eventually propelled Sly into motion. As he readied the sails to ride upon the wisps of occasional breezes, Sly steered far away from the beasts that now circled the bloodied water. Slowly, as their craft lurched away from the speck in the distance that was Reaper Island, Sly viewed Joan underneath. He cursed and shouted. At Lizzie and Antoinette's dorsal fins, he flung the headless corpse of his crewman.

"Choke on m'man's bones yo' rotten sons-of-bitches!" Sly quickly steered the boat with the maximum thrust of wind behind them. "Good fuckin' riddance yo' murderin' bastards!"

For days they sailed at the mercy of the infrequent wind. One crewman, the other man that suffered from seasickness, was still unable to keep anything down. He was becoming dehydrated and increasingly weaker. Traumatized, the other mate refused to move from his spot at the bottom of the boat. Shock had paralyzed his ability to function the slightest bit. No one spoke, except Sly. He tried desperately to keep morale up as he encouraged his mates to stay hydrated and keep warm. Virtually alone in manning the craft, Sly focused his attention on navigating their escape.

Oswald

It was time for New Zealanders to branch out from their shores and explore the state of the world. Satellite images of concentrated life force activity in Vancouver, Canada and Amsterdam, Nederland prompted the expedition. With cures for the newly mutated cancer behind them, local scientists assisted the naval journeymen in readying for their trip. Inoculated for AIDS, radiation, and a plethora of other ailments, the crew stocked their submarine with heavy doses of antibiotics and cures for the new world scourges, as well as with the necessary supplies to be gone comfortably for many months.

Assured of a manageable radiation level outside the South New Zealand biosphere, a curious crowd filled the dock next to the *Antarctica III's* aquatic crafts to bid farewell. Carefully chosen, the crew was a combination of scientists, naval officers, submarine specialists, and a few doctors. They would determine what life forms resided outside of N.Z. and how they had maintained an existence. Almost everyone had loved ones elsewhere in the world, but they had not heard from them for fourteen months. Could there be others alive and scattered about outside their borders? If so, were Vancouver and Amsterdam the only locations with survivors? It was time to discover the answers to those questions. One by one the aquatic amphibious crafts took crew members to New Zealand's restored super submarine, the *Antarctica III.*

When they surfaced to up-periscope depth for an

inspection of the empty sea, visibility was quite murky. Soon, a greyish ash covered the lens and the detector on the periscope head indicated a high level of radiation. Unfortunately, it increased the closer they came to land. Routinely, "down periscope" was ordered and the submarine submerged to lower depths, not for safety purposes, more for the conservation of RDXM, and other purifiers.

With the use of amphibious crafts to reach the many shorelines, the search parties spent week after week in hopes of finding viable life forms. Australia, Philippines, Japan, China, India, Russia, Germany, and many other countries in Europe had produced no survivors, that is, sane and healthy ones. Pockets of diseased, starving, and mentally broken individuals were found but were impossible to approach. Starvation and cancer would eventually claim these struggling souls. All seemed grey since ash covered everything. It appeared the nuclear obliteration had caused smaller countries and cities around the world to unleash any missiles and other destructive arsenals they had been hoarding. Dictators, presidents, prime ministers, and others in leadership positions had released their stockpile of dusty armoury. Of those participants and instigators, not one resisted; not one held out for a peaceful future. It was hit or be hit. This mentality had even rippled down to the neighbourhood level. Individual citizens had released their Rapid-Fire Mini Nukes (RFMNs). These miniature atomic bombs were built from easy-to-make instructions off the Internet. Over the years, guns began to lose their superior appeal. Because these metal accessories no longer carried a punch, RFMNs became the threat of choice. A few were deployed each year, pre-WWIV. Home after home was flattened, others were poisoned from radiation, and the bomb owners joined the violent criminals on death row in every country. Still the RFMN's popularity grew. Those that could not build their protection purchased it. Black market accessibility was easier than people wanted to believe. Like a pack of dogs, when the peaceful showed fear, the aggressive attacked with their stockpile of RFMNs and then attempted to rule. Cities burned and toppled. It was the best excuse the angered could use to derail any nearby enemies and settle their disputes. When WWIV began, the consensus was that no one would survive this insanity so why not empty personal weaponry on one's adversaries? After all, countries were no longer deploying manageable fission bombs. Instead, their arsenals included the two-stage thermonuclear, hydrogen bombs, a hundred times more powerful than the atomic bombs dropped on Japan during WWII. These nuclear fusion bombs had levelled the world.

Not until the *Antarctica III* reached Nederland did the New Zealanders find a thriving civilization. Everyone aboard the submarine was ecstatic. The crew ate well and consumed many pints with the Dutch locals in Amsterdam. Top government officials encouraged the interaction with their visitors. Captain Oswald and the current leader of Nederland, Norwegian-born Prime Minister, Trigg Ellestad, compared notes and discussed the details of WWIV. Pieces of the post-war puzzle soon fell into place for Oswald. Prime Minister Ellestad shared Intel he had received from a Russian immigrant, Bogdan Kozlov. Whether it was because of a guilty conscience or a direct order from his angered spouse, Kozlov had explained the pre-war events to Prime Minister Ellestad. He had provided Intel from the KGB, Mossad, China's

Triad, and Japan's Yakuza intelligence organizations. What Ellestad pieced together, with the help of Kozlov, was that if Israel took the bait and launched an attack on the U.S., Russia and China would attack America with weapons of mass destruction, as well. Directive Four would end with Russia and China unexpectedly levelling Israel and the Middle East. Only KGB and Russian top executives knew Directive Five, China would get the next nuclear surprise. What the Russians had not foreseen was the pure hatred and duplicity of its enemies. China saw a chance to seize world leadership from Russia. They had created directives of their own. It seemed many shared this delusion of grandeur. Hence, the skies had filled with the grandest show of nuclear fireworks headed for multiple destinations. It did not really matter who got the last blast, for at that moment, all had carelessly demolished thriving civilizations.

Things became much clearer for Oswald after his discussion with Ellestad. The Dutch had searched the world for survivors, as well. North and South America's Eastern seaboards had revealed no active communities and the only territories left unexamined were the Middle East, Africa, and North America's Western coastline. As Captain Oswald and Prime Minister Ellestad mapped out a future between the two surviving countries, they agreed some critical Dutch citizens would join the *Antarctica's* search team to examine those countries currently unexplored, and return to New Zealand to share knowledge. It was a fantastic find. The New Zealanders and Dutch were surprised at their similarities. Living under domed cities, making advanced strides in science and technology, and yearning for global peace, these bodies of people were committed to making the new world a more beautiful, cohesive place to live.

So they continued to search. Sadly, everywhere revealed more of the same. A thick, eerie silence lay heavily upon the daily exploration teams. Every place the *Antarctica III* crew members investigated showed evidence of nuclear genocide. Carbon footprints were a worry of the past. These impressions had long since been stomped out by fateful radiation boot prints. Pollutants of a more powerful sort now lingered in the soot that danced upon the breeze. Zinc-laced smoke from once-bustling factories had ceased metallic contamination. Herbicides and pesticides were no longer a concern. Dams had burst, causing brackish flood-waters to bury trash and debris with silt and oyster shells along the shorelines. What the *Antarctica* crew witnessed was Mother Nature battling ferociously to rebuild. Peeking through the toxic soil were new growths of switchgrass and numerous wildflowers. Those buildings not levelled by the nuclear calamity pulsated with new life as well. Spores had penetrated even hermetically sealed houses and offices. Water had fought to get inside. Flourishing mould munched on the gypsum boards, while termites feasted on rotting studs and floor joists. Carpenter ants, roaches, hornets, and small mammals became the new occupants. Swimming pools had become planter boxes filled with brambles and grapevines that snaked around rusting pipes and in some cases rotting corpses. Still other skeleton pieces were seen protruding from piles of leaf litter that lined most of the standing structures. The crew was horrified. These recovering cities were straight out of a science fiction movie. It seemed the worst insults human beings had hurled at Mother Nature only staggered her temporarily. Life was starting over, with a vengeance and minus the overindulgent humans.

Maktan

Reluctantly, Maktan made her way yet again to Mu'mad's pre-school. His teacher claimed he bit another little girl and was extremely reluctant to share. Maktan was conflicted. In her homeland, this assault was considered an acceptable male assertion, essential to putting females in their place. Biting was Mu'mad's, or little Zeren's, way of defending his position, flexing his superior gender. However, Maktan was torn; she liked her newfound freedom from oppression. But after an exhaustive period, her dead husband's voice won her mental battle. Zeren's teachers got nowhere with Maktan. Given an ultimatum carried no weight, either. Maktan played the Christian-dominated Canadian game and outsmarted the infidels. Robotically, Maktan seemed reasonable and appeared as though she belonged. Administrative reprimands completed, she avoided her confusing predicament by politely demanding a refund and her child. Mother and son marched from the building not worried for a moment that yet another pre-school was behind them. Besides, Maktan had found a non-denominational private school run by wealthy Canadians of Middle Eastern descent. Surely, they would better understand her little Zeren.

Daily, Maktan fought vehemently against the Western ways, only to vacillate between her ever-increasing doubts. After all, she had been raised to believe the infidels were evil. And Maktan had her son's future to carry out, as dictated by Mu'mad's father. However, as she lay in bed at night and was not forced to focus on tradition and duties for her son, Maktan's abhorrence toward the Westerners was allowed to become less and less fervent. Irshad's words still echoed in her head, but deep inside, doubts continued to grow ever so slowly, day by day. Not when it came to Mu'mad so much, but in dealing with her buried inner self. Darkness and peace filling her opulent bedroom, Maktan was secretly happy they were far, far away from the Middle East.

Kittelty

Aerin lay on her back feeling the perfectly sculpted lawn underneath and breathed in the mixture of wild onion and grass. Lately, her thoughts were one-dimensional. Her mind obsessed over images of Cameron's piercing blue eyes, soft blond curls, slight cleft in his chin, and towering six-foot-six-inch height. Aerin had run through those depictions so many times they were like a crazed slideshow tattooed onto her brain. Heart rushes surfaced sporadically as well, a feeling Aerin found quite foreign. Although she had found the business of love to be quite torturous, Aerin was happy. Above her, she watched the lecherous clouds grope the protective dome with searching, cottony tendrils. Slowly they slid across the surface causing a premature nightfall.

"Aotearoa . . . Land of the Long White Cloud," Aerin whispered.

Shadows crept across Aerin's body then landed upon her face. Kaikoura was silent yet not completely peaceful. For the first time Aerin knew what complications could arise when introduced to too much change in such a short period of time. An ever-present jitteriness within her soul made tranquility quite a challenge. Lately, staring skyward for hours had been Aerin's only remote chance at solace. Drifting, drifting in her mind, Aerin floated amongst those snapshots of Cameron once again.

In the distance a faint siren sounded. It grew louder. There was that chilling noise again, a sound Aerin dreaded. She sat upright, her remnants of solitude immediately banished. Constable Kittelty only released his bellowing siren for either a devastating accident or grave discovery. Plumes of smoke within the dome reached toward those lurking clouds outside. Fire engine honks and blasts joined Constable Kittelty's police craft's wails. Aerin jumped to her feet and ran uphill to the backyard to get to higher ground. In the direction of the Whaleway Rail Station was the smokey culprit. A large orange glow told Aerin something very large was ablaze.

Long after midnight, Tanid, the twins, and their cousins came stumbling into the sleeping household reeking of alcohol and smoke. As they felt their way along the darkened hallway, no one engaged in drunken laughter. Instead, a sombre mood filled the household.

Wide-awake, Aerin joined everyone in Tanid's bedroom. "Rami, where have you guys been? Jesus, you stink!"

"Sh-h-h, Aerin, you'll wake Papa. We went out for some beers after helping Kittelty."

Balic took a raspy breath then coughed. "Aerin, the rail station caught fire after a craft pod without breaks left the Tranz Coastal Tube and hit a burning jellywheel in its path."

Tanid had already stripped off his odorous jeans and sweatshirt, pulled his pajama bottoms on, and struggled with buttoning his top. "When we finally got the fire put out Constable Kittelty had us help him put crime scene tape around the perimeter of the station and burnt vehicles. He was anxious about finding out whose corpses were inside the pod and jellywheel."

"So he thinks this was a crime? How many corpses did he find?"

"Of course, anytime there's fire Kittelty has to wonder

if the Inferno Killer is somehow involved. There were five dead people, two in the stalled burning jellycraft and three in the pod that left the Tube."

It seemed an eternity had passed before Constable Kittelty received his forensic reports from Christchurch.

To the group of six detectives and forensic experts, Kittelty relayed the detailed information. "An accelerant was used on the jellied vehicle that sat burning in between the rubber crash plate and the oncoming pod that left the Tube and ploughed into it. With that said, I found the accelerant wasn't the same as what the Inferno Killer used on his first victim." He paused. Could this be the work of the same man or merely a copycat or coincidence? Kittelty felt morbidly invigorated after the accident. He was half hoping this was the work of his killer. But who could be sure? "Again, there was no evidence found amongst the cinders. Only one victim produced a viable DNA sample and piece of eye tissue, and his information was not found in CODIS or SCAN. Additionally, the burned jellywheel traced back to a couple that had reported it stolen months ago. So we have nary a clue or correlation to the first murder except a charred foreigner, possibly two.

"Now for the really interesting part, we received a report from a specialist in Auckland on our first victim . . . the one found at the Body Farm. This doctor reviewed photographs, our police report, pathology reports, and forensic expert and medical examiners' reports. His conclusion? The Inferno Killer's first victim was a level 4 on the Glassman Scale, had no clothing remnants on his body, and had an ash-like substance left in his thoracic cavity and parts of his abdominal areas. Evidently, the fat liquefied from excessive heat, which was absorbed in the victim's clothing causing it to act as a huge wick for the fire. Because of the internal fluid content in the victim's organs and cavities, his stomach, liver, heart, and bladder were not completely charred. Bottom line . . . our man was killed by SHC."

"What!" A seasoned detective blurted out. "You can't be serious." The entire group was taken aback.

"Yep, Spontaneous Human Combustion." Kittelty handed the report package to the forensic expert closest to him and left the room completely frustrated. Nothing made sense.

Within his dim office, Kittelty ran exasperated fingers through his thick light brown hair. He opened the missing person's file that lay upon his cluttered desk. Kittelty held very little hope of solving the Inferno Killer case. The long list of missing persons consisted primarily of women. Those few men reported were locals and nowhere in Kittelty's report were there names of any misplaced foreigners without a CODIS or SCAN code. The SHC victims had somehow arrived on New Zealand ground and avoided the entire DNA and optical N.Z. identification processes. So not only could Kittelty not put a finger on any suspects, but he also wondered how in the hell the Inferno Killer had tortured and killed his first victim at the Body Farm, let alone his possible second and third found in the already burning jellywheel.

Oswald & Deek

Southeast of Madagascar the *Antarctica III's* sonar picked up movement in the waters. The crew was startled. The sonar images were not enormous yet large enough to be spotted. Only when Oswald peered through the periscope and saw a glistening dorsal fin moving about did he realize the *Antarctic III* was not alone in the ocean. Oswald smiled. Even the highly protected, endangered great white sharks had flourished post-war. With less human intervention, it seemed the possibility of extinction had become extinct. In the early sunrise, a mesmerized Oswald watched the resilient sharks with fascination. That was when he spotted something floating in the water. The great whites seemed to be circling a crude raft-like boat. Oswald jerked his head back and ordered his crew to bring the submarine to the surface.

When Oswald released the hatch and stepped onto the observation platform, he discovered a sunburned Black man inside the nearly dilapidated boat. Beside the unconscious survivor lay a dead man with chunks of flesh missing from his rotting corpse. It was apparent the conscious man had used pieces of his dead friend as fish bait, for there was an almost bare carcass of a large fish tied to the side of the tiny vessel.

With a mild New Zealand inflection, "Let's get this man aboard. Get his wounds dressed and water in him immediately. Move people!"

Captain Oswald helped lift the man out of the aquatic hovercraft onto the submarine's deck.

"Sir, what do you want to do with, uh, the dead body?"

"We've witnessed a lot of dead bodies, Jacobs, that one is no different. Let the sea take him, eh?"

"Yes, sir."

Once aboard the submarine they worked hard to tend to the injured man. *Antarctica III* had not found any surviving life, sane life that is, anywhere besides Amsterdam during their months of exploration. And they had yet to arrive in Vancouver where the Dutch had discovered definite signs of a thriving society. All were fascinated with their new find. Patiently they awaited his first words.

In the quiet of the night, they finally came past blistered lips. The man kept mumbling, "Reapa."

CAPTAIN OSWALD LISTENED TO THE delirious Black man. If only he would open his eyes and focus on his audience, maybe then Oswald could piece together the man's story. All remained patient.

"Deek . . . Deek, help 'em."

"Sir, can you hear me?" The submarine's medic placed a cold compress on the man's battered forehead and continued. "Do you need more water?"

"Where's Deek? Find Deek!" His own shouting caused him to open his eyes.

"Sir, do you need some more water?"

"Who da fuck—"

"I'm Officer Sullivan. We found you on the open sea . . . in a crude raft, your boat."

"I'z didn't kill 'em! It was dat beast! Dolls eyes, dem cold dark dolls eyes. That beast killed 'em!"

"Sir, please calm down. I'm Captain Oswald, no one is judging you, mate. We were so surprised to find you alive.

Where did you set sail from?"

"Reapa . . . Island."

"Reaper? Sir, what is your name?"

He cleared his parched throat. "Sly, da name's, Sly."

"Here it is, Captain! Oh my God, there is such an island."

"Well, I'll be. Let's head west a bit and see if Sly's comrades are still there . . . alive."

It took them a good part of the morning to arrive at Reaper Island. Several aquatic hovercrafts were released and past unrelenting waves, the small fleet advanced. All made it to the jagged rocks that lined the beach except the last boat. One of the ravenous great whites had pummelled the tiny vessel before it had a chance to elevate and hover above. Victorious in her pursuit of the thrashing swimmers, Antoinette and the others helped themselves to the human trespassers. Screams were barely heard by the others already on shore. When it was clear they had lost one of their aquatic lifeboats, the exploration crew made the painful decision to continue. A few pinnipeds barked unenthusiastically; for once, they were not the hunted. The sailors noticed some of the seals had mottled skin and strange growths about their bodies. Upon the relentless winds, radiation had hitchhiked, paying every living organism a painful visit.

Atop the cliff, the exploration team was met by a group of thin, muscular men all bearing weapons. No one greeted the islanders; instead, they just stared in disbelief at the scraggly group of natives. One by one, men and women scurried down the craggy path to the beach below.

Sullivan yelled, "Do any of you know Sly? Is there

anyone here by the name of Deek?" The largest man in front of the pack stepped forward with a look of relief etched upon his weathered face.

"Oh my God, I'm Deek. Who's asking?"

"Sullivan . . . the name's Sullivan, sir. We are from the New Zealand Royal Navy, assigned to *Antarctica III* on a search for life expedition."

"Search for life?"

"Yes, sir, my orders are to bring you to Captain Oswald straight away."

"Search for life, Sullivan?"

"Deek, sir, my orders—"

"I know, I know . . ." Before Deek could move, he clenched his eyelids shut and breathed deeply. "God bless you, Sullivan. Oh, God bless you." The Lompoc tribe members lowered their spears and knives. "Let's go see your Captain Oswald."

Both men walked toward the barking elephant seals. "Sir, we are elated that you really exist and not some figment of imagination from a bleached out, delirious survivor."

"Excuse me?"

"Your friend, Sly, sir. We found him alone on the open sea close to death. He's been asking for you."

"You're serious? Is he all right?"

"Yes, sir, he's struggling but doing fine. When we found him, he was close to death. It was quite unbelievable."

From the moment he had entered the claustrophobic, steel cylinder, Deek relished in its warmth. A year of frigid dampness had been enough for a lifetime. The musky air, free of ammonia, was pure heaven. Deek breathed in deeply as he studied his surroundings. It was more than physical heat he experienced, a human comfort emanated from the crew. Laughing and sharing camaraderie while working the many gadgets and switches, the naval crew gave Deek a feeling of safekeeping. He had missed this world of advanced knowledge, free of blame and bitterness. Deek smiled. Everywhere he set his sights was evidence of advanced technology. It had been more than a year since he had laid eyes upon simple components such as EyeNet phones, mediavisions, and computers. Now he was in the presence of mechanical intelligence. It was a brilliance Deek realized he desperately craved. Sullivan stopped at yet another cramped doorway.

Even after ducking considerably to enter the captain's quarters, Deek remained hunched over from the submarine's low ceiling.

"Sorry, Mr. Jorgensen, submarines aren't built for such heights. Please, have a seat. I'm Captain Oswald."

"Deek, Captain Oswald, please call me, Deek."

Oswald grabbed Deek's hand and shook it enthusiastically. Oswald stood almost as tall as Deek; his head just nicked the cabin ceiling. Deek stared at the large white hand that engulfed his dark fingers. It also had been over a year since he had seen a man with such light skin and eyes the colour of the sea. He felt as though he was dreaming.

"Would you like a drink? I'm having a scotch on the rocks. Name your poison."

"An ice cold beer would be great."

A young sailor standing by disappeared and quickly reappeared with the men's drinks.

"So according to your fellow islanders you are their leader?"

"It seems so. My leadership started out of disgust for our group's destructive behaviour. However, we have evolved into a very tightknit, but strange, family."

"Well, whatever happened, it's apparent they trust and respect you."

"Sly and I never gave up on them. Although I saw the faults of the group, I believed more heartily in the strength of the individual. And if the ex-Lompoc group didn't co-operate, Sly and I would kick their respective asses."

"Right, quite right. Deek, we're here to help. I'm assuming you want off Reaper Island?"

"Christ, yes!"

"How, may I ask, did you end up here? The last we heard back home was the American government cleared out their prisons of all African-Americans, and volunteering loved ones, and shipped them off to Africa. In return, the United African government received enough vaccines and cures for AIDs and cancer for every one of their citizens."

"That's correct. We were dumped in barren grasslands only to battle the heat, watch our fellow prisoners become dinner for many hungry lions, and exhibit typical aggressive behaviour against one another. It was worse than prison. So many people died unnecessarily. What we didn't know was the United African government had been observing our sudden adjustment to Africa from day one. Evidently, our Lompoc tribe impressed the powers to be enough for them to invest in our bleak futures. We were saved. Ha! As if you can call it that. The prison groups left behind on the mainland soon faced a tougher war. Without assistance, those folks had to battle not only each other but also the impossible heat, ravenous, relentless lions, and extremely pissed off neighbouring United African natives. Let's just say the fatality rate most assuredly neared one hundred percent by the end of the year. This was all explained to us when our Lompoc group was extracted from the others and forced onto stealth jets. Hours later, we were dumped upon our frigid island with its ragged shoreline, high winds, and choppy, dark blue waters infested with great white sharks. We were told we were the hopefuls. If we survived a year, given monthly assistance, we would earn our United African citizenship and eventually move back to the mainland. One month went by and the care packages stopped." It felt good for Deek to vent to someone without the threat of negativity sprouting.

"That's harsh."

"Indeed. Our Lompoc community worked really hard to overcome the anger created by that betrayal."

"Mr. J—, Deek, I can honestly tell you the United African government did not betray you. In fact, in a warped sense, they saved your lives."

"Saved our lives? With all due respect, Captain, those bastards left us to starve and die slow deaths as if we were discarded trash."

"Actually, they were the ones that died. Deek, there's no delicate way to tell you this, mate, but we are all survivors of World War IV."

Confusion was etched into Deek's weary face. "Sullivan mentioned a 'search for life mission.' Is that what he meant?"

"Yes, Deek, nuclear and atomic bombs devastated most of the world. Russia stirred doubt within the minds of the Israelis. Fabricated Intel caused the Israelis to believe the United States was conspiring against them. It took only days before Israel's navy launched the first nuclear bombs . . . destroying Washington, DC.

"Believing the Russians would protect them, the Israelis pummelled Palestine as well. Little did they realize Russia was the mastermind. Naturally, the Americans retaliated, levelling portions of Israel. When the fabricated truth surfaced, the U.S. released bombs aimed at Moscow and St. Petersburg.

"Simultaneously, Russia attacked New York and San Diego, as well as China, India, and Afghanistan. North Korea hit Alaska, South Korea, and China. Iran and Iraq levelled what was left of Israel. Beyond that, no one could be sure who had attacked whom. Most of the Arab countries were devastated in addition to Tokyo, London, Toronto, Paris, Madrid, Rome, and Sydney . . . very few countries were exempt from getting attacked.

"Nuclear bombs sprung from the dirt in every major part of the world with foreign labels on them. Middle Eastern bombs made and released within America hit U.S. cities. At one point, no one knew for sure where the bombs had originated; there were too many launched into the air and headed in too many different directions. Countries that were never suspected of having a weapon of mass destruction released a bomb or two . . . or three. No one held back. There was no need to 'save' any weaponry at that point. The sole decision was which target was the most beneficial? Which target had stirred the most hatred?

"When the dust settled, Israel and Palestine were gone; radiation, ash, and rubble remained. It seems only very small, uncontroversial countries went bomb-free. These highly radiated areas are living a different hellish nightmare."

"The United States?"

"Yes, Deek."

"Africa?"

"Yes, from what we've seen so far."

"That explains a lot."

"With each country's armed services and police forces pulled to the borders looting started, immediately. Crime rose to an all-time high. Not even tranquil New Zealand was exempt. Along the borders of our North and South Islands, ships filled with desperate, diseased, and dying foreigners landed on non-contaminated beaches. Within weeks the military and police forces were overpowered. Once past the first line of defence, the panicked foreigners fought with one thing in mind, survival. Internally, these initial 'quiet zones' were soon fighting their own battles. Food, water, and shelter were suddenly worth dying over. Many, many small fortresses were activated. Eventually, not even neighbours could be trusted. Fires were lit to try and drive out the locals from their homes. Crops were burned, stores were ransacked, and bullets flying in the air were as common as breathing. In many locations, government officials remained in hiding, leaving no one in charge. No one reported to work, businesses failed, and commodities became scarce with no importation and exportation. Each city quickly depleted its resources. To put it simply, the entire world went insane . . . and that became the new norm.

"So far we have discovered our New Zealand and Nederland are the only countries to avoid being bombed and consumed by radiation. Now we can add the inhabitants of Reaper Island to our list. Everywhere our expedition has taken us, there is one consistency, many deaths and much insanity. Very few survived the nuclear holocaust. The only reason the Dutch and my fellow New Zealanders survived was because of our extensive knowledge regarding how to detoxify from any potential radiation poisoning. We still have the Northwest on the Pacific Ocean to explore;

however, we are not so optimistic. It seems Vancouver, Canada, is the only Western territory that has possibly survived a direct bombing."

"So that's what our group suffers from . . . radiation. Christ, we lost so many."

"The only reason your Lompoc community hasn't suffered complete extermination is because of frequent high winds that run through this area. Very little fallout must have reached Reaper or was allowed to settle into your bodies and surroundings."

"What about America?"

"All dead, like the rest of the world. From what the Dutch have witnessed, anyway."

"How could this happen?"

"Greed and prejudices. The Dutch confirmed all of the WWIV news from a Russian diplomat now living in Amsterdam. I guess his conscience got the better of him. Anyway, he revealed everything he knew and showed the Russian Intel correspondence he'd received. So no one held back during WWIV . . . and our world almost ended."

Deek reflected in silence for a while. "So I'll never see my wife again, or my child who no doubt was never born."

"No one knows for sure, Deek. I'm so sorry to have to deliver this unbelievable news to you, mate."

"Captain, I could use another drink. Got any whiskey?"

"Absolutely."

The young sailor reappeared with refreshed drinks for Oswald and Deek.

"Thanks."

"Deek, we can treat your sick clan members. And, more importantly, we can evacuate everyone and take you wherever you'd like. You'll have the means to decontaminate your water and food sources. And you'll be able to treat any future cancers and diseases."

"Captain, why would you want to help a bunch of ex-criminals . . . Black criminals?"

"It's not our job to judge. You remember Australia used to be a debtors' prison and look how well they turned out. Such a great country until WWIV happened. We'd be naïve to think none of those debtor prisoners found their way to New Zealand. We are proud of our citizens. Everyone deserves a second chance. Besides, it's the right thing to do, Deek."

"This all seems too good to be true. Listen, I'll present this to our townsfolk. You'll forgive me if they have a hard time trusting all of you . . . lighter folks."

"I completely understand." Deek got up from his chair and readied himself to leave.

"Would you do me the honour of having dinner with me before you go ashore? Rest assured, our crew is medicating and feeding your townspeople. They're in excellent hands."

"Do you the honour? It would be my honour, Captain."

"I'm sure you'd like to check on your friend. I'll let the cook know we'll be ready to eat in half an hour?"

"That would be great, sir. Thank you for everything."

Dinner had been prepared exquisitely for Captain Oswald and his guest. Crisp salad greens with chunky blue cheese dressing was a tasty starter. Steak, mashed potatoes and gravy, steamed green beans and carrots, hard rolls with real butter, and all the whiskey Deek could handle followed. He savoured every bite.

"Food never tasted so good. I think my taste buds are in shock."

"We're very lucky we landed a top-notch chef with an

adventurous spirit. How is Sly?"

"He's still unconscious."

"Have you read the classics, Deek?"

"Some, at university."

"Well, when we found Sly, he was sun-blistered and dehydrated; he looked like a perverse version of Hemingway's *The Old Man and the Sea*."

"I can only imagine; he still looks rough."

"He'll be fine, Deek. Don't give up hope. Please, eat."

Deek followed his host's lead and ate with gusto. Conversation was kept to a minimum.

"Sorry, I haven't eaten anything today. When we found your friend, we worked around the clock to decipher what he was trying to tell us. Then we worked to find all of you."

"No need to apologize. I've been starving for over a year. You're good people, Captain. I'll be sure and pass that onto my group. That meal was incredible. This beats the hell out of murre eggs and sea lion meat."

Oswald raised his glass. Deek clinked his against the captain's. "Salute."

"Deek, I must tell you, I know who you are. I loved watching American football, the gridiron, eh? And I followed your case on the news."

"I didn't kill that storeowner."

"I know, Deek, you were administering CPR."

"Yes, yes I was." Deek stared in disbelief at the captain.

"Deek, the real murderers stepped forward and confessed to stabbing the man. No one could have known that a couple of desperate, drug-crazed junkies were in the process of robbing and murdering the storeowner. The one who actually stabbed the man was a teenaged drug addict who couldn't live with his guilt. About the time he came forward, unfortunately, your Lompoc blokes had been shipped off to Africa. Deek, I'm so sorry. It was such an injustice."

"So the truth came out?"

"It did. If WWIV hadn't occurred, the U.S. government would have retrieved you from Africa and you would have resumed your life as a hero."

"What about my wife, Lourdes, did she know?"

"I'm not sure. She was already airborne on her way to join you, with a lot of other Lompoc relatives."

"Her plane?"

"No one truly knows. Her plane could have been diverted, but no one would know where. All flight documents originating in the U.S. were lost, of course."

"She was coming to be with me?"

"She was. Journalists made a big deal out of America's plans to come rescue you and your wife."

"But then the war—"

"The war stopped life dead in its tracks, Deek. None of us planned for our current lives and futures."

Tears fought to escape Deek's eyes. After he slammed down his empty glass of whiskey, Oswald poured Deek another.

Inferno Killer

UPSIDE ONE CHEEK AND DOWN the other, gasoline was sprayed onto the latest victim's face. He never flinched. He never blinked. His eyes were glazed over and stared at nothing in particular. Completely saturated, the man's gas-soaked dark hair clung to his pale, distorted face. A solid stream of accelerant was then squeezed over every inch of the victim's body. It was time. The gas can was placed within the attacker's hovercraft; then from his pocket, he retrieved a book of matches.

Without hesitation, the Inferno Killer dragged the match across the scratch pad, igniting the devouring monster. Flames hit the accelerant and with a *whoosh* quickly engulfed the motionless body. The killer made sure nothing was left for the police to find. Inside his pocket, he stuck the cooled matchstick. Footprints in the dirt beside the Inferno Killer's vehicle were erased with a sweeping towel; back and forth, the killer swept the dusty rag. Still running, the hovercraft was suspended in the air; no distinguishing marks on the ground were left.

As the killer took one last look at the burning body the only lingering thought was, this cold-hearted bastard would never rape another woman . . . never touch another child. It was time to flee. Into the night, the Inferno Killer vanished without a trace.

Aerin & Cameron

High drama went unnoticed by the men in the Ermani and Whibley families. Aerin kept her love life from all of them, except Tanid. Refuting a lot of what the women had advised her to do, Tanid gave Aerin the male's perspective. Enjoying the excitement from the women was intoxicating, but hearing the more reasonable advice from Tanid was invaluable. She would not push for attention from the handsome professor, remaining mysteriously aloof would have a more lasting effect. Although this was torturous, Aerin reluctantly dived back into her medical career and spiritual reform. However, being away from Cameron made her miss him even more, which made for an even more impossible situation. What Aerin was not privy to was how her absence was slowly penetrating one clueless professor's heart.

There was nothing but anguish ever since the beautiful, young Persian woman volunteered to organize his new SNZU library. Lately, Aerin graced him with her presence only twice a week, instead of daily. When she was not there, Professor Thorpe felt an absurd emptiness inside. In addition, others evoked irritation in Cameron when trying to perform Aerin's duties. These people lacked the thoroughness and ingenuity Aerin possessed.

A knock on the door sounded. "Come in."

"Hey, Cameron, what's up?"

He answered with a thick Australian accent and dialect, mixed with the precise diction of an academic.

"G'day, Tanid. Let us see, the biggest issue is I have a structural problem with the new science building. Some of the blokes volunteering last weekend did not have as strong construction expertise as they led me to believe. It seems they do not know Christmas from Bourke Street. Joists on the second floor ceiling are not flush with one another. These need to be redone by someone with the full quid. I do not want to cut corners. They have really set us back, mate."

"Aerin told me you were having trouble."

"Oh, really, great, great. How is your sister?"

"Aerin's fine. She's a busy one, always spreads herself thin, juggling family, the hospital, and your library."

"Yes, that would be right. I have noticed she has not been around as much lately."

"Well, let's get started, Cameron. I've got lots to do with our new home and all."

"Sure, sure, sorry, mate. I really appreciate all your help. You know that, right?"

"Yeah, no worries."

The two young men crossed the campus. Transforming the old Christian college into a full-blown, four-year university had been brilliant on paper, but implementation was quite another story. Dormitories would be added eventually. At present, though, Professor Thorpe and the others had to be content with enlarging the library, adding a research science building, and hiring the rest of the much-needed instructors. They had three months before classes began. With assistance from the community, SNZU would hopefully open on time.

Cameron held the door open for Tanid. Upon entering, Tanid was overwhelmed by the enormity of unfinished business. "Damn, Cameron, has everyone abandoned you?"

"Not completely. It is only Thursday and most of my volunteers show up on the weekend, when not needed at their daily jobs. They may be short the full quid, but they are definitely not a crew of bludgers. We work long hours on Saturday and Sunday and there is not a lazy one in the bunch."

"Well, that's some good news. I can help this weekend if you could use another."

"Tanid, are you kidding? With your construction background we would be honoured to have any time you can spare."

"It's a plan then."

"Great."

"On one condition."

"Name it."

"You must promise me you'll pull your overly intellectual head out of your arse, realize you're interested in my sister, and ask her out. Christ, you can't be that stupid."

"So, my favourite sister, you might want to ditch your scrubs and do whatever you girlies do to take men's breath away."

"Why on Earth would I want to take the breath away from any of you Ermani men?"

"You're gross. I'm not talking about your blood, bonehead. What if a certain professor graced us with his presence?"

"Tanid?"

"A tall university fella with powder blue eyes might want to share some food with us this evening." Tanid turned his back to his sister and headed for the kitchen.

"Tanid!" Aerin threw a couch pillow, smacking Tanid on the back of his head.

"Okay, Cameron is coming over for dinner."

"What?"

"Yep, he's got some business to discuss with you."

"Tanid, you're freaking me out! What is this all about? Tell me, what did you do?"

"What any favourite brother would do for his little sis. But I promised I wouldn't mention a word to you. So trust me and get happy with your appearance. I assure you the rest will take care of itself."

"Should I tell you I hate you now or later?"

"Hate me? You're going to love me, my sweet, celibate sister. I'll say no more."

Frantically, Aerin ran for her new bedroom. She would deal with Tanid later. Sawdust still covered much of her books and tabletops, but Aerin did not seem to notice or care. She ripped off her clothing, wrapped a large towel around her, and sprinted for the bathroom.

After a quickie shower, Aerin jumped into a fresh sundress then towel-dried her hair. The Ermanis' new shower, with all the modern day accoutrements, was not quite finished so she resorted to outdated methods. When Aerin turned on her blow dryer, she noticed in her mirror that an out-of-breath Saroya had burst through the bathroom door. Aerin's elated mama clapped her hands together signifying her excitement. Aerin rolled her eyes in exasperation but could not quit smiling. Hair dried, Aerin chatted with her mother while she applied a bit of makeup. A shaky hand told Saroya it was time to take over.

"Close your eyes." Saroya fixed Aerin's eye shadow.

"Spill it, Mama. What did Tanid tell you?"

"Nothing, really."

"You're a really bad liar."

"Relax your lips." Saroya applied some lipstick.

Aerin looked in the mirror and wiped away some of the redness. "Mama, don't change the subject."

"Oh, Aerin, I don't want to spoil the evening for you."

"Tell me, Mama, I need to be prepared. I'm no good at this boy-girl thing."

"Nope, I won't spoil a special night."

"So it will be a special night?"

"Aerin, I want you to be surprised. This is one of those nights you'll remember for the rest of your life."

"You and Tanid are the foulest of traitors. I love and hate you both, equally."

"I can live with that."

Mother and daughter peered into the mirror together. Aerin smiled. When she looked at Saroya there were tears swimming about in her loving brown eyes. "Mama?"

"I'm just happy, Sweetheart. You look wonderful. Now go, go have fun."

DINNER WAS EXCRUCIATING. SMALL TALK was thrown about as Aerin's indigestion sabotaged her comfort. Sitting next to her, Cameron, dressed in a crisply ironed button-down shirt, smelled heavenly. As per usual, Aerin thought he was stunning. This had made it difficult to swallow her Khoresht. And to further Aerin's discomfort, the professor seemed so at ease around her family. She liked this man way too much.

As the meal wound down, Cameron continued his comfortable banter. "Mrs. Ermani, this is a corker of a dinner. Can I ask what it was I just ate without offending?"

"Certainly . . . and you are not offending me, I appreciate the interest, Dear. You have eaten Khoresht, a Persian stew with lamb and fresh vegetables, over Basmati rice. The meat is prepared separately with special spices—a family recipe, actually. Now for the bread, it's another secret recipe. It's a flat bread with Persian panir, cheese derived from sheep's milk."

"It was delicious. I am entirely stuffed. You really should open a Persian restaurant someday."

"Well, thank you, Dear. That is the plan . . . eventually."

Rapid-fire conversation pinged across the dinner table from man to man while everyone ate. Failure by Aerin to interject several times led to her recession. Confused, Aerin did not recognize these childish reactions stirring within. She lost her appetite completely and finally stood. "Sorry, everyone, I need to be excused." Aerin felt nauseated.

The male banter came to a screeching halt. Cameron stood, "Aerin, are you okay?"

"My stomach is betraying me; feel a bit queasy. I think I'm going to call it a night. Everyone, please, keep talking; don't stop on my account." Suddenly dizzy, Aerin froze in her tracks, waiting for a morsel of bodily control.

Saroya sank every so slightly in her chair, whereas a proud smile swelled across Ari's face. Their enlightened daughter was a bit inept when it came to dating.

Cameron rose. "Would you feel better if we got some fresh air? Take a stroll with me, Aerin."

Colour drained from her face. "Maybe we can do this again some other time." Her eyes darted from her mother to Tanid; then she started to nibble at a fingernail.

Cameron took a step in Aerin's direction. He grabbed her raised hand. "Walk with me. My nerves are a bit jumpy as well."

"Oh." Aerin's cheeks flushed. "I don't want to disrupt the evening though."

"You are not disrupting anything. No offense to your family, but my main intention for coming here tonight was to see you." Cameron still held Aerin's hand. "Walk with me?"

Saroya's shoulders seemed to rise. Her daughter would not be scaring off this distinguished man with her desire to be alone with journals and medical texts. Saroya smiled at her husband. This professor could quite possibly handle Aerin.

While the Ermani men retired to the living room, Cameron guided Aerin out the back door; the moonlight shone brightly through the fortified glass, far above.

"Did you really feel nervous in there, or were you just throwing me a bone, Cameron?"

"I must confess, I am a bit nervous, out of my element—an attempt at misery loves company?"

"I see . . . thanks." Aerin smiled. Her embarrassment lessened.

"I do not date much."

"Neither do I." Aerin felt infatuation's playfulness intercede. "Is that what we're doing? Having a date?"

Cameron peered down at Aerin. "Well, yes." He returned her assured expression. "It took Tanid to show me what a whacker I have been for not asking you out sooner."

Aerin's heart raced. "Ha. That's my brother. He's so bossy."

"I'm glad he is." Cameron took Aerin's hand again.

Slowly, Aerin's amorous confusion lifted a bit more. She was actually enjoying herself. "So, Professor, tell me about your childhood."

"Well, let us see, I grew up on the shores of Sydney."

"I bet it was beautiful."

"Yes, that would be right. We called our Aussie land the Lucky Country; Sydney was rich with surprises."

"Did any of your relatives survive the war?"

"No, not that I know of."

"Oh, I'm so sorry, Cameron."

"No drama. I have learned to bury my past where it belongs, and I quite love Kaikoura."

"I guess you could say SNZU saved your life then?"

"Yes, that would be right. Such a great project in which to bury oneself."

Aerin mocked Cameron's studious dialect, one of the many things she liked about him, and recited the more common phrase. "Yeah, that'd be right." Aerin smiled up at him; Cameron had not noticed her playful attempt at humour. She continued. "How long did it take you to get used to New Zealand and this plastic cage we live in?"

"I will never get used to being confined. A bloke cannot even have a dingo's breakfast."

"A what?"

"Aussie's version of the perfect morning: a yawn, a leak outside, and a good look around. That is hard to come by when you live in an inverted fishbowl."

"I agree, except for the urinating outdoors part."

"Not a burning desire for a Sheila?"

"Not hardly, especially not this one."

"No surprises there. I do miss the fresh outside air; the ocean air to be precise."

"Me too."

"So Tanid mentioned your schedule has gotten quite impossible. I have missed you at the university. All the chaos is much more bearable, actually enjoyable, when you are present."

"Thanks, Cameron. I have to admit I've missed being there, as well. Another boat of pirate types hit the dock two days ago. I'm sure you heard about it."

"I did. I just was not aware it would dominate your schedule."

"Someday, I'll tell you all about the job I do in my spare time."

"Aside from being a doctor? Wow, you are busy. Now I really appreciate how much time you have spent on the library."

"I love books; that was easy. And my other job . . . well—"

"I have heard the rumours."

"Well, don't believe everything you hear."

Cameron squeezed Aerin's trembling hand. "You can tell me about it whenever you like. Maybe you could carve out a few hours from your busy schedule Tuesday night, so we can get together and yabber about anything other than the University."

Aerin's heart pounded. "I quite like our discussions surrounding the Uni. Can't get enough academia, right? Tuesday . . . Tuesday is doable. I mean, it sounds good . . . great actually."

"Fair enough then, just you and me. So it is a date?"

"It's a date."

Both stopped and looked up. "Maybe we can sneak outside the biosphere barrier and spend some time on the beach . . . watch the waves. How does that sound?"

"Oh, I'm definitely game. I have ventured outside the dome before, but then that's a story for another night."

Cameron put his arm around Aerin, pulling her closer. She smiled. Her stomach fluttered, but it was a good feeling this time. They watched the distant stars in silence as they ambled down the long driveway.

"It matters not what someone is born, but what they grow to be."
~ J.K. Rowling
Author of *Harry Potter and the Goblet of Fire*

DAWN BREAKS

Deek

Deek was never so glad to get past the circling sharks below. Being in the small aquatic hovercraft headed for Reaper Island, he got a feel for what Sly must have experienced on a much, much scarier level. The massive great whites had made it known, time and time again, this was their territory, and visitors were less than welcome. Even more troubling, O'Malley's three—Joan, Lizzie, and Antoinette—had returned to Reaper waters with the sub.

Feet planted securely upon the familiar rocky shore, Deek suddenly longed for the secure environment of the *Antarctica III*. Guilt consumed him. There had been a brief desperate moment when he had entertained the idea of abandoning the difficult Lompoc tribe. He had not wanted to leave the submarine. Besides, he was not a criminal like the others and he had more than paid his dues for his past participation in gang violence. Deek's debts to society were paid. He owed no one. At that moment, Deek would have been happy to never set foot upon Reaper, again. He was so tired. Just making a decision for his future, and nothing else, would be so much easier. All Deek had wanted was to stay aboard the sub and research Lourdes' whereabouts. Did her plane land in a bombed area? Was she alive? Deek sighed. Should he even entertain the idea of hope? His mind would not rest. When he started to climb the familiar craggy path ahead, Deek felt eyes upon him. Looking up he saw the crowd of suspicious, yet eager faces. A tightness gripped Deek's chest. How could he even consider deserting these people, his people? They had been crapped on so many times during their lives. True they had created a lot of their hell, but it was just another case of "what came first, the chicken or the egg?" Did inequities create rebellious behaviour, or did inappropriate behaviour cause deserved, harsh punishments? Refocused, Deek waved and smiled at his Lompoc family, above. If Captain Oswald was being truthful, everyone's future was about to improve . . . immensely.

DEATH HAD TAKEN A HEFTY bite out of the Lompoc tribe. Counting Sly, only fifty-six members remained. Deek spread the news that a town meeting would be held in the greenhouse immediately. He stopped at his and Sly's cabin along the way. It took him a mere couple of minutes to gather O'Malley's journals, one well-worn picture of him and Lourdes—long since shoved in Deek's sock by a sympathetic Lompoc prison guard—and Sly's meagre possessions. Inside his dreary shack for the last time, Deek held not a shred of sentimentality. He was eager to get back to the *Antarctica III*.

Within the greenhouse, everyone sat upon the ground huddled together. Questions were rifled at Deek from all directions. "Please calm yourselves. I promise to address all of your concerns. First of all, has everyone seen the naval medics? Is there anyone who hasn't?" No one raised his or her hand. "Okay, what I'm about to tell you will not only explain everything that's happened to us, but will be equally hard to hear. Trust me; there is a very good explanation for such a tough year of illnesses." For the next half an hour Deek retold Captain Oswald's news.

Stunned faces stared back at Deek. Some townsfolk cried. "What we need to decide now is where we would like to relocate."

"What are our choices?" Several individuals shouted.

"Well, the obvious options are Amsterdam and New Zealand."

A teenaged boy hollered from the back of the greenhouse. "Why can't we go to Africa, the mainland? Why can't that be our country now?"

"It can. Captain Oswald said he'd relocate us anywhere."

"You gunna stay with us, Deek?"

He was careful with his answer. "If you want me to, I'd be honoured." The clapping was unanimous. "So where to, comrades?"

Locations were shouted at Deek as the debating began. "So we agree?" Hoots and hollers sounded. "I'll tell Captain Oswald. What I need everyone to do right now is quickly gather your prized possessions. Limit your articles to what you absolutely treasure. I'm not sure how much room there is on the submarine. When you're done, please help each other to the beach. Leave no one behind."

It did not take the Lompoc family long to clear out of the greenhouse. Most of them raced for their sparse huts, forgetting their weakened state. Excitement infected everyone. Without much waffling, they grabbed the very few belongings that held any meaning. Possessions left behind would wait patiently to give hints of their island living, slowly deteriorating, until discovery by the next unfortunate inhabitants of Reaper Island.

As if deep within a long-awaited dream, the Lompoc family kept a watchful eye on the sailors, sure they would disappear never to return. Boatful after boatful carried Deek's anxious group to the *Antarctica III*. Before carrying his articles to the beach, Deek made sure all of the remaining Lompoc islanders had evacuated their township. Once he had joined the others on the beach, Deek could feel his heartbeat quicken. What if the submarine could not take any more aboard? He paced to and fro. Elephant seals barked repeatedly from all the human commotion. Deek held his hands to his ears and walked. He could hardly breathe. Where were the rescue amphibious crafts? What was taking so long? The surf pounded harder against the rocky shoreline while grey clouds congregated overhead. Deek was beside himself. Then, at the apex of an enormous swell, Deek spotted the rescue squad. One more extraction and everyone would be off the island. Deek still paced. He dreaded trespassing on the great white's territory, yet again. White-capped, choppy water increased their chances of capsizing before the aquatic crafts' hydraulics took command, raising them above the swells and massively sharp teeth below. For the moment, Deek never wanted anything so much as to be aboard the *Antarctica*, warm and secure, by Sly's bedside.

After a rough go, the rescue amphibious hovercrafts skidded onto the small stretch of sand one after the other. Excitedly, like children boarding a rollercoaster at an amusement park, the last remaining Lompoc townsfolk piled into the small oval crafts. Smiles were plastered across many elated, nervous faces. Before Deek stepped aboard, he looked behind himself for one last farewell. A gust of wind hit his chapped face. He smiled and under his breath Deek whispered, "Thank you for keeping us alive old friend." He nodded toward the grave he and Sly had dug for O'Malley's remains. Over the side of the hovercraft, Deek stepped. Two sailors then pushed the vessel into the mounting waves. Deek and the others hunkered down in the centre of the small aquatic craft to avoid the seawater that pelted them. Fuelled by excitement, no one seemed to notice the icy weather biting through their tattered clothing. Squeals of delight could be heard above the engines that had begun churning, readying for battle against the angry swells. Thunder roared in the near distance as the threatening storm grew closer. Deek yelled at the sailors, warning them to keep their heads within the boat's confines. Once everyone was safely aboard the submarine, he would tell the crew the legend of the beheading great white, Antoinette. Until then, Deek would stay alert continuously monitoring the turbulent waters. Through the ocean spray, no dorsal fins were visible. Not far from them was the *Antarctica III* where they would be free and clear. Deek felt a twinge of relief. That is when the aquatic hovercraft's hydraulics sputtered then failed completely. The amphibious craft began to whip about. Once the engines ceased to function, gravity quickly pulled Deek and the others to the ocean surface. An aqueous explosion came immediately from underneath launching evacuees and sailors into the air . . . and not everyone landed back inside the rescue boat. Three of Lompoc's townsfolk landed in the water before they realized what had happened. Joan of Arc submerged out of hiding. Cutting through the choppy surf, the agitated great white backed far away from the craft. She hesitated then with determination Joan gained momentum, hastening toward her prey. The shark's enormous dorsal fin gracefully sliced through the water. Screams heightened as awareness returned and panic set in. Quickly, the sailors dragged a young man and woman back into the aquatic craft. Deek reached for the third man who was struggling to keep his head above the choppy water. He yelled loudly trying to get the drowning man's attention. Flailing about, he had not seen the dorsal fin headed his way. Deek shrieked above the churn of the struggling engines but to no avail. Under the water the man sank. The white-capped surf made it impossible for Deek to locate the drowning man. Still he searched. Finally, the engines roared to life. Swiftly the sailors whisked the aquatic hovercraft about. Joan's sleek, enormous body continued to charge toward them, gaining speed. Watching the approaching dorsal fin left everyone frightened beyond speech. When the submerged man resurfaced, gasping and coughing, one of the sailors grabbed the nap of his sealskin cover-up and yanked him to the side of the boat. Joan dropped below the surface and remained focused on her victim's splashing legs. With mouth wide open and jaws protruded, she let her large, vacant doll eyes roll back into her head as she readied herself for a possible fight. Deek saw the flash of pearly white teeth just below the waterline as he ripped at the side of the struggling man's shirt, hurling him over the side of the vessel and into the other passengers. Searching for her prey's feet, Joan of Arc's enormous jaws came out of the churning ocean and snapped several times right in front of Deek's face. He was paralyzed with fear. Missing her target, Joan slammed her enormous head back into the darkening sea. A wall of saltwater sprayed over the entire group. Twisting her gargantuan body to and fro on the surface of the water, Joan suddenly opened her fierce, black eyes and stared right into Deek's. Chills ran through him. Inside the craft everyone, including Deek, grabbed onto each other. Before Joan of Arc could ram the craft, one of the sailors pushed the handle down, full throttle. Joan's body continued to flail about the choppy surf as she readied herself for another attack. Evading the twenty-five foot shark had nearly caused them to slam into the submarine's hull. Expert manoeuvring by the sailor brought the amphibious craft to a safe position for disembarking. Without hesitation, Deek and the others were pulled out of the vulnerable vessel and onto the *Antarctica III*. They were pushed and pulled along until they were secured within the guts of the submarine. Then, the man who had almost drowned and avoided becoming a meal for Joan of Arc threw up at everyone's feet. Nerves frazzled, all Deek could do was burst with hilarity as he hugged the drenched tribesman. Suddenly, the mood shifted. Those that were not laughing had conjured up at least a glazed smile. They had made it. Finally feeling safe, the Lompoc family could allow themselves to rest.

Deek was escorted to Captain Oswald's quarters immediately after he had changed into warm, dry clothes given to him by Sullivan.

"Oh my, Deek, we'll have to work on fixing some clothes that actually fit you, eh?"

"Sullivan was very generous, Captain. I've lost so much weight I can actually wear his garments." Deek stretched out his arms then rubbed his newly shaven head. "However, I am having a little difficulty with the length." Deek's forearms and lower legs were completely bare. Both men chuckled.

Captain Oswald handed Deek a whiskey. "I have some clothes that will fit you better. I'll have Sullivan bring them to you. Also, there are blankets in that cupboard over there if you are still chilled. Sit, Deek, sit."

"Captain, I can't thank you enough. I feel horrible

about the two sailors that died from the shark attack, earlier. I only found out a bit ago. I'm so sorry."

"Me too. I think we're all in shock. It all happened so quickly, it just doesn't seem real."

"Those great whites scare the hell out of me. I hope to never see a shark again as long as I live."

"We knew we would incur some casualties on this lengthy excursion but never expected this outcome. Hell, we were shocked when we discovered the sharks had survived the nuclear war. Deek don't feel responsible, really. Thanks for your concern."

"I'm so very sorry."

"No worries, Deek, it's not your fault. We still consider our expedition a success. We actually found survivors, so this mission is considered a huge success."

"Thanks, Captain."

"So, Deek, where are we taking all of you?"

"After much debate it seems we New Africans would like to start over in Africa. Cape Town, to be exact."

"Cape Town . . . fine choice. Cape Town it is." Captain Oswald stood to leave. "I'll alert my crew as to our new destination. Sullivan can get you some food or anything you need. He's my first mate and his cabin is right next-door. You make yourself at home here. This is my guest quarters for dignitaries. Welcome, Deek."

"Sir . . . thank you so much, really."

"You are very welcome. I'll check on you in a bit. If you're not resting, we can have another drink together. And just to warn you, there will be a lot of dead bodies, being Cape Town was never encased inside a dome. WWIV, no doubt, obliterated everyone. We will have to be prepared for the worst."

"I'll mention that to the others."

"I'm not trying to discourage your group. We have the means to battle radiation. And we have Bobcat utility vehicles to move debris, or, if necessary, dead bodies. But Deek, any city you choose will have many corpses I'm afraid."

"Fair enough."

"Well, Deek, get settled. We have a lot to discuss for Cape Town's future . . . New Africa's future, actually."

"Indeed. I look forward to it. Captain?"

"Yes?"

"Any news on Sly?"

"His fever is down. It's just a matter of time before he'll be begging for drink and real food."

"Oh, that's great news."

"Feel free to visit him and your townsfolk. We want you all to be comfortable; you've been through so much."

"Bless you, Captain. Please don't be offended if our New Africans are a bit suspicious of such kind treatment and keep to themselves."

"I understand, not a problem. I'll let you get settled."

"Thanks."

Sullivan appeared in the doorway after the captain departed. "Deek, sir?"

"Yeah, Sullivan? Come in, come in."

From behind his back, he pulled a weathered, oversized football. His cheeks flushed. "Some of my mates and I like to play a little when we go ashore. I know it's a rugby ball, but it's the closest thing to an American football that I could find. Captain Oswald was a big gridiron fan and told us all about you. You had a stellar rookie year. Um, he said you used to sleep with your football ever since you were a boy . . . your brother's ball, right?"

"That's right. Christ, he knows all that about me?"

"Yes, sir. I'd like you to have this ball as a gift from all of the crew."

"Sullivan . . . I can't take your ball. What will you guys play with when ashore?"

"We have others, sir. Please, it would mean a lot to me . . . please take it."

"Well, thanks, Sullivan, that means a lot, really. And please call me Deek; drop the 'Sir.'"

Sullivan tossed Deek the soft, bulging pigskin. "Then please call me, Sully."

"Thanks, Sully." Deek examined the ball moving it from hand to hand. "Damn that feels good; a bit fat for a football, but good nonetheless. I haven't touched a ball in over a year." Both men were reflective. "Sully . . . this has been quite a day. Promise me one thing?"

"Name it, Deek."

"If I'm dreaming, please don't wake me."

Aerin & Cameron

Who would have predicted this promising future? From Iran to Iraq then Canada, Aerin had sculpted a beautiful future in her head. Of course, this image never included New Zealand or an Australian professor. Aerin's psychic abilities rarely revealed answers for her personal life, but that left Aerin contented. She was free to dream again without restraints. And no matter how tremendous a life Aerin created in her head, experience was teaching her life often turned out better than her limited visions of it. True, the unimagined highs brought with them unpredicted, often painful lows, but the net outcome was happiness and a swelling wisdom. In the realm of science and medicine, Aerin had learned logic ruled. Only in the past few years had she discovered the strength in considering spirituality as an explanation or cure. Unseen, intangible methods, although harder to explain, were proving to be more powerful and effective. New Zealand was truly a mystical place. The locals often joked about how boring life was on the South Shore. Truth be told, the Kiwis had found the secret combination to a peaceful, rewarding existence. They had worked out a beautiful cohabitation between the foreign imports and native Maoris. Equality always needed tweaking, but for the most part, life in New Zealand was something the rest of the world thought was a sugar-coated unattainable myth.

It did not take much convincing to rely on an ethereal force. Unlike the men in the pre-war Middle East who valued nothing but Allah and their maleness, the wonderful, open-minded New Zealanders welcomed Aerin's combination of Western and Eastern medical abilities and psychic feedback. Her thriving patients healed quickly and often left the hospital with a strengthened inner peace. After all, Dr. Aerin could see into their souls. She understood them, knew which direction he or she should proceed. No longer was "pop a pill and call me in the morning" acceptable. Dr. Aerin knew what ailed her patients, both physically and emotionally.

Many worshipped this young powerful healer. That is why it was not surprising to the Ermani family that the church was bursting from the crowd of onlookers when Aerin and Cameron exchanged vows. That was not to say Cameron did not have a draw. He had single-handedly convinced the South Shore to reach for a new future. The only way to do this was by educating their youth. To give young adults hope was the best gift imaginable. This powerful union between a beloved Dr. Aerin and Professor Cameron was a promising package. With the world nearly annihilated, progress was evaluated and re-evaluated to the nth degree. New World citizens fervently wanted to avoid mistakes of the past. The future had all the potential for greatness without repeating destructive pitfalls. The marriage of Aerin and Cameron reminded many there was a loving God overseeing them. He had created these powerful individuals and brought them together in pure love. Only God could pull off this beautiful miracle. A kiss to seal the deal brought cheers and tears. Many cried for their hopeful futures, their dreams.

It was the hardest thing Aerin ever had to do. What if Cameron rejected her spiritual conversion of people? He had not judged her psychic abilities, but instead had been fascinated. Aerin's gift was just another unique thing to love about her. Nevertheless, would he feel the same when he saw the machines? He said he had heard the rumours, but what did those rumours say? Would he approve of what the Glowworm cocoons did to the troubled souls?

Balic and Rami led the dishevelled, odorous Arab toward the tubular mechanism. When Aerin lifted the lid florescent aqua light escaped, filling the darkened storm cellar with a soothing glow. Cameron stood motionless. The Middle Eastern man cursed as he struggled to free himself. Softly Aerin recited verses from the Quran in Arabic. Spittle flew from the man's enraged mouth. Balic and Rami lifted the man and placed him into the soothing, aqua-glowing jaws of Glowworm. Aerin quickly strapped the man in, inserted a needle into a bulging vein on his wrist, then turned a valve to release the deadly fluid into his bloodstream. Flipping a few switches, Aerin secured an oxygen mask then closed the lid. With their methods perfected over the past year, cumbersome breathing tubes were no longer necessary. A whirring sound began from the metal cocoon.

"Aerin, that bloke did not look conscious. Should you recheck his vitals?"

"Sweetheart, this is that occasion when I asked you to keep an open mind."

"But—"

"We want him to die."

"Aerin!"

"I know it's murder."

"You are damn right it is murder! Open that lid right now!"

"Cameron, I need for you to be calm. I have to focus."

Cameron searched for remorse in Balic and Rami's eyes. There was none. Back and forth he paced, never taking his eyes from the encapsulated man. After what seemed like an eternity, the whirring ceased and the lid released, then slowly rose. Again, florescent aqua light flooded the room. Cameron could not believe what he saw. Inside, a calm Arabic man with blinking, clear eyes stared at Aerin. Tears leaked down the sides of his face. When Aerin removed the oxygen mask, the man whispered gentle words toward his captor. Aerin brushed dampened hair from the man's forehead and repeated softly, "Allah . . . Allahu Akbar." At that instant, the once-troubled man wept. Aerin checked his vital signs, released his constraints, and assisted him out of the Glowworm pod. Balic helped the man to a chair. Rami handed him a warm washcloth and a cup of orange juice.

Aerin turned and faced Cameron. He was speechless. "Sweetheart, can we go upstairs? I'll explain everything."

Bewildered, all Cameron was capable of was following his wife. As they passed the Arab, the man jumped from his chair and locked grateful arms around Aerin's shoulders. She hugged him back. The man continued to weep.

"You saw all that? That bloke was a shonky mongrel?"

"Yes, Cameron. After taking over that elementary school he would have torturously killed many innocent children."

"But you saw a glimmer of hope? Regret?"

"Yes, he would have taken his own life eventually."

"And that is how you know these grey souls will change?"

"Exactly. Somehow these individuals get diverted onto a dark path but aren't completely comfortable with their choices. That is how I know they are salvageable."

"So you jab a needle in their arms until they are cactus, they see God or Allah, then you bring them back to life?"

"Yes, they die and see Home on the other side, which is all about God, or Allah. They see lost loved ones and experience an indescribable, unconditional love they could never imagine here on Earth. Truthfully, they probably don't want to come back to this hellish world. Gently, they're nudged back into their bodies and, when awakened, their life is marked with a spiritual evolution, forever. They have become part of that rare group that truly understands. Cameron, it's this wonderful secret. Conventional beliefs are discarded and we come back with a renewed purpose. Not a purpose governed by man's religion, but driven solely by God's love. It really is that simple . . . love and knowledge are the only things we never lose when we go Home. Makes for a less pressurized peaceful existence, eh?"

"You saw those things when Ahmed killed you?"

"Cameron, I saw so many wonderful things. If it weren't for my grandfather suggesting I come back, I could have easily been happy staying . . . dying. However, I knew I had God's work to do. I had to come back to make others' lives better, safer."

"What if in your psychic vision you do not see any remorse from a killer? What happens if you encounter a dark soul?"

"You don't miss a trick do you, Sweetheart? Well, that is a much tougher decision."

"Can you convert them as well?"

"I don't dabble with dark souls. They're hopeless.

Sweetheart, I'm tired. Can we discuss this further, tomorrow?"

"No, I want to yabber about it now. I am having a hard time with this, Aerin. Christ, you are killing people, Love . . . without their permission. You are playing God. How can you justify that?"

"They die, that is true, then I bring them back. I justify it when I see the rebirth in these people's eyes. They have a second chance at a wonderful, more fulfilling life. How can that be wrong?"

"Crikey, Aerin, you think that is your job to intervene?"

"Yes, Cameron, I do."

Deek

HIS UNCONSCIOUS FRIEND BELONGED IN a bad horror flick. Leprosy-like sores and patches of sagging flesh covered Sly's face. Deek was saddened. Sitting at Sly's bedside, Deek stared at his saviour, imagining what horrible events had led him to this moment. Four men had left Reaper Island in pursuit of help, yet only one had survived. Captain Oswald said the *Antarctica III* detected Sly's fleck of a boat upon the early morning horizon when they had discovered several circling great white sharks. Of course, everyone aboard the submarine had tempered his or her enthusiasm. Prospective survivors had proven fruitless before. Oswald and his crew had encountered massive casualties, so Sly instantly became their link to life.

"Old friend, when will you open those tired eyes I remember so well? I found O'Malley's final journal . . . his final words. Come on, you know you want to hear how he died." Sly did not move. He seemed so far away. Deek noticed the faint scars on his neck from that frightening lion attack so long ago. How their friendship had grown since then.

Deek continued, "You know, Sly, we're heroes. We outlived the rest of the world, except for Nederland and New Zealand. Can you believe it? It seems we missed the biggest firework show ever. That's right, the unthinkable World War IV happened, in all its destruction. Here we thought the United African government betrayed us. Ha! The joke's on them, Sly. We outlived all those superior power mongers, as well as millions of innocents. God, it all makes sense now. Evidently, Reaper's high winds got rid of a lot of the radiation, but of course, we were still exposed; explains why our rustic community lost so many lives. Sly, it wasn't some funky island rot, or Cholera, as we discussed. Nope, good ole radiation poisoning killed our townsfolk. Vomiting, diarrhea, bloody stools, and much later, unexplained growths . . . we should have guessed it was something more catastrophic. Don't worry though, these New Zealanders have treated and medicated all of us. They've even treated you. For the sicker ones, it's been tough. The medications can be quite harsh and side effects aren't uncommon. Everyone from Reaper is being closely monitored. We're in good hands." Sly lay motionless. "Oh, and by the way, did you know we are all on a submarine? Bet you never dreamed that would happen in your lifetime?"

Deek scooted his chair closer to Sly's bedside and lowered his voice. "I sure hope you can hear me, Chief. I haven't told the others, but I'm scared, Sly. Hell, so is everyone, yet no one discusses it. You can feel it in the air. I just can't share my fear because it would only make matters worse. I have to lead, Sly. These White folks are so kind, but a part of me doesn't trust them. Whenever we eat together, I find myself wondering if they might drug me . . . drug all of us, cart us off to New Zealand and sell us for slavery. Why not? We're so grateful to be off that damn island, many of our group would probably welcome servitude. Not me. Christ, I wish you would wake up. Is my mistrust valid or am I simply a ridiculous xenophobe? Yes, my friend, I'm going to throw big words at you until you're ready to scream inside that head of yours, and finally wake up. That could easily be all of us. Sly, I'm out of sorts. Captain Oswald has treated me with nothing but respect.

He even knows I'm not a killer . . . seems he watched me play ball, too. And he's a fan. But what if that is a load of fluff thrown at me so I'll let my guard down? What are these Kiwis getting out of rescuing us? Get this, Oswald's response was 'to do the right thing.' Do you believe that? They say they're taking us to Cape Town. How do I know that isn't a lie? I know my skepticism is overinflated, but we're under water, Sly, in a huge metal tube. How would I know if we were being duped, or not? Chief, please wake up. I need you, damn it."

FOR DAYS, THE LOMPOC FAMILY travelled, and they were not doing well. Deek had to convince them every day freedom was in reach. They needed fresh air and meals free of anxiety. Above all, the Reaper clan needed proof of their relocation to Cape Town.

"Deek, come in."

"Captain, I'm really worried about my group. They're not eating . . . and they are sure they're being lied to. Sir, you have to understand, growing up in America our distrust of White people is common. Hell, they think you're taking them to New Zealand to sell them into some underground slavery racket."

"Oh, Deek, my mate, that couldn't be further from the truth. We are all rebuilding this world; we've collectively been through hell. Not one person alive today avoided losing loved ones in the nuclear holocaust. Pain and suffering is finally diminishing. And as you'll see, we are hellbent on avoiding repetition of the world's horrible past. Deek, we don't want to move backward, only forward, and that means a peaceful existence."

"But how do they know, Captain?"

"I understand your clan's need for proof. Actually, we spotted land so I'll have my crew surface and your folks can check out the African shoreline. Maybe we'll see something that will ensure them we are in fact on our way to Cape Town."

"Captain, that would really help. I'm sorry if we appear at all ungrateful."

"No, no, Deek, if I were in your shoes I would be questioning everything as well. Go tell your mates and I'll talk to my crew."

A WARM BREEZE HIT THEIR weary faces. Equipped with power glasses, the New Africans took turns searching the shoreline for answers. The *Antarctica III* was barely moving. Even Deek took a turn. Peering through the high-powered binoculars, Deek's eyes combed the abandoned city for a clue. Whitish-grey dust covered everything making it difficult to read signs. The minutes ticked by and no one said a word. Only the whistling of the comforting wind past their faces could be heard.

Deek was growing impatient. He knew he had to support his group, but he longed to join Sly. The *Antarctica* inched southward. Then, an unexpected bloodcurdling scream erupted from one of the Lompoc women.

"I see it! A sign . . . Durban! It says Durban! It's Africa, it's really Africa!"

Those that held the high-powered glasses searched to confirm her find. Other shouts of excitement joined hers as they witnessed evidence to support the woman's claim. Another group, gathered around a man who held a large opened atlas provided by Captain Oswald, searched for the city along the Eastern African coastline.

"Here, here it is! It's in the atlas! It's Africa, it's Africa!"

Deek felt his heart race. Behind him, a hand gently grabbed his shoulder. "Welcome home, mate."

Captain Oswald beamed at Deek. They grabbed each other sharing a quick bear hug. Each slapped the other on the back. "I can't thank you enough, friend. Your word is truly golden."

With that, the rest of the New Africans began hugging and shaking hands with Oswald, thanking him over and over. Deek stepped back letting the others get closer to the captain. He gave Oswald a playful salute then left the deck to join Sly and share the great news. His steps seemed lighter. Weaving in and out of corridor after corridor, Deek could not wait to be beside his friend.

Deek stopped when he rounded the corner. "Oh my God, you're awake! Oh, thank God. Sly, it's about time!"

"So yo' found O'Malley's last journal?"

"Under some clapboards in his cabin, under the floor. Wait a minute . . . you heard what I said when you were unconscious?"

"Every damn word. Jesus, yo' could talk da ears offa jackass!"

"It's so nice to hear that wonderful foul mouth of yours."

"So we gunna be slaves or what, yo' paranoid fuck?"

"Nice . . . no we're safe. We just spotted an African city along the Eastern coastline. We are definitely on course and not far from Cape Town, Chief."

"I knew yo' would take care of us, College Boy."

"Sly, thanks for leading our expedition off Reaper. I'm so sorry you had to watch the others in our boat pass. That had to be horrific."

"Don't go gettin' all soft on me."

"What happened during the days you were gone? You looked like hell when I first saw you."

"Man, I'm not ready . . . I don't wanna talk 'bout it. Those sharks, Deek . . . those goddamn sharks. They tore us ta pieces then more and more of da bastards kept comin'. Da more we drifted . . ."

"I know, I know. Fair enough, Chief, you rest." Sly turned his head from Deek's direction. "Hey, how about I read you O'Malley's last journal?"

"Ah, now yo' talkin'. I missed those stories."

Deek raised a corner of Sly's mattress and retrieved a ratty, faded composition book. "You're not going to believe what this poor bastard went through." Deek flipped open the journal. "Okay, we left off with O'Malley finishing his crude boat."

"Yeah, he'd packed up all his belongin's with some food and was headed ta da beach."

"That's right. Okay, let's see . . ."

May 7th   I'm bleeding. An artery has been nicked. They won't leave me be. Fire is everywhere yet still they come for me. They wait for me to sleep.

Kittelty

Constable Kittelty shivered. The Christchurch morgue was never a place of warmth. Quietly, the medical examiner stood by and let Kittelty do his cursory examination. Upon the stainless steel table lay the seventh burnt corpse since the onset of the Inferno Killer's rampage. Flakes of skin ash littered the tabletop. The smell of formaldehyde laced with singed flesh caused the constable to step back. Kittelty kept his distance but could not take his eyes from the charcoaled corpse. Something about this one was familiar. Lips completely incinerated, the victim's repulsive, root-exposed teeth had given Kittelty a shred of hope. A distinguishing chipped front tooth resembled an infamous Kaikouran, Ben Pickersgill. Kittelty stared at Ben's frozen, empty eye sockets and involuntary skeletal grin. If this was Pickersgill, and he was sure it was, Kaikoura would not grieve his departure for a second. No amount of imprisonment had reformed this despicable excuse for a human being. Pickersgill's proclivity for violence included beating senseless Kaikoura's highly protected fur seal pups for no apparent reason, as well as any women who got sucked into the wake of his depravity. Yes, Kittelty thought, if this was Pickersgill, good riddance.

Pete tried to hold his ground. "This is the year for my Blues, I can feel it."

Isaac rolled his eyes. "The Blues? Go back to Auckland, mate! Your Blues will never get past the Hurricanes, let alone our Crusaders. Your team can't even solve its administrative arm-wrestling long enough to pick a permanent coach. Come on, Pete, your team is in constant disarray and you can't tell me this won't affect their play, you stubborn old bastard."

"Ari, surely you aren't as daft as your brother here, help me out, mate."

"Oh, no you don't. I'm only watching rugby because soccer has been obliterated. Hell, Pete, I'm still learning the game."

"Pete, even with the Super 14 league being whittled down to five teams now, your Blues will end up in third place at best. Our Canterbury team, as well as Wellington's, is going to give your Blues a thumping, guaranteed!"

"Bugger off you daft wanker. Everyone in their right mind knows the Hurricanes will finish dead last!"

"Ah, naff off, don't be such a Doris. The only reason your Blues beat the Hurricanes last week was because of that unpredictable breakout where you scored a kick-and-chase try in the last gut-wrenching seconds of the game. That was a fluke win, pure and simple."

Pete raised his drink. "A win nonetheless."

Constable Kittelty entered the living room. "Hi ya', mates."

"Kyle, finally a voice of reason. Pete here thinks his Blues are going to beat our Crusaders."

"I suppose you think your Blues will win after losing Tilley, the leagues' number one flanker? Ah, Pete, you're a bit of a dag, mate. Are you pissed? How much drink have you had?"

"Not nearly enough, you bunch of tossers."

"Tell him what else you said, Pete. Kyle, this buggered fool thinks the Hurricanes will finish last."

"Ha, now I know you're clean out of your mind. Christ, Pete, Wellington will finish second behind our Crusaders. Your Auckland boys will be crying the blues . . . pardon the pun. I should arrest you for being so stupid, you daft bastard."

"Ah, go on. Isaac, be a good mate and get us another spirit?"

The men were getting on with their manly fun while their offspring congregated in the hallway. Kittelty, lately, was a wealth of morbid information, such fascinating fodder for young minds.

"Kyle, take a load off, mate. You take the wahine to dinner?"

"No, no, I came home to my favourite cooked meal, homemade meat pies."

"Well at least you got that right, got the little lady trained."

"Oh, Pete, how does Victoria put up with you?"

"My loveable nature."

The men laughed. Isaac handed the men icy drinks.

"Actually, Deidre's been a gem this past year with me spending so many hours on that Inferno case. It's plaguing the hell out of me."

Ari asked, "How is that going, Kyle? Any news on that last body?"

Isaac sat in his large rocking chair. "Was it Ben Pickersgill?"

"Yes, spot on, it was Ben all right."

"Any solid leads yet, mate?"

"Pete, if I had at least one hint of a clue I wouldn't be here debating rugby and getting pissed with my mates."

"Fair enough . . . sneaky bastard that Inferno Killer."

Eavesdropping, the Ermani and Whibley young adults absorbed Kittelty's every word. When the conversation turned back to rugby, they skulked away to the nearest bedroom. They did not dare turn on the lights.

"Ben Pickersgill? Wasn't he the most recent escapee from jail?" asked Kendall an EMT who had experienced a lot of the Inferno Killer's bodies up close. He was clearly intrigued with the Inferno case. "Aerin?"

"Yes, he came to us at hospital for his homeopathic cleanse. I didn't see him after that. I will tell you, he was a rude pig, to say the least. Ahmed told me he was the gluttonous Neanderthal that got paid for letting Ahmed's shipmates, off Avoca Point, enter our biosphere; hence releasing those vermin into Kaikoura. In the privacy of the night, Pickersgill took the Arabs' gold spoils and one by one led them through the observation point ventilation system. Those with nothing to give were left to roam the beaches and wait for the silent killer to penetrate their bloodstreams. That's how Ahmed found me on the beach. It was such a pleasure jabbing the IV into Pickersgill's arm several times. And all of us were relieved when they got him out of our hospital. Everywhere he went he left his stench."

Tanid added, "Yeah, Constable Kittelty said the women weren't huge fans of his, to say the least."

"Not the nicest bloke that's for certain. I heard the constable questioned his latest girlfriend extensively. She probably had the strongest motive for killing him, eh?"

"True, Kendall, but why would she kill all those others? She can't be the Inferno Killer. Besides, Kittelty is sure the killer is a bloke. Have to be to handle the likes of Pickersgill."

"Maybe the girlfriend isn't, Tanid, but instead used the Inferno Killer's MO to get rid of the bastard that blackened her eyes."

"You witnessed that, Aerin?"

"Yes, he tore into her with heavy fists. If she is a copycat and killed Pickersgill, I commend her."

Deek

May 7th – Yes, they wait for me to sleep then come for my flesh.

My boat launch was a success. Everything unfolded as planned. Although a series of waves hit hard and left me spitting and coughing saltwater from deep inside my bronchial tubes, I could see I was past the worst of the collapsing waves. Cognizant of my beloved great whites, I was very careful to stay within the confines of my boat. Their large grey dorsal fins circled as if escorting me away from their island. That is, all except Joan of Arc. I was sure she was underneath and close. Upon closer examination, Lizzie's dorsal scars are dramatically severe. It's evident she was attacked by another shark, or sharks. It's very likely Lizzie was a partial meal when participating in a feeding frenzy. As scared as I was being in their waters, I couldn't take my eyes off their powerful, massive bodies. They are so beautiful. In comparison, I am so very, very small and unimportant.

An hour or so passed as I sailed north, or attempted to sail, toward the direction of Madagascar. The one day when I needed the boisterous wind at my sails there was instead an eerie stillness. My simple, ragged sail didn't cooperate either. Instead, it continued to luff. There I sat anxious to know Antoinette's whereabouts. She hadn't surfaced yet and that troubled me, knowing her past behaviour. The waves kept pushing me toward the shore. I didn't dare use my oddly shaped paddle. Antoinette would surely attack whatever appendage, either head or limbs, that extended beyond my craft. So I drifted and waited.

Then she hit. Joan of Arc delivered an explorative bump. I braced myself. What troubled me was I could only see Lizzie's dorsal fin. She seemed to hover close by, waiting for something.

Tension spread in the thick air. Lizzie came closer, circling the boat. I suddenly doubted my craftsmanship. I was afraid. That's when Antoinette struck hard. Flung into the air, I flailed about pleading with God. It seemed an eternity before I landed, my prayers partially answered. I fell back into my boat with one leg hitting the water. Unfortunately, my nightmare was upon me. There was a reason Antoinette's dorsal fin had disappeared before. She had lain in waiting a ways from me as if to get a swimming start to gain momentum. Charging toward the surface, before I could yank my leg out of danger, Antoinette sank her razor sharp teeth into the meat of my calf muscle. Suddenly out of the water, Antoinette twisted her body awkwardly attempting to regain some stability. All her bending back and forth caused her to rake her teeth down my leg and lock onto my ankle. I screeched from the unimaginable pain. As she slammed back down into the calm water, my anklebones snapped from sheer force. The sound was horrifying. Still, I hung onto the craft with all my might, my leg still in the great white's mouth. We started a tug-of-war for life. I was petrified about being yanked from my boat and into the depths of the ocean. My shredded flesh burned. One more tug and a pop sounded as she tore my foot completely from my lower leg. There was a delay before the pain erupted. It felt like someone had poured acid on my open wound. Also I could feel the shock approaching. Blood was everywhere. I wanted to pass out, but knew I had to stop the bleeding. Quickly I cut a piece of rope from my rigging and tied it tightly right below my knee. In the ocean my magenta life force spread, mixing in with the saltwater. Further and further the sister sharks whipped themselves into a frenzy. Bumping my craft left then right, the great whites' repeated passes drove me closer to the surf that hugged the shoreline. I was relieved. All I wanted was my rustic, freezing cabin on the cliffs. Joan of Arc hit hard one last time as a large wave buried me. I was free of my confines when Lizzie bit into the side of the boat taking it deep into the sea. Swirling within the churning water, I held my breath. Saltwater shot into my nasal passages. It burned. Over and over, I toppled until I finally hit the welcomed beach. I coughed water from my throat and nose. I was never so glad to be on land again.

It wasn't long before I began shivering. Perhaps it was just the shock upon me, but one thing was for certain, I had to get out of my soaked clothing and get warm. So I began to crawl. The pain in my leg screamed through my brain every time I bumped it. To pad the area where my foot used to be I took off my t-shirt and tied it around my lower leg.

Three hours later, hands and knees bloodied and raw, I arrived at my cabin. I was never so thankful. Even the offensive bird crap was suddenly a welcomed odour.

BEFORE FURTHER INFECTION SET IN, I built a fire. Bit by bit I singed my new stub. Swollen and ragged, I wasn't sure what to do with the protruding bone. So I burned my injured limb and screamed. Several times the pain put me out, only to awaken and vomit bile and saltwater. Seagulls began to congregate and move closer, somehow sensing my vulnerability. As long as I kept the fire stoked though, they retreated. When my nausea subsided, I took a chance at releasing my tourniquet. I had failed. Blood shot from a raw section on my nub. It sprayed everywhere. My audience of noisy gulls chirped and flapped about, never taking their eyes from me. I should have been more nervous. Without thinking, I pulled a piece of driftwood from the fire and plunged it against my tender, tattered skin. I screamed and screamed. Tears squirted from my eyes as my flesh sizzled. It was hard not to hyperventilate. Eventually the bleeding subsided.

Dusk rapidly approached. With what little strength I had left I hopped, then crawled, the rest of the way to my cabin. All I could do was huddle upon my coverless bed and sleep. There was no food or bedding. Everything was lost at sea. Sleep . . . that was my only option. Tomorrow will be another day.

May 9th – When I awakened, I could see the many yellow, beady eyes staring at me. They were stares of patient hunger. The small spaces in between some of the wall planks left the seagulls much hope for intrusion. And still they wait.

May 13th – I tried to kill one of the aggressive gulls. They found a way in! I feel like I'm in an Alfred Hitchcock movie. While in a feverish haze, I watched several of the birds tear flesh from my unprotected limbs. They are eating me! The pain though is far away now. Perhaps these gulls are getting even for all their relatives I have eaten. Mother Nature does retaliate.

May 15th – There's not much fight left in me. I'm so hot with fever. My mind wanders in and out of my memories. When I sleep, the seagulls feed. I'm too weak to catch one. I'm so thirsty. My sharks didn't want me to leave this island, but why? If only I could talk to them. Were they fond of me? Would they be pleased to see that I've become bird feed? My fever keeps me occupied. Will anyone read these journals? If so, will they appreciate my words or think them simply the ravings of a lunatic?

"That's it. Look at the dried blood smudges, Chief."

"So da birds ate O'Malley?"

"Well, they surely didn't help him. Lack of food and water and the growing infection in his leg probably had more to do with his inevitable demise."

"Christ, whatta way ta go."
"Poor bastard never knew he would save so many lives."

New Africans

Grateful for their newfound freedom and lifesaving vaccines and antibiotics, the Lompoc family buzzed with a renewed energy. Healing had begun, both physically and emotionally. Their strength was coming back ever so quickly. Aquatic hovercrafts gathered to take the first loads of New Africans ashore to their new city of Cape Town. Days had expired as Deek and the Reaper Islanders had anxiously awaited their arrival. With False Bay non-conducive for a super submarine of the *Antarctica III*'s magnitude, Captain Oswald was forced to anchor off the tip of the Cape of Good Hope.

Once the New Africans were loaded into the crafts, their smiles could not be broader. They were living a dream. The closer the Reaper group got to shore, the more Deek and the others were awestruck. Fortunate enough to have avoided a direct nuclear or atomic assault, their new city remained somewhat intact. Cape Town, in all her splendour, lay hidden, buried beneath a thick layer of ash. One did not need much of an imagination. Everywhere there were glimpses of its past beauty. Considerable clean-up lay ahead, however. Patches of pastel colours could be seen beneath the soot. Whereas Cape Town's architecture had survived WWIV, its previous occupants had not been so lucky.

On shore, Deek, Captain Oswald, the New African inhabitants, and some members of the New Zealand naval crew began to survey the ghost town before them. Children's eyes were covered when meatless skeletons were discovered. Sadness hung over the once-vibrant United African city. In a park, overgrown with unruly vegetation, the New Africans congregated for their first town meeting. Proudly, Deek stood before his fellow citizens and repeated the topics he had discussed extensively with Captain Oswald. The first order of business was less desirable—cleanup. Surprisingly, there was little resistance. To motivate everyone, Deek informed the now healthier eager faces before him that every family would be allowed to pick a home. Ownership would become theirs outright. Additionally, each family would choose a trade they would be responsible for. Volunteer N.Z. doctors relocating to Cape Town to provide and teach medical services would choose temporary residences after the New Africans were satisfied. The crowd was electrified.

"Keep in mind, we have survived hell together. Our pasts are behind us, far behind us. Take your time, choose two places you love, write down the locations, and we'll solve any disputes democratically. Cape Town citizens, if there's arguing or intimidation, you automatically lose the bid for that property. Please remember, our community is based on peace. There are plenty of beautiful homes to choose from. And don't worry about furnishing your future houses; there is plenty of furniture in Cape Town to go around. We'll work together as we always have to make everyone's home exquisite. Once again, if you feel the need to be greedy and decide looting is the way to go, you will forfeit all rights to whatever you are hoarding. Love and honour one another. Take pleasure in being a part of building an amazing community for each other. Let's show our children a better life than we had. Okay . . . after we have recorded everyone's property, all other locations will be owned by our city. When one of our offspring reaches sixteen, they will choose a home and the city will sign the property over.

"Let's stop here. We can discuss the rest of our future later. Go forth and find your homes with enthusiasm. Help each other, please. Afterwards, return quickly so we can get started on cleaning up our neighbourhoods."

Cape Town citizens scattered in all directions, squealing with joy. Deek helped Sly to his feet. "So, College Boy, where yo' gunna live?"

"On the waterfront next door to you, you cantankerous ole bastard."

"Sounds like a plan."

"I'm thinking, incredible ocean views. I know it sounds insane, but I actually miss the sounds of the ocean while on Reaper. After looking through some of Oswald's books, I'd like to find this amazing building in the Victoria and Alfred development on the waterfront. What do you say?"

"I say, hell fuckin' yeah!"

Deek mimicked Sly's dialect. "So you're lovin' these mayo-faced bastards now, ain't yo', Sly?"

"Yeah, damn New Zealand mayos makin' such a liar outta ole Sly here. I should hate 'em for it, but I don't. They some of the best folk I eva met. I'm actually happy bein' 'round whitey for once, College Boy."

"God bless da' mayonnaise."

Deek and Sly took their time walking toward the coastline through the area known as Bo Kaap. Many gorgeous homes painted in shades of bright coloured ice cream hid underneath the dull, grey ash. Cape Town had many wonders yet to be discovered.

Intrigued with the tall buildings downtown, many of

the New Africans decided to explore the skyscrapers. High winds blew ash in every direction. Several of the younger men pried open a heavy glass door to a newer, very modern angular building. It took much doing before the entrance barrier would budge. Upon entry, the young men heard the eerie echoing of birds' wings flapping and agitated chirping. The men stopped. Despite the securely sealed doors, Mother Nature had found her way indoors. Vines reached across the marble floor in the atrium. Dirt, grime, and dead leaves covered every visible crevice. As if haunted, the high-rise groaned from the whistling wind. The men shared troubled glances. The last powerful gust mercilessly shook the loosened glass. Spooked beyond reason, the young explorers could have sworn the far wall moved. That was enough for them. All three wheeled around and could not exit the unstable building fast enough. These towering ash-covered skyscrapers would remain empty. Where dynamic people once lived and worked, these unused monoliths were reduced to mere reminders of life before the war.

Deek and Sly cruised the beachfront. Some of the smaller houses had disappeared under magenta and lavender mounds of bougainvillea. Lizards and snakes skittered in and about the brush. Sly signalled for Deek to follow him down a debris-covered stairway.

"Oh my God, Sly, look over there; it's Cape Town's new subway express tube."

"Yeah? Look at it now, what's left of it."

Below ground, where the pods once flew with record-breaking speed beneath the city, flowed a muddy river.

"Let's have a look."

Deek crossed what was once an asphalt street. Now it was cracked and crumbling from uncontrolled semi-deciduous Fever and evergreen Bladdernut trees. Inside the station building was a jungle of vines and scrubs. From the moisture underneath, the structure's innards had expanded and contracted causing the joints between the walls and rooflines to separate. Rain had leaked in, bolts rusted, facing popped off, and ashen slabs of insulation fluttered in the breeze. Winds sighed through the broken windows and began to whine with a fury of the oncoming storm.

"Sly, we need to study that diagram and choose a place nowhere near the Tube lines."

"Deek, did yo' hear dat?"

"What? The wind?"

"No, dat low growl. We ain't alone."

Several pairs of large golden eyes showed from the shadows. Hairs on the back of Sly's neck prickled. Backing away, Deek and Sly slowly inched toward the Tube Station's double doors. The hungry eyes moved closer from the darkness. Deek felt for the door handle behind him. Suddenly an all-too-familiar roar reverberated as a large lioness broke from the shadows. Deek grabbed the back of Sly's naval-issued shirt and yanked him through the crack where they had entered the Station. Just as Deek passed safely through and slammed it shut, the lioness hit the large wooden door with full force. The roaring ceased. Deek could hear claws scratching rapidly against tiled floors. He began to run with Sly in tow.

"Hurry, Sly, they're running for another exit. It won't take them long to find us on this open street!"

Maktan's Vancouver

WHILE MU'MAD ATTENDED SCHOOL, MAKTAN sat on her sofa sipping hot tea and watching the mediavision morning news. Via the resurrection of the Internet and EyeNet phone service, Canada was informed about a rescue that took place near Madagascar. The news commentator buzzed with excitement. They were not alone in the world. Maktan was intrigued. Everyone had discovered the survival of Amsterdam and New Zealand not long after the war. The rest of the world, however, was presumed dead. This was the first discovery of random survivors. After a few pictures of the Reaper Island rescue flashed across the screen, the commentator transitioned to another story. Maktan took another sip of tea. Soon there was a discussion about another town meeting. Maktan yawned. Usually she ignored these group gatherings; long and tedious, the town council meetings never seemed to ignite a spark of interest for her. Issues dragged on, sometimes without resolution. The panel of newscasters explained the current dilemma further.

It had taken the Vancouver townsfolk many civic meetings before they could agree to petition the help of New Zealand. Trust would be tested. Soon to be discovered by Captain Oswald's expedition, the Western Canadians were extremely cautious. However, it was apparent they needed assistance from the outside. Corpses needed extraction and elimination, survivors needed medical care, and the healthy, fortunate ones wanted to feel a part of the world again. Once resolved, the trapped dome-livers would be able to think beyond rudimentary survival. Food, water, and shelter were simply not enough these days. Livelihoods were explored. And the renewed question of how Canada would become a world player arose. Speculation as to the future of Vancouver, actually, was quite splintered. Lumber used to be lucrative, but with the new flame-retardant materials used for construction, forests were left refreshingly untouched. Still the Canadians pondered unique ways to prosper in the new world. One frivolous suggestion at the latest town council meeting was Hollywood. Vancouver could easily become the pulse of a new entertainment industry. Over the decades, film crews had been taught the craft from the Hollywood old-timers. It had not taken long before these crews had proven they did not need the Southern California heavyweights' assistance. Film studios sprouted up all around Vancouver. Canadian hospitality drew "A-list" actors, prominent directors, writers, and producers into their city. Pleasant weather and postcard beauty were only a part of the draw that pulled productions from the U.S. The convenient ski slopes of Whistler, for weekend getaways, were the clincher. It had not taken long before Vancouver had become the elite location for film and mediavision productions. By the time WWIV ignited the skies, many of those "A-list" actors and film-maker "bigs" resided within the confines of the downtown dome. It seemed there were no coincidences in life. Surely Canada, the surviving Canada, could eventually become the Mecca for the entertainment industry, once again. Only this time, the pool from which film positions were filled was much smaller. This allowed for higher probabilities of stardom for its participants, which was quite intoxicating for entertainers.

The mediavision newscaster gave more details regarding the next town council meeting; this one emphasized investment opportunities. Maktan pointed her remote control at the large flatscreen and increased the volume. What caught her attention was the mention of the movie industry. Her Mu'mad loved movies and mediavision shows. And a lot of money exchanged hands inside the entertainment realm. Besides, Maktan had a civic duty, more like a civic charade, to keep her new city and country thriving . . . thriving for her son. Perhaps someday Mu'mad would use this industry to perpetuate his views and beliefs. Maktan put the remote control upon her coffee table and retrieved pen and paper. She waited for the newscaster to finish his spiel then jotted down the meeting details. It was time to get involved.

Far in the back corner of the historical Orpheum Symphony Hall, ironically the setting for many an entertainment production, sat Maktan. A panel of city officials sat upon the antique stage waiting for everyone to take their seats and settle down. Conversations amongst the crowd brimmed with excitement. Actors, writers, and directors occupied many a seat. Maktan recognized many of the famous faces. Like others, she was in awe. The mood in the room was electric; it was not every day one sat next to a movie idol to discuss the future of his or her country.

The new Canadians began to strategize. As had happened with those playing professional sports, salaries would not become inflated as they had been in the past. Compensation would be more reasonable and equitable. In this new film industry, the representatives decided productions would recognize each contribution more fairly. No longer would four to eight producers "sit" on a film only shelling out big bucks to a director here or an actor there. As a city, Vancouver would hire one producer, a director, and crew only after they had chosen a writer's fabulous script and fit the appropriate actors to the project. Writers would stay involved, having an active say in the visual birth of their literary efforts. Each production would be collaborative. The city's film industry would profit, or fail, as a collective entity. Fairness would bring more happiness, and much of the cutthroat past would die amongst the ashes of the old world. Art would return as the purpose of film, mediavision, and Internet webisodes.

A buzz reverberated about the city's attendees. Maktan listened with intent. Ideas for new projects were suddenly unleashed on the crowd. Everyone seemed eager to begin, right away. Yet they needed that dreaded up-front compensatory consideration to begin principal photography. That is when some of the "A-list" actors, directors, writers, and producers entered the picture. After all, they could not let their profession perish. Donations were encouraged and would remain anonymous. Financial influence would not become a factor when making decisions. The meeting was then adjourned. Pockets of celebrities chatted enthusiastically with exaggerated gestures. Uncharacteristically, for this town council meeting there was resolution. Envelopes containing considerable contributions were handed to the council members. Although the dynamics were now solely domestic, instead of international, the entertainment magnates breathed life back into their dying industry. Eyes affixed to two famous actors, a mesmerized Maktan reached inside her purse and retrieved her chequebook.

Deek's Cape Town

Luckily, the large cats had been unsuccessful in their pursuit of Deek and Sly. With swollen, tender underbellies, the lionesses were obviously protecting newborn cubs. Shaken from the experience, the men took another path to their new homes.

Evermore cautious, the Lompoc group finished their residence search fully armed. Thankfully, neither animals nor people were injured in the process. With homes chosen and appreciation at an all-time high, not surprisingly there were very few disputes. Each family recorded their names in the new Cape Town registry for proof of ownership. For almost everyone this was the first time in their lives they had ever owned property. After the last signature, the New African crowd stood and applauded Captain Oswald, Deek, Sly, and the N.Z. naval crew. Bottles of champagne were popped open and the celebrating began. Dampened eyes, every one of them, the new Cape Town citizens basked in euphoria. Contentment was a part of their lives for probably the first time in their troubled existence.

It had not taken long for all healthy citizens to get busy cleaning up their new township. Many compact utility vehicles, mostly skid-steer loaders, were brought ashore from the *Antarctica III*. These vehicles were imperative for removing the countless corpses. For the weeks that followed, Captain Oswald and crew, some recruited Dutch sailors, and the Lompoc family worked diligently to remove the debris and destruction, and dispose of the dead. Cape Town citizens' fear and suspicion of their saviours was well in the past. Innocently and naturally friendships had developed, replacing frustration and pessimism with laughter and singing.

When all was restored to an acceptable condition, the ex-Reaper islanders unpacked what few belongings they possessed and enjoyed getting settled. These Cape Town inhabitants worked diplomatically to decorate their homes with beautifully restored African artwork and furniture. No one practised aggression, no one complained. They found happiness in taking turns making each person's living quarters the best it could be. There was true New African pride. Plans were then laid out to get businesses started and ignite their community globally.

At the final town meeting, the last day before the foreigners left, the townsfolk gathered for crucial guideline and survival instructions. All were in attendance. Well-rested eyes fell upon Deek, who updated everyone on New Zealand and Nederland's future global efforts. Talk included a proposed, unified currency; the restoration of EyeNet service, mediavision, and the Internet; the continuation and implementation of solar-energized electricity, and water filtration; and the import of aquatic and terrain hovercrafts, as well as the future, local production of these vehicles. Deek assured the New Africans that mirrored efforts would take place for Africa, with aid primarily from New Zealand. Health-wise, Deek reviewed the necessary procedures to eliminate the ever-present radiation that had hitchhiked upon the winds and settled in every corner of their ash-laden city. If the New Zealand-made compound, RDXM, was used diligently, the New Africans should be able to nullify any radiation affecting their food and water.

With new discoveries implemented from N.Z.'s "think tank" an improved RDXM had emerged, which significantly reduced radiation fatalities. Without the protection of biospheric living, Cape Town citizens were told they would most undoubtedly breathe contaminated air and drink tainted water for a very long time but would have the wherewithal to eliminate any sprouting cancerous cells. Captain Oswald's men had given them aura scanners, which would identify any abnormalities. If cancer did germinate within the New Africans, they had cancer-fighting injections to administer. Beyond that, if illness won the battle, the inflicted would travel to New Zealand where stem cell rejuvenation would restore the individuals' health.

Captain Oswald took the podium after Deek. He informed his new acquaintances that New Zealand was in full support of their new community. They would return eventually with volunteers to assist the New Africans in building a protective dome over Cape Town. In addition, import/export activities would be negotiated and scheduled. Finally, he informed the crowd that Deek would travel with them to New Zealand for ideas to keep his citizens safe and have the best of the best. Captain Oswald said when Deek returned, New Zealand and Dutch scientists, researchers, and engineers would come as well to spend time in New Africa and share ideas, educate, and improve living conditions.

Before the visitors gathered to leave, Deek thanked them, calling them his new brothers. Then in front of the entire Cape Town Township, Deek signed a treaty between New Zealand, Canada, Nederland, and New Africa. Captain Oswald explained it was the same deal initially offered and executed with the Dutch and would be presented to the Canadians soon enough. These four regions would rebuild a peaceful, enriched life and an environment where these ex-Reaper islanders would never have to feel inferior to anyone, again. Fresh starts were securely in place, all equal players in a global arena.

Aerin & Cameron

Hours, days, and finally months ticked by and still Aerin and Cameron travelled different paths; their separation had shocked everyone. While their relationship had stagnated, the university thrived. Students from all surviving parts of the world, including New Africa, flocked to one of the leading intellectual institutions. Unable to comprehend Aerin's spiritual methods, Cameron had invested all of his time in expanding SNZU. The student body kept him young at heart as he fed off their youthful, hopeful energy. To have one's entire future a blank slate was intoxicating. What others did not know was amid his excessive work hours, Cameron spent much time each day secretly observing Aerin's plight. Those close to her believed in her visions. Those converted by her, loved her more. It was all too intangible for Cameron, though. He was not raised around a bunch of psychic hocus-pocus. Yet the new generations entering SNZU seemed to accept, without difficulty, this ethereal world Aerin understood. It was just another component of their everyday lives. Cameron was envious. The young possessed such faith and confidence. Many knew where they were headed without fear, even in this once-blistered world where others had lost direction and hope. Most importantly, these new world warriors loved their Dr. Aerin; in fact, they worshipped her. "Open your eyes, Cameron," he told himself. "Rewire your thinking. So many youthful minds cannot all be wrong." That is why, when approached by the SNZU student council demanding they have Dr. Aerin speak at their first graduation ceremony, Cameron gave little resistance.

AT THE PODIUM, AERIN SPOKE clearly with much conviction. Each word had been carefully chosen. After all, she was sending these graduates into the world with a hefty, thought-provoking shove. What they did with her challenges would be a testament to their "no bullshit" approach to life.

All eyes were locked upon Aerin during her entire speech. These seniors had attended other universities before WWIV and only needed a final year to complete their degrees. They were a small group but worldly and mature for their ages. Aerin approached the end of her oration. "Short-term gratification does not a future make. You know this."

A male voice bellowed from the student body. "Marry me, Dr. Aerin!"

With a wry smile, Aerin blew the young man a kiss when unexpectedly tender thoughts crashed against her vestigial heart. She found herself searching, unsuccessfully, for Cameron amongst the many faces before her. Although so much time had passed, that amorous wound was still raw. It quite possibly would never heal. No one had warned Aerin how painful love could be, and Cameron had cut deeply with his disbelieving, old-fashioned mentality. A "thinker" by nature, he had outsmarted himself by actually viewing life with conservative, outdated philosophies. Aerin had quickly adopted her "men beware" attitude with an unbending determination when Cameron had left her. What an oxymoron, the very men who professed to have superior intellects were just a pool of stunted analyzers. In such a shallow highbrow pond did they swim. Besides, it would be easy to know all in such a small, stagnant body of water. Confusion swirled about Aerin's heart. Such anger contradicted her enlightened approach to life. Unable to rise above these conflicted emotions, Aerin had buried herself in her work. There had been no time for frolicking about or ridiculous heart rushes; to this drug, Aerin was no longer addicted.

Aerin finally tuned in to the sound of her own voice. "You've sacrificed years of your lives so you can reach higher. We send you out into this battered world, your world, to live out your dreams . . . your destinies. Dare to make that future you've envisioned in your minds. There are no limits. Be happy with you. As the singer icon, Elton John, once said, 'I cannot bear successful people who are miserable.' Do not let negativity consume you.

"I speak for the older generations when I say our lives are now in your hands. We've all grown up with Jesus' words 'the meek shall inherit the Earth.' Well, historically New Zealand has collectively lived with this truth and pure intent. So, graduates, you've now inherited the Earth. What strides will you make? How will you leave your imprint on society? I have only one request. When hard times hit, question everything; conform to nonconformity . . . make us proud!" The graduating class stood and cheered. Tasselled hats flew high into the air.

"Aerin."

HER SKEPTICAL HEART STRUCK HARD in her protective chest. His deep Aussie voice was the only sound that could instantly cause that erratic insulin surge, dampening her palms with irritating perspiration. Aerin's heart raced with a wasted "fight or flight" impulse. Slowly, she turned to face her amorous attacker.

"Cameron." Aerin nibbled at a fingernail.

"That was a corker of a speech. The students loved it. They sure admire, actually, worship you, Aerin."

"I meant what I said, they are our future."

"Well, they were listening . . . so inspired."

"I'm glad someone sees the good I'm trying to perpetuate."

"It is not that we, I, do not see it. Some of us whackers are hard-headed and take longer to understand a more expanded version of 'good.'"

"Is this your attempt at an apology, Cameron?" Aerin could feel anger welling up inside her.

"Pretty pitiful?"

"And if you were me, would you slap yourself across the face for taking so long to approach me, maybe spit in your face for being so stubborn? Maybe shout that your love has expired and that you wouldn't dare attach yourself to a maybe? Because that's what you are, Cameron, a maybe. You're one of those predictable men who don't believe in anything they can't touch. You're just a maybe. So what is it, Cameron, what do you suggest I do?"

Aerin turned to walk toward the University parking lot. With heightened anger and confusion, she reeled around once more. "What incredible divine imposter informed you that you were more special, more intelligent than the rest of mankind?" A large lump swelled in her throat. "Why did you take so long?" Tears pushed to get out. "Why did you leave me?"

"Because I am stupid!" He stared at Aerin, not sure what to say. "I am so sorry."

A tear escaped down Aerin's cheek. "Cameron, I know spirituality is hard to understand. And I don't have all the answers." Aerin held her hands over her face. She spoke through sobs. "I'm just a girl standing before you with a broken heart."

With a swift motion, Cameron grabbed Aerin and planted his lips against hers. Aerin's body resisted, but her lips did not. It was their defining embrace: that moment when words could not possibly describe what was happening collectively within the two lovers' hearts. Their lips separated. Cameron grabbed the back of Aerin's head and gently held her wet face to his chest.

"I am an incurable jackass . . . but I am your jackass, nonetheless. I have missed you so."

"Temptation is a sharpened sword, Cameron. How do I know your mind will stay open to new ideas?"

"Because I have been humbled, Aerin. It took me forever to realize that just because they are my beliefs does not automatically make them right. I am a reformed intellectual with a heart that has been in a constant state of unrest since that confusing, horrible night so many months ago."

Cameron released Aerin's head. She looked up at him with dampened eyes. "I fight so much ignorance. Every day people argue about, struggle with, and curse spirituality. I can't have that energy-sucking, heart-breaking behaviour coming from my man . . . my husband. His wings have to be enormous enough for me to crawl under. I have to have a safe place to fall, Cameron, always."

"I am that bloke now, Aerin."

"Are you?"

"Quite right."

"How can I be sure? You once asked me the question regarding dark souls. What if I told you I wished these destructive individuals recycled? What if I told you I wished they would never take another breath?"

"I would say—"

"In your language, I wish them cactus, Cameron . . . dead, never to return. If given the chance, I would send them back to God in a split second only to be inserted into some poor unsuspecting woman's womb for another chance. You see God *never* gives up on us, Cameron. Yes, he even loves his precious, narcissistic psychopaths. What do you say to all of that? That has to be too intangible for you." Aerin raised a trembling hand and tore into a ragged fingernail.

"I am still here, standing before you with opened ears, mind, and heart, Dear Wife. Do you see me running? Do you see me gasping with disgust? Disbelief? I get it, Aerin. There is a bigger world out there, one I am not fully acquainted with. Have a little patience." Cameron's hands had moved to his hips. His face was flushed with frustration, desperation. He took a very deep breath then exhaled slowly. "I get it, Aerin, I get you. I am ready to be the husband you deserve." Cameron gently pulled Aerin's hand free from her nail biting and placed a feathery kiss upon his wife's lips.

After a prolonged hug, Aerin's body finally relaxed. She whispered. "I love you."

Kozlov

Sasha was maturing, nicely. She no longer resisted sinking roots in Nederland—how lovingly resilient children were. Luckily for Kozlov, Sasha had not stayed angry with her father for long after discovering his involvement in WWIV and the annihilation of her Russian friends. Painful as it was, Kozlov endured the cold shoulders of his wife and in-laws for the good part of a year following WWIV. A mundane existence set in: no highs, no lows. Only Sasha, with her unfaltering loyalty, had stayed by his side. She kept his life exciting, seeing the new world through her *tween* eyes. Kozlov remained positive with a loving spirit. With an overabundance of time on his hands, Kozlov spent many hours examining and re-examining his KGB antics. How many families had he ripped apart? How many daughters like Sasha had suffered by his hand? Day after day, Kozlov listened to his screaming conscience. His wife had been right in her hatred of him. The spy industry put country first, family second, and Kozlov had been a top agent. During his career, he never wavered. For the past three-and-a-half years, post WWIV, Kozlov had been forced to face his daily reflection in the mirror with contempt.

In need of absolution, Kozlov had spilled his past deeds to his wife. What did it matter? Russia was dead. There would be no assassins hunting him down for betraying KGB secrets. Years of loneliness, except for his teenaged daughter's love, had been his punishment for his KGB brutalities. Kozlov had embraced his chastisement by doing everything in his power to please his wife with no expectations of forgiveness. Then, one winter morning, Kozlov noticed a shift in his wife's demeanour. Gradually the iciness in his bedroom had unexpectedly thawed. Kozlov sprung alive with encouragement, resorting to every romantic cliché imaginable. Finally, Kozlov's wife showed signs of melting her frigid disdain.

Her glacial heart had warmed with flickering memories of the man she had fallen in love with years ago. It was easy for her to embrace those forgotten feelings so easily frozen in time right after the war. She had missed him, missed them. Thanks to the example set by her daughter Sasha, Kozlov's wife had learned to forgive and how to live again. Albeit it took several years, amnesty was in the air.

The Kozlovs were a family, once again. Worldly KGB affairs were not the issues at hand anymore. A new challenge plagued Kozlov, however. Sasha and her gaggle of girlfriends had discovered a more interesting topic aside from their once-revered dollies: boys. And Kozlov's concerns were much greater than the average parental paranoia brought on by a daughter's puberty. With the slender legs of a fine colt, Sasha had long since outgrown her awkward stage. These days she walked with the assurance of a thoroughbred. Kozlov knew his battles were just beginning with his maturing teenager and it scared the hell out of him. Sasha's long flowing platinum-blonde hair caught many an eye, and not only the eyes of boys her age. What disturbed Kozlov the most was his daughter and her friends seemed to prefer the older teenagers. With their facial hair, tattoos, piercings, and sexual awareness, these young men had every attribute a father despised. How had his innocent Sasha become so bored with the boys her age and so enamoured with the teens clearly headed for trouble? How had his baby girl become a woman overnight? Kozlov was petrified.

Deek

Ash swirled behind the massive JetAir New Zealand flashjet as it hit the Cape Town airstrip. Cheers erupted from the New Africans who waited inside the terminal. Two-and-a-half years had passed since Captain Oswald and the *Antarctica III* had said their goodbyes. In preparation for their friends' arrival, the New Africans had long since scoured the abandoned Cape Town airport. Everyone had buzzed with excitement as they scrubbed and sanitized the terminal. They were elated with the reestablishment of air travel. Long-awaited assistance from powerful scientists and doctors kept the New Africans highly motivated. They were given the support necessary to improve even further everyone's standard of living. Deek, New Africa's elected Prime Minister, had coordinated with the New Zealand government for another small group of New African young adults to make the return trip to Christchurch then on to Kaikoura. This apprehensive, yet excited, new batch of students had been accepted at SNZU. Upon completion of their education, these pupils would return to their country as innovators, and later, professors of the new Cape Town University that was almost completed. Once established, young people from Nederland, Canada, and New Zealand's universities would have exchange student opportunities. For everyone there were no limits. Clearly, a life of crime had become an obsolete option for the New Africans.

In a high-rise penthouse office suite, Deek paced.

Much had changed inside him. Every effort to find Lourdes had failed, yet he refused to believe she was dead. He was despondent. There never seemed to be enough people and hours in the day to accomplish what was needed to keep his city running smoothly. Equipped with an unfaltering sense of justice and genuine love of his community, Deek strived daily to spread fairness and hopefully instil happiness like an honourable parent. Unfortunately, Deek was overwhelmed. He did not possess expertise in governmental matters. While at university Deek had majored in pre-Med, and of course football, not political science or economics. Through the glassed wall of his enormous office, Deek peered at the peaceful ocean. He craved his old life, football, and most importantly Lourdes. Not that Deek was ungrateful to be off Reaper Island, but his current luxurious lifestyle had switched his thoughts from daily survival to more complicated desires. These needs brought with them a dose of viral disappointment. Deek sighed and continued to pace.

During his walk to join the others in the spacious conference room, Deek played his unwavering plans over in his head. His lifeless eyes met the eager faces seated before him. Deek's unwelcoming expression put his fellow representatives on edge. They sensed something was amiss.

"Hello, everyone."

"Deek, sir."

"Prime Minister."

"Sir."

"Well, we are looking quite happy this afternoon."

"Deek, we've finalized orders of our new product from New Zealand and Nederland for our traditional, colourful dresses. We're working on Canada. Actually, we have more work than we can handle."

"Those *dirhas?*"

"Yes, the ones we're wearing. The long tunic is the same, but we've altered the flap; it's more decorative. Deek, you should see the other colour patterns we've created too, they are quite fantastic. We've captured the eyes of the younger generations."

"They're really beautiful. Nicely done. Looks as though we have some rejoicing to do."

"Deek, yo' look like shit, what's up?"

"Never could fool you, could I, Sly? Maybe we should chat before Prime Minister Oswald and our Kiwi comrades arrive. I understand their plane has landed. Exciting times. You all know I love our country and am committed to making it better."

"But?"

"But, well, I truly feel I'm a mediocre candidate to lead our country. Cape Town deserves better. I've searched my heart and I can honestly say I do not want to be prime minister. I'm still an American at heart."

"So we'll change yur title ta president and implement a U.S. constitution, College Boy."

"Bless you, Sly, but that's not the problem. I have pontificated voraciously about everyone following his or her dreams, yet I feel like a hypocrite. Bottom line is I haven't been following mine. There is a growing emptiness inside. I feel trapped. Therefore, I'm standing before you to submit my resignation and in the same breath announce tryouts for Cape Town's new football team. I'm starting an International Football League. I want to play ball."

"College Boy, I want ta be twenty years old again, but dat ain't happenin'."

"With your permission I'd like to propose an IFL to the New Zealanders."

"Deek!"

"Sir!"

"Just listen. Within each country, there could be say eight to ten teams. Then we could have a championship playoff with the winner of New Africa, Canada, New Zealand, and Nederland."

"So we're going to repeat inflated salaries and an over-emphasis regarding athletics?"

"Yeah, what's that all about?" An argument broke out amongst the women. Deek tried several times to interrupt, but all continued to talk over one another, speaking louder and louder.

Deek pounded a fist on the conference table. "Tess! Chandra! Ladies, a little decorum please." Everyone stopped. "You are diplomats, representatives of our New Africa. Is it asking too much to have you drop the ghetto attitude? Do you realize how ridiculously you are acting? May I remind you about ego and the unconscious mind? Eloquence and sophistication is easily learned and a nice habit to maintain. Our ancestors didn't talk like that. Be the impressive women I know you to be. You have had disagreements with other countries' representatives, and you have communicated with them without shouting and bickering. Can you repeat that wisdom instead of riding on raw emotions with one another? Let's nod those heads up and down with understanding, drop the side-to-side head jerks and the wagging fingers in each other's faces. Trying to be fierce or getting one-up on your neighbour is so very passé. Agreed?"

"Oh no, you didn't just call us ghetto bitches, Deek."

"Oh, I most certainly did." Everyone laughed.

Deek put a hand on his hip and started imitating the women, his head juking and jiving about. The women especially enjoyed a good laugh at Deek's accurate mimicry. It was so much easier to communicate with the New Africans these days since they had put into practice an egoless world. Sure they regressed occasionally, who didn't?

"Okay, Mr. Fancy-Pants President, who taught you such grace and manners?"

Suddenly Deek broke into a thick southern accent. "Well, ya'll, my Mama didn't wont her li'l man actin' simple, ya' know?"

Again, laughter filled the room. Even Sly joined the playful commotion.

When everyone finally calmed down, Chandra spoke with class and diplomacy. "Deek, we have a chance to form an existence that values all areas of life. I personally don't want our youth thinking their only future is football or eventually basketball and other sports. That is all my boys used to live for pre-war, and I know now they missed out on so, so much."

"Chandra, I'm not doing this to try and regain any wealth. That was always just a byproduct of my sport. Besides, I have everything I need, except my lovely wife. I'm doing this because I love the game. I love the feel of the soft leather when it drops into my hands then spins against my fingertips . . . love the feel of my leg muscles as I dodge multiple tacklers and break free toward the end zone. I play those feelings over and over in my head every night. God, I love that sport. I'm doing this because I love football, Chandra. I mean that." With that, Deek handed his resignation to Sly.

"I can't take this, College Boy. Why can't yo' do both, be our president and play ball?"

"How? I preach to all of our townsfolk, especially the young ones, about following their dreams. My destiny is elsewhere; I feel it in my bones." A hush came over the group. Looks were exchanged between clusters in the back of the room. Deek was suspicious. "Okay what's brewing, folks?"

"Well, Deek, this is as good a time as any to inform you that a portion of us plan to ask Prime Minister Oswald if his *Antarctica III* and crew would be willing to take us home . . . to America."

"Chandra, seriously? Wow, I didn't see that one coming."

"Don't get me wrong; we love New Africa. And we will keep roots here, but we still feel American deep down, as you said. Why not inhabit the United States amidst proper circumstances and build the country the way we are building New Africa?"

"Are you sure?"

"We've discussed this ad nauseam . . . we're sure. Of course, we will need help from our friends in New Zealand, Nederland, and especially Canada. That's why we have picked the Seattle area. If it's impossible, we can always return to New Africa, our second home."

"I'm speechless. Wow. What can I say? I'm impressed with your convictions and support your decision."

"Deek, back to your dreams; I think I speak for the entire group. You must follow your heart. We will be fine in New Africa and America. As long as your IFL doesn't turn our youth into a bunch of sports-crazed, arrogant, brain-dead bores."

"Not a chance, Chandra. And I'll try and not take that last statement as a direct insult." Deek laughed. A heaviness stepped off Deek's enormous shoulders. "I'm really proud of all of you . . . extremely proud."

A knock sounded on one of the thick double doors. Oswald and five of his governmental officials entered the conference room.

With his soothing New Zealand accent, Captain Oswald said, "Deek, it's so good to see you, mate." Enthusiastically, he grabbed Deek's hand. "And Sly, great to see you looking so well."

"Captain, or should I say, Prime Minister, I think I speak for our group when I say we are thrilled to have you."

"Thank you, Deek, we have much to share."

"As do we, sir, as do we."

Justin

Excessively stressful lives kept Aerin and Cameron childless. After five years, when both resigned to the fact they might never be parents, a precious seed began germinating inside Aerin. Always a workhorse, Dr. Aerin's pregnancy was not discovered until her fifth month. Servicing her many patients and continually reforming troubled souls, Aerin could not find enough hours in the day. Cameron surprised her with meals at the hospital. Sandwiches with a slice of romantic sense of humour kept Aerin balanced. To bite into her lunch and pull out a piece of paper with Cameron's latest sentiments brought laughter to Aerin, such an effective stress release. He did anything to get his wife to eat. Massages and tenderness at home allowed Cameron to entice Aerin into much-needed slumber. Daily the South Island's power couple grew deeper and deeper in love. And at the end of nine months, they had tangible proof of their loving union.

Justin was every bit as beautiful as his parents. Olive skin from Aerin's side of the family only accentuated the baby's already penetrating sea-foam green eyes. The Ermani family were elated. Long fingers and feet were strong indicators their new addition would be blessed as well with the Thorpes' wonderful height. Justin, from day one, seemed to have it all: intelligence and an unfaltering sensitivity. Not a bit spoiled or headstrong, Justin's determination exuded nothing but a soft-spoken strength. Surrounded by excessive love and Cameron's playful sense of humour, Justin had nothing to accomplish except grow and be happy. Being the firstborn child of the Ermani siblings, he was surrounded with lots of willing babysitters.

Uncle Tanid had found love, again. A stunning Kaikouran of Maori descent had captured his eye while working at a local, overcrowded orphanage. Justin loved Hauku's *tā moko*, traditional tattoos of blue lips and Maori chin art. Hauku, meaning "dew" in Maori, was just that, a fresh start to Tanid's every day. Aerin was sure it was only a matter of time before Hauku became her beloved sister-in-law. And Hauku was so good with Justin. He released a squeal every time she greeted him with the traditional Maori greeting of *hongi*, touching her nose and forehead gently against Justin's. Hauku gently whispered a welcome in Justin's tiny ear. "*Tena koe*, my little man." Immediately, he wriggled with glee and grabbed at Hauku's chin tattoo with his pudgy, baby fingers.

With Aerin and Cameron's busy schedules, Justin spent his time away from his parents, either at the orphanage with Uncle Tanid and Hauku, in the research lab at the South Peninsula "Think Tank" with Uncles Balic and Rami, or at the Ermani/Whibley compound with grandparents Saroya and Ari. A profusion of love surrounded Justin's childhood.

Maktan

Mu'mad continued to breeze through public school. The transition from private to public in his very early years had been a seamless, effortless move. A natural born leader, Mu'mad was the favourite of his elementary school classmates and the school administration. Humble, yet intelligent and successful in every pursuit, Mu'mad was never resented for his excellent grades. More freedom was his reward. Mu'mad tried every aspect of life and with each experience his wisdom grew.

With maternal pride, Maktan watched her rare gem shine brighter. He was turning into a fine boy. Her life now was much different from her earlier days in the Middle East. Daily life was filled with many comforts. There was an obscene abundance of material things; things that Allah most assuredly found appalling. The only worries Mu'mad's mother carried was the possible seduction these *things* had on her son. He seemed to internalize the stories of his father, but then Maktan observed Mu'mad's increasing dependency on Western ways, especially technology. Were all those electronic gadgets, brainwashing mediavision shows, and warping feature films assisting the Islam plight or hindering it? If only her son truly knew where they used to live, how she had struggled to make his life better.

Like a cockroach, Mu'mad's mother had crawled from a cave. At least that was how the wretched Americans had described Middle Easterners in their many textbooks. Was it any wonder the spoiled, obese, vile Westerners were loathed worldwide? Had any of the judgmental infidels ever travelled to the Far and Middle East? Similar to the ancient Romans, the Americans led the world for many years. However, they started believing their own deceptive propaganda and gradually their culture began to implode. The Americans proved to be no exception. Greed bred more greed and violence soon followed. Without notice, the structure seemed to crumble as they viciously turned on one another, destroying the very culture their country worked so hard to build.

Questions about the father of Maktan's child were increasing in frequency lately. The other Muslim mothers badgered her. Snide remarks helped this insignificant lot feel somehow superior. Even after telling the curious crowd of women that she had been gang raped shortly after Mu'mad's birth, there was very little sympathy for her struggles. There was always another victim whose story was much more distressing. Devoid of pity, this tough pack of females were harder on one another than the men who continually inflicted physical and sexual abuse upon them. Emotional scars took longer to heal. Their only safe haven was inside their heads, not even their hearts were there for them. Ever since childhood, these women's souls had long since died. The only love Maktan felt was for her gorgeous son, who was not a product of violent rape, quite the opposite actually. She had been honoured to give herself to such a monumental man. However, this information would not be revealed until her child was grown and in his powerful position. Maktan could not risk herself or her precious son being murdered. Condemnation by her female peers made it easier to abandon the remnants of her true past. Like non-stick Teflon, Maktan let the hurtful comments slide off her without a fuss. Only when she was alone in her bedroom at night was she unable to fight off the stinging remarks. Many a night Maktan cried herself to sleep. She hated those cruel women. By morning, though, she reminded herself of her earlier heroics. Her past feats kept her going.

Truth be told, she *had* crawled from a cave like a cockroach. Under the pretence that Maktan was headed for the town market, she fled without the slightest glance in her direction. Instead of carrying out domestic duties, she and her bundled son were to meet a leader from a faraway prominent mosque. He was the very man who had hidden her in the Pakistani caves, a henchman of her great husband. Her life held temporary importance. However, when her husband was killed her self-worth went to the grave with him. In the days that followed his passing, more and more of the soldiers ignored her presence. After all, she was just their previous master's whore. What fools they had been. Tucked neatly away in a Luxembourg bank were millions of dollars, in her name. It had been such a surprise when her husband's closest friend had contacted her after months of silence. The man was to ensure Maktan and Mu'mad's safe passage to Syria. Some of these men knew the rumours were true about her son's lineage. What these helpful men did not suspect was Maktan knew their long-term plans did not include her. And more importantly, what they did not know was she held bigger plans for her child.

Many times, she retold her story within her head. If only she could safely shove the truth in the faces of those shallow-minded Muslim bitches. How good that would feel.

Chrysalis Society

"BROTHERS AND SISTERS FOR LIFE" was their motto. This was easy at first, since membership consisted of Aerin, Tanid, Balic, Rami, and Cameron. Gradually Ahmed, Aerin's attacker who brought about her near-death experience, became an inductee into their secret society. However, this was not a "Skull and Bones" environment driven by illusions of grandeur and superiority, nor was there a debilitating initiation. There were no confessions by the participants to be strategically used as blackmail in the future. This secret society was based on the love of God, Allah, Buddha, or whatever deity one believed in. No religion carried the ultimate truth. There was virtue in every form of worship, each with a different way to pay homage to one's ethereal caretaker. This clandestine society would not focus on limited views driven by man's doctrinal "do's and don'ts." Their next recruits were the world leaders, that is, depending on open-mindedness.

Aerin sat with Tanid and Cameron. "How are we going to convince the Prime Minister our organization isn't like the old secret societies, initially inspired by a spiritual purity only to sink to the lowest depths of greed, power mongering, and corruption?"

Tanid gave Cameron a quick look. "Isn't that how we are starting out? Aren't we heading for the same trap? Aerin, if our secret society is for the betterment of humankind, why do we feel the need to be so cryptic?"

"Seriously?"

"Your brother is spot on, Aerin. If we are doing the right and moral thing, why hide it?"

"Because, my two brainiacs, the human race isn't ready for our cleansing process. You know the general public would view us as evil, on par with the terrorists we convert, because of their fear and bigotry. Do we really want to take a backward step and fight such spiritual inexperience and prejudices?"

"No, but Oswald will surely challenge you, Aerin. And I think his argument will be just as compelling as yours."

"Cameron, if I can convince the likes of you, I can easily sway the prime minister. Besides, where we are united in the divine white light of the Holy Spirit we are ever stronger."

"I will try and not take that as an insult, Love."

Aerin grinned. "Take it however you like. You were a tough sell, my dear husband. If Oswald proves to be more dogged than you, we'll simply dump his butt into the machine and let God take over."

"You are scary for such a little Sheila."

To Aerin's delight, Prime Minister Oswald seemed very eager to inspect her group's handling procedures for terrorists. Any skepticism was well hidden.

"So, Prime Minister, I must begin by asking you how you feel about psychics?"

"Oh, I actually avoid supernatural discussions when they arise."

"Well, this is one situation where you cannot hide your beliefs."

"Dr. Aerin, I'm uncomfortable with that which I'm unable to see or prove."

"What if I can give you proof?"

"Then I'll analyze the facts and form an intelligent opinion."

Fully captivated by Aerin's near-death experience and spiritual beliefs, Prime Minister Oswald sat quietly, not sure how to react.

"Prime Minister, are you ready for your personal proof?"

"I'm not going to lie to you, the evidence is going to have to be quite fantastic or—"

"Trust me, it will be. Let's get started." Aerin sat in front of Oswald, grabbed his hands, and closed her eyes. For a brief moment, everyone was silent. Aerin opened her eyes and dropped his hands. "These things may be difficult to hear, so if you'll refrain from interrupting me, I would appreciate it."

"Fair enough."

"When you were a tiny boy you saw your father beat your mother unconscious and this happened often. You were wearing flannel fish; no, ah, they were dolphin pyjamas. Your home was quite large and beautiful, yet you hated it. You felt guilty when growing up because you wished you had told someone about the beatings. A letter . . . you wrote a letter when you got older. While walking it to the police station your father stopped you. Again, you felt guilty for not protecting your mother and for wanting to tattle on your father. Oswald, please understand your father wasn't right in the head. When he died, which you were relieved about, he crossed over right away. In fact, your mother was there to guide him to the light. He was cocooned for a time to get his mind healed on the other side, which I will call Home. They, your Earthly parents, want me to tell you they love you, they are very happy and to please release your guilt and any hatred you may be harbouring toward your father."

Aerin finally focused on the Prime Minister. Tears streamed down his pale face. "How can you possibly know those things?"

"Please, I have more."

"Aerin, I don't need—"

"This isn't for you; it's for your loved ones. And I can't have any doubts. Oswald, you feel guilty for leaving your wife Hannah alone for much of your married life. She went home to Australia to spend time with her family because she was lonely. She took your four-year-old son, Nathan, with her. They did not suffer when the bombs hit Sydney. The first year after the birth of Nathan you resented his constant neediness. He says he understands. He loves you and enjoys being on the submarine with you and your mates." Aerin laughed. "Nathan says he loves that you have kept Carrot his stuffed, floppy-eared bunny. Lastly, your wife wants you to know she is not upset about passing. She's with you often. Hannah knows you miss her fresh cut flowers and rhubarb pie. And she loves that you carry with you always the four-leaf clover necklace you bought her after one year of dating."

"Aerin, please."

"Oswald, I have a bit more to share so you can truly begin to heal. None of us here has secrets from one another. I know that you thought about suicide often when aboard the *Antarctica III*; all colour had drained from your life. Every morning when you awoke you felt numb and calloused. No one or nothing brought you hope. Until . . . until you stumbled upon Deek's group. Those wonderful, struggling New Africans put everything in perspective. They saved your life actually."

The prime minister cried. Tanid handed him a box of

tissues. "We've all been through this, sir. Aerin surprised, and equally upset, me when she informed me my fiancé had died during the Seattle bombings. She knew things I'd never shared with anyone."

"Same here, Prime Minister."

"Please, call me Oswald."

"Oswald, sir, the other side, or Home, is quite real. Aerin is simply our spiritual conduit." Balic smiled. Rami nodded in agreement.

"I feel as though my heart has been ripped from a deep sleep."

"I have a lot of books you can read, sir, Oswald. It helped me a lot in the beginning."

Tanid patted the prime minister on the back. Oswald wiped the tears from his face and thereafter sat a bit taller.

"Aerin, this goes against everything I believe in. I was raised in a devout Catholic household."

"So that makes the truths untrue?"

"My mother—"

"Yes, your mother was a love. She was nurturing and everything good in your life, Oswald. How could such a beautiful, loving woman be wrong? Please don't feel ashamed, Oswald, all children are brainwashed to an extent by their parents and society. You're feeling guilty that if you agree with what I'm telling you, you're somehow betraying your mother."

"Well, yes. But there's more . . . what about the Bible? My mother read it to me daily."

"Man wrote the Bible, imperfect individuals, as we all are, whose recollections of one-hundred-year-old events were interpreted and reinterpreted. The Bible was edited (words added to and deleted from) countless times. Eons ago, Constantine extracted and eliminated chapters on reincarnation as well as the suppression of the feminine principle, Mother God. One man, Oswald, changed an entire religious faction. Don't you think there were others as well?"

"Sure, but—"

"Use those analytical skills of yours. You remember the documents they found in the Vatican. Jesus didn't really die on the cross. It was a conspiracy. Oswald, I'm trying to ease you into a higher enlightenment. The brutal truth is there is no devil, Hell is right here on Earth. Mary Magdalene was not a whore; she actually came from a wealthy family. And Judas was chosen to play the role of traitor because Jesus could trust no one else to do so when playing out his death-and-ascension-to-Heaven conspiracy. Judas has been vilified wrongly for centuries just as Mary Magdalene has been judged harshly as some tramp because she refused to marry the man her domineering father had chosen for her. Satan was man's fabrication to scare the crap out of Christians hoping they would behave and attend church. Those are the cold hard facts. Mother and Father God love us, all of us. Why would they punish and manipulate? Oswald, burrow deep into your heart. You know I speak the truth."

"But Aerin, how can anyone prove those claims?"

"Yet you believe in the Bible, with blind faith?"

"It is what I was raised on."

"There is nothing wrong with your beliefs, Oswald. I'm simply asking for you to keep an open mind. We're all children of God like Jesus. And Mother and Father God want us to seek knowledge and love one another; that is all. It doesn't matter how you go about that. Oswald, for a brief moment, just entertain the idea that your beliefs might not all be correct. That's all I ask."

"I can do that. But let's discuss all this secrecy. This group you have formed appears to be based on an elitist attitude."

"Now that can't be further from the truth. We don't congregate to discuss world domination and we didn't pool a bunch of wealthy, powerful members steeped in politics and global influence. Our group emphasis isn't to manipulate worldwide epidemics, energy crises, or wars as secret societies have done in the past. We don't take oaths, have penalties for breaking these promises, or disseminate falsehoods to keep the general public in the dark or advance personal superiority."

"Then why are we here today? What is your organization's purpose?"

"I'm glad you asked. Our purest of intentions are to assist individuals in understanding how to live together peacefully."

"That's all?"

"That's all, Oswald. Where there is much confusion, we intervene. Nothing is forced upon a troubled soul except for them to witness another perspective. Each has free will in how he or she uses that knowledge."

"Well, there is no doubt I want to be a part of your cause. However, I reserve the right to be skeptical."

Aerin shot Cameron a glance. "Skepticism is expected."

"Let's proceed then."

"Take a deep breath and open your mind. What we have to show you in the cellar will startle you. Please don't cast judgment until the entire process is complete. And before we go we need for you to sign a release that states none of us can be arrested after what you are about to see." Aerin handed Oswald some forms.

Oswald held the documents and searched for deceit in each participant's eyes. His gaze moved from Rami, Balic, Tanid, Ahmed, and Cameron then to Aerin. He saw no deception. "After all that you've told me, Aerin, I'll sign anything you want." Tanid handed Oswald a pen.

"We are witnessing a very drastic global metamorphosis. These are exciting times. We have a chance to create a world with the heart as its driving force instead of the brain. It's not a coincidence that our younger generations seem to understand gentleness is not a weakness, quite the opposite. Sorry, Oswald, I'm rambling."

"And I'm listening, Aerin." Oswald signed the papers.

Aerin gave a regal nod. "Welcome to Chrysalis."

Deek

"IFL? WHY WOULD WE WANT a gridiron league? After all those years, this is back on the table? We successfully squelched the IFL proposal last time."

"Yes, ex-Prime Minister Jorgensen says it is art for art's sake. He really misses the sport. His argument is we've cut out the parasitic peripherals, agents, publicists, managers, and so on. The young these days know how to manage their careers, are quite business savvy. Our creative offspring have the ability now to publish their own books, produce their own compact discs, and manage their own athletic careers. No one is filling our youths' heads with negative constraints. No one is given the power to snuff out their blossoming careers. Greedy corporate types are a part of the past and that is why salaries are posted for everyone's viewing. These younger generations have a say in their pay scales. There's no way we will repeat the distorted world of professional athletes or movie stars. What's left, art or sport for sport's sake."

"I say we recruit Deek to the dark side, the All Blacks side. If given a chance, rugby could easily become one of New Africa's sports of choice again." Prime Minister Oswald called a verbal vote. The ayes won, it was unanimous. Deek would be invited to New Zealand. "Now, Nina and Mickey, you have an issue with your neighbourhood waste manager?"

Mickey spoke first "Well, Zack isn't able to make payments on his property and he won't take any help from any of us, his mates and neighbours."

"We all know historically handouts don't work, Mickey. We rather appreciate everyone's contributions in our communities. As quickly as money flows to a talented individual, they've been brought up to give back. Extremes such as communism and capitalism didn't work in the past. We've learned that poverty is our disease not 'their' disease. If we have blokes struggling then we've failed as a community. We've taught our babies to reach for their dreams at a very young age. They've learned to grasp their destinies with positive attitudes and ultimately their futures have brought obtainable happiness. Pessimism seems to be a dwindling part of the past thankfully. In turn, resentment and poverty should be extinct. No longer do we have members of our society that choose to do nothing. Slovenly behaviour is 'uncool' with our young nowadays. We've discovered the key to success. Blokes no longer accept handouts but are willing to work for their futures. You all know this. What needs to happen is you need to have a neighbourhood meeting and readjust Zack's fees. Obviously, he'll need more money than other waste managers do in order to live in your upscale neighbourhood. Don't be greedy, mate, let your comrades judge his pay. Diplomacy will keep justice intact. Make it fair."

"Yeah, that'd be right. Looks as though we also need to bump up the salaries for our pool and lawn manicurists as well. This is an easy fix, we'll take care of it."

"Next order of business? We have a dispute regarding excessive celebration . . . unrelenting noises?"

"Yes, Prime Minister, they continue to ignore our holidays and try to force theirs upon us."

"How are they forcing theirs upon you?"

"The noise, the decorations. They are being, well, defiant. They should follow our traditions."

"Are you serious? Can you hear yourself? Do you like being with others who think like you, have similar religious beliefs or living like you? I take that as a yes?"

"Yes, sir."

"Then why are you condemning your Chinese neighbouring community for doing the very same thing? They are simply seeking the comfort you sought and achieved when you settled here. Neighbours care for one another; neighbourhoods care for other neighbourhoods, which care for their city; cities care for the South Island and so on. What part of this are you ignoring? When did you decide acting like privileged, ungrateful citizens was acceptable?"

"Prime Minister, we're very sorry. We've judged our neighbours harshly because they're different."

"So what is your solution?" Irritation was etched upon Oswald's face.

"We've tried to solve this, but unsuccessfully."

"I suggest you celebrate their Chinese New Year. They are tolerant of your New Year's, Christmas, and Easter."

The man could feel the Prime Minister's frustration. "We can do that. We'll embrace the Year of the Dragon, Prime Minister. Sorry, somehow bringing this to council, it all sounds so trivial."

"Let me reiterate, hate will get you killed. And you are a participant in the hatred business every day you practise intolerance. None of us is exempt. Has the past taught you nothing? I need a higher level of maturity from all of you. Enough said—meeting adjourned!"

Prime Minister Oswald approached Deek in the marbled hallway. "I think I understand this whole football quest, mate. I'm so bogged down with ridiculous mind-numbing squabbles all I crave is to gather my naval officers and take one of our subs out for a very, very long trip away from every needy person in this country, sucking up my time unnecessarily."

"And I think you should. Currently, Sly is back home handling our disputes. He's much more suited for bickering and conflicts. In fact, Sly rather enjoys all that mess. He found his calling late in life." Oswald laughed. "Yeah, who knew?"

"It's worth considering . . . getting away for a while. I find the whole PM process tedious and trivial at best."

"You'd think these complainers would appreciate being alive."

"No doubt, mate."

"Let's go meet this Dr. Aerin of yours. With my brief medical exposure, I'm more than intrigued with this woman's work."

"She's truly special, unlike anyone you'll ever meet. Come, she's waiting upstairs in my office. Oh, and the gridiron proposal failed, Deek. We want to discuss you playing rugby for the All Blacks instead. Eventually, you would be a natural for resurrecting the South United African Springboks."

"Huh, I didn't envision that outcome. Let me digest that idea. I can't lie and say that I'm not disappointed."

Aerin described to Deek her death and the events that followed just as she had for Oswald. She found the New African wise beyond his years. This positive force would be a huge asset to their secret Chrysalis Society.

"So, Deek, are you ready?"

"I'm not sure what I'm saying 'yes' to but, okay, yes."

"The information that flies from me may shock you or evoke uncomfortable emotions. Please let me purge as much as I can, but if you need to interject please feel free."

"Oswald, do I have a choice?"

"No, mate, buckle down and be ready for the most amazing wild ride you'll ever experience."

"Something is telling me to run, but rugby players aren't cowards, right Oswald? I'm ready as I'll ever be, Dr. Aerin, please proceed."

Aerin held Deek's hands with closed eyes. After a few deep breaths, she opened her eyes and let her thoughts flow quickly. "Okay, I already know about your rescue, the wrong that was done to you by the citizens of Fallstaff, Montana, so I won't waste your time with telling you I see all that. Here's what else I see. While stranded upon that remote island you and a friend, Sid, ah no, Sly, found some weathered composition books. There was a story inside by a man, O', ah, O'Malley, that lived and eventually died on the island. Unbeknownst to you and Sly, O'Malley is very pleased his books helped save all of you. His death was gruesome . . . I see lots of feathers and blood."

"Miss, Dr. Aerin—"

"Just Aerin is fine."

"Aerin, no one knows about those journals except Sly and me. Initially, I read them to Sly for entertainment. He swore me to secrecy in case we could turn them into a bestselling book some day. O'Malley's journals are with Sly right now in Cape Town. How do you know about them?"

"Aerin is psychic, mate, remember?"

"This is unbelievable. O'Malley knows?"

"He was with you when you read them."

"I'm speechless."

"It gets easier, Deek. Can we continue?"

"Am I going to like what you have to say?"

"It's a lot better news than I had to share with Oswald."

"That's comforting, I guess. Okay I'm ready."

"You had an older brother, Torr . . . Terrance, who died very young. He's telling me the two of you used to dance like James Brown for your Mama. You both loved making her laugh and it was fun to see how long your Mama would let you stay up past your bedtime." Aerin giggled. "You were cute little boys. Terrance loves that you slept with his football for so many years. He's with an older woman. It's your mother. She's telling me after Terrance's death she used to call you her little TD, her little Touch Down. Your Mama is very beautiful. You have her dimples. She's telling me she was known for her southern barbeque and coleslaw sandwiches. These were your favourite."

"Oh, my God, I'd forgotten that nickname. It was TD for Terrance and Deek as well. She used to call me that at home but not in front of family or friends. She knew it made me feel special. As for her barbeque, it was legend ary. Her father, my granddad, built her a pig cooker from a metal trashcan. He cut it lengthwise in half, put hinges on the lid, and welded a grate inside with a motorized skewer. It was quite ingenious. God I love the smell of a roasting pig. No one was ever able to duplicate her barbeque sauce recipe either. Aw, that smell can bring me back to my childhood in an instant."

"Deek, there's more."

"Oh, sorry, I'm listening. Go on, please."

"You have a wife. She boarded a plane in Los Angeles to join you in Africa. That is when the bombs went off.

Lourdes was midair when WWIV began. Her plane was diverted to a lush place. It landed where no bombs were dropped."

"Lourdes is alive?"

"Very much so. Deek, she was in Auckland. She's moved, but her whereabouts on the North Island is a bit murky."

Looking upward with saturated eyes, Deek seemed to be settling a score with his maker. His wildest dreams had finally been answered.

"Your wife has built a life for herself. There are things she wishes she could tell you but there is much sadness that surrounds her. You must find her, Deek."

Deek & Lourdes

Tortured by Aerin's visions, Deek wasted no time in working with the best investigators to find his beloved Lourdes. Oswald, Aerin, and Chrysalis had to wait. Repeatedly Deek played Aerin's words over and over in his mind. Probably the most significant information was that not only did Lourdes intend to join Deek on that dreadful Reaper Island, but also she was very much alive. If he had taken the time to step outside the churnings of his heart, he would have recognized that he was potentially in the midst of a Jane Austen-esque love story. Of course, Lourdes had read every one of those classic romance novels. Thick with layers of rushed assumptions and misunderstandings, unrequited love had been left dangling in the breeze. Yes, fully committed beautiful lovers separated by life's unfortunate circumstances only to reunite unexpectedly, yet wholeheartedly, was nothing short of bliss afforded star-crossed lovers. Deek's heart was a gelatinous mess.

For more than a week, Deek sought out Lourdes' whereabouts with no rewards. Lead after lead uncovered more heartache. Anxiety consumed Deek. Nothing else seemed to matter, making it impossible to sleep. Past events with his beautiful wife played over and over in his mind. Albeit Deek was exhausted, he refused to give up. With Aerin's psychic guidance, Deek travelled out of Auckland's dead-end searches toward a charming region in the heart of the North Island known as Taupo. It was so like Lourdes to settle within a city where olive skin was predominant. It was so like her to embrace the Maori culture and habits too. A renewed vigour took over. Deek found it difficult to contain his optimism. He tried to calm himself. Breathing deeply, he wondered how Lourdes' new townsfolk would receive him. With such dark skin, Deek was quite apprehensive. As Oswald's driver approached the address given Deek, his throat resembled grainy sandpaper. Anxiousness returned with a vengeance and pounded relentlessly in his chest. If ever a man was in love with a woman, Deek was that and more. He desperately wanted to feel Lourdes' skin against his and smell her sweet scent. It had been so long since he had gazed into her penetrating deep blue eyes, the very eyes Deek wanted affixed to his until the day his heart ceased beating.

A meagre, pale green prefab home stood before Deek and his driver. He could not exit the hovercraft fast enough. Once at the door, however, it took him a while to tap upon the fresh coat of burgundy paint. He canvassed the quaintly decorated porch. Flower planters, filled with bursts of colour, hung from the awning. Peace washed over Deek as he allowed all the feelings he had suppressed over the past years to rush to the forefront. It was as if he had found a rusty filing cabinet within his mind, suddenly forced open the drawer that contained his heart, and reacquainted himself with the contents. Deek felt dizzy. He leaned against the door before lightly tapping again. Footsteps could be heard approaching. Deek yanked his head back and stood upright. Fear rushed with an unrestrained madness throughout his body. What if she was not alone? What if time had poisoned her heart? Rejection was a very viable possibility. Suddenly, the door's tacky crevices from undried paint gave way.

Speechless, Lourdes stared at the familiar face from

her frayed memories. Slowly Deek's beautiful wife raised a trembling hand to her mouth. Tears pushed free from the corners of her eyes. Still Lourdes did not move.

Deek reached for her, hesitantly. She did not recoil, causing his heart to leap with encouragement. He followed Lourdes' eyes. That is when he knew. Pushing all questions and doubts aside, Deek engulfed Lourdes with his enormous, powerful arms. In that instant, Deek had found his home. For many, many minutes, they embraced. Oswald's driver smiled and turned off the hovercraft's engine.

Realizing they were not alone, Lourdes shuffled Deek inside her home. "Oh, Deek, my God you're here. I never thought I would see you again."

"Sweetheart, I thought you died in all the bombings. Even still, I searched and searched for you but to no avail. Only when I had a reading done by a reputable psychic did I discover you were alive. She told me you were on your way to join me when the war began. We didn't know about the nuclear war until a year later. During that time, I just figured you had decided not to join me due to your pregnancy."

"Not a chance. When the U.S. government informed us of our choices, I immediately took action. Deek, the paparazzi was so relentless I had to change my name before leaving L.A."

"I know, Lorna." Deek took Lourdes' hand and led her to a tattered couch where they both sat.

"I had to sneak away very late at night to get to the airport without a bunch of snooping photojournalists following me. It was difficult, but I was successful. I boarded the plane quite anonymously."

"So mid-flight they diverted your plane to New Zealand?"

"Yes, according to the pilot the rest of the world was in the process of levelling itself with nuclear and atomic bombs. When we landed, we were decontaminated and shuffled off to a school auditorium where food and beds awaited us. The New Zealanders have been so generous, Deek. They are lovely people. Shortly after that we were transported to a motel that had been converted into housing for the displaced Americans."

"Why didn't you stay there? I was just there a week ago. Wasn't it comforting to be with other U.S. citizens?"

"At first, it was very comforting. I was distraught for quite a while. Kind of a misery-loves-company, but that turned sour for me when the government so generously put us on a temporary program to receive social welfare. Deek, you know me, I felt humiliated. Back home, I was never one for food stamps. The other wives seemed so happy with their simplified habitat. They actually enjoyed sitting around and complaining, day after day. In the beginning, I was envious of those non-ambitious women. They were content. I was not. So many nights I wanted to snuff out that burning desire for personal accomplishment. Suddenly, I became disgusted with the prevailing pathetic attitudes. That's when I began to work hard to approach my survival with positive thinking once again. How easily negativity had tried to become a bad habit in my life. Everything we taught each other, Deek, I held dear to my heart. The other surviving Americans continued to thrive on their perceived misfortunes. The happier I appeared the more they clawed at my foundation. They bitterly tried to poison the shreds of happiness I'd created. Smiles were met with ridicule, kind gestures pelted with harsh criticism. The more I succeeded in improving my post-war life the more they tried to sink their jealous, misery-drenched daggers into my back. That is why I had to leave Auckland. Those tainted Americans needed to be without me to scrape and gouge at one another. I sought to be near a culture at peace with nature. That is why I am here. Before I made my escape, though, I again changed my name."

"I know that too . . . Winfrey. That's when I knew for sure it was truly you. I'm one of the few who knows of your love for the legendary Oprah Winfrey."

"I felt somehow her namesake would help me tap into her amazing legacy."

"Sweetheart, why the tears?"

"I have a confession." She took Deek's hands in hers.

"Okay."

"Deek, I knew you were alive."

"You what?"

"I saw the newscasts and headlines regarding your rescue."

"Why didn't you try to find me?" Deek pulled his hands free. "There wasn't a morning I awakened that I didn't think of you. My heart died a slow death, Lourdes. Why? Why would you do nothing?"

"Most of the stories, especially the pictures in the newspapers, were surrounding you . . . you and a very pretty, delicate woman."

"Lourdes!" Deek stood and turned away from his wife.

"Chandra, her name was Chandra. You looked like a couple; you were hugging one another. It broke my heart."

Slowly Deek faced Lourdes. "Honey, Chandra lost her husband soon after her arrival on the island. She was so petite, which made her an immediate target. Remember who was with me on Reaper, murderers and violent criminals. What those pictures and stories didn't tell was Sly, my dear friend in Cape Town, and I both protected Chandra. Did she want more? Yes, but she soon learned there was no hope of a romantic relationship with me. She knew my heart belonged to you. The few times I allowed myself to open up, I talked incessantly about you. Chandra quickly learned of my devotion to my wife. She is just a good friend I assure you."

"Deek, I had no way of knowing. I'm so sorry. Heartbroken, I went on the run again. After changing my name, I waited to leave one night very late when the others were sound asleep. I left Auckland never to return. I'd researched where I wanted to go . . . and that was Taupo. It took a while before I convinced the local school system of their need for Latino studies. I now have a lucrative career teaching Spanish and my Mexican American heritage. So here I am."

"So here you are, my beautiful bride." Deek pulled Lourdes to her feet. "Come closer, I don't want to waste another minute. It was always you, Lourdes. It will always be you."

Deek and Lourdes embraced again, both shuddering with anticipation. Gently Lourdes pulled away and whispered in Deek's ear. "Come, my love, there is someone special I want you to meet . . . a sleeping angel awaits you."

*"The only thing necessary for the triumph of evil . . .
is for good men to do nothing."*

~ Edmund Burke (1729-97), Irish Political Philosopher

Unknown source

CLANDESTINE JUSTICE

Justin

He had grown up playing in the aisles of the stately SNZU library. It was only natural Justin would later share his mother's love of books. Every night he fell asleep with remnants of his fantasy world swirling untethered about the right hemisphere of his brain. Young Justin devoured book after book. Year after year, his ravenous literary interests swallowed more of his logical reasoning—steadfast was his creativity.

Entering SNZU as a first-year student, Justin felt proud to be a part of the popular institution. Instrumental in the development of SNZU, Justin's parents had successfully built the New World's premiere university. Albeit the emphasis initially was science and medicine, SNZU had evolved into a literary, artistic powerhouse as well. Prominent authors and artists had found their way to a progressive New Zealand, along with award-winning scientists, prior to WWWIII. Worldwide classics were preserved and newer ones created, all within the confines of N.Z.

Armed with his newly purchased required texts, Justin dragged his heavy backpack into the library. He was never happier. To spend hours with these new books stirred excitement deep within. Embarking on this promising journey, Justin dived into his new assignments. While concurrently completing his studies, Justin planned to produce the next New World classic. Secretly, Justin filled his journals with a fantastic fictional underworld. Quiet and peaceful, Justin relished his isolation with paper and pens as his comforting friends. Labelled the "sensitive" one by many of his "thinker" Ermani relatives, Justin paved the way for a new wave of creative men in the Ermani/Thorpe tribe. Aerin, Cameron, and Grandma Saroya were thrilled with Justin's refreshing view on life and whimsical existence beyond rational boundaries. Born into a sea of rejuvenated hope, Justin was part of a freer generation. History was a subject studied in school that held nothing more than a desire not to revisit their ancestors' misguided antics. Altruistic, Justin's generation was a mixture of solid hope and a confident wisdom. Even as a youngster, Justin stood his ground with the men in his family. Aerin adored her unique baby boy. Many a chuckle was had watching little Justin argue respectfully with his grandfather and uncles. Being the firstborn in the Ermani extended family, Justin set the tone for his future cousins. Aerin and Cameron encouraged Justin's refreshing points of view. He had quickly become the centre of the family's joy and peace, actually the family's heartbeat. As a young adult, Justin's position had not changed. The only difference was he had many cousins who shared his opinions. A powerful new generation had emerged.

From his book bag, Justin pulled three thick, heavy textbooks—Organic Chemistry, Advanced Microbiology, and his favourite, Quantum Physics. Major assignments in each subject were due by the next class meeting. Justin dived into his least favourite, Organic Chemistry. Coddling at the university level was a thing of the past; homework was five times the volume of early twenty-first century assignments. There was so much to learn within such a small period of time. Life was precious. One never knew when the end was near. This powerful generation found their world an open door and each was anxious to jump into his or her destinies. Instructors had learned never to allow boredom to creep into their learning environments. Driven by self-fulfilling prophecies, the professors knew if they believed in their students, they would succeed no matter how tough the curriculum. Justin reread his Organic Chemistry syllabus and sighed deeply about the voluminous pages he was required to read. Not one to procrastinate, Justin flipped back the hard cover. It made a wonderful plunk against the polished desktop. Justin could smell the fresh pages. He smiled. As much as he dreaded the topic of chemical elements, he loved his new monstrous book. And so he began.

Immediately a battle erupted inside his head. Craving time spent in the right side of his brain, Justin reread the first paragraph several times. It took quite a while before his mind eased enough to allow him to solidly enter the left lobe, focus on analytical aspects, and dive into the microscopic realm of life's building blocks. Thankfully, Justin had his uncles, Balic and Rami, and his mother to assist him with his chemistry and biology studies. Thirty minutes into his reading and Justin started to fidget in his uncomfortable, wooden chair. His eyes wandered about the tall bookshelves. Clamouring about the second floor was a herd of fellow classmates struggling with their aggressive schedules. A few pretty girls sauntered by; each did a double take when noticing Justin.

Kozlov

Hidden in a secret chamber within their cellar's vault was where Aerin and the others still housed their cherished machines. This particular morning would bring Nederland into their support system. Foreign Diplomat Bogdan Kozlov, with his wife tucked away in a scenic hotel, had joined Oswald to view the inner workings of their secret society. Chrysalis had to be pure of heart and would never include persons motivated by personal gain. So far, they had a heroic membership with the purest of intent for their spiritual, non-Darwinian movement. Next would be an invitation to Canada's newly appointed Prime Minister, Sean Ulmer. However, indoctrinating PM Ulmer would be a cakewalk compared to Nederland's Kozlov.

Down the dark stairway they moved. Aerin flicked a light switch when they hit the cement floor of the underground storm cellar. She then placed her hand on the brick next to a picture of the Ermani family. Heat from her hand eventually caused the sensor to activate. The brick façade moved to the side exposing an iron latch. Once Aerin turned it, the bulwark opposite the stairwell opened. Built into the mountainside was their secret room that extended beyond the boundaries of the vault's walls above. Inside, well hidden, were several tubular machines . . . and a man of Middle Eastern descent shackled against the far wall, his mouth gagged. His eyes shone yellow with a lifelong ferocious anger no one could possibly penetrate.

Oswald patted Kozlov on the back. "This vile man's transformation will erase any doubts you may have regarding the spiritual world as Aerin has described it. Please feel free to ask anything you like."

"There is one question that keeps nagging me, Aerin. How can you be completely sure you are dealing with a grey soul?"

"Bogdan, it comes to me as quickly as the information I shared with you about your involvement in the war and those horrible incidents surrounding your daughter. I immediately see if people have angels surrounding them. I feel a soul's heaviness. And with grey souls, there is murkiness, not the glowing white light associated with white souls. As quickly as those sensations hit me I see glimpses of that soul's future carnage."

"And you're never wrong?"

"Oh, Bogdan, if I ever had a shred of doubt I would never put that person's life in peril."

"Is religion ever an element?"

"No one religion is correct, so how could it be? It's quite irrelevant really. As long as someone practises love and tolerance, it doesn't matter what religious dogma or rituals they prefer. What I've learned is we need to love one another and search for the highest good. We all possess a unique passion we have chosen, so we need to search for it, implement it, appreciate it, then help others reach theirs. The key to getting to the core of the Godhead is positive thinking. Metaphysically, what we bring into our minds, it tries to accomplish. Feed it negative thoughts and actions and the world produces more of that. Feed it positive nourishment and the mind and body flourish. With that mindset we can receive wonderful results beyond our dreams."

"But why me and not Prime Minister Ellestad? My

past has proven I can be quite a knor. I frequently get things wrong."

"Ellestad is a very old, tired man with very traditional energy. There is no way he would listen to psychic information."

"Still, Aerin, I don't understand how you can consider me for this purest society after all the atrocities I've committed. I'm responsible for so many deaths. What if I am, as you say, a dark soul?"

"Bogdan, God knows your heart. Dark souls have no remorse. They are void of a conscience. The very fact you are so heavily burdened with guilt speaks volumes. Dark souls never question their actions. Besides, Bogdan, as misguided as you were at the time, you were acting with pure intent. You thought you were doing right by your country."

"Taking so many lives?"

"With all due respect, Bogdan, you were a victim of societal manipulation. So many countries raise their citizens to fear and hate others. It's why our history is so thickly laden with wars."

"So this man we've been discussing is a prime example?"

"His hatred is centuries old."

"And you will change that?"

"Yes, we will."

"Then I am ready, however dubious this all sounds. For Sasha, my daughter, I am ready."

Maktan

Her strategy was successful. Mu'mad thrived while in the public school system and later in his switch back to an exclusive private institution. Only when at home did nagging doubts worry Maktan. Her son had too much, too many *things*. During high school, and still at home, Maktan watched Mu'mad closely with all those things. Skateboards that hovered above the sidewalks, wristwatches that played music and movies, and videophones connected through EyeNet and the Internet, Mu'mad had it all. At home he had an enormous MV flatscreen in his bedroom where he could bring his classmates to him at all hours of the night. Mu'mad was never alone. Muffled voices had awakened Maktan frequently in the wee hours of the morning. What these young defiant males discussed so late, she was never privy to.

Yes, indeed, Westerners loved their things. But most worrisome was Mu'mad's growing disinterest with what Maktan had to say about Mu'mad's father, his past. Younger generations had proven to be disinterested in traditional conflicts. To a rapidly growing Mu'mad, the stories he once loved as a little boy had grown mundane and bothersome. Whereas he learned to cry to get out of hearing the redundant tales when younger, now, with an ever-present scowl for his mother, Mu'mad simply left the room when Maktan spoke. And he had stayed away at his private school more and more. Disregard for elders was yet another Western trait Maktan abhorred.

Mu'mad was a young man now. Finished with

university, he felt he possessed all the answers like most young adults. Maktan could not possibly understand his world. Plans to attend Amsterdam University could no longer be thwarted by Maktan. Upon turning twenty-six, Mu'mad, along with his loyal sidekicks from the University of British Columbia, declared his freedom from his mother and Muslim background. He and his friends had stayed at college as long as they could until they had exhausted every aspect of the school's curriculum. Three extra years at the university and Mu'mad was more than qualified for advanced studies. Acceptance to AU's graduate program was Mu'mad's next-to-last act of defiance against his mother. The final stinging blow came to Maktan upon Mu'mad's departure to Nederland, and a heartbreaking call from their bank. Mu'mad had pulled out ninety percent of the millions of dollars from their joint savings and chequing accounts . . . money that lay dormant, virtually untouched since Mu'mad was an infant.

Although Maktan had more than enough to live comfortably for her lifetime, she had planned for that money to be used to continue the Islamic cause. That was Mu'mad's father's dream, which he had given his life for. Maktan was crushed. She had failed. Her son was gone, with millions upon millions of dollars, to immerse himself in a life of warped ideology. Snubbed continually over the years by her icy Muslim friends, Maktan found solace more and more with her comforting infidel acquaintances. They were all too familiar with wilful, insolent young adults. Their collective advice was to remain patient and the free-spirited *career-students* always seemed to return home after a strong dose of the real world, often with their dirty laundry in tow. Maktan hung onto every infidel-spoken word.

Beads of sweat broke out across Mu'mad's forehead. The flashjet had not even left the runway and he was already feeling nauseated. He closed his eyes as tightly as he could. Blood drained from Mu'mad's head as the engines roared louder. He focused on his dreams. Mu'mad could not wait to land in Amsterdam. Besides, Nederland was wonderfully far, far away from his smothering mother. Yes, he was free. Then why was he feeling so horrible? Why was he so nervous? For the first time, far away from home, Mu'mad should feel elated, released. Facing the unknown should be much more rewarding, yet Mu'mad's leg continued to jump nervously. A short gasp escaped him as the flashjet lifted off the ground. His stomach lurched. Gripping the armrests so tightly had caused his fingers to go numb. First class was supposed to have given Mu'mad all the comforts he was accustomed to at home. However, nothing the flight attendants did seemed to help calm him. Flying for the first time, Mu'mad was anxious to exit the claustrophobic tube. How would he get through the next few hours? Mu'mad's champagne and quiche pitched about his stomach. Wild-eyed, Mu'mad searched for something to ease his panic. Erratic breathing brought a flight attendant to his side. Strategically she placed the humiliating barf bag in front of Mu'mad just in the nick of time.

Chance

Obsessed with the Art Department, Chance Montegro was eager to spend her spare time with her canvases and vibrant paints. Unfortunately, the many demands of her teacher's aide responsibilities, and nagging thoughts of her dissertation, dominated her time and often caged her within the confines of the SNZU library. Once past the intimidating doors, Chance felt a heaviness press upon her. The silence of the library rang in her ears . . . ears eager for boisterous island music. To the second floor Chance trudged, her backpack causing a tingling sensation in her right arm, her irreplaceable artist's arm. Once she reached the top of the staircase, Chance searched desperately for a study cubicle near a window as she shifted her pack to her other shoulder. She vowed to herself, as she often did, that once her backlog of research items was completed she would escape to her empty canvases in the art studio. Back in the far corner, Chance spotted the perfect study spot. Shifting her menacing book bag yet again, she quickened her pace, eager to claim her prospective territory.

As she rounded the cubicle privacy wall, Chance yanked the menacing bag of books from her shoulder and started to fling it upon the desk. With her bag in mid-flight, Chance retracted the backpack causing her to stumble. Chance righted herself then pushed a stubborn lock of curly hair from her eyes. Crouched before her was a fledgling nemesis occupying her cubicle. Hunched over several massive textbooks was an annoying freshman.

Chance had spotted the chronic bookworm with unruly sandy-blond hair her second week of school. She stared at the young man with disdain. Her time was precious, and why would this geek-ish, insolent bookworm not look her way? Chance dropped her book bag upon the tiled floor. It landed with a loud thud. Nothing fazed this stubborn young man. Hands on her hips, Chance blew several tight, light brown curls from her eyes again. Still he did not budge. Was he deaf? There were no earbuds in his ears. Chance studied him further. His clothes were marginally cool, local island garb, but his behaviour told a different story. He bordered on geek-hood, yet there was an assurance about him. Chance exaggerated a sigh, announcing her exasperation. Finally, the overzealous freshman shot an uninterested glance in her direction. Her breath caught in her throat. Past long dark lashes were the most translucent eyes. Dark circles encased the young man's light green irises, which heightened his incensed stare. Chance could not find the words to manifest her obvious charm and superiority.

Before Justin stood a gorgeous upperclassman. After ignoring several of her attempts to get his attention, Justin had given in to her manipulative feminine wiles. However, he had not bargained for such a beautiful pest. Flawless dark olive skin was what he first noticed. The young woman's fingers, arms, face, and exposed flat stomach were an intoxicating mocha colour. It took a while for Justin to lock upon Chance's jade-coloured eyes. Amber starbursts surrounding the pupils drew him in further. True, she was amazing to look at, but she obviously knew her affect on men.

When the young man finished surveying her body, he

sat back in his chair. That is when Chance noticed how tall he was. Long legs were crammed underneath the desk. Dirty blond, feathery hair, with sun-streaked highlights, framed his angular face. Every feature reeked of masculinity except the slight boyish cleft in his chin.

The not-so-geeky bookworm cocked a dark brown eyebrow at Chance and grumbled. "Something bothering you? Uh-h, trying to study here."

Chance flashed a smile that normally melted men's hearts. "This is my favourite desk. You freshmen are supposed to study downstairs."

"Really . . . news to me. And what are you, a sophomore?"

"No, first-year, I'm a grad student, a TA. Now come on, scram; show a little respect. I have a lot of studying to do."

"Well, Miss Privileged, my father built this library . . . Dean Thorpe? Yeah, that's him. I can assure you I grew up in these halls and know for a fact freshmen are free to study anywhere they please. So if you could *scram* I'd be immensely appreciative and would overlook your condescending indiscretions. I too have a lot of studying to do."

"Condescending indiscretions, who talks like that? Little Thorpe, eh, you look like your father, actually. I've heard some pretty embarrassing stories about you. Dean Thorpe is hilarious. Chickies and dollies, hmm? Are you sure you want to piss me off? I could easily trash your fragile reputation in an instant."

"Have at it. My father tells lots of stories. I believe he told me one about you."

"About me?"

"Quite right. Before I started the university, he warned me about superficial, overindulgent, self-serving female upperclassmen. Yes, as a matter of fact, I believe he was talking precisely about you."

"You don't know me . . . wet the bed lately?"

"And just because my father shared a few ridiculous stories with the likes of you, don't think for a second you know anything about me."

Chance stood steadfast. "I know you are behaving quite predictably, thinking you're favoured because daddy's a big wig."

"Is that all you've got? Not fazed—still sitting here. Just so you know, guilt doesn't work on me, Miss Priss. Go manipulate someone else."

"Listen, Little Thorpe, I would really appreciate you letting me have this cube. It's my favourite, I study here all the time."

"That's funny, I'm here every day and I've never seen you here."

"Well, I study here really late." Justin stared at the beauty and released an easy chuckle. "What's so hilarious?" Chance folded her arms across her chest.

Justin repositioned his piercing eyes and looked directly into Chance's. "You're a shitty liar." He put both hands behind his head and leaned back in his chair. "And you're used to getting your way, aren't you?"

"I beg your pardon?"

"No need to beg, Pretty Girl."

"Oh, so you think I'm pretty, Little Thorpe? Is that your way of apologizing?"

"No indeed."

"But you think me pretty."

"Quite right, you're a knockout . . . actually, more like a scary distraction."

"Are you in such a distracted state that relinquishing my desk will be an option?" Chance poured on more charm.

"Your desk?"

"You know it."

"What's your name, fourth-year?"

"Chance Montegro . . . and I am not a senior. Grad student remember?"

"Well, Chance, I have to say . . . no. I have tons of reading to do and a paper to write. Besides, if I gave you *my* desk, I would be just another spineless fool letting your beauty pummel my self-respect, hence spiralling me into eventual self-loathing."

"Coward."

"Man eater."

"Spoiled brat." Stalling, Chance gathered her backpack and peered about searching for a replacement cubicle. Two desks away, facing Justin's workplace, was an empty desk.

"Yeah, sit there. You can watch me work."

Feigning a sarcastic yawn, "I'm amazed at how beige you truly are." Chance turned to leave.

"If I'm beige, Miss Priss, then you're as blanched as a walking coma."

With no response, Chance continued to walk away. A smile crept across her face.

Mu'mad

Glad to have escaped the confines of the suffocating jet, Mu'mad quickly regained his composure. Fresh air filled his lungs. Feet planted firmly upon Nederland soil, the remnants of nausea began to subside. Arrival at the Amsterdam University felt even better. Mu'mad's corner dorm room was the best money could buy, though still cramped and inadequate. At least as a graduate student, he would not have to endure a drivelling, pest of a roommate. Staring past his shuttered window, Mu'mad could see the many canals, clusters of sandwiched buildings, and in the far distance, windmills. Picturesque, Amsterdam was a living piece of art. It was also the ticket to Mu'mad's freedom. He had no complaints. Even standing seven floors up, Mu'mad caught a whiff of cannabis from the quad below. If that was what freedom smelled like, Mu'mad would be inhaling much more in the near future.

Those days when Maktan kept a watchful eye on her son were over. Never again would she try to force Mu'mad into living like a traditional Muslim; those days were long past. To ward off his mother's wrath, he would wait a week or so before writing or calling her with his general whereabouts. The last thing Mu'mad wanted was a visit from his irrational matriarch. This was Mu'mad's fresh start.

Below, Mu'mad watched the confident juniors and seniors congregate and socialize with ease. In contrast, he watched the pathetic freshmen wander about taking their wallflower positions on the outskirts of the bell tower quad. Mu'mad studied the coeds. It did not take him long to spot the popular crowd, the cluster of overly confident, beautiful students with obviously pampered lives ahead of them. He leaned upon the windowsill and observed the group he would make his own. Mu'mad knew who he was, knew who he would become. For now, it was time to explore the campus further and find his pack of loyal friends from UBC who had arrived the week before.

Amsterdam

Pleas to Joseph R. Smith's mother by the boy's teachers had landed on deaf ears during his formative years. After a time, along with privately despising their spoiled friend, the other children grew to fear him. Daily they were reminded of Joseph's ruthlessness that carried no consequences for him. They could not look Joseph in the eyes; there was something dark within them everyone wanted to avoid. Prep school had served as Joseph's testing ground. How much pain could he inflict on his classmates without being named the perpetrator? Joseph mastered the art of getting others to carry out his despicable acts while still maintaining a superior impression with the school's administration. It had started with elementary school pranks. Loyal classmates had proclaimed Joseph their leader. By the time he entered middle school, his gags evolved into inflicting mental and emotional pain upon his enemies. If someone challenged or rejected Joseph, he waited very patiently until an opportunity for revenge presented itself. Only Joseph knew these retaliations were vengeful paybacks. Others viewed the incidents as random events. After all, Joseph and his loyal followers were just spirited, healthy mates. And prep school fostered freedom. Blessed with excessive charisma, Joseph had wasted no time when puberty erupted. Sexual gratification was easy and plentiful. Under the guise of searching for true love, Joseph tapped into the private treasures of most of his female classmates. By his senior year, Joseph was anxious about moving on to the university level.

Bored with his current university and its women, Joseph was more than overdue for new experiences and people. Amsterdam would soon house a fledgling monster. And mother would not make this trip. She had avoided visiting Joseph during his years at prep school because of a mysterious, recurring illness. Watching over her son like a lioness protecting her cub, Joseph's mother was most assuredly too protective. Joseph thought his matriarch a nuisance. He had to do something; she was cramping his style. Poison was slow, painful, and inconspicuous. No one suspected a thing.

Chance & Justin

Chance had made an impact. Of what that was exactly, Justin was not sure. She teetered between remarkable and irritatingly spoiled, simple. The latter Justin avoided with ease. High-maintenance women were not stunted by their self-absorption but were notoriously boring. Justin tired of their nonsensical, narcissistic banter that displayed shallowness at every turn. Not surprisingly, Justin's pickiness with the opposite sex stemmed from these women falling short when compared to his maternal role model. Aerin had created impossible shoes to fill. To Justin, his mother embodied the perfect female. She had raised her son with knowledge, laughter, and love in abundance, and a selflessness that fostered wisdom. Although possessing his father's unwavering stability and sense of humour, Justin remained balanced. At a very, very young age, he spent his time drawing and reading. Yes, Aerin and Cameron had successfully passed on their love of books, all books. Literary bombardment served as Justin's muse; never was he void of artistic content. Boredom had seldom entered his world until the pretty, boring girls had tried to barge into his private sanctuary. Justin seemed to crave unraveling the mysteries of life, whereas his dates sought to unravel, obtain, and confine him. Manipulative tears and many unnecessary discussions seemed to flag the end of many a trivial union. And this Chance had all the earmarks of one of these eventually smothering types. Because of her unusual beauty though, a part of Justin was terrified.

For the week that followed their introduction, it was a

race to see if Justin or Chance arrived first at their perfect cubicle. When class commenced, both engaged in the daily territorial competition. Whoever arrived first commenced studying and secretly waited impatiently for their attractive opponent to appear.

Chance had never been so motivated to study. Irritated with Justin's lack of interest, Chance turned her flirtation into a stubborn attempt to annoy this strange freshman. The way he stared directly into Chance's eyes told her there was an attraction, but there was a conscious blocking of any desired follow-through. This was foreign territory for her. Equally intrigued, Chance wanted to know what interests drove Justin beyond being just another "hottie." He was truly not like the other young men on campus. When he studied Chance's eyes, she swore he was searching for something, something to make it worth his time. This equally angered and exhilarated Chance because she knew she possessed much, much more than a pretty face. The real question was, when Justin discovered Chance's complicated sides, would he be worthy of her?

WHAT BROKE THE ICY WEDGE between their stalemate? It was a balmy day, one more conducive to artwork than schoolwork. Eager to avoid Chance's repetitive sparring, Justin chose the second-class desk, conceding the cubicle with the picturesque view outside. Upon the desk, Justin spread his charcoal drawings. Lost inside his artistic bubble, Justin scuffed the charcoal against the thick paper in a continual effort to illustrate the "shitty draft" of his latest novel. With quick purposeful strokes, Justin let the picture reveal itself onto his cherished sketchpad. Quite a while passed before Justin felt eyes upon him.

Without turning around, Justin pulled from the privacy

of his right hemisphere. "Can I help you, Chance?"

She stared at his drawing. Finally, a piece of the mysterious Justin surfaced. "Darken the rings around the irises a bit more and his expression will become the focal point."

Justin stared intently at the Middle Eastern man's eyes he had drawn. They were the feral eyes of a tiger. Justin's hand froze. Chance was correct.

Astonished, Chance could not pry her eyes from Justin's sketch. "Just wanted to thank you for the desk. I got my Art History paper ready for publication so the cube is all yours if you want it."

Justin turned to view Chance. "Wasn't up for a tussle today, nothing more."

She smiled. Upon her shoulder, Chance readjusted her backpack and proceeded toward the stairs. It was not for any other reason except to flee the library for the art building. Viewing Justin's sketch had ignited something inside her. Suddenly an overwhelming urge to paint had washed over Chance. Lately, her looming dissertation had put a definite damper on any artistic endeavours. Justin's creative energy had flooded Chance with a warm unrest. As she trotted toward the Art Studies building, Chance dodged passing students with impatience. Her forgotten easel would not be ignored.

Justin was not focused on Chance's retreat from the library. He instead worked intently on making those Middle Eastern eyes more believable. An hour went by before Justin raised his head. He was pleased with the finished product. Thanks to Chance, the man's eyes were not only piercing, but they more accurately portrayed his story. Justin looked around as he stretched hoping to see that Chance had returned to the library, but she was nowhere in sight. Suddenly Justin wished his beautiful critic had not abandoned him earlier. He so wanted to share his finished product with her.

Amsterdam

PROTESTING, AND EVENTUALLY OVERTURNING, THE Amsterdam University Dean's latest decision to impose a nine o'clock curfew was yet another milestone for Joseph R. Smith, or J.R. as he was more commonly known. Just because a rapist was preying upon AU coeds did not give the administration the right to create an educational prison. When the Dean's initial announcement had been delivered, J.R. had come unglued. Swiftly he had called upon his loyal followers. Much like Yale's secret pre-war "Skull and Bones Society," J.R. had formed AU's "Phantom Society" to ensure he and his henchmen had some say in forming their environment. J.R., of course, had broader aspirations for his infant society after his time at university. His constituency had already grown beyond campus borders. With the death of al-Husri, after WWIV, al Din needed a leader; and J.R. gave them one. Al Din members were surfacing in all the surviving cities around the new world, ready to regain power. J.R. spoke of discipline, and most of all patience, to his Phantom members. To the infidels, J.R. fed what they needed to hear; the manipulation began. His beliefs prompted the citizens of Amsterdam to tune in to his weekly radio show. Listener response was overwhelming and growing every day. There was a refreshing purity in his rants and discussions. He appealed to young and old, suggesting ways to avoid past, catastrophic mistakes and mould the new world with unity and peace. His ideas were intoxicating. Eloquently stated, J.R.'s humble, charismatic orations captured many a Dutch ear. Al Din members lay in wait.

By day, J.R. was the new saviour; however, by night his true self would not be denied. He studied them for weeks, watched their routines and habits. Vulnerability locked his eyes upon them initially, especially the petite ones with long shiny hair. Colour was of no concern, blonde, red, brunette, they all appealed to J.R. Sheen and length was the attraction. Firm bodies beneath tight jeans, these women flaunted their wares, and J.R. was buying. It had been a month since the Dean imposed the ridiculous curfew. Since J.R.'s administrative victory, no one on campus would be raped. Why lead the authorities to him so easily? Working at the local radio station near Dam Square, J.R. had a new hunting ground. Young, fresh women were everywhere riding their bicycles, hair flowing behind them in the breeze. J.R. was about to burst, needing a release badly. Possible prey flowed past him in droves. Only when he locked upon one in particular did the plotting, scheming, and fantasizing begin. His next victim would be the stunning young curator of the museum that housed his favourite coffee shop, several blocks from Amsterdam's prominent broadcasting centre. Outside on his coffee break, before going on air, J.R. noticed her long blonde hair streaming behind her as she rode her bicycle past him with grace. After parking her bike, the sophisticated woman released the clamps on her pant legs, flipped her hair from side to side, grabbed her satchel, and sauntered into the art museum. J.R. watched through the coffee shop window as she spoke to several tourists with poise and ease. She was an excellent choice.

J.R. especially enjoyed defiling blondes. His first victim had golden hair. After planting a sloppy kiss upon his conquest's full lips, the ungrateful bitch had spat upon the ground claiming she could taste the infection in J.R.'s soul. It had been so easy to strike her down, kill her. No emotions had flowed through his bloodstream, only dead silence had taken residence in his brain. Without a forensic trace left behind, no one suspected the handsome teenager. This new blonde had smiled at J.R. Desire for him burned in her eyes; he recognized that. J.R. would accommodate her soon, but there were details that needed consideration. When she was alone in the dark of the night, he would come for her.

Maktan

WHEN MAKTAN FIRST HEARD HER son's voice on the EyeNet speakerphone, she could not help herself; she wept. Annoyed, her son threatened to hang up if she did not cease her emotional foolishness.

"I am stopping, Son. But why, why did you run away?"

"I didn't run away. No more drama please."

"You cleared out the bank account and left without a word."

"I left you plenty of Papa's money. It was a joint account remember?"

"Mu'mad, it's not the money; you just disappeared with no explanation. You don't know what that does to a mother."

"How many times did I bring up Amsterdam University? You didn't want to hear it. Besides, Vancouver was stifling me. And I told you I needed more, but you weren't listening."

"Dearest, you are meant for bigger things."

"Not that again, Mama. Be glad I'm furthering my education."

"By a bunch of pot-smoking halfwits."

"How ignorant you are."

"Oh, how little you know. You'll see; they'll eventually show their true colours. Mu'mad, they'll turn on you because of your Muslim background. I kept you safe in Vancouver, raised you in a city tolerant of foreigners. Your dark skin will tell them who you really are and they will reject you."

"My friends love me for who I really am, Mama."

"For now, Mu'mad."

"Mama, some of my friends have darker skin than I."

"But Mu'mad—"

"As usual, so nice talking to you, Mama. May your cynicism keep you warm at night."

Maktan had lost him. The cold dial tone purred in her ear. She felt her beautiful boy was lost in a sea of intolerance and prejudice. Islam was surely not the prominent religion in Nederland. Her beliefs were outnumbered, buried significantly by the war. And sadly, her son would not be resurrecting any part of his father's dreams.

Was she right, Mu'mad wondered? Doubts crept inward. Were his old UBC and new AU friends lying? Did they secretly detest him because he was not White and a Westerner with a Middle Eastern background? Mu'mad tried on his mother's paranoia but for a brief moment, then discarded the absurdity. His mother did not understand him, never would. How could she know his world, his friends? Furthermore, his mother never listened to his plans. Mu'mad felt more than ever he had made the right decision to leave. One day his mother would see his successes, discover she was wrong, and ultimately be proud.

Amsterdam

Under a dimly lit streetlight, J.R. strolled. Maturity hovered around his latest choice. The beautiful blonde was older than his previous sex objects, maybe even in her thirties. This excited J.R., something new. He paced to and fro. His chosen one must be off work by now and would be pedaling her taut body past him soon. Onto the dirt path, J.R. flicked his unfinished cigarette. It was time for him to position himself in the bushes along the segment of path devoured by darkness. Just as J.R. pushed between two large bushes, concealing him from any passers-by, he heard heavy footsteps. They grew ever louder. Sweat seeped from every pore on J.R.'s body, for he had unwittingly cornered himself. There was nowhere to slip further into the night. Had someone followed him? The footsteps were weighty, belonging to a man. J.R. peeked through the thick brush at his stalker's silhouette. The stranger stared in the direction of J.R. Could the stalker see him? J.R. held his breath. Slowly the man pushed closer. Behind J.R., the weathered brick wall felt cold through his thin shirt. He wanted to run but could not. Did this stalker know he was hiding in the bushes? Hardly anyone travelled this dirt path after dusk. The night was usually J.R.'s. About this time, he should be positioning himself along the patch of road where no lights shone. About this time, his blonde prey should be pedaling by. J.R. did not dare move except to ready the Bowie knife in his hand.

From the near distance, a bicycle could be heard as it approached with a churning rhythm. J.R.'s stalker stopped.

He waited for the cyclist as well. As he stepped into the hazy funnelled beam of light from the streetlamp, J.R. recognized the rugged face, the undeniable scar that ran the length of his stalker's jaw line. He had seen this man many times on the news. What was he doing out here? This prominent figure was surely filled with secrets, but why was he here? He was a Nederland diplomat, ex-KGB. The bicyclist, startled by the man's presence, came to a screeching halt. Gravel and dirt flew into the air, trailing behind the skidding tires.

During all the commotion, J.R. was able to inch past the bricked wall.

"Papa, what are you doing here?"

"Sasha, I'm sorry I startled you, but I was concerned. Call it a papa's intuition." Kozlov stared in the direction of J.R.'s hiding place. Aerin's unforgotten words spooked Kozlov even more when he noticed the bushes, where she had envisioned Sasha's killer, were moving. "Stay here, Honey."

Kozlov ran toward the thick shrubbery. Pistol drawn, he lunged through the tangled brush. Many branches tore at Kozlov's flesh and clothing. He refused to feel any pain as he stumbled to the ground, his eyes incessantly and frantically searching for Sasha's supposed killer. There was no one there. As Kozlov struggled to get back to his feet, he noticed large male footprints in the soft, moist soil. Behind him there lay a warm cigarette butt. Aerin's words rang in his ears. Sasha's rapist, killer, had been hiding here. If only Aerin had seen the slaying rapist's face.

J.R. SLITHERED SUCCESSFULLY BACK INTO the shadows. His camouflaged car took him swiftly and quietly to safety, far away from the ex-KGB operative and his daughter. J.R.'s thwarted plans would never be revisited. Rumours swirled about the agent-turned-diplomat. And he was not a man to be trifled with. J.R. had not known his new conquest was the daughter of such a powerful man. In lieu of this new information, J.R.'s previous obsessive interest in the gorgeous young blonde went suddenly limp.

Chance & Justin

CREATIVITY HAD SUCCESSFULLY PENETRATED THEIR wilful barrier. Artistic expressions were Chance and Justin's unspoken language. What started in the SNZU library as a stubborn, youthful sparring match ended with the inseparable bond of kindred spirits. Chance's paintings and Justin's narratives and sketches retold the story of passion and unrequited love over and over, in many different forms. Only those whose hearts had been fortunate enough to feel that amorous fire understood Chance and Justin's creative expressions. To revisit that unwavering warmth kept viewers wanting more. Enough so that Chance and Justin were able to eventually open an art gallery in Kaikoura years after their university studies were completed. For the next ten years, Chance and Justin worked exhaustingly for this. Her oil paintings and his charcoal sketches hung from the many walls but only for short periods. Very few pieces were left behind to collect dust. Many works of art were sold the same day they were displayed upon the gallery walls. The young couple flourished. Quite simply, Chance and Justin were in demand. There was never any doubt they would someday marry, although an unexpected pregnancy brought that day sooner than later. Neither resisted fate. After all, spontaneity had always been their fuel.

At the altar, Justin stood handsome and proud next to his best man and awaited his bride's arrival. However customary it was for the bride to be fashionably late, this was way beyond uncomfortable. The heat made Justin's temples throb and his tuxedo collar threatened to suffocate him.

Why was Chance taking so long? Justin began to perspire. Had she changed her mind after all these years?

Justin tugged at his constricting bowtie when he spotted Chance's maid of honour. Her beautiful white smile, framed by traditional Maori facial tattoos immediately soothed Justin. Always his favourite, Justin's Auntie Hauku, Tanid's wife, was one of the few women who intricately understood his soul. Relief rushed in. As Auntie Hauku proceeded down the aisle, she winked at her nephew. Angst faded to relief and quickly reignited ardent anticipation. Chance would be next.

Justin breathed in deeply and exhaled slowly. Shifting his weight from one foot to the other, Justin continued to fidget. Through the double doors came his breathtaking future wife with child. Floating, Justin was suddenly weak-kneed. There stood Chance dressed in the most magnificent flowing, ivory dress. Sunlight framed her with an angelic aura. Justin's eyes darted to his father, Cameron, who gave an approving nod, but a sudden wave of doubt lingered. Would he be as good a father as Cameron was? How would he build that closeness with his unborn child? Infants did not come with instructions. How had Cameron been able to read him so well?

Justin smiled when remembering how at the most troubling times at University he was pulled from class and sent to the Dean's office, only to find his father wanted to take him to lunch. The talks they shared were of such help. His father was not as creative as his mother was, but he truly knew the male spirit. Justin's eyes switched back to Chance. She flashed another dimpled smile, the smile of her father. Beside Chance stood Justin's towering father-in-law-to-be.

Deek Jorgensen never looked more handsome. With his gorgeous daughter on his arm, Deek slowly walked her toward Justin, never taking his eyes from his teary-eyed Lourdes sitting proudly in the first pew. Side-by-side father and daughter sauntered down the aisle. It seemed a mere dream. Deek was engulfed in happiness. Reaper Island, surrounded by hopeless comrades, to Cape Town and on to New Zealand, Deek was swimming in a sea of accomplishment. He knew a contented heart more so than ever before. That memorable morning when Lourdes had walked Deek into Chance's bedroom, he could not believe they had produced such a beautiful sleeping angel. Deek had stared at his young daughter and had immediately fallen in love. Although she resembled her mother, even carried Lourdes' maiden name of Montegro, Chance had proven to be like her father in every other way. Yes, that day Deek realized God had really heard his many Reaper Island prayers.

As for the other father-in-law, Cameron too was a force to be reckoned with. He would be a phenomenal father-in-law. Chance had been so glad Cameron was Justin's father, so pleased to become a part of the Thorpe family. Father and son shared a male camaraderie deeply rooted during Justin's boyhood. One glance, an understanding smirk, was all it took to connect a wealth of understanding. Cameron and Justin even spoke their own language at times. Chance still was not entirely clear of the meaning behind "chickies and dollies." All she knew was the ranking of the female gender between father and son had started as early as Justin's third birthday. Cameron would nudge his small boy and exclaim "chicky or dolly?" Justin, hand-in-hand with his towering father, would whisper the response and look for that paternal wink of approval. To this day, no one could pry the definition of a chicky or dolly from Cameron or Justin, if in fact any particulars ever existed. To this day, Chance was not sure where her ranking had fallen. What she cherished was Cameron had raised the bar high for parenthood. Chance tried to swallow the enormous lump in her throat. Yes, Cameron was a force, but Chance was equally proud of the man attached to her arm. Deek had come into her world a bit late but with a loving influence that erased those plentiful sad, fatherless days. Chance treasured every minute with her father since their reunion. She was strong because of her resourceful parents. Just as Justin was a wonderful offshoot of Cameron, there were no doubts that Chance was very much her father's daughter.

Like everyone else in the chapel, Aerin turned to set eyes upon the bride. Chance was the sparkle in her son's eyes and holder of her unborn grandchild. It seemed such a short time ago that she held her newborn Justin in her arms. He and Chance were so much in love but seemed so terribly young to be marrying even though Justin was in his late twenties and Chance in her early thirties. Both were older than Aerin when she married. However, they just seemed so youthful, forever young. Post-war life had often prompted hasty unions. Uncertainty had become an accepted certainty. Unlike Aerin's parents' generation, who had once lived decently long lives, such longevity was not a given post-war. Struggling in earlier years had taken a toll on all those who had survived. Saroya and Ari had passed first. It was a terrible blow to Aerin and her brothers. Ari had died of an unexpected heart attack. Several months later Saroya died in her sleep. Aerin was sure it was from a cardiac problem as well: a broken heart. They lost Pete

Whibley next to cirrhosis of the liver. Victoria, Auntie Clara, and Uncle Isaac all passed away years later due to old age. Aerin, the Ermani brothers, and Whibley boys had gradually become the "older generation." With no assurances of long lives, the newer generations wasted no time in any endeavour. Passionate, they rushed into adulthood, marriage, having children, everything. However, a part of Aerin was pleased. At least her son had finished university and he and Chance had striven to get established before marrying. And they worked well together. Chance possessed a spirit like no other, and she and Justin seemed to fit. Even more amazing would be the child they produced together. Albeit, Aerin still felt they were too young.

She turned and stole a glance at her son. Again, that nagging doubt surfaced when Aerin's eyes shifted back to Chance. An unexplained darkness hovered about her, not her soul, but the darkness of another. Lately, the troubling images had lingered. Perhaps one of the curses of her psychic abilities was that Aerin could not always see future incidents as clearly for those closest to her. Aerin had felt Chance's darkness early on, but knowing Chance's soul was as bright white as one could get, Aerin had dismissed the bleak, heavy impulses. Meditation sessions had revealed the taste of bile by Aerin even though she felt no health issues inside Chance. Unable to pinpoint the source, Aerin had chosen to keep her visions to herself. No sense raising unnecessary concerns. Aerin took a deep breath and smiled again at Justin, struggling to force feelings of contentment to the forefront, instead of dread.

Deek

Thirteen months flew by. Safely back in Cape Town, Deek and Lourdes rushed about with everyday life trying to ward off the emptiness they felt from missing Chance and their five-month-old grandson, Lachlan. Nothing would fill that void. Embracing another season of Springbok rugby, Deek, going on his twenty-sixth year with the organization, spent hours immersed in his veteran position as head coach. Time would hopefully fly by until he and Lourdes would leave for New Zealand to watch their Springboks take on the historically dominant, reigning champions, the All Blacks. This would allow them much needed time with their daughter and grandson.

Then tragedy struck. Without warning Sly's heart ceased beating. During a congressional meeting, Sly dropped like a rag doll after an outburst to stop the bickering amongst the younger representatives. With the help of the Canadians up north in Vancouver, the New Americans had settled nicely in what used to be the thriving city of Seattle, Washington. Levelled by the war, the adventurous original Lompoc group had found only small remnants of the old northwestern metropolis. They worked hard resurrecting what was important to them. Familiar with what needed to happen during the clean-up process, the Lompoc settlers used their expertise learned during the Cape Town restoration. With assistance from their northern neighbours, the rebuilding of Seattle had gone much more quickly and efficiently than expected. Forever indebted to the Canadians, the Western Lompoc family adopted new perspectives, different values than their Eastern New African comrades. Initially, the split Reaper survivors embraced their contrasting worlds. Only in recent times had the tension grown between the newer generations of the Western and Eastern Lompoc family, and no one could pinpoint what ramifications would result from those oppositions. Perhaps the recurrent discussions regarding New Africa versus New America had taxed Sly's cardiac vessels beyond repair. Disputes between the offspring of the originally divided Lompoc group had produced two opposing belief systems. Proud native New Africans slammed up against the blended citizens of the "melting pot" New Americans. Many age-old issues of intolerance crowded their agendas. Much like a pack of siblings, the New African Lompoc family felt comfortable speaking their minds with their New American Lompoc brethren, each thinking their way was the preferred path. Neither group listened with both ears, however. Resolving the discord between the opposing countries for so many years, Sly had grown weary, tired. It was only a matter of time before the eighty-two-year-old cardiac time bomb detonated inside his chest.

Deek could feel the heaviness in the room when he entered. Younger, righteous congressional participants strutted around barking orders at one another. Sly had confided in Deek about the unfortunate changes brewing. The newer generations were absent of the loyalty and conviction that had been present when forming New Africa and New America. It was next to impossible to adequately pass on one's valued past. Reaper survivors had long given up the fight with their children and grandchildren when attempting to impose their values and beliefs upon them. As always, each generation moved forward, not backward. For each passing generation, WWIV and the Reaper stories were farther and farther removed, just another tale incorporated into the history books. Deek waited for the tension in the room to ease.

A handsome, headstrong descendant of Sly and Vera stepped to the front of the room.

"Deek, good to see you."

"Gabriel, I'm so sorry to hear about your grandfather."

"Thank you, sir."

"What can I do to help?"

"Nothing, really. As vice-president I'm sufficiently prepared to run the country." He lowered his voice. "Hell, my grandfather hasn't been making the hard decisions for the past year. It's been me, working behind the scenes."

"I see."

"My grandfather worked tirelessly to make New Africa what it is today. He was a fine man."

"I loved him as a brother."

"Deek, although there is no need, you are welcome to sit in on our congressional meet—"

"Your president wanted me here. He had many concerns and made me promise him—"

"Excuse me. Grandfather was old school. He just couldn't accept the fact that our world was no longer his. Trust me, we have everything under control."

"Gabriel—"

"Deek, sir, we're fine."

"Then you won't mind if I take you up on your offer and not only observe but participate in your meeting?"

"Not at all. Suit yourself."

"For the president's sake, I wouldn't want any of your youthful decisions to cause another world war."

"What would be the wisdom in that?"

"Indeed."

Chance & Justin

Except for his retired parents and quiet, unassuming uncles, Balic and Rami, Justin felt as though Kaikoura had become his. Most of the old influences, relatives and close neighbours Justin had grown up with, had moved on. Over the years, there had been quite an exodus from Kaikoura, the world's borders ever expanding. And the fact the small seaside town housed a serial killer did not help. Tanid relocated Hauku and their three little girls to New Zealand's North Island near Hauku's family, whereas Isaac and Clara's sons, Kendall, Quentin, and Evan, as well as Pete and Victoria's eldest, Tucker, became a part of Australia's rebirth. Anxious to take advantage of Australian riches, the New Zealand government had assembled a large group of volunteers to inhabit the once-thriving Aussie continent two years after WWIV. People branched out, staked claim on foreign territories. Harrison Whibley, Aerin's teenage buddy, had succumbed to a virus that seemed to spread throughout the South Island soon after the arrival of a ship filled with many dead and dying Aussies from the southernmost island of Tasmania. A delicate Harrison was one of the first fatalities. That was when the Whibley family had begun to unravel. Years passed before Tucker was finally sucked back into the Whibley vacuum; Australia had to wait. Reluctantly, Tucker had returned to Kaikoura to help stop the emotional family hemorrhaging, stemming from years of disrepair after Harrison's death.

Favoured by his father Pete, Tucker was forced down a path of survivor's guilt and smothering paternal disapproval.

Pete's pressure was intense. Although kind-hearted to those on the outside, his offspring never dodged his wrath. Pete felt the harder he was on Tucker, the better man Tucker would become. But that kind of pressure often produced predictable results, namely a life saturated with alcohol. Pete had eventually succeeded in his efforts; Tucker was the spitting image of Pete, definitely his father's son. Running the Whibley farm, beer in hand, Tucker was Pete incarnate.

When Lachlan was born, Cameron, Tanid, Justin, and any local and willing construction labourers built a third house on the Ermani property. It sat on the back acre in between Cameron and Aerin's home (previously Ari and Saroya's) and Balic and Rami's dwelling, which used to be Uncle Isaac and Auntie Clara's. Charming and warm, with Chance's artwork upon the many walls and Justin's published book alongside his leather-bound classics within their built-in bookshelf, the cottage left its young couple fulfilled. Lachlan's nursery was full of sunshine with walls and ceiling painted as an animated jungle. Chance had painted his bedroom with a world of unicorns, pixies, and humorous pirates. Imaginative ideas sprang from every corner. Lachlan was a truly lucky boy.

Every waking hour was spent on work or Lachlan. Chance painted, nursed her baby, washed clothes, sold paintings at the gallery, paid bills, cleaned the house, and napped whenever her son went down. Justin wrote, cooked breakfast, folded clothes, grocery shopped, ran the gallery, changed diapers, sketched, wrote some more, let his wife nap whenever Lachlan went down, cooked dinner, and slept for a short power nap when Chance awoke. Fatigue, as in most early relationships blessed with newborns, held them hostage.

Knowing this pace was only temporary kept the young couple from collapsing. With such minimal time for their creativity, Justin and Chance were especially productive during those cherished quiet moments. Lachlan dictated his cherished moments with at least one parent at a time. This meant most of the young couple's day was spent writing or painting, or tending to their precious son. However, exhaustion would never conquer Chance and Justin completely; their happiness would not allow it.

Inferno Killer

Worldwide infamy of the Inferno Killer catapulted Justin into literary notoriety. Constable Kittelty's detailed Inferno files had served as informative fodder for Justin's latest international bestseller. Kaikoura had housed a serial killer for many, many years. Although there were several theories documented by Kittelty as to viable suspects, the case was never solved. Local Kaikourans had passed on their theories regarding the Inferno Killer in the form of myths and legends. Inactive in the past few years, the vicious Inferno case became ice cold. Sadly, Justin's newly released book brought the recounted killings alive again. Constable Kittelty passed his knotted, liver-spotted fingers across a much younger version of his face that dominated the cover of Justin's book. He released a heavy sigh.

Reading the murder accounts, the Inferno Killer was mildly amused with Justin's book—such a gruesome story occurring in such a quaint town. However, N.Z.'s most notorious killer had slowed with old age. Murdering was for the young. There would be a time when the Inferno Killer would rise again with purpose. So much time would pass before the next critical burn. Two significant births had happened within different generations before and after Kittelty's reign. Two future players would engage in the Inferno battle yet again: one would be a protégé, one a future victim. The Inferno Killer read on. Justin was such an astute author. How close his legendary assumptions were. Kaikourans had no idea just how close they were to solving the Inferno case.

Aerin & Cameron

"I can't describe it, Cameron."

Cameron took a sleeping Lachlan from Aerin's arms and placed him within his portable playpen. "Are you saying the darkness you see and feel hovers around Chance? Or around Chance and Justin?"

"Well, it is just Chance, but Sweetheart, I never have visions regarding Justin. You know those closest to me, including myself, are like anyone else, simply gut reactions."

"Crikey, that really unnerves me, Aerin."

"I know, me too. Keep in mind, I've felt this darkness hovering around Chance since the day I met her, years ago, when the kids started dating."

"So we do not begin to know what or when?"

"Correct, Sweetheart. As closely as I watch her and Justin, the feelings stay the same. They don't intensify, but sometimes they won't leave me . . . they linger."

"You do not plan on telling Justin, do you?"

"Heavens, no. Besides, he would think I'm being an overly protective mother . . . and mother-in-law."

"No doubt. Well, let us enjoy our rambunctious grandson while we have him, Love."

Since the addition of a coffee shop attached to Justin and Chance's gallery, they had virtually no time for themselves. Business boomed. The locals loved their new artistic hangout. When Chance was not selling artwork, she and Justin had spent their days filling cups of coffee, making hot and iced tea, and lattes, and serving fresh pastries. Hiring a manager and an assistant had finally freed the young couple. Justin and Chance made plans immediately for a much-deserved, short getaway just for the two of them, so they could return as refreshed artists and parents.

RAPPING COULD BE HEARD AT the kitchen door. "Must be Tucker."

As soon as Cameron opened the door, a baby's wailing assaulted the tranquil evening.

"Oh, Tucker, bring me that little bloke."

"Nikki stormed out. I don't know where she went. I don't—"

"Go after her, mate. Aerin and I will watch Craig."

"Give him to me, Tucker." Craig grabbed Aerin's neck and continued to sob. "It's okay, Honey, Daddy will be back soon. Let's go see what baby Lachlan is doing, shall we?"

Craig raised his tear-streaked face and looked at Aerin. "Lala?"

"Yes, Little Man, let's go see Lala."

Cameron patted Tucker on the back. "Go, mate, go. We will take good care of little Craig." Tucker looked distraught. He glanced toward his son and baby Lachlan now happily playing together on the floor. "Go, we will put him to bed. You can pick him up whenever you wish, do not worry about us. We have Lachlan for the next few days. Go after Nikki."

"Thanks, Cameron."

"Sure, sure, no drama." Tucker raced for his garage. Cameron closed the door.

"Those poor kids, arguing again." Aerin ruffled Craig's hair as he played at her feet.

"Nikki is a tough little Sheila. She is not one to take Tucker's caustic mouth. As you have told me many times he is a mirror image of Pete when he drinks."

"Yeah, what a legacy Pete left behind. He wasn't satisfied passing on his maleness and gentle heart. No, Pete made sure Tucker inherited his chauvinism and tongue-lashings."

"Well, he'd better mellow or Nikki will stay gone for good."

Cameron joined Aerin on the sofa to watch Craig, almost two years old, and Lachlan, who had just celebrated his first birthday. As soon as he sat down, Cameron was up again to diffuse a tussle starting between the boys. Craig tugged on Lachlan's favourite caboose that lit up and talked when held. Lachlan's face was beet red with frustration. Cameron scooped up his grandson, turning him upside down. A burst of laughter escaped the baby. With his heavy Aussie accent, he cooed. "The Buds . . . Nandy's little Buds." After he plopped down his bundle of joy in the playpen, he grabbed Craig and tossed him in the air. "Who is this? Are you the Buds' mate?" Craig's giggling turned to a belly laugh when Cameron began to tickle the toddler.

Aerin quickly confiscated the culprit of the boys' squabble and hid the caboose behind a sofa cushion. She tickled Lachlan. Suddenly the living room was pregnant with toddler gaiety.

Amsterdam

He had never experienced such heights with a female. This one would be worth keeping around for a few more nights to cure his insomnia. How easy it was to hold one captive when one's insecurities took over. His latest AU freshman felt privileged, desired . . . such a youthful mistake. J.R. always feigned concern and compassion. To his female conquests, he explained his sacrifice of not being able to settle down. Tears were delicately handled. While around his trusted al Din henchmen, he voiced his despair. Only in his private confines did J.R. laugh. Such pathetic, wasted tears flowed from these ridiculous women. After a well-earned orgasm, J.R. found women's neediness exhausting and appalling. But he played the game well and slid out of their clutches with little disruption. Besides, the more powerful he became, the easier it was for J.R. to get his needs met with little conflict. His followers wanted him happy, so whatever was needed to advance the Christian movement was indulged. Secretly, J.R.'s concubines hoped they would be his Mary Magdalene, resurrected. Not the old prostitute version but the Mary Magdalene who became the wife of Jesus and lived out their secluded years together in southern France. Little did these foolish women know J.R.'s real opinion regarding their gender; to him women were truly inferior creatures. Their emotions and abundance of feelings kept them weak. J.R. could hardly stand to be around the opposite sex except when they were satisfying his sexual needs. They were so predictable, reminding him of every annoying woman in his life. Now that his popularity was bursting at Amsterdam's seams, J.R. found killing his sexual releases unnecessary. Nowadays, when he was finished with a woman al Din took care of her disposal. Local police believed the AU rapist had disappeared, moved on, or been arrested. Into the cold case cabinet his file had gone. Thankfully, J.R.'s latest conquest would not need extermination right away. She was different. This young teen knew better than to put any constraints on J.R. He was content.

Beyond the Amsterdam borders J.R.'s propaganda seeped, and it was gaining momentum. Backed with bundles of Dutch donations, J.R. headed for New Africa to spread his rebirthing of Christianity. This would be an easy task, because New Africa's founding Mothers and Fathers were ex-Americans, so there would be fewer Islamists blocking his new movement. Besides, his beliefs appealed to all religions. J.R.'s manipulations took hold with Christians, Jews, and Islamists alike. Desperate souls searching for some form of hope would have believed anyone no matter what they were selling. He just needed their ears. Five minutes with the New African strangers and J.R.'s gift of gab and charisma would soon have the gullible as part of his growing congregation . . . and their money in his pocket.

Maktan

Maktan suffered greatly. Several EyeNet calls from Mu'mad, after his initial departure to Nederland, had not gone well. Unable to reach him, she had been totally at the mercy of his obligatory whims. His calls came less and less frequently over the years. Maktan was worried. Her women's circle, which still included Muslims and infidels, were discussing "The Christian." His new movement prompted many a heated discussion. The latest debate regarded Joseph R. Smith, J.R., being labelled "Jesus Resurrected" by his beloved followers, which especially challenged the Christians. Maktan listened to the details that flew amongst the women's many critical opinions. Evidently, the ones who spoke highly of him, mostly the infidels but surprisingly some of the Muslims, listened to his speeches over the Internet. Maktan was terrified of technology and that included the cyber world. All this talk of J.R. troubled Maktan because he lived in the same city as her son. When Maktan received a lengthy letter from Mu'mad, her concerns intensified.

High marks at AU had eventually earned Mu'mad a prestigious professorship in religious studies at a smaller college nearby. He had been teaching there for the past eight years. In his letter, Mu'mad said his job was fulfilling. And there was talk of a younger Muslim woman in his life. Clad in the proper Islamic clothing and serious about honouring Allah, she sounded like Maktan's dream girl for her son. It was not the life Maktan had envisioned for Mu'mad, but he seemed happy. What else could a mother ask for her child? Perhaps grandchildren would come eventually. Maktan read further. Amidst the daily happenings in Mu'mad's life, darkness had appeared. Shocking news brought goose bumps to Maktan's skin. Out of the blue Mu'mad mentioned J.R. . . . and the man made her son nervous. Mu'mad actually sounded frightened. There were incidents on the AU campus over the years that Mu'mad had witnessed involving The Christian and young women. Without a doubt, J.R. was a force to be reckoned with and not to be crossed. As for Maktan's opinion, this Christian did not sound like a spiritual man at all, quite the opposite. That is why she was relieved when she read Mu'mad's final news that J.R. had departed Nederland and travelled to New Africa for a spiritual retreat.

Maktan reread Mu'mad's letter over and over, as well as carrying it with her everywhere. When meeting with her women's circle, she never breathed a word of her precious son's discomfort. She was there for only one reason, to listen and learn about The Christian.

Chance & Justin

Shackled within the dank, vestigial storm cellar, Ahmed cried. Not from the cold dampness or days without food but from fear of the inevitable destruction of Aerin's Chrysalis Society. The secret organization she had poured her soul into was about to be exposed. More importantly though, Aerin's life was in danger. He had to get free to warn her.

"Hey, Sweetheart, the car is all packed, snowboards, painting easels, journals, pens, everything."

"Crikey, Justin, I miss him already."

"Oh, Honey, Dad and Mum will be great with the baby."

"I know. The Buds always squirms with delight when he sees his Nandy Cameron."

"Listen, this skiing trip will be a great chance to rest, play, and let our creativity re-emerge."

"Oh, believe me; I'm so ready for a break. I just don't want my baby Lachlan to think his mum and daddy have abandoned him."

"I guarantee my parents won't give him the opportunity to even miss us. I'm more worried about how spoiled he'll be when we return."

"That I can live with."

Justin hugged Chance until he felt her tenseness ease. "Come, Sweetheart, the ski lodge with an oversized fireplace, and spa, awaits us."

With the laser and electrical barriers deactivated,

the dark Middle Eastern eyes were free to survey the beautifully decorated house. Yet another rich capitalist's obscene display of wealth. Into the living room, a tall blond man entered. The observer could see he held a toddler in his arms. For days he had watched their every move, and he would not be rushed. He watched and waited for his time to meet the evil woman doctor. When the observer finally made his move, he passed through the piggish murderer's unlocked door.

Aerin took Lachlan from Cameron and placed him in his crib. Little Craig was fast asleep in Lachlan's playpen. As she approached the bedroom door, Aerin's knees buckled as she doubled over in pain. Cameron raced to his wife's side.

"Oh, God, Cameron, my chest!"

"Dearest, what is wrong?"

"I'll be fine." The feeling of doom crashed in upon Aerin, which had caused her to collapse. "I'm feeling sharp pangs on both sides of my ribcage and throat. We've got to get the boys to the storm cellar, now!"

Without hesitation, Cameron grabbed Lachlan and Craig despite their tired protests. "Aerin? Love?"

"I'm right behind you!"

Just outside the South Island dome, Justin and Chance broke free. Over the years, air quality had improved immensely and the milky, corrosive rain had ceased falling. More and more people ventured outside dome living. Deeply entrenched in wintertime, Justin and Chance would join many others at the ever-popular ski slopes and resorts in Mt. Lyford, about an hour from Kaikoura. It felt strange to watch actual snow hit the hovercraft's windshield. Neither spoke. This trip was sorely overdue.

Without warning, their craft began to sputter. After a few violent jolts, Justin was compelled to bring the hovercraft to the ground. When he exited the vehicle, snow pelted his face. It felt wonderful. Before Justin could get to the engine to have a look, however, two sets of headlights, hovering low to the ground, were headed toward the stranded couple. Justin was elated. He waved frantically hoping the crafts would see his distress signal. Slowly the approaching vehicles descended the rest of the way to the ground.

Cameron regained consciousness. He could hear the babies crying, screaming. As he crept into the hallway, Cameron could barely see past a blanket of smoke filling the living room. The intruder had a rope around Aerin's neck. He screamed at her in Urdu. When the attacker started to drag Aerin out the front door, Cameron made his move. He lunged forward and tackled the intruder. As they wrestled about, he could hear Aerin choking. The Arab fought hard. Cameron's punches were not bringing the man down. Their battle intensified, each landing piercing blows. Aerin was not moving. This enraged Cameron further. He slammed the Arab's head against the floor until the attacker went limp, then rushed to Aerin's side. He clawed at the thick rope. Finally, he could see colour returning to her skin. With a huge gasp, Aerin breathed in a welcomed breath. Cameron held his wife close to his chest.

"Get the babies, Cameron." Aerin's voice was a raspy whisper.

Cameron jumped to his feet. His eyes burned and he coughed from the smoke. With a heavy throw blanket, he snuffed out the flames crawling their way up the drapes. Hysterical cries led Cameron to the bathroom where he found both boys confused and red-faced from wailing. Neither looked injured, so he quickly grabbed Craig and Lachlan again and ran for the storm cellar. A dazed Aerin stumbled behind him.

That is when he found poor Ahmed, gagged and chained to the cement wall. Cameron gently placed the boys on a blanket then struggled to release Ahmed. As soon as he pulled the gag from Ahmed's mouth, the shouting began.

"Where is Dr. Aerin? We have to get to her! Where—"

"Ahmed, hold still, mate! She was behind me."

"Go to her! Leave me! They're coming for her! The man with a knife!"

The lock finally clicked open releasing the chains that bound Ahmed's wrists. "Watch the babies, Ahmed."

Cameron ran back toward the house panicked. Where was Aerin? He screamed for her. The attacker no longer lay unconscious on the floor. He was gone. Cameron screamed Aerin's name over and over as he darted from room to room. Fresh air rushed in through an open window in the kitchen. That is where he found his battered wife.

"Aerin, Love, I thought you were behind me. Oh God, I am so sorry." Cameron started to look Aerin over more closely. He pulled her to a sitting position.

Aerin winced. "Sorry, I'm so dizzy."

Blood had soaked through the back of Aerin's sweatshirt. "Oh, Dearest, you are injured."

"Don't call 111, Cameron. Call Oswald."

Cameron grabbed one of Lachlan's diapers from the kitchen table and placed it over the knife wound on Aerin's hip. He lifted a weakened Aerin as he tried to keep pressure on her bleeding injury.

Aerin's eyelids fluttered. She whispered, "Oh God, Cameron . . . I taste bile."

Maktan

LONELINESS CONTINUED TO TEAR AT the core of her beliefs. All Maktan's dedication to Allah had come to this, nothing but a bunch of bitter, rigid Muslim acquaintances and an unappreciative son who ran far, far away and created a new life in a foreign country.

While the sadness of Mu'mad's absence clung to Maktan's broken heart, day after day, year after year, the only person who had been remotely comforting was a redheaded Western infidel named Beth. Each painful day that crept by, Maktan had found herself drawn to the condo down the hall. Warmth exuded from Beth's home. Widowed by WWIV and left to raise two boys by herself, Beth knew all too well the crippling feelings of a shattered heart.

Riddled with grief from her husband's death, she had laid a heavy burden upon her twin boys. That is why after high school graduation both sought to further their education many miles away in Australia, far from their emotionally crippled mother. When Beth spoke of that maternal loss, Maktan felt that agony deep in her soul. Maktan's Muslim friends saw her as weak. Pity never entered a conversation. Beth not only identified with Maktan's pain, but she offered ways to release the debilitating ache inside.

Yes, Beth spoke of independence, both hers and Maktan's. With such pure intent, Beth schooled her friend in the ways of self-love and inner peace. Maktan was just vulnerable enough to devour every word, even those regarding a loving God. These words were hard to hear, but at night, Maktan pondered them as she always had in the past. Beth was right. Allah had not felt so loving over the years. But her version of Allah was only unkind and terrifying via man's interpretations.

Beth never judged Maktan's beliefs; she simply challenged them. Slowly, as the years passed, Maktan had tested her Islamic boundaries, pushing further and further, each day, week, and month. Reading her first romantic novel had not ended with Allah striking her dead. It was entertainment for entertainment's sake. Allah did not even seem to mind that Maktan had abandoned her burka and regularly wore jeans. And it had actually felt good to wear the denim pants when gathering with the harsh Muslim group.

Defiance rapidly reduced Maktan's repressed frustrations. Allah had not punished Maktan even after she had had her first glass of wine. She was still alive. Rejection and condemnation came from Maktan's Islamic constituents, not Allah. She had actually welcomed the ever-increasing disdain thrown her way from the judgmental Muslim women; it made her stronger. Maktan felt liberated. As for Beth, she had become a wonderful distraction, such a compassionate person.

Especially torturous for Maktan had been her failed attempt at visiting Mu'mad in Amsterdam. Arriving unannounced in Nederland one month after Mu'mad left Vancouver, Maktan had felt lost among the tsunami of fair-skinned faces. Only when she found her hotel and checked into her room had Maktan felt safe again. Being so far from home had stirred such feelings of fear and insignificance. Three days of waiting patiently at Mu'mad's dorm room door caused Maktan's maternal protectiveness to override all else. What if her son was hurt somewhere? What if the Syrians had found him? Maktan became sick with worry. When a pimple-faced student approached Maktan and informed her Mu'mad was out of town on holiday with some of his mates, her anxiety waned. Never planning to stay more than five days, Maktan returned to Vancouver quite dejected. She missed her boy terribly, but staying in Amsterdam had left Maktan vulnerable to any Middle Eastern WWIV survivors who still searched for her. Leaving the Vancouver International Airport after her return, Maktan stayed covered under her raincoat hood, making sure no one followed her home.

Fifteen minutes later, Maktan's hovertaxi had arrived at her high-rise unaccompanied. As soon as she got to her penthouse level, Maktan walked swiftly, almost ran, to her redheaded friend's condo. When Beth opened the door, Maktan's tears flowed. She grabbed Maktan and hugged her, not letting go until her friend was ready. Beth was such a comfort. Ironically, she too had tried to surprise her boys while in Australia. However, Beth's visit was accomplished but horrifically unsuccessful. Both boys were furious with their mother's intrusion. Smothering by nature, Beth's innocent attempt at a casual visit spiralled into yet another manipulative way to control her offspring. Beth had boarded her flashjet with a heart filled with dejection and humiliation. At least Maktan had avoided that heartache. Beth patted Maktan as she let her cry out completely. How lucky she was to have someone who understood her pain. And Maktan knew Beth was the only person who could comfort her. She had learned so much from this Western friend.

After so many years, the internal calm Beth had spoken of repeatedly had gradually taken hold inside Maktan. Beth had truly given Maktan an eternal gift. Inner peace was a treasured commodity never to be lost once gained. Best friends who had shared grief throughout the years now shared crow's feet at the sides of their eyes, intruding grey in their hair, and hopeful talks of daughters-in-law and grandchildren. Sharing their habitual morning cup of java or tea together, Beth and Maktan found comfort reading the newspaper and investigating the Internet. Maktan had opted for tea this chilly morning, for coffee often gave her the jitters. While Maktan sipped her steamy chamomile tea, Beth fiddled with a cordless keyboard on her lap. Soon she brought a picture onto the MV flatscreen positioned over the living room fireplace. She tapped her fingertips quickly across the keys. Maktan put her newspaper down and watched with fascination. As fast as Beth's fingers moved, the screen seemed to jump from one confusing picture to another. Maktan was highly educated but never in the intricacies of the World Wide Web. The clicking of the keys slowed as Beth arrived at her cyber destination. Suddenly there were hordes of people on the screen with a man providing the commentary.

Beth addressed Maktan by the only name she had gone by since her frightening encounter with Irshad many, many years ago. "Yonca, it's him, look, the one they call The Christian."

They listened to the man describe the events taking place in Cape Town, New Africa. Then the camera zoomed in on the reason for the crowd. There he was, the man Mu'mad had spoken of often in his infrequent letters.

"My son calls him J.R."

"What does Zeren think of him?"

"He fears him, Beth. That is hard for my proud son to admit."

"I can see why he scares him. Look at those people, Yonca. They worship this man as if he is God himself. I don't know . . . I don't trust him. Where did he come from? No one knows."

Maktan was mesmerized. She could not take her eyes from the chiselled jaw line covered with a slight, dark beard peppered with grey. The young messiah's shoulder-length hair was dark brown with blond streaks, which gave him a sunny, weathered look. Vanity, now there was a spiritual contradiction. What really bothered Maktan were his dark sunglasses. What was he hiding? Why not let the world gaze into his eyes, study the depths of his soul?

"This man preaches tolerance for every religion, yet he criticizes each and every one. There's a side of him that is very inconsistent."

"To believe this man is to go against one's core beliefs. He bothers me too, Beth."

"It's just hard to pin down what he is really preaching. I'm worried he has ulterior motives."

"As horrible as my Islamic upbringing was, this Christian causes me to want to defend those repressive fibres of my youth."

"What was it like, Yonca, being a child in the Middle East?"

"Oh, Beth—"

"I'm sorry; it's none of my business. I know you don't like to discuss such things."

"No, no, Beth, I trust you. The sad thing is I didn't know it was horrible until I arrived in Canada. That has been a very hard pill to swallow."

"A different perspective, eh?"

"Definitely... the maltreatment of women is ingrained in Islam. There is forever a need to cover up all distinctive features of our female bodies, lest we commit the unpardonable sin of arousing men's desires. A Muslim man's accusing finger always, always finds a woman, Beth. When we became teenagers, my sisters and I were promised to men with no choice. I was lucky, I felt honoured at the time to be the wife of Zeren's father, even though he was quite a bit older. I was so pampered after providing him with an heir. But then, most of my female friends, and all my sisters, were married to older men. It was the norm, to be expected. However, the majority of their husbands were wrinkled, grey-haired and generally so disgusting that one's stomach contents easily curdled. At least my husband was handsome and powerful."

"That's horrible. How old were the women?"

"Fifteen, sixteen, some a bit older."

"Oh, that's disturbing."

"It's how we were raised, Beth. It's all we knew. We were not servants of Allah; we were slaves of man. The Quran is not a holy document. It is a historical record written by humans, a version of events as perceived by the men who wrote it 150 years after the Prophet Muhammad died. And it is a very tribal and Arabic version of events. It spreads through a culture that is brutal, bigoted, fixated on controlling women, and harsh in war. This too took me years to accept. Additionally, we were taught the Quran in Arabic, which many Muslims don't even speak, let alone understand."

"Well, we all know no religion is perfect, Yonca."

"I used to think Islam was. That is until I arrived in

Canada and listened, a lot. I spent many months, years, pondering Allah and Islam. And I spent many months, years feeling forlorn and adrift. I have discovered the cause of backwardness and misery in the Muslim world is not Western oppression but Islam itself, a faith that proclaims contempt for enlightenment. It teaches hatred to children, promises a grotesque version of an afterlife, and elevates the cult of martyrdom. Islam flirts with the mad idea of forced conversion of the non-Islamic world onto others – can you believe that? How arrogant is that belief? What boils my blood the most is Islam deprives societies of the talents and energies of fifty percent of their members, our female half. Beth, I've grown to believe that my marriage was even a farce. The more I have grown up I've realized how naïve I had been with my husband. I thought I was an exception. Now looking back, I know he had other women. I was so stupid to believe I was enough for him. Our culture encourages infidelity on the man's part. I was so young."

"Maybe he didn't cheat, Yonca. Maybe he was the exception."

"No, I'm sure of it. I was so busy hating the Westerners I didn't pay attention to those times when he returned home late smelling of someone else. I wasted so much time hating our collective enemies. My struggles were blamed on the West. So many of my relatives and ancestors taught me it was not because of Quranic fanaticism that our children's teeth rotted, disease and illiteracy was rampant, and nothing much except the police system seemed to work. No, it had to be because of Jews and Christian Crusaders that Muslims suffered."

"Well, it would have been nice if WWIV had changed

those atrocities. Unfortunately, I fear our chance for a clean slate never took hold after the war. And now, look at this Christian creep; he's not promoting peace and harmony.

"He says he is."

"But that's just it, Yonca, it's all talk."

"Talk is powerful when not recognizing hurtful practices."

"You are so right. I'm sorry your earlier years were so painful, Yonca. I feel so lucky to have you as my friend."

"Same here. You are a daily reminder that Allah does really love me. You are my wonderful Western infidel, Beth, and I'm thankful you are a non-believer. You have uncovered a life, my life that for so long was helplessly buried by fanatical ignorance. You helped me rise above childhood hatred and find myself, Beth. For that I am eternally grateful."

Kittelty

"I'M ADAMANT! THIS WAS A copycat killing!"

"You don't know that for sure, Kittelty. There's been so much press on the Inferno Killer, not to mention Justin Thorpe's book. Our killer could have easily changed his MO to create more confusion. There's never been any doubt that we are dealing with an intelligent sonofabitch."

"Nonsense, young man; this killer copied exactly what I released to the media, and young Thorpe for his book, but failed to be consistent on every other detail I didn't mention."

"Kittelty—"

"Baker, the autopsies showed the organs in the victims' thoracic and abdominal cavities were intact, no ash-like substance. The accelerant used was not a petroleum derivative. The killer used alcohol, which was a slower burn giving him time to escape. And their clothes—"

"So the bodies didn't have a chance to burn all the way through, that doesn't mean anything. The Inferno Killer has surfaced again and we can't be careless, dismissing these deaths as a singular grudge kill."

"Listen, Baker, the clothes weren't burned off them."

"Oh, you can stop all that internal combustion crap!"

"Young man, you weren't here to examine those Inferno corpses."

"Just because I'm new to this district doesn't mean I'm not familiar with the case. Inferno burns his victims plain and simple; inside out, or outside in, it doesn't matter."

"Well, you obviously didn't read everything."

"No, you listen here, old man. I don't have to take your impertinence. Enjoy your retirement and leave the Inferno Killer to us. You've been obsessed with this case from the get-go. You needed a collar-jerk way back when, Kittelty. Your head was so buried in detail you started reading nonsensical fabrications into this case. Inferno owes his infamous, sensational, mastermind bullshit to you and you alone. Your theories are ridiculous. The man douses people with accelerant and strikes a match, no more no less."

"You couldn't be further from the truth. Your youth betrays you and it's left your forensic expertise a lot to be desired. This ruthless bastard used his victims as a human wick. The fat liquefied from the heat inside the victims' bodies, absorbed into their clothing, which caused each to act like a wick when eventually catching fire on the outside."

"Kittelty, that's—"

"That's the multiple wick effect, look it up! Inferno burns his victims from the inside out. That's a huge difference, don't you think? One last thing you haven't considered, which is probably bigger than internal combustion, Inferno murdered despicable people. The Thorpes in no way fit that description. They were valued citizens on their way to Mt. Lyford, ambushed, murdered, then lit on fire. We have a copycat killer plain and simple."

Ex-constable Kittelty finally penetrated the young constable's rational approach. He had his attention for the first time. Both stared at Chance and Justin's partially charred bodies lying upon the steel autopsy gurneys.

Aerin & Cameron's Escape

SECURED WITHIN THEIR SECRET CELLAR, Cameron, Aerin, Ahmed, Oswald, Balic, Rami, and the babies were all silent. No one from the outside could get to them in Balic and Rami's impenetrable cement building. The doors were filled with reinforced steel like the building walls. Window vents made of unbreakable glass would only open by a central computer system, no locks or latches. Any intruders would activate boundary lasers and electrical charges if they passed through the barrier, killing the perpetrators instantly. And so they sat together in silence and disbelief. Shock had taken hold of Cameron and Aerin. Like petals plucked from a rare flower, Chance and Justin had been on Earth for such a brief stay.

Prime Minister Oswald held a sleeping Lachlan. Little man Craig was sound asleep, curled up next to Ahmed with his head in Ahmed's lap. Gently he stroked Craig's hair.

Oswald spoke softly, "Ahmed, the man attacked you first?"

"Yes, sir. He followed me on my way into the cellar a couple of days ago, put a knife to my throat. He kept repeating that Dr. Aerin had killed his son."

"Killed him?"

"Brainwashed him. His son was one of the grey souls we converted. Because his own son renounced Islamic ways, the father felt compelled to kill him, all in the name of Allah, naturally. The man claimed Dr. Aerin was the infidel bitch who ruined, killed his son."

Oswald looked confused. "But didn't Aerin say these reformations of grey souls, using Glowworm, leave the individuals feeling cleansed and reborn? Why would they share their experience with rigid fanatics?"

"Most of us are so appreciative of a second chance at life; we cut ties with those ignorant, destructive believers of a distorted Islam. Evidently, this converted man thought he could convince his fanatical father otherwise. Dr. Aerin was the receiver of this older man's hate."

A tear rolled down Cameron's cheek. He stared at his beloved Aerin, unconscious and fighting for her life; she lay horizontal on the bench, her battered head in his lap. "Oswald, mate, I have got to get Aerin out of Kaikoura."

Ahmed said, "Cameron, sir, you need to get her out of New Zealand. Talk amongst the Muslim community is, Dr. Aerin must be killed. She is corrupting the followers of Allah. None of you are safe here. These are the same men who killed Chance and Justin."

"I will release to the press that both you and Aerin died in the fire, Cameron. Ahmed's right, we need to get you two and the baby out of the country."

"Oswald, call Deek and Lourdes. With the loss of Justin and Chance, they will need to see their grandson. Maybe we can stay in Cape Town."

"Will do. Balic—"

Rami stood. "We'll take care of it, Oswald. If you'll make the call, we will orchestrate their escape."

Aerin's eyes opened. Balic gently grabbed his sister's arm. "Come on, Aerin. You need to be strong for your grandson. He needs you now." He turned to Oswald. "Make the call and release the false death information. We'll take care of little Craig. Is there a ship going to New Africa where we can stow away everyone safely?"

"I'm not sure, but rest assured, we'll make it happen."

Aerin cleared her scratchy throat and whispered to her husband. "I tasted bile, Cameron."

"You were stabbed, Dearest."

"No, no it wasn't my fluids I tasted, it was Justin's. Those Arabs stabbed him and cut Chance's throat."

Cameron swelled with grief yet again. "Oh god, my precious son. Oh god." Cameron wept. No one knew how to comfort him. Cameron spoke softly to Justin above. "We will take care of The Buds. He will not forget you, Son." Cameron drew Aerin closer as they both sobbed.

THEIR STAGED ESCAPE WAS A success. No one suspected Aerin and Cameron were still alive. Cremated, Chance and Justin's remains were preserved in an urn aboard the ship that would take the Thorpes to Cape Town. The Desert Muslims took the bait when sealed, empty coffins were used at Aerin and Cameron's memorial service. Rid of the evil Dr. Aerin, they felt vindicated. Ahmed was relieved the Chrysalis Society had not been exposed or compromised because many deaths would have followed if it had. Tearful goodbyes were all that remained at the Wellington docks. A shattered neighbourhood and seaside town would sorely miss the Thorpe family.

DURING THE VERY EARLY HOURS of the morning, Cameron, Aerin, and baby Lachlan stole away into the fog-filled night. Tucked within the captain's quarters, Cameron and his precious wife clung to their grandson's bursts of joyful oblivion for days. Never having been on New African soil before, Aerin welcomed another foreign beginning. Nothing, except Deek, Lourdes, Cameron, and Lachlan, would remind her of her adored son and daughter-in-law.

Cape Town was truly spectacular. Its inhabitants were gracious enough to accept Cameron, Aerin, and baby Lachlan. Any relative of Deek's was considered part of the New African family.

"As much as we appreciate your hospitality, Deek, it is not safe, mate. I could not live with myself if we brought more death to our extended family. Our skin, mate, is much too light, not very inconspicuous, when trying to remain hidden. We three must feel free to hide in broad daylight in the company of many."

"Listen, I too would not have our grandson harmed, nor you or Aerin. My conscience won't allow it. There is a tightly knit Dutch community on the northern outskirts of the city where I know you'll be safe. They don't take kindly to newcomers, but rest assured if I take you to them you'll be accepted immediately. You see, I helped them settle within Cape Town years ago. Seems they left Nederland because of radical religious oppression in the post-war government. Corruption started in Amsterdam but has since been flushed out. These people are a quiet farming township that keep to themselves."

"Predominantly Christians?"

"More spiritual than religious. I can tell you this, I know of no Islamists in the bunch. These Dutch farmers are peaceful, non-violent believers more than anything."

"That sounds refreshing. And you are sure they will accept us?"

"From the looks of that blond fuzz on Lachlan's tiny, bald head, and those powder-blue eyes he obviously inherited from his Nandy, you'll have no trouble at all. Your light skin, eyes, and hair will do nicely. However, Aerin's hair needs to be lightened and of course, we'll need to fabricate new identities for you all. Play up Aerin's Canadian background. That can be easily explained: Australians and Canadians used to participate in work exchanges. That can be how the two of you met years ago. We'll work together to create a believable story. Current friction in North Vancouver will support your supposed move to New Africa."

"I am nervous, Deek. How can we be sure word won't get back to those shonky bastards back in Kaikoura?

"Because you're dealing with a peaceful bunch as I said. They'll accept your delivered identities. They're not an overly suspicious group, just private. Of course, Aerin will have to keep a low profile, meaning no more medicine."

"I do not think she could concentrate on saving lives even if she tried, mate. Taking care of Lachlan seems to be the only thing keeping her sane these days."

"For those close to me who know you, Cameron, consider you and yours part of my family. You are without a doubt family as far as Lourdes and I are concerned. The Cape Town citizens will keep your anonymity. Besides, we don't want troubled Muslim conflict on our soil. Believe me, it will be a safe place for Lachlan to grow up. Lourdes and I will help you with any communications to Balic, Rami, and Tanid initially, until this tragedy quiets down. We've secured a beautiful, modest farm with a quaint Dutch cottage. I'm sure you'll learn to love it. Lourdes took great care in fixing it up and stocking the kitchen with lots of food. The whole process kept her mind off Chance, for brief moments, here and there. I know it will be quite a while before you'll feel like venturing out into your new township. Take your time. Your new neighbours won't push. Welcome home, Cameron." Deek's eyes welled up. "God, I miss the kids. Sometimes when I think about Chance it hurts so much I feel as though I'm having a heart attack."

Cameron's eyes were damp as well. "I miss them too, mate. I think about them off and on every day." Deek nodded. "Thank God we have our grandson."

"Indeed."

Across the room sat Aerin, deep in thought. While she rocked Lachlan to sleep, she gnawed at a ragged fingernail. Cameron sighed. That bad habit had resurfaced after twenty-plus years, a trait Aerin indulged in during her most troubled times.

Lachlan

YEARS AND YEARS INCHED BY and life became comfortable again, perhaps too comfortable. History's repetition unfortunately found a place in modern existence. Such a dusty cliché had lain dormant in the shadows for generations only to re-emerge with a slothful gluttony. Threatened by the power-hungry, fanatical elite few, peace again would become a scarce commodity.

Vulnerable from her stab wound and broken heart, Aerin's life was cut short. Although she was committed to making Lachlan's childhood fulfilling, inside, Aerin battled an unending depression. Playing melancholy songs on her flute and biting her nails repeatedly had returned with a vengeance. Shortly after Lachlan turned three years old, Cameron was not surprised when Aerin's pneumonia took a turn for the worse. A weakened spirit for years had eroded Aerin's health. Even her unwavering spiritual convictions were not enough. Unable to practise medicine, or more importantly, feel the touch of her treasured Justin again, Aerin had been left completely hollow. No amount of dedicated spirituality could pull her from a debilitating sadness that eventually devoured her from within. A hard psychic truth was that extreme grief blocked the desired dead person from appearing. This exacerbated Aerin's condition for she could not get Justin to appear.

Ironically, Lourdes died only a year after Aerin. Deek, too, had a despondent wife on his hands. For years, her heart ached for Chance. She was everything to her mother and father, but a strong bond had grown between Lourdes and Chance after WWIV. Lourdes had rebuilt her life in New Zealand alone with her baby girl. It was mother and daughter against every other human being left on the planet until Deek entered the scene. Lourdes had listened to Aerin's visions in the past and was equally frustrated when Aerin was unable to conjure up Justin or Chance. Even if she had, it would not have lessened Lourdes' saddened state. She wanted to hear her daughter's voice, touch her beautiful hair and skin, and watch her be a mother to Lachlan. What Lourdes had not internalized was that Aerin, psychic intuition or not, privately fought the same internal battle.

Cameron and Deek did their best to keep the memory of Lachlan's Nana Aerin and Grammy Lourdes alive within him. Snapshots covered the walls of Lachlan's home as well as his Papa Deek's. Childhood stories were told and retold of his parents and grandmothers. Whereas Deek taught his grandson rugby and American football, Cameron carried on the tradition of fairy tales and books, "chickies and dollies,"and those mysterious rustling bushes. Six-year-olds were easily fooled into believing someone was hiding in the shadows while walking the long path home each evening. Deek showered Lachlan with sports and stories of sharks and lions, and Cameron kept his grandson firmly planted within Justin's footsteps. For such a small boy he was quite wise. To say Lachlan was a highly intuitive child was an understatement. Deek and Cameron often discussed an all-knowing smirk Lachlan often wore upon his face and the bright intensity he carried in his eyes. Both grandfathers agreed their grandson saw more than they could ever see.

Lachlan's New Zealand

When Lachlan had finished high school, Balic and Rami finally convinced Cameron it was safe to return to New Zealand. Several fanatical Islamic movements had begun on the South Island only to be disbanded as quickly as they began. Many of the men who held disdain for Dr. Aerin had long since died or were rotting in prison. Cameron jumped at the chance to relocate. Living with a broken Aerin for years had scarred his heart. He longed for happier days when he and Aerin had shared joy and were filled with hope. Kaikoura beckoned him and his phenomenal grandson.

It was difficult leaving their Dutch community, however. These people had been good to the Thorpes. Excited about his journey to New Zealand with his Nandy, Lachlan was equally saddened about leaving his friends and Papa Deek. Assured he would get to visit as often as he liked, Lachlan worked hard to keep the sorrow from taking residence inside his inexperienced heart. Papa Deek planned to visit Kaikoura soon, which would ease much of Lachlan's sorrow.

Being back in New Zealand felt more like a dream than a distant memory for Lachlan. Many of his built-in mannerisms, which were not any part of the Dutch culture, suddenly made sense. This allowed Lachlan the transition into his new life to be much easier. Somehow, in Dutch Africa he never felt like he fit in completely. As a young child, Lachlan had been drawn to the Maori people even though he was miles away. And he thanked Nandy for that.

Throughout Lachlan's formative years, Nandy Cameron had kept the Kiwi world alive inside his grandson. Cape Town was a beautiful place to live, but New Zealand held many family memories and secrets to discover. Kaikoura was simply home.

From the first week of settling in, Lachlan had dived into restoring the musty, abandoned family home. His Nandy helped when he could but was growing tired. Either from old age or from melancholy it did not matter, Cameron had earned the right to rest. Filled with an abundance of youthful energy, Lachlan worked tirelessly. It warmed Cameron's heart to see his grandson alive with purpose. While in Dutch Cape Town, he felt he was ever so slowly losing Lachlan. Troubling dreams and night sweats for the boy had increased in frequency, and these bouts of insomnia had begun to affect his grades at school. Some ethereal force was summoning Lachlan to return to Aotearoa, "Land of the Long White Cloud," a magical New Zealand. When he had confronted his Nandy after a morbid nightmare about returning home, there was no resistance. Without hesitation, the Thorpe men packed their lives in boxes and headed for their homeland. Lachlan had his first week of solid sleep on Kiwi soil in the heart of tranquil Kaikoura. Even more of an indicator that he, Nandy, and Papa Deek had made the right decision for him to return came in the form of a stunning blonde.

Toddler, little man Craig, had turned into a fine young man. Filled with stories from his Nandy how he and Craig played together as babies, Lachlan felt immediately drawn to his laconic neighbour. Always clad in his free-spirited colourful New African shirts and Vans® tennis shoes, Lachlan was quite the opposite of Craig who wore drab clothing and a withered look across his weathered face. Aged beyond his years, there was nothing youthful about Craig. Abandoned by his mother, Nikki, as a baby, all Craig had known was his borderline-abusive father, Tucker. Born with a demeanour more like his deceased Uncle Harrison, Craig took parental "tough love" quite hard. Constant disapproval led to massive doses of shame and disappointment. Upon Tucker's early death, Craig, with his sensitive constitution, felt a prolonged sadness. Yet another heavy burden, Craig's guilt soon replaced the sluggish depression from his overwhelming relief when his father finally passed. When he had a son, if he had a son, he would never make him sink to the depths of self-loathing as his father had done to him. Constantly told he was worthless, Craig was content to live an isolated existence running the Whibley farm. Human contact was much too painful. So what if he never contributed much to the world, at least his animals loved him. That had to be enough. It had to be or he might go insane.

Little had Craig known his future was about to change abruptly with the arrival of his childhood friend, Lachlan. Immediately the two young men became inseparable. Living next door was simply a convenient perk. Their friendship had started as babies, destined to be rejoined and last through adulthood. Whereas Lachlan was amazed with, and drawn to, Craig's quiet wisdom, Craig was astounded by Lachlan's ability to attract people, especially the opposite sex. Women were quite creative when trying to get Lachlan's attention. However, he was unfazed. Lachlan thought women were wonderful, but he never exploited their attention. He kept things balanced, as his father had. Craig on the other hand was terrified. Women had been a source of heartache and anger for his father. What Tucker had passed on to Craig was raw fear. Bring a woman into your life and she will eventually rip it to shreds. That is why Craig resisted vehemently when Lachlan planned a night out to survey downtown Kaikoura … specifically, the Kaikoura Police Station.

Several years Lachlan's senior, Hailee Kittelty was Kaikoura's new chief of police. Law enforcement had skipped a generation in Hailee's family. Her father, bitter from his father's constant absence, was never drawn into that time-sucking, all-consuming lifestyle. He wanted more for his children, at least an active father in their lives. When Hailee had followed in her grandfather Kyle Kittelty's footsteps, it had stirred those familiar feelings of resentment once buried by her father. He was dead against Hailee's career path. Fighting his eldest daughter at every turn had proven fruitless, for Hailee had long before made up her mind. Wilful, tough, and highly intelligent, Hailee was the epitome of her grandfather. Add a powerful dose of feminine beauty and Hailee was an impossible battle for the young Kaikouran men to conquer. Most of the locals had vied for a date at one time or another, when courage or self-abuse was at its pinnacle, and failed miserably. A few lucky chaps had landed maybe one or two outings at the most, but none had ever sustained a long-term relationship with her. Hailee knew what she wanted and she was not afraid to wait until she found that man.

Beaming with the prospects of his new life, Lachlan was the happiest he had ever been. No one could ruin his rested state of mind. With an impenetrable confidence and infectious demeanour, Lachlan was not impressed so much as amused when he literally ran into the tough, somewhat haughty Hailee at the local market. He had witnessed attractive women before with that arrogant "pick and choose" attitude. True, Hailee made Lachlan's heart beat faster, but he was not about to join the ranks of the other poor sods and drool all over her. No, Lachlan knew if she was worth pursuing, the last thing he should do was just that: pursue her. Hailee would have to meet him halfway. Yes, the "new boy in town" with his multi-coloured shirts, well-worn tennis shoes, and latte in hand would skilfully draw the local princess Hailee from her comfortable throne. So when Hailee batted long eyelashes that framed translucent green eyes at Lachlan, he had responded with a heart-stopping smile, quick handshake, and "pleased-to-meet-you" goodbye. After all, Lachlan knew what he wanted in a woman and was willing to wait as well. That is why he let eight full days pass before he dragged a reticent Craig with him to the local police precinct. It was time to find out more about this mysterious girl.

"Sometimes grace is a ribbon of mountain air that gets in through the cracks."

~ Anne Lamott

Author of *Grace (Eventually): Thoughts on Faith*

RIPPLE EFFECT

Evil Arises . . .

Kaikoura, New Zealand

So I DARED TO SPEAK of the past; I stirred regretfully those sleeping hornets. Lachlan was astonished and exhausted. I had laid tough discoveries upon his youthful shoulders.

"Miss Hailee, chicky or dolly, Lach?" I closed the last of the journals and nodded at Deek who had joined us earlier in our discussion.

"Both, Nandy. You know Hailee is both. Can I see that last journal?" Lachlan flipped through the pages looking at nothing in particular. Deep in thought, he ran his fingers over the faded, tired pages.

"That is my boy. Buds and Hailee—"

"I know, blah, blah, blah . . . boy meets girl and they make a most unlikely union. Let's leave the love story for Vollywood in Vancouver, shall we? I want to discuss this outrageous, dodgy story you and Papa Deek have just unloaded on me."

Sitting on the divan, amongst Aerin's journals, news clippings, and father Justin's book, Lachlan's head reeled with disgust, love, and disbelief.

"It is not a story, Buds; every word we have spoken is the truth. It is important you know your family history."

"But you want me to believe Nana Aerin was some kind of hero. I'm not buying it. She manipulated people's souls."

"Buds, an open mind, remember, mate? There is a very specific reason we are dredging up the past."

"Well, please get to the point, Nandy, I have a lot to do. This hasn't helped a bit."

"Very well, the point of this long-winded narrative is to prep you for what is to come." Deek and I exchanged a quick, apprehensive glance.

"Nandy? This tale is—"

"It is not a tale, Lach."

"Papa Deek, why unload all this—"

"Because you are your Nana's lad. And it is time you face who you really are," I interjected.

"What are you talking about?"

"You may have Papa Deek's athletic abilities, your Grammy Lourdes' beautiful skin, and my powder-blue eyes, Buds, but your intuitiveness was passed to you from your Nana Aerin's lineage. I am not trying to diminish your uniqueness, Lachlan. True, you possess pieces of all of us, especially your parents, but you are very much your own bloke. However, it was very important for you to hear about your history so you do not miss any opportunities to reap the benefits of your gift."

"Gift?"

Deek added, "We watch you. We hear you at night when you sleep hot. Your dreams speak the truth, don't they? Ever since you were a tiny boy your slumber state never lied, Lachlan."

"Papa Deek, Nandy, a lot of people claim to be psychic, so what? We have free will. What may be envisioned can change in a heartbeat. Frankly, I think it's all a bunch of bollocks."

"Is it? Your dreams speak to you if you will listen. Your night sweats are severe . . . and you talk in your sleep."

"Lots of people talk while asleep."

On the end table next to me, I grabbed a remote control. When I pressed the top button, we were flooded with Lachlan's voice as a boy. His words were clear and accurate.

"Lachlan, you were five years old. You heard your words, mate . . . the Beast is alive. That is how I knew you had the gift of sight like your grandmum. Your Nana Aerin comes from a family, of psychics. On her mother's side of the family, Aerin's lineage can be traced back to the famous French seer, Nostradamus. Your gift is not to be taken lightly. Buds, Nana Aerin had night sweats too."

"Nostradamus?" We nodded; waited for the information to penetrate. Unimpressed, Lachlan's complexion flushed with anger. "Nandy, Papa Deek, so you are telling me I'm destined to live Nana's life? Why wait until now to tell me all of this?"

"We did not think it necessary to burden you with pertinent predictions. We wanted you to have a quiet childhood."

"Then why now?"

"You said you needed help; none of the elders are listening. You have repressed your talent, ignored your visions, while growing up. Well, it is time to embrace your lineage, welcome your abilities, Lachlan." Deek squeezed his grandson's broad shoulder.

"So you're telling me I'm to fight them with psychic mumbo-jumbo? Wow, this has been a colossal waste of time."

"We are not trying to tell you what to believe, Buds. There are dark souls in that group and genocide is their goal. We have discussed this. And what about the evil one?"

"He is a monster that is for certain; I know it . . . feel it with every fibre of my being. What I've been trying to get from both of you is how I am supposed to conquer pure evil."

"And what we have been trying to get you to see is you

need to discuss this very topic with the elders, Buds, using your gift. Know this . . . if they will not listen, then you may need to act alone." Arms folded, Lachlan had reached the pinnacle of his aggravation. "And you know your troubling dreams will not subside until there is resolution."

"Alone? Nandy? Papa?"

"Alone. Search your soul, Buds, like your Nana. There has to be a way to trap this embodiment of evil."

Lachlan

Despite our best efforts to ease him into his transformation, Lachlan, lost in thought, would not speak to me, or his Papa Deek, for two days. Late on the third night, he came to me, very troubled.

"I've been dreaming hot again, Nandy."

"I know . . . I heard you, Buds."

"What did Nana do with her visions? How did you deal with her?"

"We searched for meaning, picked every aspect apart. Know this, we treated her vision as a gift, not a burden. What did you see, Buds?"

"Powerful blokes crawling from caves and the underground. Those close to the leader follow and stay loyal."

"Are you able to untangle what it means?"

"These dreams are so upsetting but out of focus; and they seem to be coming in more frequently. I almost hate to sleep at night, Nandy. I can't tell if these blokes are bad souls or if there are some good ones worth saving."

"Maybe the future can be changed. Maybe that was your warning, to simply be alert."

"How do I change the outcome though when I can't identify the enemy?"

"Lachlan, in time those answers will be revealed. Do not choke the process . . . let the visions flow and be patient. This is what your Nana had to learn. Buds, Papa Deek will be back tomorrow. Maybe as a family we can decipher what you have seen. Let us see what tonight brings. And do not be afraid to sleep. Ask God to guide you through what you see."

"These are nightmares, Nandy, not visions. Laced amongst the Middle Eastern cave dwellers were images of my Hailee."

Lachlan tried to rest. He watched shadows dance across the moonlit ceiling of his bedroom. His mind raced. How had his life gotten so complicated?

Lachlan remembered how exciting New Zealand was during earlier times, when he and Nandy first arrived home. Unpacking that first day in Kaikoura, eight years prior, had been slow and uneventful. Though the Thorpe farmhouse, previously Cameron and Aerin's (and before that Ari and Saroya's), was incredible, Lachlan's room was especially amazing.

Occupying the entire third floor, an addition built on years ago by his great uncles for lookout purposes and easy access to the hovercraft garage, Lachlan had a raw undeveloped area to convert as he wished. He had quickly assessed the room, noting where he planned to install partitions, closets, and shelving. Phenomenal hardwood floors, freshly painted walls, two gabled rooms positioned on the front side of the house, and many, many windows, including three window seats, were just a few of the alluring aspects in Lachlan's new sanctuary.

After he sketched a rough plan, Lachlan shoved his many unpacked boxes into the corner of his space that would become his sleeping quarters, adjacent to one of the gabled rooms. The view of the ocean would be visible from his bed. Lachlan was thrilled. Like his father, built-in bookshelves were Lachlan's first necessity; lumber abandoned in a shed out back did nicely. All afternoon Lachlan had measured, sawed, hammered, and stained the new shelving into place. That is when his childhood friend, Craig, had stepped back into the picture.

Nandy Cameron had already given Lachlan a bleak synopsis of Craig's upbringing, probably more details than should have been repeated. Tucker, Craig's father, was a tough man to live with. He had taken his father Pete's chauvinistic attitude to an impossible level, causing Nikki and a small Craig to move near Nikki's family in Auckland. Shortly after that, Nikki had moved to Australia with a new boyfriend leaving Craig to be raised by his maternal grandparents. Burdened with many years of guilt layered upon his young shoulders, Craig finally succumbed to his paternal pressures and rejoined his bitter father in Kaikoura after high school. Craig endured the wrath of Tucker's unhappiness and poor choices in life. Although wisdom told Craig his father's failings were not his, it still did not diminish the emotional pain. To Tucker, poor Craig was Mr. Shoulda, Coulda, Woulda but Never Did. Avoiding Tucker at all costs, Craig buried himself in his work, perfecting his Granddad Pete's farm. Just a good ole bloke, Craig stayed in the shadows until Tucker's alcoholism hollowed him into an early grave. Craig, the only surviving Whibley child, inherited the farm. This became his only purpose, besides being a loyal friend to Lachlan.

CRAIG NEEDED HEALTHY MALE COMPANIONSHIP. Somehow, he instantly trusted this New African. He knew the minute he set eyes upon Lachlan's flawless face the female population in Kaikoura would be awestruck. It was in his eyes. Not the powder-blue colour but the way Lachlan looked inside your soul when he addressed you. His fierce warmth. Not devoid of good looks, Craig favoured his mother. The only difference was Craig's wavy, light brown hair and dark blue eyes were constantly ridiculed over the years by Tucker. Even after his father's death, Craig could hear his insults. And sadly, Craig believed every word of that brutal, internal harsh voice. Besides, Lachlan being exceptionally handsome was a constant reminder of how inadequate Craig's looks were to him. He did not resent his New African friend, however. Lachlan could not help the fact he had an appearance others envied. No, Craig blamed his father's harsh critiques.

Those first few weeks with his new best friend were a blur for Craig. Perhaps so many years of isolation had kept Craig's surroundings consistent yet mundane. In a flash, he had a new mate who was dating the hottest young woman in Kaikoura, possibly the South Island, and who had an equally beautiful, at least in Craig's eyes, younger sister. Jacqui Kittelty, though a bit shyer, was a brunette version of Hailee. Comfortably tucked within Hailee's shadow, Jacqui was an enigma, awaiting discovery.

MONTHS HAD FLOWN BY AS Lachlan immersed himself in the university environment, the very SNZU his Nandy built during his younger years. Playing rugby and studying Eastern and Western medicine, Lachlan soared. His thirst for knowledge, inherited from his parents and both sets of grandparents, was insatiable. And on a sentimental note, this university was where Lachlan's parents had met. Justin and Chance's art gallery had been sold and converted long ago into an import retail shop. There were no memories there for Lachlan. Everything for him was encapsulated within SNZU. Days at the university were Lachlan's happiest. Darker days unfortunately were ahead.

Hailee & Lachlan

LEARNING AND LOVE FORTIFIES MY grandson as he battles his God-given gift. Hailee's intelligence and criminal justice pursuits intrigue Lachlan and keep him grounded. To say she is special minimizes Lachlan's growing feelings for Hailee. Surrounded by his Nana Aerin's many journals on the divan, Lachlan has finally fallen asleep. He goes before the Youth Council elders tomorrow night. I worry for him. He seems so overwhelmed. Thankfully, though, Lachlan sleeps. I never tire of watching my amazing grandson. It has always fascinated me how our offspring take the best from their parents genetically, and our Lachlan is living proof of that. A wonderful byproduct of merging distinctly different gene pools, he has pulled the strongest from his mother, father, and grandparents. Physically, he could not be handsomer. Of course I am biased, but I hear others talk. Lachlan's got Grammy Lourdes' flawless olive skin, Chance's small nose and perfect teeth, a broad smile like his Papa Deek with dimples to match, his Nana Aerin's thick, feathery hair mixed with my blond colouring, and a powder-blue version of Justin's eyes, framed with dark circles around the irises, and dirty-blond eyelashes and eyebrows. Proudly, my grandson also has the Thorpe and Jorgensen men's exceptional height at six feet six inches and a very slight Thorpe cleft in his chin. As many have commented, Lachlan is, well . . . beautiful.

Inside, he is creative like his parents, has a wonderful fiery disposition when needed like his Grammy Lourdes, is masculine and athletic like his Papa Deek, possesses my logical approach to life and quirky sense of humour, and sees inside the souls of others as his Nana Aerin did. Do you see? Lachlan is the embodiment of everything amazing and dynamic. The best was plucked for his genetic tree, and God has a purpose for this powerful being, of that, I am certain. There are truly no coincidences in life.

All was going well until that horrible night. Hailee hurried to rid herself of the heavy casserole dish. Her greetings went unheard. Annoyed, she quickened her pace across the manicured lawn as she tried to keep her sneakers from getting wet from the excess dew.

Then she saw her young man cutting wood in the shed. No shirt, tattered blue jeans, and well-worn black PF Flyer® high-tops, Lachlan switched off the whirling saw. Safety glasses pulled from his face and propped on the top of his thick head of hair, he peered at Hailee with concern. Lachlan shook his head.

In slow motion, the casserole dish hit the pavement below and shattered. Hailee looked at the fragments of glass and food that now covered her black velvet heels. Where were her sneakers? Hailee's eyes crawled up her body, revealing a beautiful evening gown. Walls had grown around her. Above her, a chandelier shone brightly in the centre of a boisterous ballroom. She was no longer at Lachlan's.

Unsteady on her high heels, Hailee felt a large hand grab her arm keeping her from falling. She recognized the man with the big brown eyes and shoulder-length, light brown hair, obviously dyed. Relieved, Hailee leaned into the newest Tribune elder. The Christian whispered something then lured an intoxicated Hailee into a darkened hallway. She thought the nice man was leading her to Lachlan's whereabouts.

Once inside the nearby stairwell, the nice man slammed the champagne-saturated Hailee against the cement wall. She winced from a searing pain in her head and spine. As her attacker grew closer, Hailee saw the grotesque, wiry grey hairs that climbed from his nostrils. His breath smelled of stale garlic and alcohol. Before Hailee could react, the evil Christian planted a sloppy hard kiss upon her lips. She could not move. Warm blood seeped from the back of Hailee's head. The Christian's hand squeezed her throat as the other fondled one of her breasts, causing her pain. His touch burned.

Lachlan tossed and turned from a fiery sleep. Nandy had been right; he was able to taste the blood in Hailee's mouth. Sharp pangs penetrated Lachlan's chest. He could feel The Christian's hands upon her. When Hailee's attacker ripped her panties free and forced himself into her, Lachlan felt a searing sensation in his groin. Everything was so vivid. He could smell the man's sweat and taste the garlic and alcohol in his mouth. But what would forever be etched into Lachlan's memory was the taste of Hailee's fear. She knew this evil man planned to kill her after the brutal rape. That impending doom would never leave Lachlan. Yes, Nandy was right; this dream state was most certainly a heeded warning. If only he could wake up, wake up and end the nightmare.

SWEAT COVERED HIS ENTIRE BODY. Sleep futile, Lachlan was suddenly wide-awake. Without question, he had experienced another premonition. There had been Hailee, Lachlan's beautiful fiancée, bloodied before him. He had been too late. Hailee's final screams of terror still echoed in Lachlan's ears. Trying to remember every detail, Lachlan closed his eyes and ran through the specifics.

The man they called The Christian, referred to as Jesus Resurrected or J.R., spotted Hailee at the Youth Council gala given by the Tribune. Off to the side of the posh hotel's crowded lobby, the lecher had waited in the shadows. With a champagne flute in one hand and a black clutch purse in the other, Hailee sauntered across the marble floor in search of Lachlan. After finishing her third glass of champagne, a frustrated Hailee planted herself in an obscure corner of the room. Her head swam. Lachlan had been dragged away by some prominent Tribune elders. He was in such demand. Hailee hated these pompous revelries. Trying to shake the foggy alcohol haze, Hailee flung her long, shiny golden-white hair from both sides of her face. She was dizzy. Against the flawless, tanned legs swished the beautiful blonde's silky black dress. The Christian's gaze was perversely locked upon Hailee as she walked toward her killer.

Lachlan opened his eyes. The upcoming Tribune party would play out just as it had in his dream. However, the outcome would be quite different . . . and much more memorable.

Amsterdam

Clad in a muted ski jacket, toque, and jeans, J.R. relished the chance to blend in with the commoners. Back from his most recent retreat, "God according to J.R.," he was overly exhausted. For the first time since his spiritual crusades began decades ago, he was wearing down. As J.R. stared at the antlike people scurrying about the sidewalks fifteen floors below, he felt compression on his chest. It was hard to breathe. The Amsterdam observatory tower was vacant of others, yet J.R. felt the glass walls closing in upon him. He had to have air. J.R. rushed for the exit, descending the stairs two at a time.

At the ground level, J.R. burst through the heavy metal door. He clutched his chest as he gulped the fresh air with a starving desperation. J.R. sat on a nearby bench to settle his vertigo. Passers-by stared at the panicked man. J.R. ignored the insignificant gawkers; not a one realized they were amidst greatness. Minutes passed and he regained his composure, although J.R. still felt uneasy inside. Danger was near. For the first time in his adult life, he yearned to leave Amsterdam and retreat to the safe haven of Vancouver.

Much like pre-war Norway, Nederland had historically stockpiled food in refrigerated vaults, released the goods, then repeated the process. From early on, the Norwegians had a survivalist mentality that rubbed off on their surviving Dutch neighbours. It paid off, for Nederland had thrived post-war. And they were pleased over the years to be considered a world power. Evidence of this was the recent invitation to attend another annual Peace Summit hosted by New Zealand. The Dutch government's only dilemma this year was who to send. It would convey worldwide solidarity if they sent Prime Minister Ellestad, but he was so very old, approaching one hundred years of age. Besides, PM Ellestad would retire soon, so instead the Dutch chose to send their most avid promoter of peace, The Christian.

J.R. was delighted. What better place to access and implement his machinations but at a gathering with his adversaries? Diametrically opposed, the peace advocates also attracted those vehemently against global tranquility. The Christian's Superjet would leave for New Zealand in two nights, carrying him and several of his most faithful al Din henchmen.

In the past, the elders had been an easy lot for J.R. to coerce at the Tribune's infrequent gatherings. They loved "the boys club," so any male hobknobbing that also made them filthy rich was a slice of heaven for the elders. What concerned J.R. the most was the disruptive Youth Council, which was growing ever so popular and strong.

Idealistic and optimistic, as most young people are, this current group perplexed J.R. They possessed purity in their energy and this made him very uncomfortable. There was something especially vexing about the leader, Lachlan Thorpe. In his presence, J.R. felt naked with the inability to manipulate. Thorpe's penetrating eyes tore past J.R.'s façade and ripped at his soul.

On the summit agenda were topics of discussion to include world trade and commerce. Nederland had the market on fishing and technology, New Africa excelled in hovercraft production and exotic textiles that were in high demand, New Zealand contributed wool and medicine, and then there was J.R.'s forte, Vollywood, the Canadian film industry. It was his perfect breeding ground, an artistic environment rich with sensitivity where everyone seemed to wear their vulnerability on their sleeves.

It had been easy to secure his superior position, claiming he could raise even more money to produce films for Vancouver. J.R. feigned hard work when delivering the massive investment. What the Canadian council did not know was he had simply made a sizeable withdrawal from his Dutch bank. No one ever audited his accounts. If by chance someone had, he or she would have been dizzied with confusion.

J.R., a master at finances, practised kiting, maintained hidden accounts, and falsified accounting records, which allowed him to keep monies in transit indefinitely. Most of the funds J.R.'s father had misappropriated were from Christian donations initially. The irony was most of these investments came from pre-war players in the film industry. "Loony Left, bleeding-heart liberals," as the Americans used to call them, had generously attached themselves to J.R.'s father's wonderful, love-filled spiritual reformation. All of these vain, self-serving contributors, long dead from WWIV, would surely be pleased to know their enormous donations had not been used for God but to resurrect their precious, superior entertainment world.

J.R. relished in the fact that all the once high-powered Hollywood Jews would no longer dominate film, mediavision, or web entertainment. No, unbeknownst to the masses, the new Vollywood's leader was a Muslim who abhorred their Western Jewish egos and vanity, and these new entertainment miscreants were being set up to take a huge fall. Vancouver and the cesspool of creative, mentally numbed idiots would never know what hit them. J.R.'s army of al Din soldiers would seize Canada and the small American city of Seattle very easily. He would then own a fourth of the world, all in the name of Allah.

Once Canada was in his pocket, J.R. would make sure al Din's strength had grown before completely reeling in New Africa. A bunch of rejected thugs, these ex-American criminals and their ancestors would be easy to recruit. J.R. sighed. Like his father, the world, now more than ever, was his playground, and he juggled all the balls. Only one annoyance stood in his way . . . Lachlan Thorpe. And he would be taken down within days.

Lachlan & The Elders

SOMETHING HAD SPARKED INSIDE LACHLAN the last time he and I read excerpts out of Aerin's journals. She had delivered quite a few scathing lectures in her lifetime. Outspoken and jarring, they were so apropos for Lachlan's Youth Council speech, a task dumped upon him by his peers. No one relished trying to reach the elders' archaic minds; they were so set in their ways. Lachlan chose to shock them into listening; it was the only solution. Tonight, of all nights, his Nana Aerin's blood would surge through his veins. Lachlan would speak passionately as his Nana had in the past and proudly stand alone.

A WEATHERED, GREY-HAIRED GENTLEMAN in the back of the room snorted his disapproval at Lachlan's words. He rose to leave.

Lachlan went after the obstinate gentleman. "You, sir, the one so cowardly running away, I take it you think war solves everything?" The Tribune elder folded his arms as Lachlan continued. "The past tells us you are dead wrong. What gives you the right, under any circumstance, to take another person's life?"

Some of the younger members voiced their frustrations. "Sit down and open your ears, you relic! This is our world now!"

"Yeah, old man, your type had a chance at the steering wheel and drove us into a ditch!"

"Sit down you sheep's arse!"

The man threw up his arms and started for the auditorium doors.

"Coward!"

"Loser!" The YC members verbally accosted the old man. They were tired of taking this same kind of abuse from the elders; time for the older men to get a taste of their own bad behaviour.

Lachlan's voice could be heard above the others. "Sir, you walk out those doors and you will no longer carry a vote. Be a man and take some harmless criticism. We endure your harsh words week after week. Please, take a seat."

A couple of the other silver-headed blokes stood. They signalled for the fuming old man to sit down. And as a hushed moment hung in the air, the obstinate elder finally took his seat.

Lachlan continued. "You know, I was going to save this passage I found in my Nana Aerin's journal for another time, but the content is desperately appropriate right now. This heated exchange was between my grandmum and her stodgy chief administrator while at Kaikoura Hospital.

"Evidently, a psychic vision prompted her to perform a risky surgery on a newborn. Knowing it would be successful and also knowing her boss's method would kill the infant, my grandmum had proceeded without approval. Of course, her chief administrator was furious. However, attempts at reprimanding my grandmum were futile.

"The chief criticized psychic phenomena, labelling it complete nonsense. And my Nana Aerin retaliated by accusing the chief of using archaic medical practices, being arrogant, and only seeing his viewpoints. To jar the hard-headed administrator, my grandmum let her visions humble him. She successfully reamed out her boss by telling him his wife was having an affair with a young resident doctor; she was pregnant as a result; and he had never bothered to tell his wife he was sterile from contracting mumps as a young adult.

"The chief administrator was in shock. When he was able to speak again, my Nana Aerin was fired, of course." There was sparse laughter. "You see the bloke she verbally accosted was quite limited in his thinking, yet he fancied himself an intellect. My grandmum reached her breaking point when enduring all the administrator's scholastic snobbishness and well, quite frankly, his abundance of ignorance.

"After a few days, the chief had my grandmum come back to the hospital. They spoke further about her visions, the unapproved operation, and his wife's affair. It didn't take long for my Nana Aerin to be rehired at the hospital and with quite a promotion. In other words, the chief administrator was reformed. And if she can convert the likes of hospital administrators, presidents, and prime ministers, then there's hope for all of you pikers.

"The psychic realm is real, accept it and move on. I had to. If you are one of these superior, rigid-thinking males like my Nana's hospital administrator, this speech is for you. Don't let pride clog your reasoning. So tough language for tough blokes, open thine ears.

"Let's begin . . . We have started our new world with purity. It's now being threatened once again. Winston Churchill warned the British prior to WWII and no one listened. His perceptions were correct regarding Hitler. Whatever title we put on our evil, Hitler or Anti-Christ, the result is the same, these forces are not happy until they dominate. War is not an option, so let's get creative. I have the solution. It's not easy to accept, but we must avoid war. Before I reveal our spiritually driven approach, you doubters and pikers need to understand . . . thoroughly comprehend. Once again, I challenge you blokes who think you have all the answers to step forward and realize that just maybe you could be wrong.

"You, sir, the gentleman who challenged me earlier but was brave enough to stick around and hear me out. Be a leader and step forward."

"Psychic visions are nothing but hocus-pocus stunts that belong in a circus, young Thorpe."

"Sir, I know you are having a rough week; you lost your beloved parakeet and didn't tell anyone. You thought it un-masculine to have a pet bird in the first place. You told your comrades it was your late wife's pet, when in fact it was yours. When you buried Bella you wrapped her in one of your wife's silk scarves, the teal and burgundy one, and buried her next to your wife, unbeknownst to anyone of course. Your favourite movie is *Gone*—"

"Have a little respect, young man! Are you trying to humiliate me?"

"No, I'm trying to reveal information that no one else could possibly know. I'm trying to make a believer out of you. I know you're buggered."

"Damn straight, I'm livid! You young people don't have any idea what kind of world we inherited!"

"Oh, yes we do! We are trying desperately not to repeat our ancestors' mistakes, plain and simple."

"You stand up there and criticize!"

"I'm trying to penetrate your fossilized way of thinking. In the past, the Youth Council has yabbered on and on only to have our words fall on deaf ears. We don't want war! Are you listening, yet? So if criticism works, so be it.

If you think about it, this is the first time in the history of the YC that we've had a decent dialogue without the elders condescendingly chuckling at our solutions. Your smugness got you here. You preach your macho shite, yet you run when new ways of thinking arise. What are you so afraid of? We live in a much different world today. You've all seen the changes. For example, women are onto you old codgers. How many of your daughters and granddaughters have an unfaltering ambition like you when you were a young bloke? How many of you have daughters who tell you to get your own damn dinner?" Laughter broke out. "How many of your sons seem to be more compassionate? Yet you interpret their empathy as un-manly. Within my generation, we are more equal today. We are trying to do things right this time."

"It's not fear that cause us to act this way, it's your insolence, your lack of respect!"

"Then earn our respect, damn it!"

A standoff ensued for a brief moment. Lachlan felt a shift. Young and old stared at one another, neither budging.

Finally the elder spoke. "I do value the Youth Council's feedback. And I apologize if we discounted your solutions with condescension in the past. Bottom line is, young Thorpe, I'm still here. I'm not leaving."

"But are you listening? Really listening?"

"I am . . . we are."

"Well, then, I thank you, sir."

"As for those painfully accurate visions?"

"Yes, sir?"

"Pick on someone else for a change." Laughter began to relieve some of the tension.

The Youth Council meeting with the elders continued

for several hours. As Lachlan had made some progress, he would not ease up. He had stood alone but was gaining ground with the older men as his grandfathers had predicted.

"In the past we've been guilty of a lack of empathy. Take the United States government, for example, they never took the time to really see America through its enemies' eyes. It was always 'strike first' in the name of keeping their democratic freedom. The old America did not survive, did it? We've been taught to get to the root of each situation and negotiate a solution. Well, this is different. We are dealing with Earthly evil and that calls for a spiritual defence. I'll say it again, that beast needs to be contained!"

"Young Thorpe, your words are contradictory. All that you've said sounds like aggression to me. How is imprisonment not some form of war?"

"It is not imprisonment or war, sir. This solution I am proposing is to reveal the cruel bugger's past, humiliate him in front of the world. If we stick together and ignore his propaganda, he will run for the hills and hide, hopefully for the rest of his miserable life."

"You've seen that, young Thorpe?"

"I have." Lachlan paused. "But . . . this is going to take a very strong hand and a cohesion among us that cannot be broken."

Lachlan

"Tell me something, Lach, why wear tennis shoes every day?"

"I can't justify killing an animal for the sake of covering my feet. Besides, I like how the rubber soles feel when walking on gravel and dirt, kind of a soothing crunching sensation."

"You're a whacker."

"You going to eat those, mate?"

"No, have at them."

Lachlan began to eat Craig's French fries. "So how was your date last night with Little Miss Feed Store?"

"Crikey, Lach, you keep eating chips like that day after day and you're going to turn into a damn spud. A tennis shoe wearing potato."

"Nice . . . don't change the subject."

"Naff off."

"Seriously, what's wrong with this one?"

"She's like the others."

"Young and pretty?"

"Immature and boring. What's with that Springbok rugby shirt, too? Need I remind you you're in All Blacks territory now? You should burn that nasty old rag."

"Leave my Papa Deek's jersey alone."

"You know, Lach, if you weren't such a pretty boy, women would find you quite odd."

"Doesn't matter, mate, I only have eyes for one wahine and she likes me just fine."

"Hailee's blind."

"You know, if I didn't know better I'd say you were having a Tucker kinda day, mate. Why all the criticism? You listening to his voice again in your head?"

"I am not my father."

"Then quit acting like him. In a matter of minutes, you have insulted my starchy tater addiction, retro tennis shoes, and beloved Springbok's jersey. What's up, mate?"

"I'm frustrated . . . nothing changes. Little Miss Feed Store reminded me of that last night. I've felt like crap all morning."

"You haven't given her much of a chance."

"She was nice, Lach. We had a decent time but—"

"She's not Jacqui."

"Yeah, that'd be right. Little Miss Feed Store is far from being Jacqui. So tell me about this dance."

"Gala actually, Tribune Gala; normally it would be a lot of fun, but I'm really worried about losing Hailee, Craig. This J.R., or The Christian, is so strong and has quite a loyal following. Hell, his father was a beast. Who can forget what that bastard did to the world?"

"But you've been blessed with the vision. You can change the outcome, Lach. And you have a lot of us on your side."

"But I need the elders. Everyone has to be on the same page. Otherwise, The Christian will have protection all around him. We won't be able to get close enough to make things happen."

"You talk with the Tribune elders again Thursday night, right?"

"I do, but what if all goes well, but then I can't get to Hailee in time? What if this is her destiny to die by J.R.'s hands?"

"I don't believe you received this premonition simply to be rendered helpless and sit on the sidelines watching the love of your life struck down."

"He's powerful, Craig. I feel him. He's rotten to the core."

"That's rubbish; you're giving him that power by fearing him. He's just a bloke, Lach."

"Yeah, that'd be right. He is just a bloke; a bloke whose narcissism will be his downfall."

"That's the spirit."

"You ready to go?"

"Yes, yes. So is Jacqui coming to the Gala?"

"Hailee asked her."

"That means no."

"That means maybe. Why don't you ask her?"

"No way, mate. She acts like I don't exist."

"Jacqui's just shy, Craig."

"After all these years and she still avoids me every chance she gets."

"You need to erase that voice of your father from inside your head."

"Easier said than done. Lach . . . um, do you ever see us together in any of your visions?"

"Sorry, mate, my gift doesn't work on those closest to me." Craig fell silent. "You've been wanting to ask me that for eight years now, haven't you?"

"Bugger off."

"Look, I know that was hard for you to ask. The bottom line is Jacqui would be a fool not to think you special, mate. You have to start believing in yourself first, though."

"That's just it, I don't ever feel special."

"Then start."

"What have I done to deserve such a distinction? What's so special about a meagre bloke with a meagre farm? You tell me that."

"Because you do the right thing, always, even when others aren't watching. That kind of character is rare in people. It takes the strongest of blokes to live like that day after day. Especially when your alcoholic, abusive father tried to tear you down every chance he got. You stood firm in your beliefs. That takes gargantuan balls my friend." Craig grinned. "Listen, tomorrow has to be different."

"Maybe—"

"—uh, still talking here. You've been pining your heart out for Jacqui for years now. Enough is enough. Saturday night, every time you hear your father's negative voice I want you to say 'rack you' inside your head. Then when you've won that monumental battle, I want you to swig a shot of tequila. When the burning liquid is felt all throughout your body, I want you to walk up to Jacqui and offer your hand for a dance. Look her straight in the eyes and don't move your hand until you feel her fingers interlaced with yours, then Bob's your uncle."

"Naff off, don't give me that Robert's your Mother's Brother shite. It's not that simple . . . at least not for me."

"Don't be such a piker. You've given up before you've even begun; you can do this. Make her notice you, mate."

"And what if she doesn't?"

"Then it still sucks to be you."

"That I'm comfortable with."

"If you want to be alone for the rest of your life. Aren't you the one who said none of the other wahines measure up? Then, for the first time in eight years show Jacqui Kittelty the Craig I know." Lachlan patted his best friend on the back. "No holds barred."

Craig looked ill.

Maktan

Beth and Maktan sat watching the news. Two octogenarians bundled up on the couch sipping hot coffee on a crisp winter evening. In recent years, the Vancouver citizens had voted to open the dome roof permanently to allow rain and snow to fall and accumulate inside. Within the living room, an all-too-familiar aroma hovered about the women. In the oven, Maktan cooked a large dish of macaroni and cheese. Good ole Western comfort food, perfect when snow flurries continued to tick against the ice-frosted windows.

For years, the women had been inseparable. Despite the absence of their sons, Beth and Maktan had learned to live for themselves, and helping others had become a part of that discovery. Beth volunteered at the local Vancouver Christian Youth Association, and Maktan donated her efforts to the Vancouver Muslim Youth Centre. Spiritual advice was avoided within both organizations. Instead, they focused on developing a kind, secure environment for Canada's younger generations. However, as the women crept into their eighties, their time became precious. It took every bit of strength to get to the mailbox downstairs and visit the corner market every few days. Both Beth and Maktan had learned to pace themselves. Waking from their late afternoon nap a short time ago, both women relied on their coffee to give them that welcomed caffeinated burst of energy.

"That Christian is such a scam. Why can't these worshipping fools see what we see? For years, he's preached a frugal life. Robes and sandals, who is he kidding? Jesus Resurrected, my butt."

"Beth, you are a funny one."

"Look at him, Yonca; he's dressed in an expensive suit now. What a phony. Why isn't Dutch Prime Minister Ellestad there to meet New Zealand's Prime Minister Oswald and our PM Sean Ulmer? The Christian isn't a diplomat. Look how arrogant he is. He's loving all the attention."

J.R. strutted in front of the cameras, waving to the crowd of New Zealanders congregated at the Christchurch Airport. Even with dye covering his salt-and-pepper hair, The Christian was still handsome. He flashed a perfect, white smile to the crowd as he removed his sunglasses.

Maktan gasped. "Oh, Beth, oh no, no, no."

"Yonca, what's wrong?"

"The Christian—"

"Yonca, are you all right?"

"I think I'm going to be sick. I feel dizzy."

"Oh dear, what can I get you?"

"Oh my, oh my."

"Yonca? Talk to me. You're scaring me."

"The Christian, Beth . . . The Christian is my son. Zeren, Beth, The Christian is Zeren. Actually, he is my Mu'mad. His name is Muhammad al-Ypaaht."

"Al-Ypaaht?"

"Yes, Beth, the son of Abbud al-Ypaaht."

"*The* al-Ypaaht? The blue-turbaned Anti-Christ? *That* al-Ypaaht?"

"The very one."

He was associating with other faiths. Mu'mad's mother should be proud of his accomplishments. Throughout his childhood, Mu'mad had endured Maktan's stories of his powerful father. Only when he was old enough to understand did he grasp the enormity of what his mother had repeated over and over.

With access to unlimited funds obtained by his patriarch, Mu'mad had a very bright future of wealth, comfort, and the crushing of Christians and Jews. Mu'mad would become his father's son. When al Din discovered his identity, they had forged an easy path for their adolescent caliph to follow. They spoke with Mu'mad, nightly, in the comfort of his bedroom.

During Mu'mad's high school years, he voiced concerns regarding his mother, to his al Din senior council. Maktan's Islamic convictions had lessened. At times, she even questioned his father's crusade ... so hypocritical. Maktan's revolting Western friends had slowly poisoned her mind. Al Din's de facto leader decided it was time for Mu'mad to leave home.

It took little effort for Mu'mad to convince Maktan he was ready for prep school. Instilling trust in their young caliph, al Din did not intervene between mother and son. Their posturing was subtle. Mu'mad loved his mother once and would handle her when necessary.

While away at prep school, he had tried poisoning his irritating matriarch on many occasions, when visiting. However, it seemed he never used high-enough dosages to finish her off. A part of him was relieved though. He was young; she was devoted to him. During his college years, Mu'mad's disdain toward his mother deepened. Progressively, Maktan was displaying more infidel traits, beliefs. The gap between mother and son grew.

Amidst Mu'mad's UBC graduate studies, al Din's

senior council applied more pressure. It was time for their caliph to sever his childhood ties completely. For Mu'mad, Amsterdam had much appeal. It had been so easy to slip away from Vancouver and his mother. Lacing her entire refrigerator's contents with arsenic, Mu'mad thought he would be completely free of his infidel mother and stifling past. What a surprise it was for Mu'mad when he had called home for the first time from Amsterdam and Maktan answered the phone. Again, there was a twinge of relief. As confusing as it was, an extremely miniscule part of Mu'mad still loved Maktan.

Fully expecting never to hear from his mother again, due to ingesting the planted poison, Mu'mad decided to amp up his disguise, instead. Facial stubble, dyed hair with highlights and sunglasses had been a strong start. Ceasing to call home and opting for letters had helped Maktan forget her son's voice.

Upon arrival in Amsterdam, Mu'mad had researched an alias that would symbolize his feigned Christian roots. Besides, he was tired of his fabricated Turkish name, Zeren Killic. Mu'mad had quickly changed from his Syrian-born name to Joseph R. Smith, J.R., an easy choice. He would give the naïve Christians back their precious Jesus.

After that first month at AU, when Mu'mad found out about Maktan's unannounced visit, Mu'mad's cover was almost blown. Showing Zeren's classmates his picture had led her to his dorm. When she had asked the pimpled-faced neighbour of Zeren's whereabouts, he had recognized Zeren's face in the picture immediately and tried to help the flustered Muslim woman. When the acne -complexioned teen had recounted the story to the new J.R., after his weekend holiday, Mu'mad knew he had to implement damage control and fast. Moving off campus was the first step.

Luring the pimpled coed to his new digs was easy and snapping the teen's neck had been even easier. Instantly, the incessant questions about Zeren and his mother had stopped. Al Din had succeeded, their jihad begun. No one would ever call him that ridiculous Turkish name again.

Many doors opened for Joseph R. Smith that may have remained securely locked if he had remained Muhammad al-Ypaaht. A common Western name of Smith mixed with high marks at university brought many accolades and secured Mu'mad's freedom. Teaching religious studies at a small college had helped his plight further. After two years, J.R. had gone on sabbatical never intending to return. Spreading Christian love and understanding was an easy task. He had been reborn, supposedly, to prevent the world from repeating its perverse, immoral past.

With ease J.R. reached into many a rich pocket via donations, all in the name of secured salvation. Having funds galore, J.R. enjoyed many retreats around the world, especially in his new country of Nederland. It was here he kept secretive, ever-bulging bank accounts. Dressing and living frugally maintained his spiritual façade. Yes, Joseph R. Smith had grown quite powerful over the years. Slowly, more and more poor, hopeless Christians began to follow him.

J.R.'s wealthier converts tithed large sums of money to their new leader. Assured their contributions were spent to combat poverty around the world, these Christians felt a restored hope unlike any other. Finally, God had answered their prayers and sent His Son back to live amongst the less fortunate. Unlike most holy men entrenched in wealth,

The Christian would lead God's children to their holiest of holy salvation.

Instead, a wake of shattered lives would soon fan out behind him. Ahead, the carnage would be unimaginable. Remembering history and how many people his father eliminated during WWWIII, J.R. knew his wrath would be much worse. Since the current world was much smaller, J.R.'s targets would be more specific. Anti-Christ Junior would bring this new world threat into many a backyard.

Maktan & The Christian

Now it all made sense. How sick Maktan had been when Mu'mad fled to Amsterdam so long ago. Beth had nursed her back to health. Believing her friend suffered from a severe case of food poisoning, Beth had immediately cleared out all potentially damaging foods in the refrigerator. If she had not, Maktan would surely have died.

After an exhausting night of comparing mental notes of the past, Maktan and Beth had the entire story pieced together. Maktan told Beth everything, even her real name; Yonca was buried for good. She sobbed for her son, and her stolen youth, as she had many times in the past. Maktan had spent so many years raising Mu'mad in the footsteps of his father. Pregnant at sixteen years of age from a man she worshipped, Maktan knew now that she had been the victim of youthful brainwashing. Sadly, she passed on many of those fanatical brain twists to her precious, unsuspecting son.

Beth snapped Maktan from her shock and grief. "Come, Yonca . . . sorry, I mean Maktan, we have to act quickly."

"Beth?"

"Not only are you in danger, Maktan, but also this Christian could be plotting to harm many others. Come, we need to get you out of your condo. Grab some clothes and any important papers you would like to keep with you."

"Hold on, Beth. My son has known that I am alive for years now and hasn't tried to kill me."

"He will when you blow the whistle on him."

Maktan was shocked. Beth helped her from the sofa. "Beth—"

"Sweetheart, don't panic. Gather some clothes, I'll help. We'll take them to my place."

Maktan knew Beth was right, but she was so old, so tired.

The ladies shoved Maktan's belongings into several suitcases and rolled everything to Maktan's front door.

"Beth, I can't run."

"Maktan, you know as well as I do that your son will come for you, especially if you breathe a word of his origin."

"Then let him come, Beth. I created Mu'mad. I created the monster that is now J.R. I am solely responsible."

"Oh, no you're not! Maktan, Mu'mad is an adult and has been for many years. He is and was in control of his conscience, his actions, for decades. It is not your fault."

"In a lot of ways it is. I taught him the ways of Islam, a very fanatical version . . . his father's version. It is my fault. Besides, I'm too old to run."

"You're not running; you're staying with me. Your son never met me and your Muslim friends never gave me the time of day. Do any of them know we're friends, Maktan?"

"No, I never told them much about my personal life, Mu'mad either. He knows I have Western friends but doesn't know of you specifically. Besides, he was always too self-centred to ever ask about his mother's life. Sadly, I raised him to be that Middle Eastern boy, superior to women. While he worshipped his male parts, as you call it, my existence went unnoticed. Many times, I tried to explain to Mu'mad about women and oppression, but he was having none of it. I was his mother; I was a woman; I was unimportant. Everything was for and about my son. I really did this, Beth."

"Nonsense, you raised that boy with love and devotion like any mother who adores her child."

"But your boys didn't grow up to think of nothing but themselves."

"Oh, yes, they did. How often do they visit, Maktan? Never."

"Oh my . . . Mu'mad said he believed The Christian raped women at the university. I think he was giving me some kind of warped confession, Beth. I think he hurt . . . killed those girls. Oh, dear."

"Maktan, the point is you raised your son with love. I saw it. He made the decision to hurt others, not you."

"I gave him everything. I glorified his father. Only during his years at university did I try to discuss a peaceful Islam, not focusing on world dominance. I wanted more for my Mu'mad, a better life than his father's, one with honour. Oh, Beth, I still can't get over the fact he laced my food with something harmful. That hurts. I kept that boy safe, got him out of the Middle East and sacrificed everything to give him every opportunity in life."

"I'm afraid we gave our children way too much, Maktan."

"Perhaps. I thought I was being a good mother, exposing Mu'mad to as much as I could. And look what he's done with that education: he kills and rapes women and tries to poison his own mother."

"That scares me, Maktan. I'm certain he'll try to harm you again, if he thinks his cover has been blown."

"I know, it is very plausible, Beth. I'm just in shock. He's my child, I raised him."

"I'm sorry. This is a horrible situation; I just want you safe. Trust me?"

"I do, I trust you, Beth."

"Then let's drag your bags down to my condo. It's really late. Besides, most of our neighbours are never around. And I'm not answering my door these days. J.R. and his thugs won't know you're with me. My security system will keep us safe. Come on, no arguments."

"Beth, how can we warn people about my son? How do we warn the world?"

"We're going to send an email to my sons from an Internet café that I know has no visual surveillance. University students saw to that. The Christian and his men won't be able to trace it back to me, to us. You'll stay in my condo while I grab some groceries then send an email to my boys regarding J.R.'s, Mu'mad's true identity. They both work closely with the Tribune and they'll be attending the Peace Summit. Once you're at my place you must promise me you will not come back to your condo until all of this has blown over. Are you sure you have everything you need?"

"I do and I promise, Beth. I won't come back. I wish I could do more to help you."

"It's about time someone looked after you for a change, Maktan. Let's go."

Chrysalis

"OSWALD, I'M CALLING WITH DISTURBING news. The Anti-Christ of WWWIII, Abbud al-Ypaaht, fathered a son. Not that there is a mysterious super-human quality surging in his veins. Hell, to dwell on that bastard would make his life somehow notable. He was no deity. The Beast was a murderer and a liar with the gift of gab. Upon his death, I'm sure he bled like everyone else. Oswald, you there?"

"He fathered a son, Deek? How do you know this?"

"Our Lachlan inherited his Nana Aerin's psychic abilities. Cameron and I had quite a long go of it to get him to accept this. He's always been highly intuitive, but what really convinced him was hearing himself on disc when he was five years old."

"He predicted this as a boy?"

"Yes, that night while in a feverish haze Lachlan stated clearly the Beast was still alive. What clinched it was hearing his five-year-old voice whispering that he feared for Hailee Kittelty's life."

"Lachlan's fiancée?"

"Yes, he found that phrase buried in with all the others."

"Aerin always said evil would rise again."

"And so it has. Cameron said he's been waiting for this dreaded day. Oswald, my grandson is in danger. The Anti-Christ's son wreaked havoc in Vancouver, my sources tell me. Seems his henchmen killed a lot of people. The RCMP have killed five men and imprisoned the others. Of course, J.R.'s thugs are not talking; the only information gleaned was that these assassins were searching for Maktan al-Ypaaht, The Christian's mother. Yeah, his mother was the one who revealed his true identity. This bastard's blood runs ice-cold like his father's. He has taken a lot of wealth from innocent people in Canada, New Africa, and Nederland. He, evidently, donated millions to the Vollywood film industry a few years ago when they went through a rough patch. Just recently, he's bilked more than he invested from those very same, naïve film moguls. And he has murdered many who have stepped into his path. Oswald, he's in New Zealand planning to attend the Peace Summit."

"Crikey."

"Anti-Christ Junior goes by the name of The Christian, J.R., or Jesus Resurrected, you pick. His birth name is Muhammad al-Ypaaht; and his soldiers are al Din. Lachlan's been working with the Tribune elders, but that won't be enough."

"We'll be ready for him. Where are you staying, mate?"

"I'm with my family at the Thorpe homestead. Lachlan has taken Cameron to the doctor. He's been fighting chest pains."

"That's not good."

"Well, we're all older than dirt, hey? Soon we'll all be dropping like flies."

"No doubt."

"All kidding aside, Cameron should be fine."

"That's good, mate. Well, I know why you're calling; I do remember Aerin predicted the rise of evil."

"Yes indeed, Oswald, indeed . . . it's time for us to resurrect Chrysalis."

Maktan

It had not taken but a night for J.R. to retaliate. Beth and Maktan heard the splintering of a door and the men's deep voices. Both women sat in darkness too afraid to call 911 for fear they would be heard. Several neighbours' voices responded to the commotion going on outside their condos. That is when the hell started. The al Din Jericho guns, with their silencers, were discharged dropping several people to the ground with a thud. Beth squeezed Maktan's hand. Deep voices grew louder as they proceeded to knock on every door. When someone answered, the silencer's sharp whistling sound could be heard. Footsteps were soon headed toward Beth's condo. Maktan stood upon the chair, which she and Beth had positioned by the front door, and peered through the peephole. A large man's face was coming into view, closer and closer. The al Din assassins repeatedly kicked the door. Fortunately, Beth's was made from wood and reinforced steel. Her door refused to buckle as Maktan's had. J.R.'s loyal followers grew impatient.

"Open the door, old woman. You have betrayed your own people, your own son. You sleep with the infidels. You eat their tainted food. J.R. says you disgrace the memory of Abbud al-Ypaaht . . . you disgrace Allah, old woman."

An al Din assassin slowly turned the doorknob that was inches from Maktan's hand. Her heart pounded. Maktan and Beth were petrified.

"Come out here and face your destiny . . . die with honour, old woman."

Suddenly, Beth and Maktan could hear the scuffling of feet and a woman screeching.

"You're hurting me! Let me go!"

"Is this the place?"

"Yes, yes, I told you that. Those two old ladies are inseparable. I saw them go in there earlier. I did! I swear it!"

"Maktan?" The vocal assassin seemed to be enjoying himself.

"No, the Muslim woman is Yonca, not Maktan."

He leaned closer to Beth's door. "Oh, Yonca, your young infidel neighbour is heeeeere . . . she wants to borrow a cup of suuugar." The al Din assassin laughed.

"Open the door, Maktan, or we kill her!"

Panicked, Maktan and Beth looked at one another. Beth shook her head vehemently from side to side.

"Oh, Maktan, I can hear you breathing. You're going to force me to put a bullet in your precious neighbour's head."

J.R.'s assassins continued to laugh and taunt them. Beth's young neighbour pleaded for her life. Still Beth shook her head then gave her friend the sh-h-h sign. Maktan did not know what to do. Then the gun released three quick eerie blasts past its silencer. Beth's neighbour dropped to the floor.

"I know you're in there, infidel bitch! I know you see me!"

From beneath the door, a scuffling sound could be heard. Beth and Maktan looked down in time to see a long shiny knife being lunged inward then swept from side to side within the crack beneath the door. The al Din assassin searched for Maktan's feet. He sliced the glimmering blade back and forth. Finally, he lodged the knife into the leg of Maktan's chair. As she wobbled from the impact, Beth steadied her from behind and began to pull Maktan toward her on the stairs leading her to the second floor of the condo. In a split second, the bullets were upon them. The sickening sound of the silencer discharged again and again, raining bullets through wood and hitting steel as they hunted for Maktan al-Ypaaht.

Lachlan & Chrysalis

"Not one of you blokes disputed my visions when it pertained to you personally during our last meeting. Why would you question what I see with regards to The Christian, or shall we call him by his real name, the spawn of the Anti-Christ, al-Ypaaht?"

"Lachlan, my boy, how can we be sure there isn't some personal motivation to condemn this man? You claim you had these horrific dreams. How can we be sure they are more than a frightful nightmare?"

"Because I've seen these visions while awake as well. Sir, have I ever given you cause to mistrust me?"

"No, not at all."

"Answer the question, young Thorpe."

"Because what you are suggesting goes against everything I believe. If I have a personal vendetta and desire to rid the world of this beast only for my behalf, that makes me no better than the bloke I condemn. I've seen the atrocities The Christian will commit."

"You have to give us more. This is all too intangible."

"He will attend our Tribune Gala in two days. That is when The Christian will rape and fatally attack my fiancée, Hailee. And if he gets away with this tragedy, his followers will plant a bomb, Mr. Hansen, in the café you have just purchased as a warning to us of just how powerful he is and that we must succumb to his terrorist ways. The day this bomb detonates, your entire family will be obliterated. Mr. Naslund, you will lose your oldest daughter, Kiera, in the blast as well. She is Danielle's best friend isn't she, Mr. Hansen's daughter?" He nodded.

"Lachlan, tell us everything you've seen and then we'll make a decision. Just so everyone knows, my wife and I just put in a bid to buy the Sunrise Café. It's our first retirement project. None of you knew about this, so there is no way Lachlan could have been privy to the information. Proceed, young Thorpe. This is serious business."

"We just need to isolate him and confine his al Din henchmen. Revealing the truth will humiliate The Christian. He will flee, never to be heard from again."

"IT WAS UNANIMOUS, OSWALD, SIR. The Tribune elders agreed to quietly apprehend The Christian's bodyguards."

"Very good. Deek, Cameron, has everything been set up?"

"Rami and Balic said everything is functioning properly. They are standing by, mate."

Deek squeezed our grandson's shoulder. "Lachlan, how did you convince the elders The Christian wouldn't wreak havoc after his sudden disappearance?"

"I walked them through my detailed premonition then finished with The Christian being fully humiliated and fleeing for good. I ran it all together so the elders would think it part of my vision."

"Well done."

"Nandy, are you and Papa Deek going to reveal everything now? What do Uncle Rami and Uncle Balic have to do with the Anti-Christ's spawn?"

I sighed. "It is time you were privy to some things I omitted from Nana Aerin's journals, Buds. Upon signing those documents Oswald holds, we will tell you the entire truth and you will become the newest member of the Chrysalis Society."

"Why Chrysalis, by the way?"

"It is the name associated with those aqua-glowing worms; our glowing cocoons—transformation, rebirth, and the like? Anyway, trust me, it will all make sense soon enough." Deek continued as Oswald handed my intrepid grandson the Chrysalis papers. "Once Lachlan, Hailee, and Craig are sworn in we need to review our plan for The Christian. Yes, the Anti-Christ's legacy is complete . . . the Beast has risen. We have to be very precise, everyone. Any error could result in Hailee's death . . . and many more down the road."

Glowworm

Against the flawless, tanned legs swished the beautiful blonde's silky black dress. J.R.'s gaze was perversely locked upon Hailee as she walked toward her nemesis.

As Lachlan watched the interaction between Hailee and The Christian, his heartbeat quickened. He had to trust their plan.

Unsteady on her high heels, Hailee felt a large hand grab her arm keeping her from falling. She recognized the man with the big brown eyes and shoulder-length, light brown hair, obviously dyed. Relieved, Hailee leaned into the newest Tribune elder. The Christian whispered something then lured Hailee into a darkened hallway. She knew the evil man was not leading her to Lachlan's whereabouts.

Once inside the nearby stairwell, the man tried to slam the sober Hailee, who feigned drunkenness, against the cement wall. She grabbed the evil man around the neck and giggled. He pulled her head away from his neck obviously pleased with this easy conquest. As her attacker moved closer, Hailee saw the grotesque, wiry grey hairs that climbed from his nostrils. His breath smelled of stale garlic and alcohol. Anticipating the evil spawn of the Anti-Christ's every move, Hailee giggled, took a sip of her drink then planted a sloppy kiss upon his lips.

Inside the vile man's mouth, Hailee had slipped an ice cube. Laughing, he revealed a white toothy smile and let the small piece of ice slide down his throat, unaware of the tiny, powerful sleeping pill inside. As The Christian's hands started to squeeze her throat, Hailee grabbed them and put them around the back of her neck. Hailee took a deep breath and kissed the revolting creature again, long and hard. She kept her eyes opened. Behind The Christian was supposed to be Lachlan and Papa Deek. It seemed to take forever for the man's grip on Hailee to weaken. His hands were groping Hailee's body with a painful force. Men were milling about, but Lachlan and Papa Deek were nowhere to be found. Suddenly, the evil son of the Anti-Christ slammed her against the cement wall. She winced with a searing pain in her head and spine. She could not move. Warm blood seeped from the back of Hailee's head. The Christian's hand squeezed her throat as the other fondled one of her breasts, causing her pain. His touch burned.

Hailee could not scream. She felt dizzy. Just as Hailee's attacker was about to rip her panties free, blood spattered across her face and The Christian's grip loosened. Hailee coughed and grabbed her bruised and swollen throat. With a severely bloodied nose, The Christian dropped to the floor. To the side of Hailee stood Craig, brandishing a rubber jimmy stick. He threw an arm around Hailee.

"Crikey dick, Craig, what are you doing here?"

"In case Lach wasn't able to get to you. It was his biggest fear."

"Where is he? Is he all right?" Hailee spat upon the floor. The Christian's taste lingered in her mouth. She spat again.

"I don't know, but you need to help me if you can. We have to get this piece of shite through that door; Balic and Rami are waiting."

When Craig lifted the new Beast's limp body a sharp stiletto fell from the man's sleeve. Craig froze. Lachlan had not mentioned this from his dreams. He had not witnessed the sharp dagger. Hailee's widened eyes met Craig's.

"Come on, Hailee, let's go. Lift his feet."

Hailee grabbed the Beast's feet. Once outside, the two of them threw him roughly into the back of the Ermani hovercraft.

PATIENTLY WE WAITED INSIDE THE dank Ermani storm cellar. An excruciating forty minutes passed before the heavy steel, retractable wall began to move. A breathless Lachlan burst into the dimly lit room.

"Hailee, you're safe!" The young couple clung to one another.

"I'm a little bruised and battered but safe nonetheless."

Devoid of youthful adrenalin, Deek, Oswald, Kozlov, and I gingerly moved our elderly bodies deeper into the secret portion of the cellar and closed the door. Kozlov's fists tightened as the urge to throttle the Beast arose from his deep-seated paternal protectiveness. The Christian had almost accosted his precious daughter, Sasha, years ago in Amsterdam. Lachlan had shared the visions with the rest of the Chrysalis members, which revealed the Beast as Sasha's stalker. In his younger more impetuous years, Kozlov would have cut short this monster's life with a quick snap of the neck. He pumped his aged, white-knuckled hands again and again. How good it would feel to sink a fist into the Beast's mouth, shattering his perfect smile. Kozlov moved closer to The Christian. Only the anticipation of this vile creature's suffering he was going to endure kept Kozlov from reacting. Thoughts of Sasha and her two daughters rushed in. Kozlov grew impatient.

"Lachlan, what happened?"

"The bastard's al Din soldiers somehow locked us in the conference room. Papa Deek finally got the door off the frame."

I flipped a switch on the near-death machine. An aqua light seeped from the lid's cracks. Hailee, Lachlan, and Craig stared in amazement. I hastened, "We do not have much time. Let us get started while this mongrel is still unconscious."

"Positions everyone."

Kozlov volunteered to place The Christian's body in the cocoon. No one was surprised when he slammed the unconscious Beast's body into the machine's bed. Deek and I secured his restraints. Rami prepared the IV containing the bacteria that would induce a deadly fever and ultimate heart failure. Balic turned the Beast's forearm over to expose his veins. Rami squirt some fluid from the needle into the air before sliding it into one of The Christian's bulging blood vessels. The Beast began to stir. Kozlov tightened the restraining straps. Their prisoner's eyelids fluttered. Rami readied the machine making sure all the necessary features were working. The heat sensors, sternum compressor, and oxygen tubing were all operational. When it was time to bring a dead prisoner back to life, the near-death machine would maintain an even temperature, begin chest compressions, and administer air mixed with oxygen into the victim's respiratory tract. But then again, those procedures were for the grey souls. This dark soul would be handled much differently.

"What the fuck are you doing?" The Beast tried to move his arms and legs.

"Watch your mouth," Deek said.

Ahmed tightened a leg strap. "We're ready."

I looked at Lachlan. "Make your Nana Aerin proud, Buds."

Lachlan stepped forward. "Well, well, well, we finally meet." Sweat poured from the Beast's forehead.

"What's this got to do with? So you're angry because I fondled your girlfriend? I meant no harm, too much drink. I can compensate you greatly; name the price, young Thorpe. Please, release these straps. I'm— "

"Claustrophobic? Yes, I know that about you. You're really going to piss yourself when I close the lid."

"No, no please don't. I have lots of money. It could help the Youth Council greatly."

"You have lots of other people's money."

"You can have as much as you want. I'll return it to the people, I promise. Just please release these straps." Desperation flooded the Beast's eyes. They darted to and fro.

"Oh, we already have our hands on much of that hidden currency. Our Chrysalis Society will make sure it gets put to good use, rest assured."

"Who are you people? Oh, Oswald, Kozlov, thankfully familiar faces, please help me." Neither budged.

"They have no interest in helping you. Focus on us . . . all of us non-believers in your scheme to resurrect a fanatical Islamic society. I have news for you, Scumbag. Your Middle Eastern homeland is dust in the wind, and it will remain that way. You're nothing but a lunatic like your father. You think your people are privileged because God, yes I said God, not Allah, sent you Muhammad? Don't you realize, historically, God sends prophets to the most buggered areas? Is it really getting back to your purist form of Islam or a desire to hold on to a small powerful faction?

Your father's arrogant, fanatical group chose power disguised as pious conformity. Some of his fellow Muslims weren't Islamic enough, so he didn't agree with them. Suddenly he had justification for murder: he killed off his Islamic competition for power. Do you really think we are going to let you stir that ancient hornets' nest once again? From what angle do you see the world? Are you so ridiculously stupid to think you have the complete picture, the all-knowing answers? Then, you inflict your warped beliefs on others. Will you die ignorant . . . or wise? I say you're destined for stupidity."

"You—"

"Shut up, I'm not finished!" The Beast was soaked with sweat. "As my grandmum so accurately stated, you are simply afraid of change. Well check this out, your treasured maleness isn't held in high regard where you're going. No seventy virgins or white grapes for that matter. Yes, I said grapes. If you knew the Quran you would understand your reward isn't virgins but an ancient delicacy of white grapes. It's a metaphor, you sheep's arse, for Heaven's riches. Do you really believe Allah would condemn fifty percent of the population; imprison women for eternity for Muslim men's sexual pleasure? You can't be that stupid. Pisses you off, doesn't it? Your entire life has been one enormous, grotesque lie."

"I don't feel so good, young Thorpe."

"Well, you shouldn't. My uncle injected a deadly virus into your vein. Your system is shutting down. This cocoon you're in has been designed to kill its occupants, show them the real life on the other side, then bring them back, healthy, with a renewed outlook on life and spirituality."

"Right, right, so let's get started. Do you have to close the lid? I—"

"Oh, vile swine, you don't get it, do you? I've dreamt of

your planned takeover and destruction. All those innocent people annihilated, and yet you laugh. You laugh as you stand over their dead bodies. And all those women you raped and killed, you're nothing but an animal, a miserable piece of shite." Lachlan raised a syringe so the Beast could see it. "This contains phosphorous, not the normal solution of herbs, epinephrine, atropine, vasopressin, amiodarone, and niacin. No, only phosphorous, you see phosphorous is highly flammable." Lachlan jammed the needle into the Beast's vein. The bastard screamed. "You are going to burn. Your organs are going to bake until they turn to ash." The Beast screamed louder. "You're not coming back, you diseased fuck. Your foul body will implode, burning from the inside out."

As the Anti-Christ's son continued to screech, Lachlan recited his Nana Aerin's prayer. "Dearest Mother and Father God, you've given me the gift of sight." The Beast fought hard against his restraints. He began to froth at the mouth. Lachlan continued. "With the purest of intentions and shrouded by the white light of the Holy Spirit, I send this dark soul back to you with the hopes of a reformed heart."

Around the deadly casket, the Chrysalis members gathered. Everyone stared at the yellowed creature. Sheer panic was the last thing they witnessed on the Beast's face. As Lachlan closed the lid he hissed, "Meet Glowworm you rotten sonofabitch."

Florescent blue light seeped from the closed lid. A whirring sound began. That is when everyone smelled the sweet sickening smell of burning human flesh. Glowworm cooked the hatred of mankind until all that was left of the Beast was internal ashes and a soulless corpse.

Lachlan released a heavy sigh and slumped in a nearby chair. "Well, I've successfully followed in the path of Nana Aerin's footsteps. Like my grandmum I have become Kaikoura's newest serial killer." In an instant, the Inferno Killer had returned to New Zealand's South Island.

Maktan

She mourned the little boy with the large brown eyes. Whereas the news reported The Christian was on the lam, Maktan knew the real truth. He was not eluding Tribune persecution. Maktan's little precious boy was dead. The same tiny baby that broke into a smile when Maktan entered the room; the adorable child that possessed an angelic face when he slept; the same little fellow that cried large tears from his huge eyes and batted away the drops with long, soft eyelashes. That son, little Mu'mad, Maktan longed for, grieved for. She had put her son first always; taught him everything she knew; gave him everything he desired. Maktan had always wanted Mu'mad's world to be better, better than hers. Where along the way had all this love and devotion soured? Maktan's heart ached for her child, ached for the grandchildren she would never hold. Maktan had created life and been instrumental in taking it back, giving it back to Allah.

Beth's front door, riddled with bullet holes, had released a silent alarm alerting the security company of an intrusion. When Beth did not answer her confirmation EyeNet call the RCMP were notified. Before long, a barrage of Vancouver police filled Beth and Maktan's penthouse floor. The Christian's al Din henchmen were trapped, nowhere to run. Those that survived were taken to jail very late that night, after quite a battle.

Beth brought Maktan some hot tea. She sat next to her best friend on the couch. No words could erase

Maktan's grief. The two elderly women sat side by side and sipped their steamy Earl Grey comfort. Slowly, Maktan reached over and took Beth's hand in hers. Their eyes did not meet. Nothing was said. Quietly, hand-in-hand, they watched the large snowflakes float about outside the living room windows and dreamed of what might have been.

"Be good, love God, then shut up, and go Home."
~ Sylvia Browne
Renowned psychic and author of *Psychic: My Life in Two Worlds*

Stay tuned for the next novel in this series by L. J. Dionne . . .

PORCELAIN MINDS

Echoes of Broken Dreams

By L. J. Dionne

Prologue

My nandy, Cameron Thorpe, grows tired. He has endured two world wars and raised me, his grandson, Lachlan Thorpe. An exemplary grandfather, no one has earned complete respect and a peaceful exit from this world more than he. Every day is a struggle for Nandy. Whereas, he was there for my first breath, I will be there for his last. From that first moment I was welcomed into the world, Nandy never left my side. He became my father and best friend. This lifelong dedication has made my decision to continue his work an easy one. Therefore, I dutifully take up the mantle to inform . . . teach. However, he has extremely large shoes to fill. I will diligently protect the masses, warning them of potential catastrophes. And my wise nandy, the best of teachers, has adequately prepared me for this journey. He was instrumental in forming our secret Chrysalis Society; prepping me for a monumental battle against evil by revealing family secrets; and destroying Muhammad al-Ypaaht, the infamous murderer known as The Christian, along with his closest al Din henchmen.

Following the elimination of The Christian in our Glowworm cocoon, the Chrysalis Society issued a press release unveiling his evil doings. His bank accounts were frozen. All upper level al Din activity was silenced. It appeared The Christian had crawled back into the shadows from whence he came, like his father, the Anti-Christ of Worldwide War III. Unfortunately, al-Ypaaht's reign of terror did not end with his death. Naïvely, I thought al Din would crumble after the loss of their precious caliph.

It seems we have only stirred the fanatical Muslim hornets' nest, once again. Much death and destruction awaits us. Evil just will not die.

Besides The Christian, there were seven other Chrysalis murders. As a teenager, I read and reread my deceased father's book about the Inferno Killer. Do you know how hard it was to realize that my wonderful Nana Aerin was the monster he theorized about, searched for? The very fiend he described was the woman who gave birth to him, lived under the same roof, and nurtured him into adulthood with an unwavering sense of right and wrong. What a hypocritical morality. However, each of the Inferno Killer's murders was a concerted effort. Great Uncle Tanid dumped the first internally combusted corpse at the Think Tank body farm after obtaining access to work on their heating system. Oh, and my favourite, Great Uncles Balic and Rami tampered with the braking system at the Tranz Coastal Tube Station successfully obliterating two already combusted corpses and taking out three Islamic terrorists when their pod crashed into the stalled vehicle, instead of the rubber safety cushion. Yeah, bravo Nana Aerin, you snuffed out five fanatical dark souls with that one, all in a day's work. Then, there was the seventh murder. I was secretly applauding the Inferno Killer after reading what my father wrote about that *victim*. All those innocent women and animals he hurt. That is when I stumbled off my righteous pedestal, when my argument unravelled. Pickersgill was a despicable pig. I was able to feel Pickersgill's victims. Therefore, I could not judge Nana or Chrysalis.

Overnight, the weight of the world was upon my twenty-five-year-old shoulders. The most heinous version of my grandmum was portrayed to me then I was dragged into her murderous obsession. To save lives, I was complicit in the killing of The Christian. At first, my conscience was bruised. Like my Nana Aerin, I discovered how difficult God's work could be. The ability of sight, a gift or burden? I was assured that every Glowworm slaying was chosen only after many torturous hours of meditation and Chrysalis discussions. Each decision was not an easy choice; I know how that feels. I share my Nana Aerin's gift of sight . . . the gift of glimpsing into the future, avoiding mass murders, and, therefore, reducing shattered lives. You see, my great, great, great, great, etc. grandfather was the famous seer, Nostradamus. Intuitiveness is in my blood. Night sweats bring me many visions and when I touch an individual my ability heightens. These techniques were used to ensnare The Christian and save my Hailee's life. Now, I am honoured to tread in my grandmum's footsteps. Nana Aerin never took a life without the purest of intent. I too felt what she must have felt. I tasted Hailee's death in my mouth, altered the outcome, and ultimately saved her life. There was no other way to stop the Anti-Christ's spawn, Muhammad al-Ypaaht. He had damaged so many lives and would have continued. In the deep recesses of my soul, I knew if we had put The Christian on trial, and had him imprisoned, loyal, brainwashed al Din followers would have found a way to release him back into society. Then we would never have been able to stop him.

Over the life of Chrysalis, only eight lives were taken—eight versus thousands, maybe hundreds of thousands. God gave me the ability to feel heartache on a cellular level, like my grandmum. I have been assigned, by the powers that be, as the catalyst to a more peaceful world. All I have to do is meditate on each situation with the purest of intent. Answers are eventually revealed. Chrysalis comrades are there for a second layer of conscience. Fortunately, my night sweats will bring informative visions. Taking a counselling job at the very university my Nandy resurrected, South New Zealand University, I will be able to use my psychic abilities quietly to identify those fledgling dark souls with a quick handshake. And just maybe, once again, we will find it necessary to employ Glowworm . . . a mere battle instead of a war.

One of our biggest challenges I have foreseen will be to cease the stinging blows delivered by al Din. Perhaps we will thwart al Din's machinations during their recruitment of vulnerable, troubled prisoners and teenagers. I plead for those hopeless souls to pay attention. For those of you unfortunates who were raised with abuse or misfortune, believe there is a better life ahead. Do not be lured into a hate-infested nest of fanatical pestilence. Someday the very jihad you fight for will be the jihad declared against you by your mentors. Betrayal amongst these vile, bigoted racists is common practice. Break free of your fragile pasts, letting hopes and dreams re-enter your hearts. Do not allow the cycle of cruel mistreatment to perpetuate. For those fortunate enough to dodge abuse during their formative years, pay attention to those seemingly forgotten, battered souls hiding in the shadows. Overnight these fragile, broken children just might become tomorrow's heroes.

"I'm talking about not having a voice . . . not being seen, not being heard."

~ Pamela Masik

Artist of "The Forgotten" paintings

THE AFTERSHOCK

Al Din

Frenzied confusion was abuzz deep within the caves of the White Mountains of Tora Bora in Eastern Afghanistan. Low-ranking al Din commanders swarmed about, agitated. For the past three days, not one jihadist pestilence, neither al Din fighter nor commander, was able to locate their leader . . . their caliph, The Christian. From what they could piece together, their revered leader was last seen at the Peace Summit gala. Inebriated and fondling every beautiful woman in his path, The Christian had sampled his just desserts—nothing out of the ordinary for their Muslim saviour. However, al Din's top commanders had vanished as well. Not even the al Din fighters arrested in Vancouver after their murder attempt on The Christian's mother, Maktan al-Ypaaht, knew of their leader's whereabouts. Paranoia settled in; had their caliph double-crossed them? The Christian's bank accounts were now empty, and no al Din commander of real importance remained. Their search for the unified Muslim leader would never stop until they had definitive answers. Each layer of information al Din peeled back when searching for The Christian only imparted more confusion, and provoked more questions.

Considered the scourge of the Earth, al Din emerged from the Afghan caves during that first post-WWIV year. Their work was done. Word had reached them from deformed, diseased loyalists claiming the rest of the world was quiet yet contaminated. However, in their eyes Islam had triumphed. The extremist group had been planning this destruction for decades. This elite class had studied radiation poisoning, its long-term effects, and discovered how to decontaminate the infected. Cancer was a disease of the past. Arrogant Anglos thought Muslims living in caves were unable to remain at the cutting edge of medicine and technology. Where were the pasty-faced infidels now? Ignorance infected those countries that did not survive WWIV. Evidently, manicured lawns and white picket fences had not aided in the Westerners' superiority after all. Yes, al Din was victorious. What the Muslim men had not prepared for, though, was how their harsh living standards would affect their women. When news reached their caves that first year, informing them worldwide annihilation had occurred, many of the females severely grieved lost loved ones. A deep resentment took root.

WITH HEIGHTENED TEENAGED ANGST, THIRTEEN-and fourteen-year-olds throughout the new world were easily lured away from the safety of their families with a one-way ticket to the secret headquarters of al Din. Promised a loving, pious life dedicated to Allah, these impressionable teenagers arrived in Afghanistan excited and hopeful. Sadly, almost immediately, they realized their decision was a colossal mistake. None of al Din's promises were delivered, especially for the females. Instead, as soon as the teen women arrived in Tora Bora they were passed amongst the men sexually. Brutal rapes occurred daily by multiple sexual partners. These disillusioned teenagers were bruised physically and mentally. Cooking and cleaning from dawn until late into the night kept their spirits broken and submissive. Pregnancy was inevitable. These courageous teens resigned themselves to the abuse from al Din men, as long as their sons and daughters were safe from such cruelty. However, the older their children became, the harder it was to protect them from the men's perverted sexual appetites. Excessive crying, and anal and vaginal bleeding from their toddlers left the young mothers devastated.

Exhausted from their daily routine of cooking, cleaning, and numerous sexual attacks, the younger mothers joined the older women in their dark, dank quarters. Emphatic whispers were heard from all corners of the room. Smothered by a mired lifestyle and deep-rooted resentment, the al Din women had finally reached their limit. It was inevitable that they would stage and execute a massive rebellion. While the men slept, after their bellies were filled with drink and food and sexual organs relieved of any pent-up pressure, the women quietly congregated at the cave's entrance. They knew the men's sexual appetites would not cease with the absence of adult females. Lust had already seeped horrifyingly into the children's world. With the women gone, pedophilia would only worsen. They watched their beautiful offspring with overwhelming maternal love, knowing many of them were already stripped of their innocence. Sodomy and rape would never again tear at their boys' or girls' dignity. One by one, the tired, second-class gender fed their children the tiny white, bitter pill. Death was not instantaneous. Every mother tightly held their precious offspring to their bosom until the convulsions ceased. They gently wiped the white oozing foam from their babies' mouths. Then, quietly, each woman quickly ingested her own cyanide pill. To Allah they went.

Sunrise over the ash-covered White Mountain Range was spectacular, a distorted beauty. Several men headed toward the cave entrance in search of their morning meal. A blanket of Muslim women and girls, but more importantly their precious sons, fanned out before their bare feet. No one moved. Death was an intimate friend. To these calloused soldiers nothing but ire crossed their faces. With vitriolic banter, the men stepped over the mound of corpses. Their caliph had abandoned them and now their women and children. The al Din fighters retreated into the bowels of their cavernous nest to report their findings.

The interim al Din top commander rubbed his bearded chin. Devoid of women, there would eventually be no more men born; the Muslim world would cease to exist. Devoid of women, and their delicious offspring, the Muslim men would not have their manly needs met. Devoid of women, it was obvious what al Din's first mission had to be, search other territories for feeders and breeders. If those they found were of non-Arabic descent, then those women would have to suffice. Besides, the dark Arabic features would surely dominate genetically. Allah would forgive the mixing with infidel blood. The interim commander gave the order to visit foreign shores. Desperate times lay ahead.

Author Biography

As a Certified Public Accountant, L. J. Dionne's vast exposure to the corporate world through auditing, introduced Dionne to the entertainment industry via work experience at Turner Broadcasting Systems Inc., Warner Bros., and Universal Pictures. As Universal's production controller, Dionne spent years in the unenviable position of having to interface between the "creatives" and accountants. Needless to say, Dionne decided to join the "creatives" and write. After years of researching the prophecies of Edgar Cayce, Nostradamus, and Sylvia Browne, studying the consistencies surrounding psychic revelations and near-death experiences, and witnessing the deterioration of racial cohesiveness in America, the story of *Dying to Live* emerged.

L.J. can be found online at Facebook, LinkedIn,
Pinterest, and Twitter.
LJDionneAuthor@gmail.com
www.InflucnccPublishing.com

Please join L.J.'s Echo Series Book Club Blog at:
www.lj-dionne.com

If you want to get on the path to becoming a published author with Influence Publishing please go to www.InfluencePublishing.com

More information on our other titles and how to submit your own proposal can be found at www.InfluencePublishing.com

CPSIA information can be obtained at www.ICGtesting.com
Printed in the USA
LVOW07s0204230915

455309LV00002B/14/P

9 781771 411318